THE SECRET OF NITRIC OXIDE

Bringing The Science To Life

Brick Tower Press
Habent Sua Fata Libelli

Brick Tower Press
Manhanset House
Shelter Island Hts., New York 11965-0342
Tel: 212-427-7139
bricktower@aol.com • www.BrickTowerPress.com
All rights reserved under the International and Pan-American Copyright Conventions. No part of this publication may be reproduced, stored in a retrieval system, or transmitted in any form or by any means, electronic, or otherwise, without the prior written permission of the copyright holder.
The Brick Tower Press colophon is a registered trademark of
J. T. Colby & Company, Inc.

Library of Congress Cataloging-in-Publication Data
Bryan, Nathan S.
The Secret of Nitric Oxide—Bringing The Science To Life
p. cm.
1. Health & Fitness—Diseases—Heart.
2. Health & Fitness—Diet & Nutrition—Macrobiotics.
3. Biography & Autobiography—Science & Technology.
4. Science—Life Sciences—Cell Biology.
Nonfiction, I. Title.

ISBN: 978-1-899694-30-3, Trade Paper • 978-1-59019-014-2, Hardcover

Copyright © 2025 by Nathan S. Bryan

February 2025

THE SECRET OF NITRIC OXIDE

Bringing The Science To Life

Nathan S. Bryan, Ph.D.

Also by Nathan S. Bryan, Ph.D.

Blood and Tissue Nitric Oxide Products: Formation and Physiological Significance

The Nitric Oxide (NO) Solution (With Janet Zand and Bill Gottlieb)

Beet the Odds (With Caroline Pierini)

Functional Nitric Oxide Nutrition: Dietary Strategies to Prevent and Treat Chronic Disease

"It is not the critic who counts; not the man who points out how the strong man stumbles, or where the doer of deeds could have done them better. The credit belongs to the man who is actually in the arena, whose face is marred by dust and sweat and blood; who strives valiantly; who errs, who comes short again and again, because there is no effort without error and shortcoming; but who does actually strive to do the deeds; who knows great enthusiasms, the great devotions; who spends himself in a worthy cause; who at the best knows in the end the triumph of high achievement, and who at the worst, if he fails, at least fails while daring greatly, so that his place shall never be with those cold and timid souls who neither know victory nor defeat."

—President Theodore Roosevelt

Legal Disclaimer

The information contained in this book is provided solely for educational and informational purposes and is based on the personal research, experiences, and opinions of the author, Dr. Nathan S. Bryan. The content of this book is not intended to be a substitute for professional medical advice by a licensed health care practitioner. Readers should always seek the advice of a qualified healthcare provider with any questions regarding a medical condition or treatment and should never disregard professional medical advice or delay in seeking it because of something they have read in this book. The content of this book is based on factual observation and not intended to be critical or defamitory.

Dr. Nathan S. Bryan, the author, and the publisher make no representations, warranties, or guarantees, express or implied, as to the accuracy, reliability, or completeness of the information provided in this book. The information is provided on an "as is" basis, and any reliance you place on such information is strictly at your own risk. The author and publisher expressly disclaim all liability for any errors, omissions, or inaccuracies in the content of this book and for any loss, injury, or damage of any kind incurred as a result of the use or application of the information presented.

The statements and claims made in this book have not been evaluated by the Food and Drug Administration or any other regulatory body. The products, methods, or protocols discussed in this book are not intended to diagnose, treat, cure, or prevent any disease. The author and publisher do not endorse or recommend any specific tests, products, procedures, opinions, or other information mentioned in the book.

Furthermore, the author and publisher shall not be held liable for any claims or actions arising from the use of the information in this book. This includes, but is not limited to, any direct, indirect, incidental, special, or consequential damages that result from the use or application of the information provided.

In purchasing and/or reading this book, you acknowledge and agree that the author and publisher shall not be held responsible for any liability, loss, or risk, personal or otherwise, incurred as a consequence of the use and application of any of the information contained in this book. The responsibility for the consequences of your decisions or actions remains with you, the reader.

This disclaimer is intended to be fully enforceable to the maximum extent permitted by applicable law. If any provision of this disclaimer is found to be invalid or unenforceable, the remaining provisions shall remain in full force and effect.

Table of Contents

	First Foreword	xi
	Second Foreword	xv
	Third Foreword	xix
	Preface	9
	Section I—Who Is Nathan Bryan?	17
1	The Early Years & Growing Up Independent	19
2	Education And Training	25
3	Introduction to Research And Science	29
	Section II—History Of Nitric Oxide	41
4	The Discoveries That Led To The Nobel Prize	43
5	How Is Nitric Oxide Produced In Humans?	51
6	What is Nitric Oxide and why should you care?	58
7	What are the consequences of insufficient nitric oxide production?	71
8	The Longevity Molecule	86
	Section III Discoveries That Changed Everything	95
9	Thinking Differently	97
10	Traditional Medicines And Nitric Oxide	110
11	Professional Challenges	127
12	The Explanation On The Benefits Of Certain Diets	133
13	The Role Of Bacteria And Stomach Acid In Nitric Oxide Production	139

	Section IV Bringing Discoveries To Market	149
14	If It's To Be, It's Up To Me	151
15	Putting The Pieces Together	155
16	Nitric Oxide Diagnostics	167
17	Is This What Nature Intended?	174
18	Academics To Entrepreneurship	185
19	Diversity And Risk Management	193
	Section V The Future Of Healthcare	203
20	NITRICEUTICAL®	205
21	The Future Of Healthcare	211
22	Lessons Learned From Failure, Challenges And Persistence	225
23	What's Next?	229
	Case Reports	233
	Home On The Range	243
	Glossary	245
	Scientific Publications	246
	Books	264
	Book Chapter Contributions	265
	Authored Books	279
	Invited Lectures	271
	Meeting Presentations	294
	Meeting Organizer	299
	Media Events	299
	Intellectual Property	300
	Acknowledgments	301
	About The Author	303

First Foreword

By David Perlmutter, M.D.

In April, 2023, I attended a medical conference in Chicago, specifically because of my interest in a fascinating molecule, nitric oxide, having previously invested countless hours over many years in its exploration. What I hadn't anticipated was how the course of that day would redefine my perceptions, largely owing to one outstanding individual: Dr. Nathan S. Bryan.

Every so often, a lecture transcends the traditional boundaries of academic presentations and becomes a transformative experience. Dr. Bryan's discourse was precisely that. He wasn't just speaking; he was weaving a rich tapestry of knowledge, history, and groundbreaking findings, centered on nitric oxide's pivotal role in human physiology. I was aware of the celebrated discovery in 1998, where the Nobel Prize in physiology and medicine was awarded for the discovery of nitric oxide's function as a signaling molecule in our cardiovascular system. Yet, as Dr. Bryan unraveled his research, it became evident that we had only scratched the surface.

Nitric oxide, as Dr. Bryan's work has unveiled, is not just a molecule but a marvel. Beyond its known functionalities, Dr. Bryan's research showcased its profound and wide ranging influence throughout the body in areas like the nervous system, metabolism, glucose regulation, erectile dysfunction, and even the mysterious area of longevity.

But clearly the most riveting and impactful revelation was nitric oxide's role as a fundamental regulator of metabolism across every organ system in the body. For decades, the scientific community segmented the body's metabolic functions, viewing each organ system in isolation. Dr. Bryan's research revolutionized this perspective. He posited, with substantial evidence, that nitric oxide functioned as a universal regulator, orchestrating a symphony of metabolic processes that worked in harmony across our entire physiological system. This revelation was not just academic; it bore profound therapeutic implications.

Dr. Bryan's dedication to this molecule went beyond pure research. Recognizing its vast potential, he ventured into the domain of therapeutic applications. He was not content with just understanding nitric oxide; he sought to harness its potential to alleviate some of the most perplexing disorders that had, for long, defied medical solutions. The fruits of his labor have and will continue to manifest pioneering interventions, promising hope where there is despair.

As the days of the conference unfolded, Dr. Bryan and I found ourselves drawn together by a shared passion. Our discussions, initially centered on nitric oxide, expanded into broader realms of potential collaboration. Our synergy was palpable, and before long, I found myself at the helm of a groundbreaking research project. Our focus? Tapping into the idea of enhancing nitric oxide availability in the brain as a potential beacon of hope in the grim battle against Alzheimer's disease.

The Secret of Nitric Oxide—Bringing The Science To Life is an embodiment of Dr. Bryan's journey with this miraculous molecule. It is not just a testament to his scientific prowess but a chronicle of his unwavering dedication. Through its pages, readers will journey from the rudimentary understanding of nitric oxide to its vast expanse, witnessing its rise from a mere molecule to a revolutionary force in medical science.

But more than its scientific revelations, this book stands as a beacon of hope. With the global health landscape marred by numerous disorders that defy solutions, Dr. Bryan's work with nitric oxide offers a fresh and encouraging perspective. By highlighting its role in every facet of our physiology, he not only underscores its importance but paves the way for innovative therapeutic approaches. These aren't just solutions; they are revolutions, set to redefine healthcare on a global scale.

As you delve into the depths of this book, anticipate a transformative experience. Whether you're a seasoned medical professional, a student, or someone with a penchant for groundbreaking science, Dr. Bryan's work promises to enlighten and inspire. It stands as a testament to the limitless bounds of scientific inquiry and the promise that perseverance holds.

To embark on this journey is to witness history in the making. So, as you turn each page, remember you aren't just reading a book; you're partaking in a scientific revolution, one that promises to reshape our understanding of health, wellness, and the very fabric of human physiology.

—David Perlmutter, M.D.

Second Foreword
By Antonia C. Novello M.D., M.P.H., Dr. PH.,
14th U.S. Surgeon General

There are moments when the best of humankind comes forward but is not recognized for doing the best work. Dr. Nathan Bryan endured this type of treatment during his research as depicted in this book. The molecule of nitric oxide (NO) discovered in 1980 – revolutionized vascular biology and the understanding of chronic diseases. The discovery was so unique and extraordinary that three scientists were awarded the Nobel Prize in Physiology or Medicine in 1998 for their work. After its discovery, the field stayed dormant because of the inability and difficulties in managing the NO gas and the lack of safe and effective NO therapies. One man persisted for almost two decades in unlocking NO. He was able to crack the code on developing a solid dose form of NO, an oral delivery system, and a dual-chamber delivery for topical applications of NO.

This book is the story of Dr. Nathan Bryan's life. He believed that NO-based therapies and product technology had the potential to change the world and make people healthier. Not all work on NO has come from his laboratory, however, this is clearly acknowledged in his writings. It was only by seeing what others had seen, while incorporating thoughts that others had not thought, that he became the first and only scientist to develop a solid dose form of bioactive NO gas. He, different from the rest, thought differently by sticking purely to science and human physiology, and accomplished what others deemed impossible.

As Colin Powell used to say – "A dream does not become a reality through magic! It takes sweat, determination, and hard work to become a reality." In this personal story, Dr. Bryan lays it all out – both the good and the bad. And as we read beyond the scientific discovery we get immersed in the strong character, perseverance, high principles, and extraordinary resilience that this man possesses.

As a result of his frank revelations, we are allowed to see into the heart and soul of a remarkable human being. Through every chapter, the reader is mesmerized by his ability to keep going despite so many failures and life hurdles that include the death of a child, betrayal by friends and peers, multiple lawsuits, accusations of theft of trade secrets, breach of contract, false advertisement, unfair competition, scientific fraud and even attacks on his own life! Despite everything, he survived. The reader will understand that although Dr. Bryan has achieved many victories in his life, there were far more defeats and failures along the way.

He has experienced and survived so many obstacles. A less courageous person would have given up or crumbled under the pressure. But he weathered the storms. As he has said – (a man of faith), "God had plans for me!" Dr. Bryan is also a true example of what Friedrich Nietzsche says "what does not kill you, makes you stronger."

In his own words, even though he has survived – and has mastered forgiveness, he still has not mastered forgetfulness. Sadly, he has become less trusting as a result. He, however, is very aware and cognizant that revenge can only take you so far. Living a fully successful life is the only way to show who has become the real winner. Today, he has discovered and created the most innovative product technology in the world – that when used and administered in the right form of NO, will change, and eventually save many lives. Many have already been changed because of the power of NO technology, for which he is proud and grateful.

The technology that Dr. Bryan and his scientific team have developed will undoubtedly transform healthcare and the treatment of patients with diseases ranging from Alzheimer's to diabetes, to name just a few, in the next hundred years.

By reading this book, I have learned a lot about NO, and you will too. I have learned even more from the life history of this unique trailblazer. Through his accomplishments and failures, I have learned that as Calvin Coolidge said, "perseverance is not just the willingness to work hard, but the ability to keep going, when the going gets tough."

—Antonia C. Novello M.D., M.P.H., Dr. PH., 14th U.S. Surgeon General

Third Foreword

By Louis J. Ignarro, 1998 Nobel Prize Winner
in Physiology or Medicine

The Secret of Nitric Oxide—Bring The Science To Life is a must read for anyone interested in improving their overall health and living a longer and more productive life. As Dr. Nathan Bryan clearly points out, there's one miracle molecule in your body that is largely responsible for your health and longevity...NITRIC OXIDE. The discovery of this molecule, also known as NO, has revolutionized our understanding not only of cardiovascular disease but also many other chronic diseases including dementia, gastrointestinal disorders, and erectile dysfunction. Your body produces NO and it is essential that you live a lifestyle that promotes the production and action of NO. This includes a healthy diet and physical activity. Dr. Bryan provides extensive and convincing evidence that certain nutritional supplements, which he terms "nitriceuticals", can boost the production of your own NO in the body, which can prevent and even reverse numerous chronic disorders.

In this fascinating and timely treatise, Dr. Bryan opens up and shares intimate details about himself and his journey, and his accomplishments and heartbreaking setbacks both in science and in life on his "rollercoaster ride" up and down the road to his remarkable success as a scientist and entrepreneur. In addition to teaching us about NO and all of the therapeutic benefits of this miracle molecule, the one lesson to be learned from the author is that one key to success is never giving up no matter what obstacles lie in your path. The emotional stories behind Dr. Nathan Bryan's success portray a person who is dedicated and committed to developing and marketing NO supplements, products and drug therapy that he believes will improve your health and extend your longevity. Long live NO.

—Louis J. Ignarro, 1998 Nobel Prize Winner in Physiology or Medicine

Preface

"As long as men are free to ask what they will, free to say what they think and free to think what they must, science will never regress. Freedom itself will never be wholly lost."

—J. Robert Oppenheimer

I clearly remember during my inorganic chemistry class in college thinking that I never want to deal with nitrogen-based chemistry after this class. The chemistry seemed so complex with five valence electrons and 8 different oxidation states. Nitrogen can either accept up to 3 electrons or donate up to 5 electrons. I thought if I can ever get through this class, I will never have to deal with nitrogen chemistry ever again. Boy, was I wrong and I'm glad I was. Fast forward thirty years and now I have spent the better part of those thirty years doing nothing but trying to understand nitrogen biochemistry and specifically the biochemistry and physiology of nitric oxide. It just goes to show that God has plans for us regardless if they are in line with our own plans. That is part of my motivation to write this book. I've authored several other books for consumers that I have self-published. I've authored medical and scientific textbooks and served as Editor on several scientific books on nitric oxide. I published over 100 peer-reviewed scientific articles in some of the top journals around the world. This book is different. There has been such an emergence of nitric oxide research and innovations over the past 10-15 years that it is time bring new science to the fore. My motivation and objective are two-fold:

To continue to provide science based, accurate information and education on nitric oxide so the masses can become informed and educated on its importance. Once people understand what nitric oxide is and what it can do, they can become empowered to take control of their own health.

To motivate and inspire people to follow their dreams and never give up despite what may sometimes seem like insurmountable hurdles and resistance. It is my hope that my personal journey and story will provide some inspiration and perspective on your own personal journey. Nothing worthwhile is ever easy and sometimes it seems easier to give up than to continue the fight. My story is one of perpetual drive and fighting against all odds. Never give up and never give in.

In the words of Winston Churchill in the midst of WWII when the Brits were losing, he made a very famous speech that I have chosen to live by. In part he said, "this is the lesson: never give in, never give in, never, never, never, never-in nothing, great or small, large or petty — never give in except to convictions of honour and good sense. Never yield to force; never yield to the apparently overwhelming might of the enemy."

Many people see the fruits of the labor but many times don't understand or recognize the labor that it took to eventually harvest the fruit. My 20 plus years in academic basic science and clinical research has opened my eyes to the many problems and deficiencies in today's health care system. In the United States today, we spend more money on health care than any industrialized nation and yet we have one of the sickest populations on earth. More than 37 million Americans have diabetes, this is more than 11% of the population. Another 9 million are estimated to have undiagnosed diabetes and another 96 million Americans have pre-diabetes on their way to full blown diabetes. That totals 142 million Americans that have metabolic disease or nearly half of all Americans. More than 30% of Americans are overweight and 42% are obese. That is 3 out of 4 Americans that have a weight problem. About 115 million of Americans have hypertension and another 59 million have prehypertension. It has been estimated that there is another 11 million Americans that have hypertension and do not even know it. That reveals that 2 out of 3 Americans have an unsafe elevation in blood pressure, the number one risk factor for the number one killer of men and women worldwide, cardiovascular disease. One in three seniors suffer from Alzheimer's disease and there are more than 6 million Americans living with Alzheimer's. The percentage of the US population living with Alzheimer's Disease has increased by more than 145% over the past 20 years. Despite billions of federal dollars spent on research each year, Americans are not getting healthier. In fact, we are getting sicker.

For me, this is simply unacceptable. Scientific research and discoveries over the past 30 years have revealed the root cause and mechanism of every major chronic disease. We've known for decades that Type 2 diabetes is completely preventable, treatable, curable and reversable. We know how insulin signaling works. We know the problem with glucose uptake. We understand insulin resistance. We know what causes high blood pressure and how to treat, prevent and cure hypertension. Alzheimer's is a metabolic disease often called diabetes Type 3 characterized by decreased blood flow to the brain, insulin resistance and an impairment in glucose uptake and utilization. We know how to address all aspects of metabolic diseases. So, what is the problem? The problem is the translation of basic science into clinical medicine and the proper dissemination of information to the health care practitioners and their patients. We know historically that it takes an average of 17 years for new discoveries in science and medicine to become integrated into clinical practice. If you go to your primary care physician, an endocrinologist, a cardiologist, a neurologist or any other health care practitioner, they will not even mention nitric oxide deficiency as a potential contributor to your disease or symptoms. Nitric oxide was named Molecule of the Year in 1992, more than 30 years ago. A Nobel Prize was awarded in 1998 for the discovery of nitric oxide. It is taught in medical schools. Since nitric oxide is not an official diagnosis and there are no nitric oxide labs or drugs for which a diagnosis can be made and a prescription can be written, physicians have no way to get paid for such a diagnosis or recognize any safe and effective nitric oxide product or drug they can feel comfortable recommending or prescribing. I've spent the past 20 years trying to educate physicians and health care practitioners about nitric oxide in clinical medicine. We have made some progress and today we have many integrative and functional medicine doctors that recognize nitric oxide as a cause and a solution for many of their patients' conditions, but most of these physicians are a cash practice and do not accept insurance.

However, main stream allopathic medicine will not recognize nitric oxide deficiency as a diagnosis and will not utilize nitric oxide as a therapy until there is an FDA approved nitric oxide drug on the market that insurance will pay for. It is unfortunate, but that is the way the current health care system works. It is called the standard of care. As illustrated above, the standard of care is failing us all. That is one of the main reasons I am actively moving my nitric oxide technology through FDA clinical trials so, for once, we can offer safe and effective nitric oxide drugs to patients who need them and would benefit from them. The pharmaceutical industry is one of the largest industries in the world. In 2023, the worldwide pharmaceutical revenue exceeded $1.5 trillion with more than 50% of this coming from the U.S. Market. This means that physicians practicing in America prescribe 50% of the world's medications to American citizens and yet we have the sickest people. This also reveals that prescription medicine is really not making anyone better. Moreover, most Americans are on more than one medication. An estimated 44% of men and 57% of women older than age 65 take five or more medications. When people are on more than one prescription medication, this is referred to as polypharmacy. Polypharmacy accounts for almost 30% of all hospital admissions and is the fifth leading cause of U.S. deaths. This is a staggering statistic. Another rarely mentioned fact is that FDA approved drugs are rarely, if ever, tested for polypharmacy risks, meaning that polypharm "drug to drug" interactions, risks and benefits are not studied at all. Worse, there is no risk or benefit to big pharma to conduct such polypharm research. Hopefully you are starting the see the problem and understand why our health care system is broken and why people are not getting healthier. The medications that are used today to treat the common diseases and illnesses are simply not working and yet they are the fifth leading cause of death. To explain this, we must understand how most drugs work. There is an entire field and discipline of pharmacology. Historically, scientist look at what happens in specific diseases, recognize what may be contributing to that disease and then they develop a synthetic compound (which is patentable) that inhibits a certain biochemical reaction that is associated with that disease. It is important to remember that association is not causation. The body always responds to any insult or stimulus. The human body typically does not make mistakes. Our creator is all knowing and designed our bodies to respond appropriately to every situation. We have certainly adapted or evolved over the years as our environment and food supply has changed. When we inhibit specific biochemical reactions in the human body, there will be side effects. That is why most drugs have side effects. Furthermore, there are off target effects of most drugs as well that interfere with other biochemical reactions but maybe not as potent. There are always consequences of inhibiting reactions that the body is designed to perform.

What I want to introduce to you is a new concept of drug development called restorative physiology. After all, the original concept of medicine was called applied physiology. Today, unfortunately, the practice of medicine is applied pharmacology. We must return to the basics of physiology and medicine. Through my studies and degrees in Biochemistry and Molecular and Cellular Physiology, I have come to realize that all chronic disease is caused by two things and two things only.

The body is missing something that it needs to do its job.

The body is exposed to something that is interfering with it doing its job.

The late Linus Pauling recognized this decades ago when he suggested that most diseases are caused by nutrient deficiencies. I certainly believe this is still true but now we recognized that so many people are exposed to toxins that even if they have repletion of nutrients, the toxins in their body prevent them from performing. This is the basis of restorative physiology. Let's recognize nutrient deficiencies through micronutrient testing and analysis and then let's begin to recognize and eliminate any toxins in the body. These toxins could come from symptomatic or asymptomatic viral or bacterial infections, such as root canals and dental infections, they could be from herbicides or pesticides sprayed on the food we eat. Toxins come in the form of electromagnetic radiation such as 5G. Heavy metals are a common problem in many people and other environmental or occupational exposures. If we can restore missing nutrients and remove any toxins in the body, then the body can heal itself. It is that simple and think about how cost effective this would be. In this model there is no need for pharmaceutical drugs since our body is never missing a synthetic compound that inhibits a biochemical reaction. In fact, many drugs are toxins and are contributing to chronic disease as revealed in the statistics above.

Based on this concept, I have learned that the mechanism of action of nutrients deficiencies and toxins is that they disrupt nitric oxide production and this causes the 4 hallmarks of every chronic disease:

- Decreased blood flow/circulation or what we call ischemia and hypoxia
- Inflammation
- Oxidative Stress
- Immune dysfunction

This is what we call mechanism of action. If we can restore the production of nitric oxide, then we are able to address every aspect of chronic disease. However, this requires specific nutrients and co-factors to produce nitric oxide and it requires the elimination of toxins in order to maintain steady state nitric oxide production. I have witnessed hundreds of patients that have contacted me with all kinds of terminal chronic disease, including terminal metastatic cancers. Some were only given weeks to live. I have applied these simple principles to these individuals and they not only survive their terminal illness but they thrive. This is after they have seen all the so-called best physicians at the top hospitals and institutions around the world. Physicians and drugs do not heal patients and that is certainly more evident today than ever before. Give the body what it needs and remove from the body what it doesn't need and the body heals itself. That is what I hope you gain from reading this book. The book is focused specifically on nitric oxide and how to prevent the decline in production. That said, it is my hope that I stimulate you to think a little differently about your own health and how you are able to take control of your own body and overall health. Nitric oxide is foundational for our health, wellness and human optimization, but it is not an end all, cure all panacea. You must still address other aspects of your health. My objective is to properly educate and inform the masses so that we have the right information to implement and live a healthy life and never have to see a physician or doctor due to illness. I not only understand and teach what I have learned over the years, but I also live it. I have not been sick in over 20 years. We also practice these principles at home. My kids have only missed a couple of days of school due to illness in 15 years and we all know schools are a cesspool of communicable infections. It is not that we live in a sterile environment. I've been on an airplane nearly every week for the past 5 years and have flown more than one million air miles. I'm in a new place every week. I've traveled internationally for the past 20 years certainly exposed to different pathogens than what I'm exposed at home and yet I do not get sick. I know that my body is able to respond to any pathogen or insult and deal with it as designed before it has a chance to make me sick. That is my hope for all of you reading this book. So, not only is the science valid that explains this but it is completely and simply applicable to anyone. This book is meant for two types of people. First, it should be read by anyone who is dealing with any chronic disease that has been poorly managed by their health care practitioners. I know these people are sick and tired of being sick and tired. This may be what has been missing in your care. The other group is for people like me who are healthy and want to stay healthy and not get sick. We know that this is possible and this book will provide you the foundation for doing that. This book is really for everyone whether you are sick or healthy. If you get anything out of this book, please share this information. As Stephen Hawkin said, "the greatest enemy of knowledge is not ignorance, it is the illusion of knowledge". We live in a world where there is an illusion of knowledge and misinformation and this is dangerous. Ignorance is curable with education and knowledge. I hope this book provides you with the knowledge and information that will change and transform your life. I know it has for me, my family and friends.

—Nathan S. Bryan, Ph.D.

Section I
Who is Nathan Bryan?

CHAPTER 1
The Early Years & Growing Up Independent
"God reminds us that he is with us and will never forsake us."
—Isaiah 41:10

I was born November 26, 1973 in Bryan, Texas. I grew up in a loving family in Lexington Texas. I was the second child by my parents. I have an older brother Marty who is 20 months my senior and a younger half-brother from my father, Justin who is 10 years my junior. My dad was an entrepreneur and owned several businesses growing up. My mom was a housewife.

We were not rich growing up but we always had what we needed and my brother and I felt loved by both of our parents. My parents divorced when I was 7 years old and that really was a traumatic experience for my brother and me. When my parents divorced, initially I lived with my mom. My brother stayed with my dad. This was very disruptive and caused even more separation of the family unit. After a few months, my brother and I both decided to stay with our dad in our small town where we had grown up until that point. I remember staying a lot with my paternal grandparents and aunts as a young child.

Family photograph, 1976.

Although our parents were divorced, my brother and I always had family take care of us as we moved from town to town. My older brother and I attended six different schools from elementary to middle school as we moved around sometimes staying with our mom and other times moving back with our dad. As you may imagine, we had to constantly adapt to new environments and continuously make new friends. The only constant in our lives was change. It seemed that as soon as we became comfortable at one place, we were moved to a new place.

Family photograph, 1978.

Somehow, we always ended up in our hometown of Lexington, Texas as kind of our home base. My brother and I found some stability in our lives living with my dad when I was in sixth grade and my brother was in eighth grade at Lexington Middle School. Early one morning on October 19, 1984, my brother and I were called to the principal's office and notified that our dad was involved in a very serious car accident on his way to work. My dad had re-married recently, but at the time of his wreck they were separated and living apart. Our dad always left for work really early before day light.

That day it was a light misty rain. We later learned a deer ran out in front of my dad's car and when he hit the deer, it forced his car into the ditch where he hit a tree on the driver's side door and compressed my dad's spine upon impact. He sat in the ditch for more than an hour before someone saw his car in the ditch and stopped to help him. He later revealed that fire ants had covered his body in the car when he was finally found. When we got the news, he was in the hospital in surgery and the doctors did not know if he would survive his injuries. My dad spent several months in the hospital with multiple surgeries but the injuries left him paralyzed from the mid-back down.

During the time he was in the hospital, my brother and I would live with my grandparents, we stayed with our aunt and moved around quite a bit from home to home. Once dad was released from the hospital, we moved in an old house in Lexington. My brother and I helped take care of our dad for several years, including working jobs at 11 and 12 years old to help pay bills. We mowed lawns, did yard work and took on whatever jobs we could to earn money. We lived there for a couple of years and helped my dad with his rehabilitation. With my dad being injured and unable to work, we had to get on welfare and my brother and I were put on the free lunch program at school. During that time, at school before lunch, the teachers would hand out yellow free lunch cards to all the "poor" kids. This was the most embarrassing experience my brother and I had encountered up to that point in our lives.

Other kids would look at us and make fun of us for being poor and getting a "free lunch." Although traumatic at the time, I truly believe that experience has motivated my brother and me to work hard so we would never have to experience that situation again. Just like the old saying, it is not what happens to you that defines you, it is how you respond to what happens to you that matters and defines you. These experiences early in life certainly cemented our drive and motivation to work hard and be the best at what we do. One thing for sure was that we did not ever want to be embarrassed or humiliated like that again.

Kindergarten, 1978.

Once dad had completed rehabilitation, adjusted to his new way of life confined to a wheel chair, we were still living in Lexington and dad's new wife moved back in. They had previously separated weeks before his car accident. He felt she could help take care of him and ease the burden of me and my brother. She was an alcoholic and was very confrontational. My brother and I would spend many nights in beer joints and pool halls. I think I won my first pool tournament at age 9. One night, my stepmother and dad were both drinking and completely drunk. She was about to push him in his wheelchair down a really long ramp and kick him out of his own home. My brother and I tried to stop her

5th grade class picture, 1983.

but she pulled out my dad's 38 special pistol and held it to my head and threatened to kill my brother and me if we tried to stop her. My brother ran to the other room and called my cousin to come rescue us.

After that, my dad ended his relationship and fortunately we were never subjected to that again. It certainly made us realize how quickly life can turn. God certainly protected us. Once dad was able to work, he took a job at Texas Department of Criminal Justice in Navasota, about 90 minutes from Lexington. It was also during this time, he was awarded full custody of our younger half-brother, Justin who was 3 years old at that time. My older brother, Marty and I did not want to move again to yet another new school. Instead, we elected to move in with our uncle who lived about 25 minutes from Lexington. We had just spent the summer with him

Calf Roping Days, 1987.

Learning to Rope, 1986.

and it was a good change and fun place to be as a kid. For the next two years, we lived with my Uncle Johnny, my mom's older brother. It was there we learned to ride horses and rope calves. We would get up every morning during the summer, ride horses, break young horses and train horses for roping. It was truly the wild, wild west.

Two young boys riding and taming wild horses, learning to rope and even started to learn to ride bulls. The bull riding did not last too long after one of our first practice sessions, I got bucked off and the bull came down and stepped in the middle of my chest. I was rushed to the emergency room and fortunately only had severe bruising but no broken bones. That was the end of my bull riding efforts. Riding horses and roping was much more fun and safer. Although many times I got bucked off young horses. It was a wonderful time in our lives learning the farm and ranch life. We got good enough to start competing. We competed in youth rodeos all through middle school and high school. Some weekends we would enter into 3-4 different rodeos all over Texas.

National Honor Society Induction, 1990.

When we decided to permanently move in with Johnny, we did however have to start yet another new school in Caldwell when I was in 7th grade and my brother was in 9th grade. We made many new friends at Caldwell and many remain close friends today more than 30 years later. It was in Caldwell that my brother and I met our wives.

Our mom had recently moved back from Illinois and my brother and I moved in with mom just up the road from where we were living with our uncle. These were good times but we were very poor and struggled to make ends meet. When I was 15 and my brother was 17, we moved into our own apartment to finish high school. We had an apartment above a 4-car garage owned by Dan Alford. Mr. Alford and his sons owned a full-service gas station just a few blocks away. I stocked groceries at a local grocery store and my brother worked at Alford's service station. After one year, my brother graduated high school and moved out.

I kept the apartment and lived by myself for the last 2 years of high school. I also took over his job at the gas station and worked there after school my last 2 years of high school. I would get out of school around 3:30 and then work at the gas station from 4-8 Monday through Friday and then work 12-8 on Saturdays. On weekends, I would check and gauge oil wells for an extra $90 per day. I would start at 5 am and would be finished by 11am so I had the remainder of Saturday to work in the afternoons at the gas station.

I was heavily involved in school as President of my class, President of National Honor Society, President of Future Farmers of America, where we finished third in the State UIL Parliamentary Procedure my freshman year. I was President of Business Professionals of America and even found time to play football one year and continued rodeo periodically. I was the only kid in school who could sign his own report card since I was independent and on my own. As a result, I developed a strong sense of independence and responsibility very early on. I made good grades in high school despite working two jobs after school and on weekends to pay my bills and I graduated fourth in my high school class. As one may imagine, my apartment was the place to be for all my high school friends. Although it was detached from Mr. and Mrs. Alford's main house, our parties were a disruption and a nuisance to them but they were always so kind and gracious.

After I moved out, I don't think they ever rented that place again. I will never forget their generosity and the accommodations they made available to me at such a critical time in my life. They often lent me money to help me through tough times. I was always able to pay back their loans even though I was barely living paycheck to paycheck. I still maintain contact with the Alfords and always let them know how much I appreciate what they did for me so many years ago. My early and teenage years were not easy but I would not trade those experiences and life lessons for anything as they helped shape me and prepare me for tougher times down the road.

CHAPTER 2
Education and Training

"Apply yourself. Get all the education you can, but then, by God, do something. Don't just stand there, make it happen."
—Lee Iacocca

It wasn't until after high school that I had an idea of what I wanted to do and what I wanted to be when I grew up. Before that, I never really gave it much thought. I was accepted into the University of Texas at Austin out of high school. I went to Austin to go through orientation but I had no idea how much it would cost to live in Austin on top of tuition, fees and books.

I had also applied to Texas A&M University and was accepted. I decided to continue living in Caldwell with my best friend Victor Mendez in a small 10 feet x 40 feet mobile home and commuted to College Station where I took classes at Texas A&M University and Blinn College. I can remember not having enough money to buy food. Victor and I both still worked at the gas station while going to college. Victor would get a few tortillas and cheese from his mother's house and we would have cheese tacos many nights. Victor and I both worked and went to school trying to survive financially. After one year, I transferred from Texas A&M University to the University of Texas at Austin to continue my studies in the College of Natural Science pursuing a degree in Biochemistry.

just Getting Off Work From Alford Oil, Co., With My Buddy Victor Mendez, 1990.

I've always had an interest in science and medicine but this really became apparent to me when I was a student at UT Austin. My high school counselor and teachers encouraged me to pursue a degree in Engineering since I was really good at science and math. I did take some Engineering classes early on at UT but that did not interest me at all.

During my sophomore year at UT, I had an opportunity to do undergraduate research in biochemistry in the lab of Jon Robertus, Ph.D. Dr. Robertus was an expert in protein purification and X-ray crystallography. While most undergraduates I knew were going to ballgames and fraternity parties, I learned how to over-express specific proteins in bacteria, then isolate the protein from the bacteria in order to study its structure and function. This provided science a strategy to gain a better understanding of what may go wrong in many diseases by understanding specific proteins' structure and function.

Throughout my time at UT, I worked evenings at Outback Steakhouse, cooking and waiting tables. I would take classes in the mornings and early afternoons and then work from 4-10 and sometimes later 6-7 days per week in order to pay bills. This was really good money. I would make $100 or more per shift. This was big money for me back then. I had the same girlfriend for several years at this point and we decided to get married my Senior year at UT. In retrospect, this was probably not a great idea since it increased the pressure to earn enough money to support my wife and me.

Once I graduated from UT with a Bachelor's degree in Biochemistry, I tested out the job market. There were not a lot of high paying jobs for graduates with a Bachelor's degree in biochemistry. I had a ton of experience waiting tables and working in restaurants but nothing related to biochemistry, except for the 2 years of undergraduate research.

I realized that I needed further education and training in order to achieve what I wanted to do in life and to utilize my science degree. At the time, my then wife, was insistent that I get a job and start earning a living. After all, she had worked for the past 4 years to help support us financially and now she thought it was my turn to return the favor. The Monday after I graduated from UT, I started a Ph.D. program in Biochemistry, Biophysics at Texas A&M University in the lab of James Sacchettini, Ph.D., a colleague of Jon Robertus and also a protein and X-ray crystallography expert.

I spent the summer learning protein crystallography. I really enjoyed the work but a few short months into my graduate work, my wife and I separated and I dropped out of the program. I spent the next year going back to wait tables at Outback Steakhouse with a bachelor's degree in Biochemistry. Not exactly what I had aspired to do.

After about 6 months of separation, my wife and I tried to reconcile. We moved to Conroe, Texas and I found a job at Fina Oil and Chemical as an analytical chemist. This was the only job I could find that somewhat fit my degree and background. I worked as an Analytical chemist analyzing petroleum and plastic samples as they came off different processes in the plant. This was part of their quality control process. It was a very mundane job with no real intellectual challenge. I would do the same thing every day. It was boring and I was making less than $25,000 per year with a degree in Biochemistry. Fina was located in Deer Park, about an hour drive from Conroe.

I would leave my apartment in Conroe every morning at 4:30 to arrive at Fina by 6am. I worked until 3pm and then drove about an hour drive into Houston to wait tables at Outback until 11pm or sometimes midnight. After my shift I would drive back to Conroe to get into bed around 1:00 AM and then get up at 4:30 AM to repeat the same schedule day after day. I did this for about a year and as you may imagine I was in complete burn out, personally, professionally, matrimonially and financially. I was broke as a stick, despite working 2 jobs.

As the saying goes, "I was so broke, I could not afford to pay attention". My wife was unhappy. I was unfulfilled in my career and I was depressed. It was no surprise when my wife left me and filed for divorce. I moved in with my brother and his wife in San Marcos and went back to work at Outback Steakhouse.

The year was 1997, I was 24 years old with a college degree, no real home of my own and no real job. I won't say I was homeless because I always had a place to stay with friends or family and some nights, I would just sleep in my car in the Outback parking lot and be ready for work the next day. My good friend Trey Novosad also let me stay with him and sleep on the couch for several months in Austin. I did this for about 3 years and was in a state of limbo with no real direction.

I was lost, heart-broken, financially broke and had no idea how to move forward. My dad always encouraged me to go back to school to give me the training and credentials to do what I always wanted to do which was science and medicine.

At that time, my mom lived in Shreveport, Louisiana. She and her business partner owned and ran a funeral home. I started spending time in Shreveport working at their funeral home, helping embalm bodies and sewing up cadavers after autopsy so they would be presentable for the family at the funeral.

I've always had an entrepreneurial drive but never really knew where to start. With the help of my mom's partner in the funeral home, Chuck Curtis, I secured a contract from the Veterans Affairs (VA) hospital in Shreveport to transport disabled veterans to and from their VA appointments. I bought a basic life support ambulance with a loan from my dad and I started transporting patients to and from the VA. The business made money but I still did not feel like this was what I was meant to do. It was not fulfilling at all. I knew there had to be more to life than this. I had to wait 30-90 days to get paid for my transportation services which caused a cash flow issue. To address this my mother's partner in their funeral home suggested I use his "factoring company."

Factoring companies are a bit like "loan sharks." They will immediately pay a portion of an outstanding invoices direct but will take a substantial portion of what you are owed to cover their risk during the 30, 60 or 90 or 60 days they have to wait to receive 100% of your invoice payment from insurance companies or contractors.

The bottom line was that I was working my tail off and he was keeping almost half of the money. As a result, I was unable to make payments on the ambulance and was forced to sell it to pay off the note. This created enormous conflict between me and my mom's partner that eventually led to a physical altercation that did not end well for him. I knew I had to move on and move out. I got my own apartment in Shreveport and again was at a cross road to decide where do I go and what do I do.

CHAPTER 3
A New Direction and Purpose in Life

"The mystery of human existence lies not in just staying alive, but in finding something to live for."

—Fyodor Dostoyevsky

Still interested in science and medicine, I answered an ad in the Shreveport paper from a physician scientist at LSU School of Medicine looking for a technician in pathology to help with tissue biopsies from diabetic foot ulcers.

I met and interviewed with John Valulius, M.D. He reviewed my resume (I didn't really have a *Curriculum Vitae* at that point). Dr. Valulius refused to give me the job because he said I was over qualified and I would be wasting my time working in the pathology lab. He encouraged me to apply to LSU School of Medicine and further my education. That was really the moment my life and direction changed. He was a complete stranger who believed in me, and realized I was wasting my time and not living up to my full potential. I was actually very excited about something in my life for the first time in a long time.

I applied to both the graduate school and medical school at LSU. I first met with Robert Specian, Ph.D. in the Graduate School. He was faculty in the Department of Molecular and Cellular Physiology. He reviewed my application and was very encouraging. A few months later I received my letter of acceptance. In 2000, I enrolled at LSU School of Medicine in their Ph.D. program in Molecular and Cellular Physiology.

The first two years was devoted to didactic lectures similar to the curriculum track of the first two years of medical school. We were also required to rotate through research labs to provide us exposure to different areas of research. I really enjoyed the classwork and learning new things.

It was during my first year at LSU when I was introduced to the science of nitric oxide. Two years earlier in 1998, a Nobel Prize in Medicine was awarded to three U.S. scientists collectively for their discoveries of nitric oxide as a signaling molecule in the cardiovascular system.

Lou Ignarro and me at the Nitric Oxide Gordon Conference, 2023.

As part of the lecture series at LSU, they invited Lou Ignarro, Ph.D. to come and give a lecture to the students, faculty and staff at LSU Health Science Center. Dr. Ignarro was one of the scientists that was awarded the Nobel Prize in Medicine or Physiology for his work and discoveries around nitric oxide. I had a chance to meet Dr. Ignarro, join him and the department for dinner that night and have a conversation with him. It was my first time to ever meet and interact with a Nobel Prize winner.

Dr. Ignarro was such a humble man who was encouraging and seemed to have a genuine interest in supporting young students in the nitric oxide field.

I will never forget how he made me feel that day and I felt more motivated than ever. Dr. Ignarro indicated that although the science of nitric oxide was pretty well defined and its importance established, it was not clear how to develop safe and effective therapeutics for nitric oxide since it is a gas and once produced, dissipates and is gone in less than one second. It immediately became clear to me that this was an important area of research with so much to be discovered. This was really the turning point in my life. I had a new passion for science, creativity and innovation and I had a path forward with meaning. Dr. Ignarro has remained a supporter of my research for the past 20 years and he continues to inspire me. I have Dr. Bob Specian to thank for giving me a new direction in life and a sense of purpose. I also thank Dr. Valulius for not hiring me for the pathology technician position and encouraging me to do something more meaningful.

The first 2 years of the program was mostly taking classes and outside of classes, doing research rotations in different labs to find a line of research of interest and also faculty members willing and able to take me under their

The Secret of Nitric Oxide

wing for training. Shortly after attending Dr. Ignarro's lecture, during one of my several rotations I was introduced to Martin Feelisch, Ph.D. Most faculty mentors allowed a 4-week rotation to get a good understanding of their individual research programs and also to learn specific research methods. When I first met with Martin, along with two other student colleagues, he informed us that he would require a minimum of 6 weeks and we would be required to stay in the lab until our work was finished. This was not a 9-5 job.

Martin was very strict, very demanding but very focused on nitric oxide research. It scared the other two students to death but I quickly realized, this is exactly the structure and discipline that I needed. Lou and Martin had been friends and colleagues for many years. Martin had returned to Academia after he left a position in a relatively large pharmaceutical company in Germany so he was familiar with the process of taking basic science discoveries to create new drugs.

From the International Nitric Oxide meeting in Monterrey Ca. From left to right: Dr. Bill Sessa, Dr. Ruben Zamora, Simona Matherne, me, Dr. Tienush Rassaf, 2005.

My first day in the lab, I met Tienush Rassaf, M.D., Ph.D. a physician scientist from Germany working on his post-doctoral training in Martin's lab. Tienush and I quickly developed a very close friendship.

He and I had the same motivation and drive to do good work and make important discoveries. Tienush and I moved in together shortly after we met. We would get to the lab before 7 am and most of the time did not leave until after 7 pm at night. After a long day of work, we would frequent our favorite bar in Shreveport called N'Cahoots. After a couple of cocktails, we would have really great conversation on how we should start a company and take our work and research of nitric oxide into some tangible product or service. This was always a great way to end the day and put our work into proper perspective.

At that time in the early 2000's nitric oxide was recognized as a gas produced in the body and once produced it is gone in less than a second. It is produced at very low levels, nanomolar concentrations (one billionth of a mole or the number of atoms of a molecule). However, over time our body's ability to produce nitric oxide decreases.

We learned that the decrease in nitric oxide is, in large part, what was responsible for age related disease, including cardiovascular disease, the number one killer of men and women worldwide. At that time, it was extremely difficult and complicated to measure nitric oxide gas or detect low concentrations of nitric oxide metabolites. My first challenge was to develop a method to detect nitric oxide gas in biological systems at such low levels.

Tienush and I were able to accomplish this within a year. That provided those of us in the field with an incredible tool whereby we would be able to measure nitric oxide in many different diseases. At that time, we were investigating different disease models in mice and rats.

We would harvest their blood and organs and analyze them for nitric oxide metabolites to gain an understanding of what goes wrong with nitric oxide production in different diseases or conditions. What became clear to us is that any disease process we studied, there was always less nitric oxide metabolites than in animals with no disease. It appeared that in these specific diseases, there was always less nitric oxide being produced.

I was fortunate to be able to attend my first International scientific meeting in Prague, Czech Republic in 2002. It was the International Nitric Oxide meeting. There were several hundred nitric oxide scientists, physicians and students at this conference. I was able to learn what other labs and researchers were working on. I learned so much at that conference and had the incredible honor of meeting one of the other Nobel Laureates, Dr. Robert Furchgott.

Dr. Furchgott was such a kind man, very humble and really encouraging to young investigators like me. I learned of his story and how sometimes simple observations can lead to life changing discoveries. I left that meeting feeling confident and excited to continue the research.

Tienush and I continued our research and we began to collect blood from monkeys and humans to continue our analysis into different nitric oxide metabolites and their stability. We also continued our work into specific tissues, such as the heart, brain and blood vessels of experimental animals.

One morning we had harvested the blood and organs of several mice that we had perfused free of blood and analyzed. We found in these particular tissues that their levels of nitric oxide metabolites were extremely high. Much higher than what we had normally seen. We showed our results to Martin and he indicated that something must be wrong. These values are impossible.

Tienush and I went back and tried to re-step our experimental methods and make sure we did not make any mistakes. We tested their drinking water in their cages and low and behold, their drinking water had been contaminated with nitrite. We had always deprived the animals of food and water at least 12 hours prior to researching so we could get fasting levels of the nitric oxide metabolites.

Although they had not had anything to eat or drink for the previous 12 hours, their blood and tissue levels of relevant nitric oxide metabolites were still elevated. We later discovered that on occasions the facilities maintenance personnel would put sodium azide through the pipes of the water supplying our research lab and animal vivarium. Sodium azide produces nitrite in solution and that turned out to be the source of the contamination.

This simple observation led us to start administering certain amounts of nitrite in the drinking water to test this molecule in mice and whether it would provide any harm or benefit to the animals.

At that time, nitrite and nitrate were considered inert oxidative metabolites of nitric oxide. In other words, we could trace the levels of nitrite and nitrate and use these molecules as a measure of the ability to produce nitric oxide in the animals. Until that series of experiments, no one had considered that these metabolites could actually contribute to nitric oxide production through some sort of recycling.

Our observation was an important contribution to other nitric oxide labs in the sense that it brought awareness to potential contamination of these molecules in buffers or other experimental media and how this may change the biochemistry in biological samples. We published several papers in 2003 and 2004 on the effects of nitrite causing changes in nitric oxide mediated physiology and sample processing.

Lab photo at Boston University School of Medicine. From left to right: Visiting undergraduate student at University of Rolla in Missouri, me, Alexandra Milsom, Selena Bauer, Martin Feelisch, Juan Rodriguez, Fumito Saijo, 2003.

If our data were true that most disease processes we had studied, all showed a decrease in nitric oxide production based on the metabolites we were measuring and nitrite in the drinking water appeared to restore these metabolites. Could then nitrite restore nitric oxide based signaling and protect the animals from injury or from the progression of disease? This is what initiated our work into the effects of nitrite and nitrate from the diet as a means to overcome nitric oxide deficiencies. This started an entire new field of study in nitric oxide. We were publishing 10-12 research papers a year at the time. I published over half a dozen original papers as a student and completed my Ph.D. within 2.5 years. Martin Feelisch provided really great training and an environment where I could learn, think on my own and develop as an independent researcher.

Tienush completed his post-doctoral fellowship with us and then moved back to Germany and begin his career as a Physician scientist and Clinical Cardiologist. Tienush and I remain great friends today and he is Chair of Cardiology and Vascular Medicine at University of Essen Hospital.

Martin then took a job at Boston University Medical Center. He invited me to join him to complete my post-doctoral fellowship at Boston University School of Medicine where I continued my research on nitric oxide in cardiology and drug design. I was still single at the time but had just started dating a friend from high school, Kristen Young.

After one year in Boston, Kristen and her son Grant moved to Boston and we got a house in Mendon, about an hour outside of Boston. I would get up every morning at 5 am to catch the 5:45 train into Back Bay station in Boston. I then had to walk one mile from the train station to Boston Medical Center. I would work until 6 or 7 in the evening and then catch the train back to Mendon and get home around 8 or 9pm. I actually enjoyed the one-hour train rides since it allowed me time to read the published literature, think about the data we had collecting during the day and what potential problems we could solve.

The winter months were brutal walking from the train station to my office and lab in freezing temperature and lots of snow. This was also a completely new life for me with Kristen and Grant. When Kristen and I started dating, Grant was 2 years old. About one year after I moved to Boston, Kristen and I got married. Now I had a wife and a 4 year-old step son to provide for. It didn't help that I was not making much money as a post-doctoral fellow.

Kristen starting teaching special needs students at Mendon-Upton High School. I always knew I wanted to be a dad and now I had my first opportunity. It was a fun time but very stressful.

Being from Texas, we never really got to experience a lot of snow. Living in the Boston area certainly allowed us many opportunities to experience the snow New England winters and all that came with it.

During my 2 years at Boston Medical Center, we continued to publish many important discoveries around nitric oxide. Martin had a team of about half a dozen students, technicians and post-docs working in the lab in Boston. The move allowed me to witness and experience setting up a lab, hiring and training new people and collaborating with other labs with different areas of expertise. We were also doing contract work for a company called NitroMed, a Boston based biotech company with nitric oxide drug development program. We were conducting some of the pharmacokinetic testing on their lead drug Bidil, a fixed dose combination of isosorbide dinitrate and hydralazine. We were using sodium nitrite as a negative control for these studies. We found that nitrite was indistinguishable from the organic nitrate drugs.

For me, this was an important observation because I believed nitrite could have therapeutic potential as a drug. This brought us back to our original observations that nitrite itself may have important biological and therapeutic potential.

We were also conducting experiments showing that nitrite could protect organs from injury after a complete disruption of blood supply. We call this ischemia-reperfusion injury.

My idea was that we could create a nitrite solution which would allow organs from donors to be transported to the recipient thereby improving organ transplant success. Interestingly, it is not the complete lack of blood supply that causes damage during transplantation, but it is when you reconnect the blood supply to the transplanted organ, that is when the injury occurs. We call this reperfusion injury.

My thought was that the nitrite in the donor organ could protect from the reperfusion injury and improve the function of the transplanted organ.

With a lot of excitement, I went into Martin's office and offered my wonderful idea and suggested that we start filing patents on some of our ideas and research. Martin commented that patents are difficult to get and most people never make any money on patents. He had several issued patents but had never received any money from them since no company had ever used those patents for a commercial drug or product.

That was really devastating to me. Why are we doing all this important research if we can't protect it with patents so that maybe someday it will improve the lives of humans and help prevent, treat or cure human disease?

I did not want to continue research in mice or cells if what we were doing could not be translated to humans and offer new information on the diagnosis and treatment of human disease. After all, I was not a veterinarian where my work was to treat mice or other animals of disease. I was interested in human medicine. This was the moment that I realized that it was time to move on and start my own independent research program where I could

Blizzard of 2005 where we had several feet of snow. we enjoyed jumping off the balcony into the bed of snow below.

make decisions and direct my own line of research and control my own destiny.

The year was 2005, Kristen's mom was recently diagnosed with pancreatic cancer. She was in the hospital in Houston. We had spent the past 2.5 years in New England and I realized that I really wanted to move back to Texas.

The notion that Kristen's mom may not have long to live further cemented that idea. We decided that we needed to move back to Texas to be closer to family. All I needed was a job offer in Texas.

I had previously met Ferid Murad, M.D., Ph.D. at a few nitric oxide meetings. Dr. Murad was one of the three scientists that had shared in the Nobel Prize with Lou Ignarro and Robert Furchgott. I sent my CV to Dr. Murad just to test the waters on any potential job opportunities within his lab or department at the University of Texas Health Science Center at Houston. I received a call from Dr. Murad a few days after I sent him my CV. He offered me an opportunity to come to The University of Texas Health Science Center at Houston to give a departmental lecture for a faculty position. I did not notify Martin that I was actively looking for a faculty position.

I flew to Houston, spent the day at the Institute of Molecular Medicine and presented my work over the previous 5 years, some of which was unpublished. I met with different faculty members and then ended the day with Dr. Murad. He was impressed with my research and offered me a faculty position. Although he liked my line of research, he indicated he did not believe my data on nitrite because he said he had tested nitrite back in 1977 and it did not work. I was super excited that had been offered my first independent faculty position and have the opportunity to work alongside a Nobel Prize winner.

Afterwards, I walked over to Memorial Hermann hospital at the Texas Medical Center to visit Kristen's mom and let her know that I was offered a job back here in Texas and we would be moving back. She was in really bad shape. I called Kristen and told her the good news about my job offer in Texas. I also had to tell her the bad news about her mom. I told Kristen she needed to get on a plane and fly to Houston immediately. Her mom did not have long to live. Kristen arrived the next day and was fortunate to get to spend the last few hours with her mom before she passed.

This event really solidified our decision and need to be closer to home. One of the pre-requisites for my hiring at UT was a letter of recommendation from Martin Feelisch, my mentor for the past 5 years. This really caused me concern since I had not even told Martin that I was actively seeking a faculty position nor that I was intended to leave his lab as a post-doctoral fellow.

Once we returned to Boston, I worked up enough courage to inform Martin of my job offer and to ask him for a letter of recommendation. I knew Martin would not be happy but felt he would support my decision to move on. I walked into Martin's office in Boston and informed him of what I had been up to and that I had been offered a faculty position with Ferid Murad at University of Texas Health Science Center at the Institute of Molecular Medicine. Once I told him, he was shocked and very disappointed.

His main frustration was that I had sought a faculty position elsewhere without his support or any discussions. He thought I was not ready or prepared for an independent career. After all, I had only spent two years in post-doctoral training and most everyone needed several multi-year fellowships before becoming an independent investigator. I told him it was my decision he could not change my mind and I needed to get back to Texas. In truth, I had already been offered the position. I just needed his support and a letter of recommendations. He agreed to write a letter of recommendation for me but insisted that I was not ready for an independent career.

As a compromise, I agreed to stay for 6 more months in his lab to finish up some projects and train new people as my replacement. My last day, Martin and I shook hands, I thanked him for his support and years of mentorship. In hind sight, I wish I would have informed Martin of my intentions of moving on. After all, a mentor's primary role is to help and prepare young investigators for the next step in the progression of their careers.

I denied Martin that opportunity and now understand why he was upset. We have since reconciled our differences and remain very close friends and colleagues. After all, it was the mentorship of Martin Feelisch that is largely responsible for my current success. I would not be where I am today without Martin. I am forever grateful for his tough love, mentorship and discipline.

Not long after that, we loaded up our U-Haul truck and started the journey from Boston to Houston. We had recently bought a home in the northwest part of Houston, about a half hour drive from the medical center where I would be working. Kristen and Grant who was 6 or 7 at the time were about to start a new life back in Texas.

We were super excited. I moved into my office at the Institute of Molecular Medicine, the department gave me $500,000 to purchase equipment and build out my research laboratory. One of the most memorable moments occurred during my orientation as new faculty.

Bruce Butler, Ph.D., who was head of the Office of Technology Management gave us an introduction into his office and the process for disclosing inventions or discoveries. He remarked that if we ever made a discovery, no matter how big or small, to contact his office, fill out an invention disclosure form and his office would review and determine if the University should file a patent for the discovery or if there was any intellectual property to protect from the disclosure. All we had to do was inform them of our idea or research and they would handle the rest. I thought of all the experiments I could design in order to prove my idea about creating a nitric oxide drug or therapeutic.

During my first year as an Assistant Professor of Molecular Medicine, I didn't hire anyone. I really did not have the funds to bring anyone on. I also spent most of my time writing grants and doing some crucial experiments that I thought would be useful for patent applications. I would design experiments, collect the data and then file invention disclosures with the University. The office of Technology Management would send their patent agents over to my office to discuss the inventions.

Looking back, I must have worn them out. It seemed they were in my office every week where we would discuss the concepts, they would give me feedback and I would go back to the lab

With Dr. Ferid Murad at the awards ceremony where I received a Young Investigator's Award at the Institute of Molecular Medicine, 2007.

to conduct more experiments. Eventually the University starting filing patents based on my ideas and data.

Over the next few years, my patents were issued and today I have dozens of issued U.S. and International patents. I felt confident we had made a lot of progress in research and discovery but now we had to make a viable product, test it for effectiveness and ultimately make it available to the masses. This would be an enormous undertaking.

At this time, the nitric oxide field was booming with more than 100,000 scientific publications. There were many companies, both small start-up biotech companies and large pharmaceutical companies that had tried to develop nitric oxide-based drugs but all of them had failed. It was time to think differently.

My personal life was great. I was back home in Texas reunited with my childhood friends. I was married in our new house in Houston and Grant was now 8 years old. I was coaching his little league football team. I had a great job that I really enjoyed making lots of exciting discoveries. Before I move onto my own personal journey in product development and drug design, let's review a bit more detail into the importance of nitric oxide and what led to a Nobel Prize for its discovery.

With my childhood friends singing on stage with the Texas Unlimited Band. From left to right: Randal Matcek, Brent Pertl, Victor Mendez and me, 2005.

SECTION II
HISTORY OF NITRIC OXIDE

CHAPTER 4
The Discoveries that led to the Nobel Prize

"The discovery of nitric oxide and its function is one of the most important in the history of cardiovascular medicine."
—Valentine Fuster, M.D. 1998 President of the American Heart Association

The Nobel Prize is announced every year in October and the awards ceremony takes place in Stockholm Sweden on December 10th every year, the anniversary of Alfred Nobel's death. According to the Nobel website, Alfred Nobel's last will and testament established the prize in 1895. Below is the actual language from his will to establish the prize.

"All of my remaining realizable assets are to be disbursed as follows: the capital, converted to safe securities by my executors, is to constitute a fund, the interest on which is to be distributed annually as prizes to those who, during the preceding year, have conferred the greatest benefit to humankind. The interest is to be divided into five equal parts and distributed as follows: one part to the person who made the most important discovery or invention in the field of physics; one part to the person who made the most important chemical discovery or improvement; one part to the person who made the most important discovery within the domain of physiology or medicine; one part to the person who, in the field of literature, produced the most outstanding work in an idealistic direction; and one part to the person who has done the most or best to advance fellowship among nations, the abolition or reduction of standing armies, and the establishment and promotion of peace congresses. The prizes for physics and chemistry are to be awarded by the Swedish Academy of Sciences; that for physiological or medical achievements by the Karolinska Institute in Stockholm; that for literature by the Academy in Stockholm; and that for champions of peace by a committee of five persons to be selected by the Norwegian Storting. It is my express wish that when awarding the prizes, no consideration be given to nationality, but that the prize be awarded to the worthiest person, whether or not they are Scandinavian."

The first prize was awarded in 1901. There is no greater honor or award than the Nobel Prize. It recognizes discoveries or productions that "have conferred the greatest benefit to humankind." As a scientist, there is no greater reward or acknowledgment for your research than winning the Nobel Prize.

In 1998, the Nobel Prize in Physiology or Medicine was awarded to Robert Furchgott, Lou Ignarro and Ferid Murad "for their discoveries concerning nitric oxide as a signaling molecule in the cardiovascular system." The announcement that year read as follows: "Nitric oxide (NO) is a gas that transmits signals in the organism. Signal transmission by a gas that is produced by one cell, penetrates through membranes and regulates the function of another cell represents an entirely new principle for signaling in biological systems. The discoverers of NO as a signal molecule are awarded this year's Nobel Prize."

The fact that a gas, that once produced, is gone in less than one second could initiate specific and deliberate signals in the human body still fascinates me today. All three of the Nobel prize recipients made important discoveries independently but it was when all three were put in context that

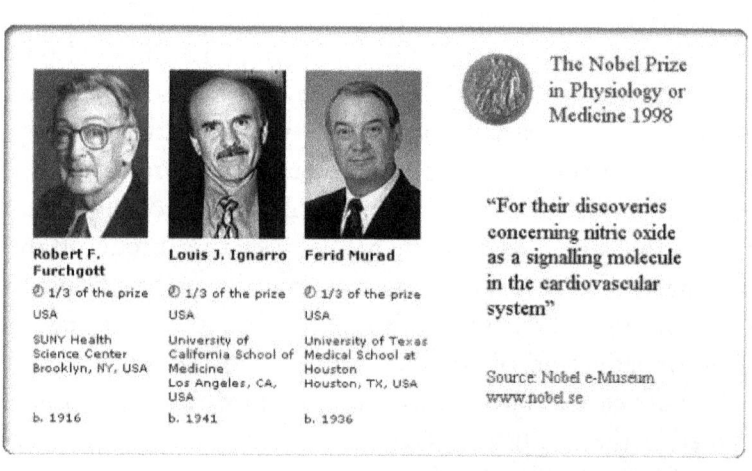

Announcement of the Nobel Prize, 1998.

The Secret of Nitric Oxide

the story was revealed. The discovery of nitric oxide was the culmination of three independent lines of research in pharmacology, vascular biology and immunology that together realized the natural production of this molecule and its effect on cardiovascular physiology. How did these fields come together to tell a complete story?

In 1977, Ferid Murad discovered and published that organic nitrates (nitroglycerin, isosorbide dinatrate) which had been used for more than 150 years for the treatment of acute angina (chest pain from compromised blood flow to the arteries of the heart due to atherosclerosis or hardening of the arteries) actually were metabolized into an intermediate substance that caused activation of a second messenger. That second messenger was cyclic guanosine monophosphate (cGMP) which was known to cause smooth muscle relaxation that resulted in dilation of the blood vessels. This allowed

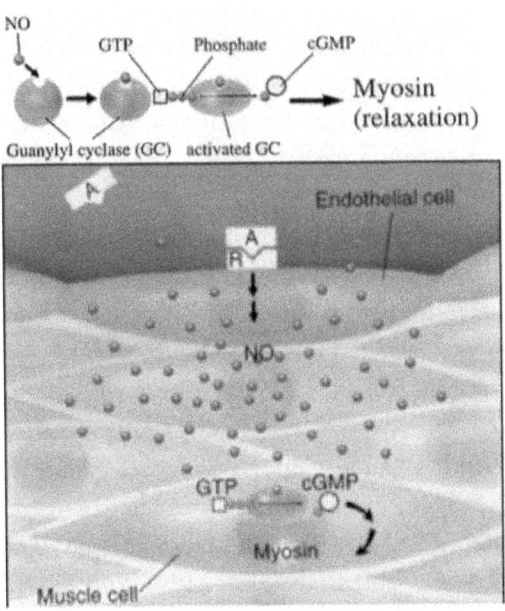

Dr. Murad knew that nitroglycerine caused relaxation of smooth muscle cells. The enzyme, guanylyl cyclase, was activated and increased cyclic GMP, causing relaxation of the muscle. Did nitroglycerin act via release of nitric oxide, NO? He bubbled NO-gas through tissue containing the enzyme; cyclic GMP increased! A new mode of drug action had been discovered!

more blood flow and increased circulation through the blood vessels. The increased vasodilation is what led to complete alleviation of the chest pain associated with heart disease.

Dr. Murad had intimated that the active component of nitroglycerin may be nitric oxide or some nitrogen containing molecule. He called these types of molecules "nitrovasodilators."

Interestingly though, drugs like nitroglycerin had been used clinically for more than 150 years prior to Dr. Murad's discoveries which finally revealed the mechanism of how they worked. These drugs were used because they were effective. However, physicians and scientists really did not have an understanding of how they worked.

Interestingly, Alfred Nobel's fame and fortune came from the use of nitroglycerin as an explosive but was also prescribed nitroglycerin later in life for his heart disease. You may ask what is the connection between dynamite and heart disease. The answer comes from astute observations by the people who worked in the dynamite factories. Many of the workers in the dynamite factories reported headaches when they were at work that resolved as the week went on. Chronic and repeated exposure to nitroglycerin causes tolerance, meaning it loses its therapeutic effect over time.

Over the weekend, the workers would lose the tolerance, and when they were re-exposed on the following Monday, the re-exposure to nitroglycerin caused drastic vasodilation resulting in a fast heart rate, dizziness, and a headache. This was often referred to as "Monday disease." It was also observed that many of the workers had "Sunday heart attacks."

A physician William Murrell had experimented with the use of nitroglycerin to alleviate angina pectoris (chest pain associated with heart disease) and to reduce the blood pressure. He began treating his patients with small diluted doses of nitroglycerin in 1878, and this treatment was soon adopted into widespread use after Murrell published his results in the journal *The Lancet* in 1879.

A few months before his death in 1896, Alfred Nobel was prescribed nitroglycerin for this heart condition, writing to a friend: "Isn't it the irony of fate that I have been prescribed nitro-glycerin, to be taken internally! They call it Trinitrin, so as not to scare the chemist and the public." The medical establishment also used the name "glyceryl trinitrate" for the same

The Secret of Nitric Oxide

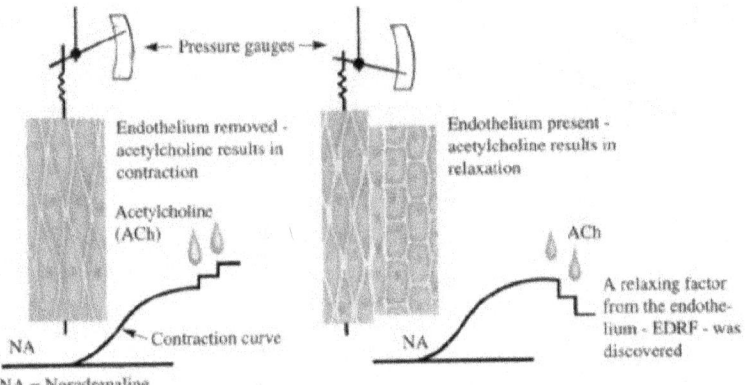

Robert F. Furchgott showed that acetylcholine-induced relaxation of blood vessels was dependent on the endothelium. His "sandwich" experiment set the stage for future scientific development. He used two different pieces of aorta; one had the endothelial layer intact, in the other it had been removed.
(Furchgott, Zawadzki: *Nature* 1980)

reason. It was the research and discoveries of Ferid Murad that explained the mechanisms of action of nitroglycerin and other "nitrovasodilators."

For me, this is what leads to innovation and discovery. First you start with an interesting clinical observation and then work backwards to determine the how. If you can answer the how and why in science and medicine, then that is when great discoveries are revealed. Dr. Murad did just that.

In 1980, a few short years after Dr. Murad's report on the mechanism of action of nitrovasodilators, Robert Furchgott discovered that endothelial cells, the cells that line all blood vessels throughout the body, when activated produced a molecule that caused smooth muscle relaxation.

At the time, he did not know the identity of the active molecule but in his 1980 *Nature* publication, he termed this molecule endothelium derived relaxing factor or EDRF because of what the molecule did. Again, this very important discovery was based on astute observation.

Dr. Furchgott's research scientist, John Zawadzki would prepare rat blood vessels in an organ bath to test different molecules. On some days, the blood vessels would dilate when an agonist such as acetylcholine was added to the organ bath. On other days, the blood vessels would constrict when acetylcholine was added.

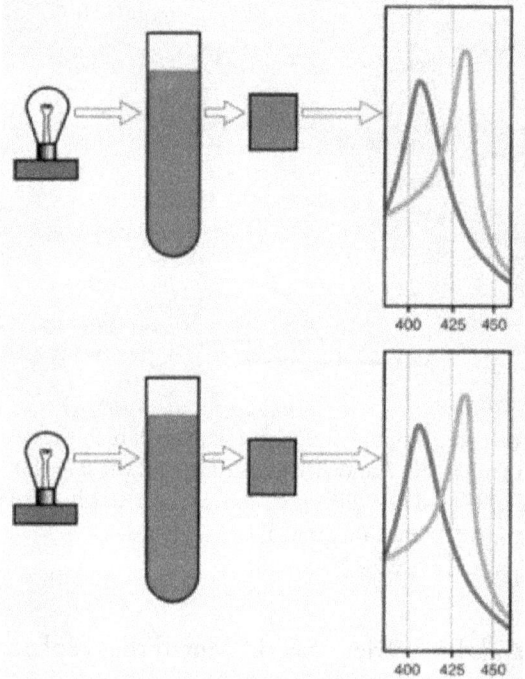

Hemoglobin (yellow) exposed to endothelial cells that were stimulated to produce EDRF (green).

Hemoglobin (yellow) directly exposed to NO (green).

The shift of absorption curves is identical, hence EDRF is NO. (Igarro, LJ et al PNAS, 1987.)

How could the same molecule cause the exact opposite response? In trying to solve the problem, Dr. Furchgott recognized that if care was taken when removing and cleaning the blood vessels, from the animal, the blood vessel would always dilate in response to acetylcholine. If care was not taken and the endothelium (the innermost lining of the blood vessels) was inadvertently damaged or if they intentionally damaged the inner lining of the blood vessel, then the vessel would always contract when acetylcholine was added. It appeared to them that the presence of a functional endothelium (the innermost lining of the blood vessels) was required in order to get vasodilation.

I can only imagine the frustration of Dr. Furchgott in getting complete opposite results and not being able to reproduce a basic experiment. However, his persistence to solve the problem, led to what I believe is one of the greatest discoveries in vascular biology. Because of the earlier work of Ferid Murad, Dr. Furchgott suggested that EDRF that he had described in 1980 may be nitric oxide but he had no concrete proof.

The Secret of Nitric Oxide

The scientific community realized how important EDRF was and the race was on to try to identify EDRF. Lou Ignarro was a pharmacologist at Tulane University who later moved to UCLA to further his research. Dr. Ignarro also had a hunch EDRF might be nitric oxide.

He just had to design a meaningful experiment to unequivocally prove EDRF is nitric oxide. He knew that nitric oxide could bind to hemoglobin in red blood cells and would cause a shift in the absorption spectrum of hemoglobin.

If EDRF when released from endothelial cells would also cause the same spectral shift, then he felt confident the scientific community would agree that EDRF is nitric oxide. In 1987 at a scientific meeting, Dr. Ignarro reported his findings that EDRF is nitric oxide. His results were published later in 1987.

At about the same time, Dr. Salvador Moncada also independently reported that EDRF is nitric oxide. However, the fact that Dr. Ignarro had first reported his findings at a meeting earlier in the year, gave him precedence and priority on the discovery. The beauty of Dr. Ignarro's experimental design and discovery was in its simplicity. He showed that EDRF is identical to nitric oxide through a simple and fast spectrophotometric measure.

Also, in the early 1980s it was being discovered that our immune cells generate nitrite and nitrate from L-arginine as part of our host defense system. Collectively, nitric oxide, whether administered through pro-drugs like nitroglycerin or through activation of endothelial cells or immune cells causes blood vessel dilation to increase blood flow. The pieces of the puzzle had been completed and the story of nitric oxide was born. Now the question became, how do we harness the therapeutic effects of nitric oxide to benefit humans? Were there other ways the human body produced nitric oxide.

At this point, the primary pathway for nitric oxide production involved the enzymatic conversion of L-arginine to nitric oxide gas by an enzyme called nitric oxide synthase. It appeared that this NOS enzyme is what became dysfunctional that led to a decrease in nitric oxide production which caused many different diseases.

Experiments later revealed that the production of nitric oxide from L-arginine by the enzyme nitric oxide synthase may be one of the most complicated and complex reactions in the human body. This did not make sense to me. If nitric oxide was the critically important and essential molecule that the entire scientific community believed, why was there only one way to make this molecule and why is the primary way to produce it so complicated that required almost perfect conditions for its production?

What I had learned as a biochemist and physiologist is that there is enormous redundancy in the human body. In other words, there is more than one way to skin a cat. There had to be other sources of nitric oxide that could act as a backup system or rescue system to always provide a source of nitric oxide signaling.

CHAPTER 5
How is nitric oxide produced in humans?
"Things are there when you can't see them, present but invisible."
—2 Kings 6:15-17

After the Nobel Prize was awarded in the field of nitric oxide, there was explosion of research. Today, we recognize that nitric oxide is one of the most important molecules produced in the human body. It regulates many important cell functions including regulation of blood flow and blood pressure, communication between cells in the brain as well as how our body defends itself against pathogens. We now know that there are two primary pathways for the production of NO.

As discussed in the previous chapter, nitric oxide is produced by the enzyme nitric oxide synthase from the conversion of L-arginine to nitric oxide gas. Today, we know there is a backup system or redundancy in the production of nitric oxide that comes from the food we eat and the presence of select bacteria that live in and on our body as well as our ability to secrete stomach acid.

Each pathway contributes about 50% of the total body NO production. When one fails the other can compensate. When both fail, bad things happen and people begin to get sick due to decreased blood flow and increased inflammation causing dysfunctional cells and organ systems.

It is crucial to understand how the body normally makes nitric oxide and what goes wrong in people that cannot make it. If you don't understand these two fundamental principles, then you can never effectively and efficiently restore your body's nitric oxide production and as a result, you cannot optimize your body's performance and health.

Today, the scientific literature reveals that there are two ways the body makes nitric oxide. At the time the Nobel Prize was awarded it was recognized that an enzyme nitric oxide synthase or NOS produces nitric oxide through a very complex reaction converting L-arginine into nitric oxide gas. In the 1990's there was work being published on an enzyme independent source of nitric oxide that appeared to be dependent on oral bacteria and stomach acid production. Nitric oxide (NO) through this pathway could be enhanced through the consumption of green leafy vegetables.

The origin of the nitric oxide was from inorganic nitrate found in green leafy vegetables. The bacteria in the mouth were utilizing nitrate that was found in food and secreted in the saliva and converting nitrate into nitrite and nitric oxide.

These observations revealed that through the eating and metabolism of inorganic nitrate found in green leafy vegetables and some root vegetables, the bacteria could provide the human body with an additional source of nitrite and nitric oxide. However, earlier in the 1970s it was revealed that nitrate from our food is absorbed in the gut and concentrated in our mouths, in our salivary glands. There are nitrate-reducing bacteria that live

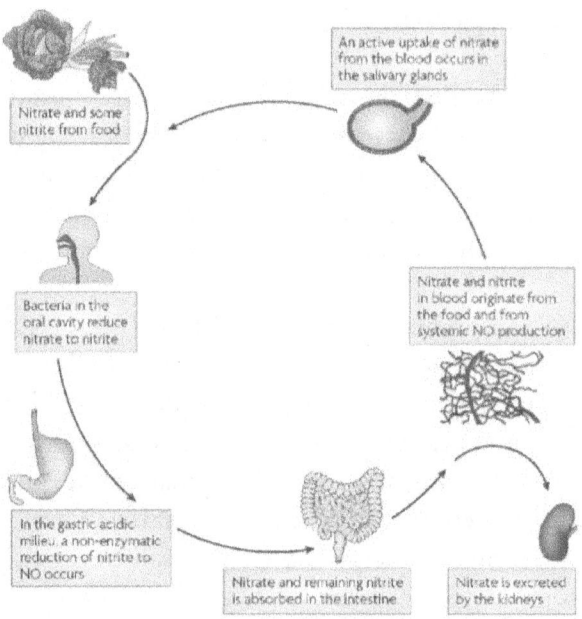

Nitrate-Nitrite-Nitric Oxide Pathway.
Lundberg *et al Nat Rev Discov.*, 2008.

in the crypts of our tongue that convert nitrate to nitrite and nitric oxide. Our saliva then becomes highly concentrated in nitrite and when we swallow our own saliva, we get nitric oxide produced in the inside space of the stomach provided there is stomach acid.

For this pathway to work, people must consume sufficient nitrate from their diet (300-400mg), must have the right oral bacteria and must have sufficient stomach acid production.

This reveals that if we eat food enriched in inorganic nitrate such as green leafy vegetables and we have a diverse oral microbiome with nitrate-reducing bacteria and our stomach makes sufficient stomach acid, then we can supplement and enhance nitric oxide production through our diet.

Would it be possible to provide enough nitric oxide through the diet, oral bacteria and stomach acid to overcome a deficiency in the enzymatic production of nitric oxide by the NOS enzyme? Could either pathway compensate for the loss from the other? Could this explain why certain diets and food lead to nitric oxide deficiency and cause chronic disease? Is using mouthwash really bad and unhealthy since it kills the good nitrate-reducing bacteria in our mouth that disrupts nitric oxide production through this pathway? What effect do all the antacid drugs have on nitric oxide production since we need stomach acid to produce nitric oxide? These were all very important questions that needed to be answered in order to fully understand how to optimize our ability to produce nitric oxide.

This nitrate-nitrite-nitric oxide pathway was focused on oral bacteria that lived in the crypts of the tongue. The NOS enzyme is found in cells throughout the body, but primarily in the cells that line all blood vessels, our endothelial cells. L-arginine is a semi-essential amino acid, meaning that your body makes it through normal metabolism in the urea cycle and it is also found in many proteins we eat.

When we eat protein and the protein is broken down into amino acids, L-arginine is provided to the body. Unless you have an inborn error in metabolism (which is extremely rare), then your body will always make enough L-arginine to produce NO. The reaction to convert L-arginine to nitric oxide is complex and complicated and requires many different co-factors and substrates. For this pathway to work, the NOS enzyme must be active and functional.

L-arginine is classified as a semi-essential or conditionally essential amino acid because the ability of the body to synthesize sufficient quantities to meet its needs varies according to developmental age and the incidence of disease or injury. The biosynthetic pathway produces L-arginine and it is then shuttled to the enzyme that makes nitric oxide.

This pathway creates more than 20-50 times than what is needed to fully activate the nitric oxide synthase enzyme. Consequently, there is rarely ever a need to supplement with L-arginine.

L-arginine is found in many plant and animal proteins including dairy products (e.g., cottage cheese, ricotta, milk, yogurt, whey protein drinks), beef, pork (e.g. bacon, ham), gelatin, poultry (chicken and turkey light meat), wild game (pheasant, quail), seafood (halibut, lobster, salmon, shrimp, snails, tuna); Plant sources such as wheat germ and flour, buckwheat, granola, oatmeal, peanuts, nuts (coconut, pecans, cashews, walnuts, almonds, Brazil nuts, hazelnuts, pinenuts), seeds (pumpkin, sesame, sunflower), chick peas, cooked soybeans.

Humans never become deficient in L-arginine with the exception of a rare genetic disorder that we will discuss later. There are conditions that

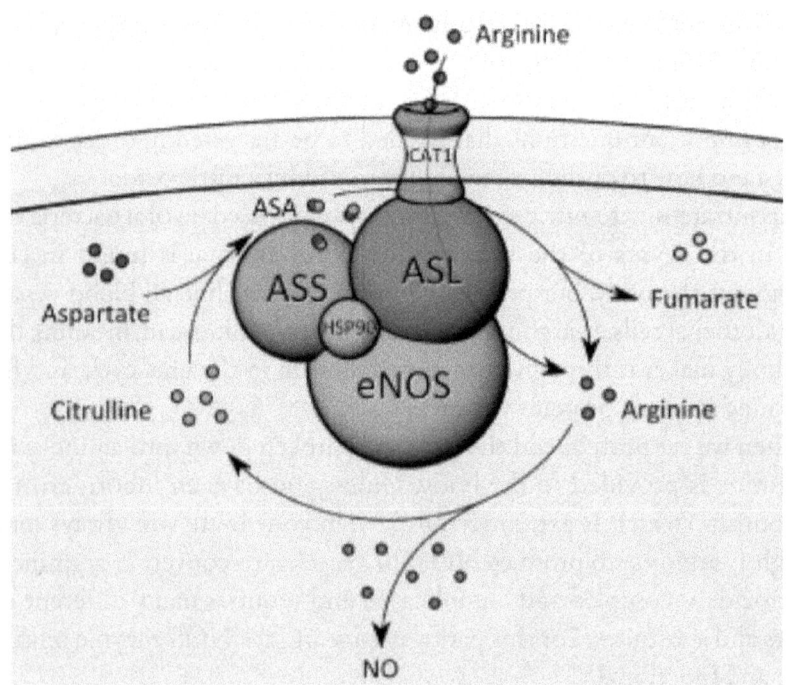

Model for the NOS complex in arginine channeling.
Arginine from de novo cellular synthesis by ASL or via transport from extracellular pools by CAT-1 can be channeled to NOS via ASL.

affect metabolism of L-arginine which may shuttle it away from nitric oxide production but very few cases of clinical L-arginine deficiency.

For NO production to occur through the NOS enzyme and conversion of L-arginine, it requires the NOS gene to be transcribed from DNA and then translated into an active protein within each cell. Once the protein is expressed and active, the production of NO can be affected by certain inhibitor e.g., NG-hydroxy-arginine and asymmetric dimethyl-arginine (ADMA), and reduced cofactor availability, e.g., tetrahydrobiopterin (BH4).

It is estimated that only about 3-5% of the intracellular L-arginine is directed through the NO pathway. As a bi-product of the NOS reaction to produce NO from L-arginine, L-citrulline is also formed. L-citrulline is not a pre-cursor to NO production but rather a bi-product of NO production. Citrulline can, however, be recycled back to L-arginine by argininosuccinate synthetase (ASS) and argininosuccinate lyase (ASL), forming the citrulline-NO cycle. What is clear is that L-arginine availability does not necessarily mean more NO production due to many competing catabolic processes.

However, for years scientists and physicians have investigated L-arginine supplementation as a means to enhance NO production. This strategy may work in young healthy individuals who have normal expression of the NOS enzyme and all the required co-factors needed and who do not have any inhibitors present.

Patients with endothelial dysfunction, however, by definition, are unable to convert L-arginine to NO and, therefore, this strategy has failed in clinical trials.

In fact, L-arginine therapy in acute myocardial infarction: the Vascular Interaction with Age in Myocardial Infarction (VINTAGE MI) randomized clinical trial published in the *JAMA* in 2006, concluded that L-arginine, when added to standard postinfarction therapies, did not improve vascular stiffness measurements or ejection fraction and was associated with higher postinfarction mortality.

Simply put, the patients who received L-arginine got worse and died more often than those who received a placebo. The summary of the study was that L-arginine should not be recommended following acute myocardial infarction (MI). This is because the NOS enzyme is uncoupled in patients that have suffered a heart attack.

Further, supplementing L-arginine to promote nitric oxide production in people with risk factors for heart disease such as smoking, obesity, high blood pressure, diabetes, high cholesterol, sedentary lifestyle and history of heart disease does not work as it does not increase the production of NO. By definition these people have endothelial dysfunction, a clinical diagnosis which means that their endothelium (the cells that line every blood vessel in the body) cannot convert L-arginine into Nitric Oxide.

In a completely separate study investigating the effects of L-arginine on patients with peripheral artery disease (PAD), the results were the same. L-arginine supplementation provided no benefit and actually made the patients worse. This study was published in the journal *Circulation* in 2007.

The authors concluded that "in patients with PAD, long-term administration n of L-arginine does not increase nitric oxide synthesis or improve vascular reactivity. Furthermore, the expected placebo effect observed in studies of functional capacity was attenuated in the L-arginine-treated group. As opposed to its short-term administration, long-term administration of L-arginine is not useful in patients with intermittent claudication and PAD."

Once we understand the complexity of systems that metabolize L-arginine combined with the complexity of the reaction to convert L-arginine to NO, we can begin to understand why L-arginine therapy is not effective, especially in the aging population or in patients with known cardiovascular risk factors and endothelial dysfunction.

The production of NO from L-arginine is one of the most complicated reactions in the human body. This reaction is a five-electron oxidation requiring 8 different co-factors and substrates and is an energy consuming process. There are many steps that may be altered and affect ultimate NO production along the reaction pathway. Providing the enzyme NOS with supplemental L-arginine because of lowered availability of L-arginine does not appear to be rate limiting since the intracellular levels of the amino acid are in the millimolar range, and the enzyme's Michaelis constant (KM) for substrate is in the micromolar range (2.9 μmol/L).

Circulating L-arginine measured in plasma of healthy humans as well as in plasma of patients with vascular disorders is in the range of 45–100 μmol/L. This is up to 15 to 30-fold higher than the concentration required to saturate the binding sites of the NOS enzyme. This biochemical discrepancy is called the "arginine paradox."

Hopefully you begin to see the problem with L-arginine-based supplements designed to enhance nitric oxide. The people that need nitric oxide the most cannot utilize the L-arginine that is readily available to convert it to nitric oxide, regardless of how much L-arginine they receive. This is due to only 3-5% of available L-arginine going through the NOS pathway and the fact that the NOS pathway is dysfunctional and unable to convert this portion of the L-arginine pool into NO. It is clear that L-arginine supplementation is not the right therapeutic strategy for a number of patients with vascular disorders.

However, research shows there may be some therapeutic benefit of L-arginine supplementation in children with sickle cell anemia. It may be that these kids have a higher concentration of specific inhibitors of nitric oxide synthesis that may be outcompeted with additional L-arginine. There may also be other mechanisms in play. Regardless, we know our body cannot and will not heal or function properly without sufficient nitric oxide.

CHAPTER 6
What is Nitric Oxide and Why Should you Care?

"There may be no disease process where this miracle molecule does not have a protective role."
—Louis J. Ignarro, Ph.D., a 1998 Nobel Laureate.

At the time this book is written there are nearly 200,000 scientific studies published on nitric oxide. The preponderance of evidence reveals that nitric oxide is an essential signaling molecule that is responsible for many important biological and physiological functions. We have an understanding of how this critical molecule is produced. We now understand what leads to a loss of nitric oxide production and we now understand how to replete and restore nitric oxide production and signaling. It is this understanding that will change the world and improve health care globally.

Let's consider the facts:

- Nitric Oxide is one of the most important molecules produced in your body to prevent a number of human diseases including cardiovascular disease, the #1 killer of men and women.
- Pharmaceutical companies have been attempting to develop drugs around Nitric Oxide for years.
- Literally hundreds of thousands of studies have been published on the importance of Nitric Oxide, in the most credible medical journals in the world.
- L-arginine is still a popular product sold in the nutrition and dietary supplement industry as a way to improve nitric oxide, yet grossly ineffective.

However, in the United States, most people first heard of nitric oxide as L-arginine or beet derived supplements used before a workout to get a better "pump" or in over-the-counter erectile dysfunction products.

If you Google Nitric Oxide, the first several pages are all links related to someone trying to sell you a workout product or an erectile dysfunction product. This is due primarily to the fact that a number of companies have exploited Nitric Oxide as a vasodilator that can enhance exercise performance, muscle gain, endurance and sexual performance by supplementing L-arginine. The vast majority of these products have no scientific basis for the claims they make. In order to understand the limitations of L-arginine based products, as we reviewed previously, we must first understand how the body utilizes L-arginine in the cell to produce NO.

When I started my career in nitric oxide more than 25 years ago, the scientific community was excited and certainly informed about nitric oxide, but the public in general was not aware of nitric oxide or its importance whatsoever. Let's review what is known about nitric oxide so hopefully everyone who reads this book will understand why everyone should be aware of nitric oxide and how it affects their own health.

Nitric oxide has been recognized as extremely important for more than 30 years. In fact, in 1992 it was deemed "Molecule of the Year" by *Science Magazine*. Nitric oxide is now considered one of the most important molecules produced in the human body. This single molecule can:

- normalize high blood pressure (hypertension), a disease that damages your heart, brain, and kidneys.
- keep your arteries young and flexible.
- prevent, slow, or reverse the buildup of artery-clogging arterial plaques.
- help stop the formation of artery-clogging blood clots—the result of plaques bursting and spilling their contents into the blood stream.
- lower triglycerides.

And by doing all of the above, reduce your risk of heart attack and stroke, the #1 killers of men and women worldwide.

Nitric oxide has also been shown to reduce the risk of diabetes and disastrous diabetic complications, such as chronic kidney disease, blindness, hard-to-heal foot and leg ulcers, and amputations, limit the swelling and pain of arthritis, and boost the power of pain-relieving drugs, reverse erectile dysfunction (ED), calm the choking inflammation of asthma, protect your bones from osteoporosis, help provide the mood-lifting power behind antidepressant medications, assist the immune system in killing bacteria and viruses, limit skin damage from the sun and improve your overall performance.

To the contrary, a lack or deficiency of this molecule is what causes most diseases, including cardiovascular disease, the number one killer of men and women worldwide. That is why the scientific and medical community are so excited that this molecule can be restored and optimized through nutrition from specific foods and diet but also now through rationally designed therapeutics.

Nitric oxide's primary function is to regulate blood flow and circulation. It is required for oxygen delivery to every cell in the body and it is responsible for killing invading pathogens such as viruses and bacteria. The older you get the less nitric oxide you make. We call this endothelial dysfunction. It is the loss of nitric oxide that is responsible for age related disease. Nitric oxide is NO, one atom of nitrogen and one atom of oxygen (N_1O_1), as simple as can be.

Simple, in fact, that it's a gas, not a liquid or solid when it is produced within the body. When it's created and released by cells, this gas easily and quickly penetrates nearby membranes and other cells, sending its signals. In less than a second, NO signals:

- arteries to relax and expand.
- immune cells to kill bacteria, viruses and cancer cells.
- brain cells to communicate with each other.

In fact, NO sends crucial signals within every cell, tissue, organ, and system of the body. This all occurs when our body produces nitric oxide upon demand. We now know that there are two pathways to make NO in the human body.

The endothelial cells, the cells that line all our blood vessels throughout the circulatory system, generate NO from L-arginine. In young healthy blood vessels, this pathway is functional and generates sufficient NO to maintain normal blood pressure and to maintain the integrity of the circulatory system.

The Secret of Nitric Oxide

Dietary nitrite and nitrate consumption. Nitrate found primarily in green leafy vegetables and root vegetables is broken down into nitrite and nitric oxide based on bacteria that live in and on our body.

Each pathway can compensate for the loss of the other but when you lose the ability to produce nitric oxide from both pathways, then that is when you start to develop symptoms and if not corrected, will develop chronic disease. There are a number of factors that lead to a loss of nitric oxide production.

Aging is considered the single largest risk factor related to cardiovascular related diseases and deaths. Clinical data reveal that the older we get, the less nitric oxide our body produces from the NOS enzyme that utilizes L-arginine to make NO.

Sufficient nitric oxide protects the heart and blood vessels. This level of cardio-protection decreases with increasing age and is attributed to a decline in NO. Aging is the most common risk factor for loss of nitric oxide production. Most of the functional and structural vascular alterations that lead to cardiovascular complications are similar in aging and the development of high blood pressure.

Moreover, these vascular changes associated with essential hypertension are generally considered to be an accelerated form of the changes seen with aging. When we are young and healthy, the endothelial production of NO through L-arginine is efficient and sufficient to produce NO; however, as we age, we lose our ability to synthesize endothelial derived NO. There is also evidence that the cells of the body produce less of the nitric oxide synthase enzyme the older we get. So not only do we have less of the enzyme but the enzyme that is present is typically not functional the older we get.

There is a gradual decline in endothelial function due to aging with greater than 50% loss in endothelial nitric oxide production in the oldest age group tested as measured by forearm blood flow assays. In 70-80 year-old patients, there is 75% less nitric oxide being produced in the blood vessels of the heart compared to young healthy 20 year olds.

Increasing age was one predictor of abnormal endothelium-dependent vasodilation in atherosclerotic human coronary arteries. Other studies have concluded that age was the most significant predictor of endothelium-dependent nitric oxide production.

Collectively, these important findings illustrate that endothelium-dependent vasodilation in resistance vessels declines progressively with increasing age. These data are illustrated in the figure below.

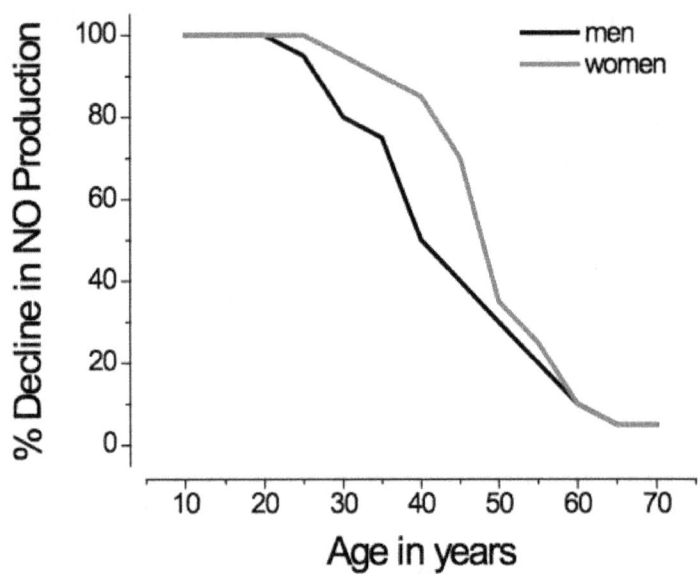

This abnormality is present in healthy adults who have no other cardiovascular risk factors, such as diabetes, hypertension, or hypercholesterolemia. Most of these studies found that impairment of endothelium-dependent vasodilation was clearly evident by the time people reach the age of forty.

The older you are, the lower your NO, because of the age-related decline in endothelial function. We lose about 10-12% of our endothelial produced NO per decade. In fact, by the time we are about 40 years old we have lost about 50% of our ability to generate NO from our endothelial cells. In one study, Italian researchers evaluated forearm blood flow—the standard measurement of endothelial health—in 47 people with normal blood pressure and 49 people with high blood pressure. They found that in both groups, those who were older had poorer endothelial-dependent vasodilation: the NO-sparked ability of arteries to widen and permit health-giving blood flow. And that weakening of the endothelium was in perfect parallel to aging—decade by decade, NO-powered, endothelial-dependent vasodilation declined. Specifically:

- 30 years old and younger. Endothelial-dependent vasodilation was strongest.
- 31 to 45 years old. Vasodilation was 11 percent weaker than in the 30-and-younger set.
- 46 to 60 years old. Vasodilation was 13 percent weaker than in the 31- to 45-year-olds.
- 60 and older. Vasodilation was 28 percent weaker than in the 46- to 60-year-olds.

All in all, those 60 and older had vasodilation that was 52 percent weaker—less than half as strong—as those 30 and younger. And these were older people who did not have high blood pressure.

"Advancing age is an independent factor leading to the progressive impairment of endothelium-dependent vasodilation in humans," concluded the researchers in the journal *Circulation*. The functional changes in the endothelium precede the structural changes seen in vascular disease by many years, sometimes decades.

Why does the endothelium weaken with age?

"A progressive reduction of NO availability," wrote the researchers. In fact, they wrote, their findings suggest that "in aged individuals NO availability is almost totally compromised." In a similar study, Japanese researchers tested vasodilation in 18 healthy people, aged 23 to 70.

A list of the patients and their response to the vasodilator is striking, showing a near-perfect correlation between age and endothelial health. The 23-year-old in the study had an artery that expanded more than five times its width when the individual was given a vasodilator; the artery of the 70-year-old expanded a little more than two times. "Coronary blood flow response to acetylcholine (an endothelium-dependent vasodilator) decreased significantly with aging," concluded the re-searchers in the journal *Circulation*. Why? Because of the age-related decrease in the release of "endothelium-derived relaxing factor or NO."

Another study by the same team of Japanese researchers found a loss of 75 percent of endothelium-produced NO in people 70 to 80 years old as compared to 20-year-olds. It's important to emphasize that this decline happens not only to people with CVD but to healthy older adults: people who don't have high blood pressure . . . people who don't have vascular disease . . . people who don't have circulation-damaging diabetes. In other words, it happens to everybody who gets older.

So, if this molecule is so critical for optimal health and disease prevention, then if we could figure out how to prevent the decline in NO production with aging, then perhaps we could prevent many age-related diseases. This would truly be the "holy grail" in cardiovascular medicine. That is why this book is so important because we know how to do this and hopefully reading this book you will be armed with the information to prevent the loss of nitric oxide in your own body.

The scientific and medical literature tells us that loss of NO production and availability is the earliest event in the onset and progression of cardiovascular disease, the number 1 killer of men and women worldwide.

Understanding the two primary pathways for producing nitric oxide, we can now understand conditions where either one or both of these pathways become disrupted.

As a way of review, the two pathways are:

- The Nitric Oxide Synthase (NOS) enzyme that converts L-arginine to NO.
- The Nitrate Nitrite Nitric Oxide Pathway that utilizes nitrate from our diet and requires oral bacteria and stomach acid production.

If one system goes down, the other one can compensate and pull the weight for the other. However, it both systems fail, then you are in trouble and disease will start to set in. The endothelial pathway becomes disrupted with age. Since pathway 1 becomes compromised with aging, older people must then rely on pathway 2. Under ideal conditions, both pathways provide about 50% of our total body NO, so when both are working and functioning properly, we make sufficient NO and all systems in our body are functioning properly. Not only have we figured out how to "fix" the problem with the loss of NO from pathway 1 with age, we have also figured out how to optimize pathway 2 so that no matter how old we get, we can still have sufficient NO production so that we are resistant to disease.

In contrast, the response to nitric oxide does not change significantly with aging. This is extremely important because all we have to do is improve nitric oxide production and the body will always respond.

These observations enable us to conclude that reduced availability of endothelium-derived NO occurs as we age, and to speculate that this abnormality may create an environment that is conducive to atherogenesis and other vascular disorders, including Alzheimer's disease. It appears that aging interrupts NO signaling at every conceivable level, from production to inactivation. Given that NO is a necessary molecule for maintenance of health and prevention of disease, restoration of NO homeostasis may provide a new treatment modality for age and age-related disease.

Understanding the normal biochemical pathway for NO production and the effects of aging on NO production, we can begin to implement therapeutic regimens to overcome NO insufficiency and monitor patient symptoms. There are currently only 3 FDA approved products on the market directly related to NO:

1) organic nitrates, such as nitroglycerin for the treatment of acute angina (these have been used for centuries long before the discovery of NO);

2) inhaled NO therapy for neonates for treatment of pulmonary hypertension due to underdeveloped lungs;

3) phosphodiesterase inhibitors, such as sildenafil, which do not directly affect NO production but act through affecting the downstream second messenger of NO, cyclic guanosine monophosphate (cGMP).

There are a number of over-the-counter products designed to enhance NO production using supplemental L-arginine. We now understand the limitations of L-arginine and how this is not an effective strategy to restore NO production in the majority of the patient population.

My research over the past 25 years has revealed a safe and effective way to restore nitric oxide production. I was the first and still the only person to create a solid dose form of a bioactive gas. I developed an orally disintegrating lozenge that when placed in the mouth and as it begins to dissolve it produces nitric oxide gas. If your body cannot produce nitric oxide, my technology does it for you. This technology provides an alternate source of NO to compensate for insufficient NO production associated with aging and other risk factors.

Since NO is a gas that is gone is less than a second after it is produced within the body, it is not simple to supplement with body with NO gas. Therefore, we have to understand how the body makes NO, and then provide the body with the raw material and nutrients it needs in order to efficiently produce NO.

We have discovered and identified these essential nutrients necessary and sufficient for generating NO in the human body. Nutrients, remember, are substances that are essential to life which must be supplied by food. Since NO itself cannot be delivered in foods, we must identify the precursors to this molecule that become the nutrients necessary for NO production. The unknown nutrients necessary and sufficient for NO production that is found in food are nitrite and nitrate.

What we now know about NO may explain very early concept around what "animated" humans.

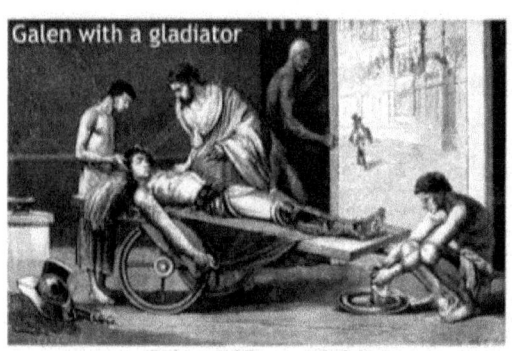

Galen (129 - c. AD 216)

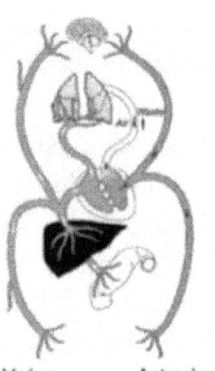

Veins   Arteries

Galen believed that food was absorbed by the intestines and transported to the liver, which transformed it into blood. Blood ebbed and flowed through veins and was consumed by body tissues. Some blood seeped from the right side of the heart to the left, mixed with air (pneuma) and became vital spirit, which flowed through arteries to body tissues.

The early Roman physician Galen based his description of the vascular system on the concept of "pneuma" or spirits, a vital principle consisting of matter in a finely divided or ethereal state that flowed through the vascular and nervous systems and animate the entire organism. Many diseases were thought to owe their origin to some disturbances of these ethereal spirits.

The Secret of Nitric Oxide

Although these ideas were fanciful, this paradigm actually prevented the advancement of medical science for centuries. Today evidence on the production and effects of such an ethereal substance, NO, exists.

Nitric oxide is indeed formed in many organs and as previously mentioned has important roles in physiology and pathophysiology. Nitric oxide is produced in the lungs and then carried by our red blood cells to fully oxygenate and animate us humans. Galen understood this concept nearly 2000 years ago.

Even earlier in Ancient Chinese medicine and culture, the concept of Qi (pronounced chi) was introduced. "Qi"(氣) literally means gas in Chinese. Chinese medicine has long recognized that gasses within the body play a role in the warming, holding, energizing and providing communication within the human body.

Medically there are names for many kinds of gasses based on their actions in the body. While they lacked the technology to identify and measure the exact gasses, the early Chinese were keenly aware of how these gasses permeated the body and the points at which they exited the skin.

Nitric oxide has been suggested to be Qi. It can pass freely through membranes, transmit signals from neurons to target cells. Nitric oxide has well-defined functions. It sends messages to tell cells how much energy they should be producing. When the right proportion of NO reaches fat stores, they begin to transform fat into useable energy and heat.

The new emerging paradigm that NO is modulated by dietary nitrogen oxides and other bioactive food components is exciting. It appears that we may have identified a critical component of our diet that many people are missing. In fact, certain compounds we have been taught to fear and avoid in our diet, nitrite and nitrate, may be saving our lives from inflammatory diseases.

Need more reason to understand nitric oxide? It is the molecule responsible for erections in both men and women. The role of NO in penile erection was first revealed after researchers observed that the injection of nitric oxide synthase (NOS) inhibitors prevented penile erectile responses in rats.

However, this inhibitory effect was not observed when NOS inhibitors were injected concomitantly with L-arginine, one of the substrates for NO. This was soon confirmed by other studies showing that NO donors injected into the periventricular nucleus (PVN) induced penile erections. It is worth noting that these rats have a functional NOS enzyme that can convert L-arginine to NO. The mechanism by which these compounds induce penile erection is apparently secondary to the release of NO, which in turn causes the activation of oxytocinergic neurons.

Direct measurements of NO in the medial pre-optic area (MPOA) of the brain showed NO release associated with copulatory behavior, meaning it stimulated sexual desire and activity. NO production increased in the PVN during noncontact erection and copulation.

The PVN is one of the brain areas containing the highest levels of NOS, and the enzyme is present in the cell bodies of oxytocinergic neurons.

Erection in men and women is a hemodynamic process involving relaxation of smooth muscle of the corpus cavernosum and its associated arterioles. This relaxation process results in an increased flow of blood into the trabecular spaces of the corpora cavernosa. Smooth muscle relaxation is mediated by NO which, during sexual stimulation, is synthesized in the nerve terminals of parasympathetic non-adrenergic, non-cholinergic (NANC) neurons in the penis and clitoris and also by the endothelial cells lining blood vessels and the lacunar spaces of the corpora cavernosa.

NO activates guanylate cyclase resulting in an increased conversion of guanosine triphosphate (GTP) to cyclic guanosine monophosphate (cGMP). cGMP provides the signal which leads to relaxation of the smooth muscle of the corpus cavernosum and penile/clitoral arterioles.

The level of cGMP is regulated by a balance between the rate of synthesis by guanylate cyclase and the rate of hydrolytic breakdown to guanosine 5´-monophosphate (GMP) by cyclic nucleotide phosphodiesterase (PDE) isozymes.

Therefore, agents that inhibit cGMP hydrolysis (phosphodiesterase inhibitors) may increase the cGMP signal and could be expected to enhance relaxation of smooth muscle in the corpus cavernosum and thereby facilitate penile erectile responses. In fact, this is the mechanism of action of drugs like Viagra, Cialis and Levitra.

The Secret of Nitric Oxide

WHAT GOES WRONG IN PEOPLE THAT CAN'T MAKE NITRIC OXIDE?

As part of the aging process, we make less nitric oxide. This is because the enzyme NOS becomes dysfunctional and no longer converts L-arginine to nitric oxide. This is termed endothelial dysfunction. The other problem is that most Americans do not consume sufficient vegetables to get enough nitrate.

The typical American diet only contains 150mg per nitrate per day. We know we need at least 300 mg of nitrate per serving to lead to any appreciable production of nitric oxide, provided the person has the right oral bacteria and stomach acid production.

We know that more than 200 million Americans wake up every day and use an antiseptic mouthwash. This represents over half of the US population. The antiseptic mouthwash does a good job killing bad breath but unfortunately it also kills the bacteria essential to nitric oxide production.

If you use an antiseptic mouthwash, you receive no nitric oxide benefit from eating a diet enriched in dietary nitrate. Oral antibiotics also destroy the oral microbiome as well as the gut microbiome. There are over 200 million prescriptions written for antibiotics every year in the U.S. alone.

To make things even worse, there are over 100 million prescriptions written every year for proton pump inhibitors (PPIs) which reduce stomach acid and even more for antibiotics that kill the good bacteria. These are drugs such as Prilosec, Prevacid, Nexium, Protonix or any generic drug ending in "prazole" such as omeprazole and pantoprazole.

Now, many of these antacid drugs can be purchased over the counter. Therefore, there may be another 100 million Americans that take antacids that are not reported by the prescription data. As a result of poor diets, the use of antiseptic mouthwashes, antibiotics and antacids the majority of Americans become nitric oxide deficient.

For me, it is no wonder Americans are the sickest people on the planet. Our way of life and our way of practicing medicine and prescription medications are completely shutting down nitric oxide production.

Things that completely shut down nitric oxide production:
    Antiseptic mouthwash.
    Fluoride toothpaste

Antacids

Antibiotics

If you find yourself using one or more of the above products or drugs, and you have symptoms of nitric oxide deficiency, you may now know the reason. Do your best to wean off of any drugs and immediately stop the use of mouthwash and fluoridated toothpaste.

There is sufficient published data today showing that the use of mouthwash causes your blood pressure to go up and if you use mouthwash, you lose the protective benefits of exercise. Of course, there are alternatives to antiseptic mouthwash.

Think about this for a minute. You may be doing everything you have been taught is right. Eat a healthy diet with lots of vegetables, exercise daily but if you use mouthwash, you do not get the nitric oxide benefits from your diet or your exercise. This is an incredible epiphany.

There is also overwhelming data revealing that people who have been taking antacids for 3-5 years have about a 40% higher incidence of heart attack, stroke and Alzheimer's disease. The use of mouthwash and antacids is leading to chronic disease and now we know why. They are inhibiting the body's ability to produce nitric oxide.

We will reveal the consequences of insufficient NO production in the next chapter.

CHAPTER 7
Consequences of NO insufficiency

"The aim of medicine is to prevent disease and prolong life; the ideal of medicine is to eliminate the need of a physician."
—William J. Mayo

Now we know how the human body produces nitric oxide. We have an understanding of what causes a loss of nitric oxide production. So now, what happens when we lose the ability to produce nitric oxide? The lack of NO production can lead to hypertension, atherosclerosis, peripheral artery disease, diabetes, heart failure, and thrombosis leading to heart attack and stroke, the leading cause of death for all Americans. Remarkably, if we can recognize these conditions and early symptoms, all evidence points to the fact that they can all be prevented. Since there is really no diagnostic test for nitric oxide production/availability, we must rely on symptoms. There is a growing list of symptoms that may reveal an early loss of nitric oxide production. We will now review a few of the most common conditions/symptoms your patients may present and its relationship to NO production.

It appears that there is a hierarchy of symptoms that manifest as the body loses its ability to produce nitric oxide. I'll review them in the order in which they first appear. This is not always the case, but holds true most of the time.

Erectile/Sexual Dysfunction

For many years and for many patients, the first sign of cardiovascular disease was a heart attack. Symptoms included shortness of breath, heavy chest, pain in the chest or jaw, or radiating pain or numbness in the arm. The heart attack and subsequent symptoms indicated patients had developed overt coronary artery disease that had taken place over many years. Their first symptom was a heart attack, and in many cases, sudden death. At this stage of the disease, it is too late to take preventative measures. This concerning reality directed scientific research to find subtle cardiovascular warning signs that could be recognized sooner, enabling corrective measures and even reversal of the disease. Cardiovascular medicine may have found its answer in erectile dysfunction (ED). We now know that sexual dysfunction is actually the first sign of insufficient NO production that sets the stage for the progression of heart disease.

Under normal healthy conditions, when stimulated for sexual activity, the nerve endings in the sex organs and the blood vessels serving the sex organs are activated to produce nitric oxide. NO is then produced in the sex organs of both men and women and that signals the blood vessels to dilate and accommodate more blood flow. It is engorgement from blood flow that causes and sustains an erection, both a penile erection and clitoral erection in women. Without sufficient NO production, there is no vasodilation, no increase in blood flow, no engorgement and thus no erection or a poor erection that is insufficient for intercourse.

When erectile dysfunction is mentioned, most people think it is a male disease. The same holds true for women. Without proper blood flow to the clitoris, women cannot have orgasms or enhanced sexual sensitivity. In women, orgasm occur when there is an increase in clitoral or labial pressure.

That pressure comes from an increase in blood flow that is a consequence of an increase in nitric oxide production. If there is no nitric oxide produced, due to endothelial dysfunction, then there can be no increase in blood flow and no increase in pressure and thus no orgasm. Can't you see how all this is tied together now? The more serious problem though, is if you have endothelial dysfunction and nitric oxide deficiency in the blood vessels of the sex organs, then you have that same dysfunction in the blood vessels of the heart, brain, liver, kidney and every vascular bed in the body.

Male or female patients with endothelial dysfunction are unable to generate sufficient NO and therefore, are unable to attain a normal sexual response. Erectile dysfunction is classified as a vascular disorder that is a red flag for the presence of endothelial dysfunction and developing cardiovascular disease. Although ED is typically classified as a male symptom or disease, it also affects females. As endothelial dysfunction is defined as the loss of NO bioavailability, erectile problems present a clear indication of the need for NO.

The Secret of Nitric Oxide

Whether it is in the male penis or in the female clitoris and vagina, erections are initiated through increased blood flow into the corpus cavernosum of the penis in men and clitoral engorgement due to increased blood flow in women. In fact, sexual dysfunction is linked to cardiovascular disease in both men and women.

A significant proportion of men with ED exhibit early signs of coronary artery disease (CAD), and this group may develop more severe CAD than men without ED. The time interval among the onset of ED symptoms and the occurrence of CAD symptoms and cardiovascular events is estimated at 2-3 years and 3-5 years respectively. ED in both men and women is associated with increased all-cause mortality primarily due to increased cardiovascular mortality. Sexual dysfunction is now considered an early marker/risk factor for cardiovascular disease and consequently a life-threatening condition. Treatment of sexual dysfunction in men and women

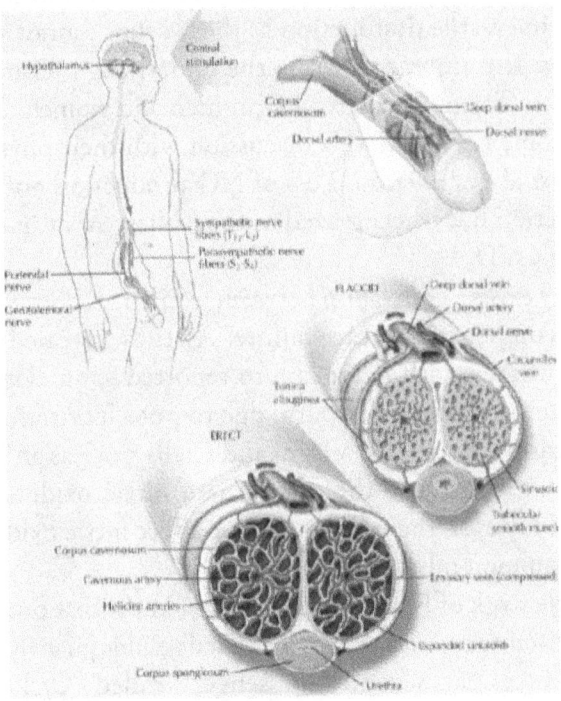

Nitric oxide causes erections due to dilation of blood vessels allowing for more blood flow which leads to engorgement.

as purely a lifestyle disorder may severely underestimate the seriousness of disorder. If you have ED, you have early stages of cardiovascular disease.

Mechanistically, we can explain how this works. Estrogen positively affects NO production and this may be responsible for the anti-atherosclerotic effects of estrogen. During menopause, estrogen production declines in women and this leads to loss of activation of endogenous NO production.

Multiple studies now show that estrogen replacement therapy increases NO availability and production in post-menopausal women. Without estrogen production, there is less NO resulting in reduced blood flow creating inability to produce and sustain an erection and orgasm in women. Current medical treatment for men with ED utilizes therapies such as oral phosphodiesterase type 5 inhibitors (PDE-5) which attempt to prolong the NO vasodilatory effect.

However, this therapy is not approved for women with sexual dysfunction. This does however serve to underscore the importance of the NO pathway in erectile dysfunction as these drugs cannot work without NO adequacy. Therefore, correcting the underlying NO insufficiency is necessary and sufficient to correct ED in men and women. This is exactly the reason people need to have a discussion with their physicians if they suffer from sexual dysfunction. Loss of NO production not only leads to sexual dysfunction but is recognized as the earliest event in the onset and progression of CVD.

In fact, there exists a correlation between women with sexual dysfunction and chronic compensated heart failure. A study revealed that 87% of middle-aged women with heart failure reported some degree of sexual dysfunction (unsuccessful intercourse due to poor lubrication and unable to achieve orgasm). Drugs like Viagra and Cialis work as an improvement in sexual function because they potentiate nitric oxide signaling and vasodilation. However, these drugs do not affect nitric oxide production and that is a common misconception.

Based on the work of Ferid Murad, we now know that once nitric oxide is produced, it activates another enzyme called soluble guanylyl cyclase. This enzyme produces a second messenger called cyclic guanosine monophosphate or cGMP. It is cGMP that leads to a mobilization of calcium inside the cells that leads to smooth muscle relaxation and this leads to dilation of the blood vessels causing an increase in blood flow.

As part of the normal cellular regulation, there is also an enzyme called phosphodiesterase that breaks down the cGMP which turns the signal off. Drugs like Viagra and Cialis are called phosphodiesterase inhibitors. These drugs prevent the breakdown of cGMP therefore potentiating the effects of nitric oxide enhancing blood flow. This is how they work to improve sexual function. In other words, nitric oxide turns the switch on and drugs like Viagra keep them on and that is the reason you are warned against 4-hour erections, an unsafe drop in blood pressure, headaches, loss of vision and other reported side effects.

Many people do not understand the risks of a 4-hour erection. In men, during an erection there is an inhibition in the outflow of blood in the penis. If all the oxygen is consumed over a period of time, then the penis can become hypoxic, a lack of oxygen. A prolonged period of low oxygen can lead to tissue necrosis and tissue death within the penis. If this occurs, the penis will never work again. Understand and appreciate that warning. We must have a continuous supply of oxygenated blood to every organ in the body.

These drugs were approved in 1998 and now with more than 25 years on the market, the clinical data reveal that 50% of the men that are prescribed these drugs for ED, do not respond with better erections.

Why do some men not respond to this type of therapy? Well, once you understand the mechanism, one can provide a valid explanation. In order for these drugs to work, there must be some level of nitric oxide produced in order to activate the second messenger cGMP. Without any nitric oxide production, there is no cGMP and therefore nothing for the phosphodiesterase inhibitors to prevent breakdown. This tells us that sexual dysfunction is a sign and symptom of insufficient nitric oxide production.

If we can increase nitric oxide production or restore its production, then these drugs can and will work. In fact, once we restore nitric oxide production, the need for these drugs may be reduced or at least one can lower the dose making them safer and more effective.

This mechanism is just not isolated to the sex organs. They work systemically. That is the reason they may cause an unsafe drop in blood pressure. This is why they cause headaches in many patients due to the increase in dilation of the cerebral arteries increasing intra-cranial pressures.

Today these types of drugs are even approved for pulmonary hypertension due to their systemic effects at dilating blood vessels. Initially these drugs were being developed for heart disease before it was realized that they worked in such a sexual way. However, this makes sense since both are a result of endothelial dysfunction. If you have ED, you have nitric oxide deficiency. ED is the proverbial "canary in the coalmine."

Take note of this very important symptom. It is reported that 50% of men over the age of 40 self-report erectile dysfunction. I would predict that same statistics in women. That means that the majority of Americans are nitric oxide deficient and if not corrected an additional long list of symptoms and diseases are coming. If you suffer from ED, then you must take corrective steps to restore your nitric oxide production.

Hypertension/high blood pressure

Hypertension, or high blood pressure, along with aging is a well-known cardiovascular risk factor that leads to functional and structural alterations in the heart and blood vessels that leads to cardiovascular disease. Nitric oxide is the major vasodilatory molecule produced in the lining of the blood vessels that regulates normal blood pressure.

Blood vessels respond to a number of different molecules. Some cause vasoconstriction such as caffeine, nicotine, endothelin, etc. and some cause vasodilation such as nitric oxide, adenosine, etc.

Blood pressure is controlled and regulated by the balance of vasoconstrictors and vasodilators. When your body loses its ability to produce the major vasodilator, then the vasoconstrictors win out and this leads to an increase in blood pressure. Think of what happens when you partially pinch off a garden hose. It causes an increase in pressure and the water sprays out with much greater force. This is because you have the same volume of fluid going through a much smaller tube which causes an increase in pressure.

When your body cannot produce nitric oxide the blood vessels are constantly constricted causing an increase in systemic blood pressure since we now have the same volume of blood traveling through smaller hoses. High blood pressure is the number one risk factor for the number one killer of men and women worldwide—cardiovascular disease.

Two out of three Americans have an unsafe elevation in blood pressure putting them at extreme risk of cardiovascular disease, heart attack and stroke. The older we get, the less nitric oxide we make. These results indicate that essential hypertension is characterized by an age-related reduction of nitric oxide. In order to combat hypertension, we must focus on the restoration of nitric oxide.

We know nitric oxide-based therapies can normalize blood pressure. Transdermal nitroglycerin which acts as a NO donor has been shown to reduce blood pressure in patients with a recent stroke. Dietary intervention with nitrite and nitrate has been shown to modestly reduce blood pressure in humans showing remarkable efficacy using this natural dietary approach. In fact, we published years ago in the *American Journal of Clinical Nutrition* that the efficacy of the Dietary Approaches to Stop Hypertension (DASH) diet works through its ability to restore nitric oxide based on the consumption of nitrate rich foods. My nitric oxide product technology has been shown in clinical trials to support healthy blood pressure.

Blood clotting disorders/Thrombosis

Thrombosis or formation of blood clots affects nearly 1 million patients in the United States annually. Out of those million, nearly 300,000 will die from these clots. That means that one third of people with blood clots die from it. A majority of current treatment options are centered on preventative anticoagulants, drugs such as warfarin, Plavix, or other blood thinning medications but with a real risk of bleeding.

In the early 1980s, it was discovered that nitric oxide produced by our own platelets prevents platelet activation and blood clot formation. This is part of the body's control and regulation of platelet function. Platelets have the same NOS enzyme as that found in our endothelial cells. If that enzyme becomes dysfunctional and unable to produce nitric oxide, then our platelets become hyperactive and are prone to become activated to form clots. So, patients who have endothelial dysfunction have the same dysfunction in their platelets and become compromised in their ability to produce nitric oxide. In addition, nitric oxide promotes platelet disaggregation meaning that if you have blood clots, nitric oxide can actually help resolve them and prevent additional platelets from sticking to existing clots.

In conjunction with its vasorelaxation properties, these anti-platelet effects of NO maintain blood fluidity and tissue perfusion. Nitric oxide derived both from the endothelial cell and the platelet, modulates platelet activation, adhesion, and aggregate formation, thereby serving as an important deterrent to platelet-mediated arterial thrombosis and even deep vein thrombosis (DVT).

The nitric oxide produced by our endothelial cells and by platelets also down-regulate adhesion molecules to prevent microvascular inflammation and transmigration of immune cells, fats and cholesterol. NO insufficiency, either through reduced production or oxidative inactivation leads to thrombotic events such as stroke, heart attack, pulmonary embolism, deep vein thrombosis, etc.

Efforts to restore the normal vascular redox balance and/or to restore normal NO availability may provide one therapeutic avenue for reducing platelet-dependent arterial thrombosis in patients. In fact, there are studies showing that dietary nitrate in the form of beetroot juice can inhibit platelet aggregation and blood clot formation demonstrating this dietary approach to replete NO may provide first line of defense for NO insufficiency.

If you are prone to blood clots, you should consider nitric oxide-based modalities as a first step in addressing the issue, rather than taking anti-platelet therapy that may increase your risk of bleeds.

Let's understand the root cause of the problem and address that. Loss of nitric oxide is at the root cause of many clinical conditions. You should always consult with your physician or health care practitioner regarding any weaning off or lowering any of your prescription medications.

NO Insufficiency is the root cause of Cardiovascular Disease (CVD)

CVD is a group of disorders including congestive heart failure (CHF) and ischemic heart disease that are the leading cause of morbidity and mortality in the world. CVD is the number one cause of death in both men and women around the globe. CVD can result from a quantitative or functional NO deficiency that can limit NO–dependent signal transduction pathways to the detriment of normal cellular function.

Atherosclerosis is the hardening and clogging of arteries and is the major source of morbidity and mortality in the developed world. The magnitude of this problem is profound, as atherosclerosis claims more lives than all types of cancer combined and the economic costs are considerable. Reduced nitric oxide production is a hallmark of atherosclerosis. Nitric oxide is what provides all the protective properties that prevent atherosclerosis including vasorelaxation, inhibition of leukocyte-endothelial adhesion, vascular smooth muscle cell (SMC) migration and proliferation, as well as platelet aggregation.

The Secret of Nitric Oxide

The concept of endothelial dysfunction arises from variations in blood flow observed in patients with atherosclerosis compared with healthy subjects. In healthy people, activation of eNOS causes vasodilation in both muscular conduit vessels and resistance arterioles. In contrast, in subjects with atherosclerosis, similar stimulation yields attenuated vasodilation in peripheral vessels and causes paradoxical vasoconstriction in coronary arteries, thus indicating a decrease in the production and/or bioavailability of NO.

Interestingly, endothelial dysfunction can be demonstrated in patients with risk factors for atherosclerosis in the absence of atherosclerosis itself, demonstrating that the functional loss of nitric oxide production precedes the structural changes in the blood vessels we see during the development of disease. These observations lend credence to the concept that endothelial dysfunction is integral to the development and progression of disease.

Impaired endothelium may abnormally reduce vascular perfusion, produce factors that decrease plaque stability, and augment the thrombotic response to plaque rupture. It is the plaque rupture in patients that have cardiovascular disease that causes heart attack and stroke and cause of death.

There are a number of studies showing that insufficient NO production from the endothelium is associated with all major cardiovascular risk factors, such as hyperlipidemia, diabetes, hypertension, smoking and severity of atherosclerosis, and importantly also has a profound predictive value for the future atherosclerotic disease progression. Restoration of nitric oxide, therefore, seems a logical means to inhibit atherosclerosis. My research group published years ago that supplementing nitrite, as a precursor to NO formation, in the drinking water inhibits the adhesion and emigration of leukocytes to the vascular endothelium, one of the earliest events of atherogenesis suggesting this nitrate-nitrite-NO pathway may be useful in preventing chronic vascular disease.

NO formation by our endothelial cells that line our blood vessels plays an important role in the regulation of blood flow, circulation and oxygen delivery throughout the entire circulatory system. The problem is that a loss of nitric oxide production leads to decreased oxygen availability to cells and tissues causing hypoxia (low oxygen) and ischemia (low blood flow). The production of NO by the NOS enzymes requires oxygen. Loss of NO leads to less oxygen which leads to even less NO production. This is a feed forward mechanism that if not corrected leads to death by heart attack and/or stroke.

Loss of endogenous nitric oxide production has a number of detrimental actions, most notably, vasoconstriction, increased activity and adherence of platelets, and accumulation of inflammatory cells at sites of endothelial damage. Endothelial damage is associated with most forms of CVD.

NO possesses a number of physiological properties that makes it a potent cardioprotective-signaling molecule. First, NO is a potent vasodilator which allows for regulation of blood flow and essential perfusion of tissue to improve tissue oxygenation.

Secondly, NO improves mitochondrial energy production and also increases the number of mitochondria per cell. The net result of sufficient nitric oxide production is that you have more mitochondria producing more cellular energy more efficiently. Sounds like a great thing to me.

Thirdly, NO is a potent inhibitor of neutrophil and monocyte adherence to vascular endothelium. Neutrophil adherence is an important event initiating further leukocyte activation and superoxide radical generation, which in turn leads to injury to the endothelium and perivascular myocardium in patients at risk for heart disease.

Fourth, NO also prevents platelet aggregation, which together with the anti-neutrophil actions of NO attenuates capillary plugging which keeps our blood vessels healthy and open. Without sufficient NO production, the body loses its ability to regulate and control normal vascular function.

Therefore, strategies designed to enhance NO production and reduce reactive oxygen species production will likely limit injury and improve recovery from CVD or perhaps even prevent onset and progression of CVD. If you have been diagnosed with heart disease, atherosclerosis or have had a heart attack or stroke in the past, then your body cannot produce sufficient nitric oxide and you must focus on nitric oxide repletion.

Diabetes

Clinical diabetes mellitus is a syndrome of disordered metabolism with inappropriate hyperglycemia (elevated blood sugar) due either to an absolute deficiency of insulin secretion or a reduction in the biologic effectiveness of insulin or both.

The risk of death for those with diabetes is twice that of their non-diabetic age-matched counterparts. Persons with diabetes mellitus tend to suffer unduly from premature and severe coronary atherosclerosis and diabetes is a major independent risk factor for the development of coronary artery disease. In 2003–2004, 75% of adults with self-reported diabetes had blood pressure greater than or equal to 130/80 mmHg, or used prescription medications for hypertension. The cost of treating diabetes is staggering. It is estimated that it cost $116 billion for direct medical costs and $58 billion for indirect costs (disability, work loss, premature mortality).

Insulin has vasodilator actions that depend on the cell's ability to produce nitric oxide which is why in healthy people insulin is a potent organ protector in many clinical applications.

We've learned a lot from mice lacking endothelial nitric oxide synthase and unable to produce nitric oxide. When mice are genetically manipulated to lack the enzyme that produces nitric oxide, these mice develop insulin resistance, hyperlipidemia and hypertension mimicking metabolic syndrome and patients with diabetes.

This suggest that a lack of nitric oxide production may cause diabetes. There is a clear association between diabetes and disruption of endothelium derived NO through the insulin signaling pathway. Restoring this pathway will likely have positive effects in diabetes mellitus. Numerous clinical studies have clearly documented severe endothelial dysfunction and nitric oxide deficiency in humans that suffer from diabetes mellitus. The dysfunctional NO pathway in diabetics is thought to be the cause of the increased incidence of cardiovascular complications.

The increase in circulating glucose, insulin, and cytokines that occurs in type 2 diabetes have all been independently shown to impair eNOS enzyme activity and reduced nitric oxide production in experimental studies. Furthermore, advanced glycosylation products that are generated in diabetic patients can very readily quench any NO that is formed by the endothelium and this is thought to be a major mechanism responsible for defective endothelium-dependent vasodilation in diabetics.

The increased sugar can also glycate the NOS enzyme making it dysfunctional and further decreasing nitric oxide production. Remember sugar is sticky and when in high concentrations in your body, it sticks to proteins, enzymes, hemoglobin (HbA1c) and makes it where they cannot function. Elevated blood sugar (glucose) also sticks to the enzyme that makes nitric oxide making it unable to produce NO gas.

Another mechanism responsible for endothelial dysfunction in the setting of diabetes mellitus is mediated by vessel wall oxidant production. Generation of reactive oxygen species by smooth muscle cells and by the endothelium has been shown to inhibit nitric oxide production. The physiological significance of impaired eNOS function and reductions in vascular NO bioavailability may serve to reduce blood flow to various organs in patients with diabetes mellitus. Therefore, strategies to correct or prevent the progression and development of vascular disease in the diabetic and even non-diabetic population can dramatically improve their prognosis and quality of life and ease the burden on the health care system.

Several years ago, we published for the first time, the role of nitric oxide in insulin signaling and glucose uptake. After a carbohydrate rich meal, our body senses an increase in blood sugar. This signals the pancreas to secrete insulin. Insulin then circulates throughout the body and binds to insulin receptors on most cell types but primarily on skeletal muscle, fat and liver cells.

Through a series of intracellular signaling cascades, eventually GLUT4 a protein that is responsible for binding glucose and clearing it from the circulation thereby reducing blood sugar levels.

It was not known at the time how and if nitric oxide was involved in this process. We discovered that nitric oxide is the signal that tells the GLUT4 protein to go to the membrane and bring glucose inside the cell. We will discuss this in detail later. If the cell cannot produce nitric oxide, then GLUT4 never gets the message or signal to go bring in glucose from the circulation. As a consequence, the patient develops insulin resistance and type 2 diabetes. Therefore, insulin resistance is a symptom of nitric oxide deficiency. In fact, we recognize that all the collateral symptoms that occur in diabetes such as poor wound healing, diabetic macular degeneration, peripheral neuropathy, and others can be explained by a lack of nitric oxide production. Simple restoration of nitric oxide or providing nitric oxide as a therapy can completely overcome insulin resistance and type 2 diabetes.

Vascular Dementia/Alzheimer's Disease

The most feared disease of the geriatric population is Alzheimer's disease. In the United States, around 5.4 million people live with Alzheimer's, a type of dementia. Patients with Alzheimer's lose brain function, resulting in problems with language, perception and memory. Alzheimer's can start before age 60 (early onset) or after age 60 (late onset). The risk for Alzheimer's increases as a person ages—and that rising risk is being seen as the baby boomers start turning 65 years old.

The Secret of Nitric Oxide

Out of every eight baby boomers, one will get Alzheimer's after he/she turns 65 years old; at age 85, that risk grows to one in two. With the 65 and over population in the United States expected to double by 2030, there may be up to 16 million people with Alzheimer's by 2050; there may be almost 1 million new cases diagnosed each year.

Each year in the United States, more than 800,000 people die from this neurological disease. It is the sixth leading cause of death, with the number of deaths rising 66 percent from 2000 to 2008.

There is becoming a clear and convincing association with Alzheimer's and NO. Decreased levels of nitrite and nitrate, markers of nitric oxide production have been detected in patients with different forms of dementia especially Alzheimer's.

The exact etiology of sporadic Alzheimer's disease is unclear, but it is interesting that cardiovascular risk factors including hypertension, hypercholesterolemia, diabetes mellitus, aging, and sedentary lifestyle are associated with higher incidence.

The link between cardiovascular risk factors and Alzheimer's has yet to be identified; however, a common feature is endothelial dysfunction, specifically, decreased bioavailability of NO. The pathogenesis of Alzheimer's disease is closely associated with the accumulation of amyloid-β (Aβ) peptides, which eventually form neuronal deposits known as senile plaques on the outside surface of the neurons and lead to neuron death.

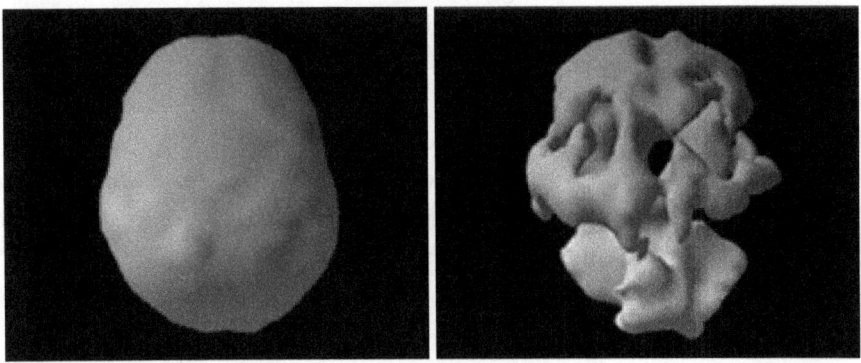

On the left is a picture of a healthy brain from a SPECT scan and on the right is a patient with Alzheimer's. The SPECT scan shows us blood flow to part of the brain. As shown in the Alzheimer's patient, there is a disruption in blood flow and circulation to many parts of the brain. (Courtesy of Daniel Amen, M.D.)

Alzheimer's is characterized by progressive loss of neurons, cognitive decline, and two defining histopathologies: extracellular amyloid plaques and intracellular tangles composed primarily of amyloid beta (Aβ) peptide and hyperphosphorylated tau, respectively. Furthermore, Alzheimer's is often accompanied by cerebrovascular dysfunction, as well as amyloid deposition within the cerebral vessels, termed cerebral amyloid angiopathy.

NO in the brain can be produced either by inducible NOS (iNOS) in microglia and astrocytes, or by constitutive NOS in neurons and endothelial cells (nNOS and eNOS). A large body of evidence suggests that the NO produced by neuronal and endothelial constitutive NOS is responsible for neuroprotection during Aβ-induced cell death, while NO production in the case of iNOS activation plays a neurotoxic role due to the inflammatory response caused by the over generation of other reactive nitrogen species from NO.

A decrease in neuronal NOS and an increase in hippocampal iNOS have been demonstrated in aged rats, suggesting the dual roles and complexity of NO signaling in the brain and during Alzheimer's. In mice, higher levels of constitutive NO produced by NOS protects beta-amyloid transgenic mice from developing most typical human symptoms of Alzheimer's. Treatment with NO donors and cGMP analogues suppresses cell death, and increasing intracellular cGMP levels prevents inflammatory responses in brain cells. It has also been shown that NO modulates expression and processing of amyloid beta precursor protein. However, an accumulation of Aβ inhibits the NO signaling pathway and therefore may suppress the protective effects of endogenous NO in the brain. In postmortem temporal cortex from a series of Alzheimer's patients there was reduced NO responsive the enzyme soluble guanylyl cyclase providing the first evidence for a loss of NO production in the Alzheimer's brain.

There are well established hallmarks of Alzheimer's disease.
1. Focal ischemia (reduced blood flow and circulation to the brain)
2. Insulin resistance (diabetes type 3)
3. Inflammation
4. Oxidative stress
5. Immune dysfunction

Nitric oxide is what controls and regulates all five of these processes. As we have discussed, nitric oxide improves cerebral blood flow, it improves insulin signaling and glucose uptake, it reduces inflammation, prevents oxidative stress and inhibits the immune dysfunction seen in all chronic disease. A single molecule gets to the root cause of every major chronic disease, including one of the most feared, Alzheimer's disease.

Collectively, the literature demonstrates a critical role for NO in the onset and progression of Alzheimer's. It appears that normal and sufficient NO production/availability can modulate and inhibit the expression and formation of the beta amyloid (Aβ) but once Aβ becomes present it further compromises NO activity. This creates a perpetual system of NO insufficiency and a feed forward mechanism that may accelerate Alzheimer's progression.

The NO pathway may be an important therapeutic target in preventing and treating mild cognitive impairment, as well as Alzheimer's. In fact, a high nitrate diet has been shown to increase regional cerebral blood flow to the frontal lobe in older patients. Patients who have been on phosphodiesterase inhibition therapy (Viagra, Cialis, Levitra) have been shown to have lower risk and incidence of dementia and Alzheimer's. This is due to improvements in cerebral blood flow which nitric oxide itself can accomplish.

All of the major, poorly managed chronic diseases we deal with today, are all symptoms of nitric oxide deficiency. If your body cannot produce nitric oxide, this sets the stage for the onset and progression of most, if not all, age related chronic disease. There then exist an opportunity to intervene early during this process, implement strategies to restore NO homeostasis, and, perhaps, delay or prevent the onset and progression of certain diseases. Fortunately, I know how to make nitric oxide and my products can help restore nitric oxide production and overcome many of these conditions.

CHAPTER 8
Nitric Oxide is the Longevity Molecule
The Unified Theory of Aging

"Science has profoundly altered the conditions of man's life, both materially and ways of the spirit as well."

—J. Robert Oppenheimer

Today people may be living longer lives, but they are not living long healthy lives. Due to development of drugs that can prolong death and treat symptoms, people can live longer but today we know we have the sickest population than ever before. We have learned a tremendous amount about cellular biology and what constitutes good health and what biomarkers are associated with longevity, the science of living a long life. There are even tests and objective measures of longevity. The three most studied and validated measures of longevity are:

1. Telomere length
2. Mitochondria number and function
3. Stem cells

I will review each of these one by one and show you how it is nitric oxide that controls and regulates each of these three main markers and controllers of longevity.

Telomeres

Telomeres are the ends of the chromosomes of our DNA. Humans have 23 pairs of chromosomes with half coming from our mother and the other half coming from our father. When we turn genes into proteins, the DNA within the chromosomes must unwind and with each cell replication, the end of the chromosomes, the telomeres can become shorter. This is dependent upon an enzyme called telomerase. When telomerase enzyme is

The Secret of Nitric Oxide

fully expressed and functional, then this enzyme prevents the telomeres from becoming shorter over time by providing the proper sequence to replace the otherwise missing ends of the telomeres.

This discovery was deemed so fundamentally important, Nobel Prize in Physiology or Medicine was awarded to three scientists in 2009 for their discovery.

From the Nobel website: "The award recognizes the discovery of a fundamental mechanism that has added a new dimension to our understanding of the cell, shed light on disease mechanisms, and stimulated the development of potential new therapies." Their work began in the 1980s that eventually revealed how the ends of chromosomes can be protected and preserved over many years. Now more than forty years later we certainly understand how we can develop potential new therapies to prevent telomere shortening and prolong life.

In 1998 it was discovered that the loss of the function of the telomerase enzyme precedes telomere shortening and if we introduced a functional telomerase enzyme into human cells, it would prolong the life of those

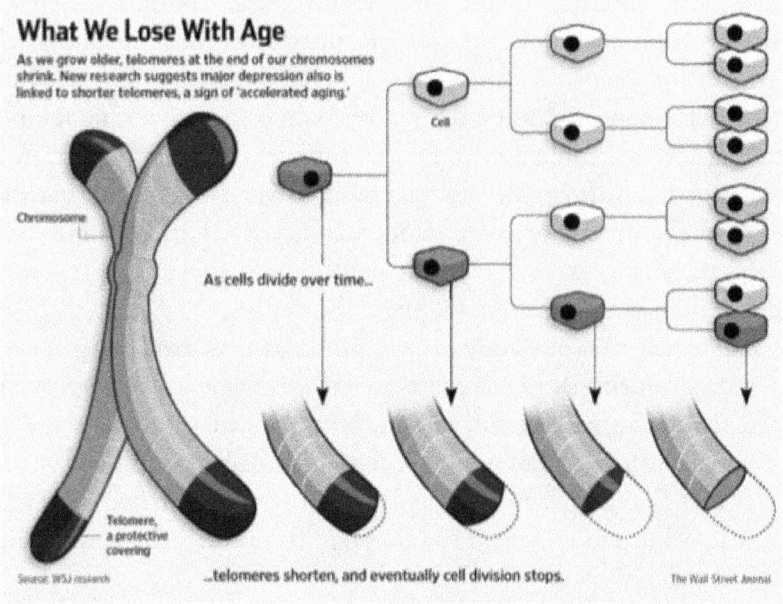

human cells. In 2003 it was revealed that shortening of the telomeres was associated with increased mortality rate from all age-related diseases. Furthermore, individuals with shorter telomeres had a mortality or death rate nearly twice that of those with longer telomeres. I would say this is pretty important. We certainly want to prevent our telomeres from shortening if we want to live longer. So how do we do that?

In the early 2000s there was research published that revealed that nitric oxide could stimulate the telomerase enzyme and prevent telomere shortening. There was a very similar story playing out in the nitric oxide field showing that people who lost their ability to produce nitric oxide had earlier onset of cardiovascular disease and many other diseases.

Was the loss of nitric oxide leading to a loss of function of the telomerase enzyme leading to shorter telomeres and early death? Other investigators starting looking at the regulation of the genetic coding of the telomerase enzyme. These geneticists found that the nitric oxide synthase enzyme, the enzyme that actually produces nitric oxide is required for the cell to actually transcribe the telomerase enzyme from DNA.

This means that nitric oxide is required to take the genetic instruction from our own DNA and make a functional protein. Wow, so if we lose the ability to produce nitric oxide, we not only get less telomerase enzyme produced in each cell but we also lose the function of what enzyme is being produced.

Nitric oxide appeared to be the master switch for preventing telomere shortening and extending life. To further support this argument, scientists knocked out the nitric oxide synthase gene in mice and found that these mice lose the ability to regulate telomerase activity but if the mice were administered nitric oxide generating compounds, they could rescue the telomerase activity and prevent telomere shortening.

This means that if your body cannot produce nitric oxide, if you take a nitric oxide producing substance, you can restore telomerase activity, prevent telomere shortening and extend your life. Nitric oxide is the master regulator of telomere length. Without nitric oxide, telomeres get shorter and you live a shorter life. The take home message is that if you want to live longer, you need nitric oxide and you need to take steps to restore your body's ability to produce it on its own.

Mitochondria

Everybody knows we need energy to do our job. Cells need energy to do their job. It is the job of the mitochondria to produce energy for every cell in the body. Each cell contains approximately 1000-2500 mitochondria. In fact, mitochondria make up as much as 25% of the volume of some cells.

These mitochondria must continuously produce adenosine triphosphate (ATP), the energy currency of the cell in order for the cell to do its job. ATP cannot be stored in the cell so it must be produced upon demand or else the cell becomes dysfunctional and dies. Every cell must have sufficient mitochondria but also the function of those mitochondria must be maintained. The mitochondria of older animals are often larger and less efficient than those in younger animals.

Studies between different species have demonstrated that longer-lived species typically have lower mitochondrial DNA oxidative damage and lower free radical production. This means that the mitochondria of species that live longer produce less free radicals than those species that don't live as long.

When cells have lower numbers of mitochondria, they produce less energy, obviously. However, cells can have large numbers of mitochondria but if the mitochondria do not efficiently produce energy, then again, those cells become energy deficient and they cannot do their job. Efficient mitochondria produce very little free radicals, they very economically generate ATP from oxygen and they sensitively detect when the cells in which they reside become damaged and they signal the cell to die. We call this apoptosis or programmed cell death.

A chain is only as strong as its weakest link. Organs and tissues are made of cells. It is the job of our organs, tissues and cells to recognize the weak cells and replace them with strong cells fully equipped to do their job. If the mitochondria do not sense this weakness, then the cells simply necrose or die a slow death and eventually kill the cells, then the tissues become dysfunctional and eventually leads to organ failure. We call this cellular senescence. That is one of the many functions of the mitochondria.

We now know from several decades of research that it is the nitric oxide produced in the cell that controls the metabolic function of the mitochondria. Nitric oxide controls and regulates:

    1. ATP production of the mitochondria
    2. Production of reactive oxygen species (oxidative stress)

3. Cell signaling by the mitochondria (apoptosis)
4. Mitochondria biogenesis
5. Metabolism/Bioenergetics

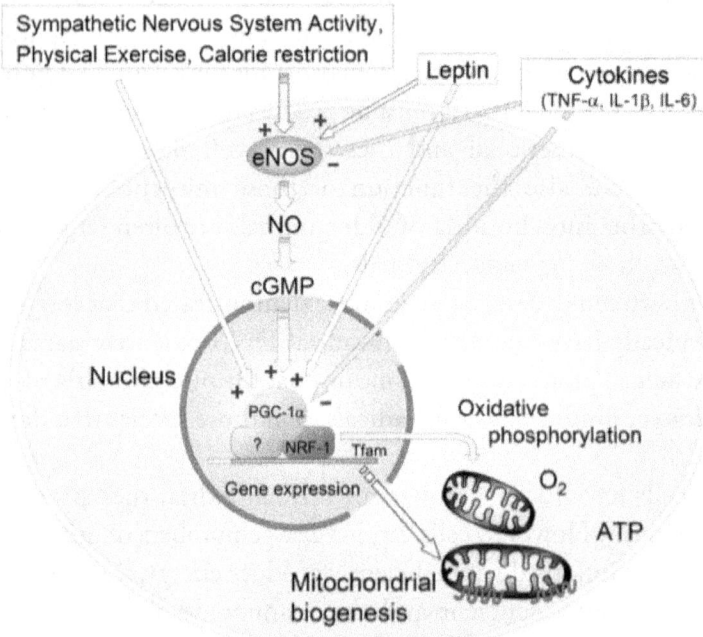

Everything we know about mitochondria numbers and function within individual cells is dependent upon the cells ability to produce nitric oxide. Without nitric oxide, the mitochondria cannot do their job of efficiently producing energy and the cells cannot function.

Another very important function of nitric oxide involves a process called mitochondrial biogenesis. This is how each individual cells increases the number of mitochondria per cell. If you have more mitochondria producing more energy more efficiently, then you become a well-oiled machine and can perform at the top of your game.

There are a number of important interventions that are known to increase mitochondria and improve health and longevity. These include caloric restriction, intermittent fasting, physical exercise and other clinically proven modalities.

However, all of these pathways are dependent upon the cell's ability to produce nitric oxide. If you practice intermittent fasting or caloric restriction but your cells cannot produce nitric oxide, then you will not get the benefits of mitochondrial biogenesis.

We must first fix the enzyme in the cells so that when stimulated or activated by these interventions, the cell can actually produce nitric oxide and lead to activation of the pathways that lead to mitochondria biogenesis and improved energy production. See figure above on the mechanism. Nitric oxide is foundational for many important scientifically proven modalities that lead to improved health and wellness and increase longevity.

Stem cells

Each day we live, we are constantly wearing ourselves out. Some of us faster than others depending on our diet and lifestyle and occupations. We must constantly repair and replace dysfunction cells and tissues. That is the job of our own stem cells.

In normal healthy people our skin renews every 27 days. The cells of our gastrointestinal system replace every 5-7 days. In our brain, there are 700-1500 new neurons created every day. Our liver can completely regenerate up to 90% of itself within days. The cells in the lung have to renew every 2-3 weeks. What happens if we don't have enough stem cells in our body or worse, the stem cells in our body do not get the message to mobilize to go and replace and repair other cells and tissues. The answer is that we wear ourselves out and we get sick and eventually die, likely years before our true potential.

There is an abundance of scientific evidence that nitric oxide is essential and fundamental for stem cell function. The number of stem cells in our bone marrow is much higher when we are young and slowly decline as we age. This is one of the reasons young people recover from injury much faster and are in generally better health.

There is evidence over the past 20 years that our fat cells contain stem cells. This may be good news since most people accumulate more fat with age. Now we understand that perhaps it is not the number of stem cells in our body that matter but the ability of our own stem cells to get the message to go do their job and increase in the circulation. Aging is not just a matter of the increased damage to our bodies but the inability to repair.

Back in the early 2000s it was discovered that nitric oxide is the requisite signal for stem cell mobilization and differentiation into different cell types. In this study, the scientists deleted the enzyme that makes nitric oxide in mice and observed that the mice could not mobilize their own stem cells or progenitor cells. The authors concluded that the loss of nitric oxide production was what caused impaired regenerative processes in patients with cardiovascular disease which are known to have decreased nitric oxide production. This means that as we lose our ability to produce nitric oxide, our stem cell function is compromised and we lose the ability to repair and replace dysfunctional cells. This means we age faster, we don't recover from injury, and we feel awful.

There are hundreds if not thousands of stem cell clinics popping up all over the U.S. and the world. These clinics take your own stem cells or stem cells from placenta or umbilical cords from new mothers and infants respectively and then inject it into patients.

Now knowing what we know, does this even make sense? We have established that it is likely not the availability of stem cells that leads to aging but rather the lack of the signal to the stem cells, nitric oxide. If we can simply activate our own stem cells and increase the number of circulating stem cells in our body, then we can heal, we can replace and repair dysfunctional cells and regenerate ourselves.

One of my objectives is to educate these stem cell clinics on using nitric oxide in their patients prior to the deployment of stem cells so the cells know where to go and what to become. It only makes sense to make these treatments more effective and allow the body to do what it is designed to do, heal and perform. It cannot and will not do that without nitric oxide. If we can normalize nitric oxide production in patients prior to the deployment of stem cells, then scientifically and clinically the stem cells work better and patients get a much better response to the therapy. If you want to heal faster, feel better and live longer, you need nitric oxide.

We've established that the three objective read outs of health and longevity, telomere length, mitochondrial function and stem cell function are all dependent upon the ability of the body to produce nitric oxide.

There are many products on the market that are marketed as telomere products to prevent telomere shortening. There are hundreds of mitochondrial products on the market and as I mentioned thousands of stem cell clinics around the world offering stem cells.

The Secret of Nitric Oxide

Let us not forget that our body is much smarter than any scientist or physician. How about we give the body what it needs and let it do its job? If we restore and replete nitric oxide, the telomerase enzyme becomes more functional, extending our telomeres. If we restore and replete nitric oxide, the number of mitochondria per cell increases and the function of each mitochondria improves. The net effect is we have more mitochondria making more cellular energy more efficiently and giving us more energy. Who would not want that? If we restore and replete nitric oxide, our own stem cells get the message to go and repair and replace old dysfunctional cells and our organs work better.

My job is to understand the mechanism of disease to the extent we can address the root cause of any condition. I'm not saying that nitric oxide will fix everything but I can confidently say that nothing else will work without first correcting nitric oxide production. Fortunately, we know how to do that. Now my hope is to take you through the discoveries that have led to our current understanding of nitric oxide.

SECTION III
DISCOVERIES THAT CHANGED EVERYTHING

SECTION III
DISCOVERIES THAT ENHANCED TYPE THINKING

CHAPTER 9
Thinking Differently

"Discovery consists of seeing what everybody has seen and thinking what nobody has thought."
—Albert von Szent-György, 1937 Nobel Prize in Physiology or Medicine

I got started in the nitric oxide field in 2000 when I was a student at LSU School of Medicine working on my Ph.D. in Molecular and Cellular Physiology. Certainly, at that time, it was accepted in the scientific and medical field that nitric oxide was critically important and had the potential to change the landscape of healthcare and on the treatment and prevention of many human diseases.

The Nobel Prize had just been awarded a couple years earlier for the discovery of nitric oxide as a cell signaling molecule in the cardiovascular system. However, there were still four unanswered questions that I thought were very important to advancing nitric oxide-based therapies. Once I began my own independent research program at University of Texas Health Science Center at Houston, I devoted my career to answering these four fundamental questions:

1. How does the human body produce nitric oxide? Part of the story was revealed through L-arginine and the nitric oxide synthase enzyme but there was also an emerging story on the role of bacteria in and on the human body and their contributions to NO production.

2. Why do people lose the ability to produce nitric oxide? What goes wrong in these people? There were data showing a loss of nitric oxide production as we age due to loss of

function of the nitric oxide synthase enzyme but that was about all that was known.

3. What symptoms or diseases do people get as a consequence of insufficient nitric oxide production? The literature suggested that people develop high blood pressure and sexual dysfunction which made sense since nitric oxide acts to dilate blood vessels and increase blood flow. Was there more?

4. How do we restore and improve nitric oxide production in people that have a dysfunctional enzyme? Is there a way to deliver bioactive nitric oxide gas to humans?

Once I was an independent investigator at UTHealth and had my own research group at the Institute of Molecular Medicine, I was excited to start my career. I was very fortunate to have several mentors early on that I could call on and discuss experiments, the meaning of specific data and just to look for advice.

People like Jonathan Stamler, M.D., one of my early heroes in the NO field. I become good friends and colleagues with Joe Loscalzo, M.D., who was Chair of Medicine at Harvard Medical School. I had routine meetings with James T. Willerson, M.D. at Texas Heart Institute and he was also

Left to right, me, Jonathan Stamler, M.D., and Ferid Murad, M.D., Ph.D., 2008.

The Secret of Nitric Oxide

Dinner with James T. Willerson, M.D., Ali J. Marian, M.D., Joseph Loscalzo, M.D., me, John Hancock, M.D., Ph.D.

President of the University of Texas Health Sciences Center. I was in the presence of world experts and really famous people in Cardiology and nitric oxide biology. These people took me under their wing and helped me early on when I needed guidance and direction.

During my time as a student and a post-doctoral fellow, we had published on the biological effects of nitrite and that many of these effects seemed to be very similar to nitric oxide. Nitrite itself was a signaling molecule. Nitric oxide was a gas that was very reactive and unstable. Nitrite was a salt that was much more stable, soluble in water and could be used as a substrate or pro-drug to make nitric oxide. However, nitrite had a bad reputation as a food additive found in cured meats like bacon and hot dogs.

Nitrite is used as a "curing" agent. Perfect. If nitrite could be used as a pro-drug to make nitric oxide it certainly would "cure" many diseases.

For the past 60 years, we have been taught to avoid nitrite cured meats because they cause cancer. However, with the discovery of nitric oxide and the realization that nitrite is formed naturally in the human body, this raised many questions about nitrite as a carcinogen.

The National Toxicology Program (NTP) investigated nitrite in the early 2000s as a carcinogen and submitted their final report in May 2001 concluding that there is no evidence of carcinogenicity or cancer risk by nitrite at any dose. In fact, at some doses it appeared to prevent some forms of cancer. We now know that nitrite is a signaling molecule that prevents food borne illnesses, prevent lipid peroxidation, oxidative stress and immune dysfunction that occurs in all chronic diseases.

One of our first critical experiments was to test nitrite and nitrate at doses one could reasonably achieve through eating certain foods or following certain dietary patterns could protect the heart from a heart attack. Cardiovascular disease leading to heart attack and stroke remains the number one killer of men and women worldwide.

This occurs when diseased blood vessels become constricted due to plaque build-up and rupture. This shuts off blood supply to the heart or brain and if not restored in a timely manner will lead to death. However, if patients made it to the hospital in time and underwent cardiac catheterization to remove the blockage and restore blood flow, then in some cases, patients would survive. However, in many cases the heart would suffer severe damage and would lose part of its pump function.

Our goal was to restore the normal pump function of the heart if patients suffered a heart attack. Could we demonstrate this if we provided a source of nitric oxide?

Many people suffer sudden cardiac death from heart attacks. Others have a heart attack, survive and suffer very little injury to the heart. Why do some people die and some people have very little injury from the same heart attack? Could it be due to their diet or their last meal?

We set out to test this in mice. We fed mice a western diet depleted of any nitrite and nitrate from their diet We had another group where we gave nitrite and/or nitrate in their drinking water to mimic a diet rich in vegetables and then we of course had a control group on a normal diet without any added nitrite or nitrate in their drinking water.

We actually gave these mice a heart attack by completely shutting off the blood supply to their heart for 60 minutes. After 60 minutes we would restore the blood supply to their heart. What we found was fascinating. The mice on the western diet without sufficient nitrite and nitrate suffered sudden cardiac death (about 9 out of 10) and the ones that survived had significantly much more damage to the heart.

The mice that had supplemental nitrite and nitrate in their drinking water did not die from the heart attack (100% survived the heart attack) and their heart function was almost normal after the heart attack. This was incredible and perhaps offered an explanation of why some people die suddenly from heart attack and others not only survive, but survive with very little injury to their heart.

Well, if all we had to do was provide a standardized dose of nitrite and/or nitrate to patients or people at risk of heart attack that would be simple, easy and affordable and could possibly keep them from dying from a heart attack and protect their heart from injury.

Our next important experiment came in collaboration with Dr. David Lefer, a good friend and colleague. David had created a transgenic mouse that had the nitric oxide enzyme over-expressed in the heart. He had found and published that his mouse had enormous protection from injury from heart attack.

This protection from injury from heart attack was due to more nitric oxide being produced in the heart prior to the heart attack. This was consistent with what we were seeing in our nitrite and nitrate interventions.

I was interested in studying the other organs in this mouse to determine if the nitric oxide that was only being produced in the heart would have any protective effects in other organs like the brain, liver, kidney and lungs. We harvested the different organs of this heart specific nitric oxide producing mouse and found the biochemistry of the liver looked very similar to that of the heart of this mouse.

Now understand the nitric oxide being produced in the heart is gone is less than one second so the nitric oxide being produced could not and would not survive in the circulation to reach the liver or any other organs for that matter. The next question was whether this increased nitric oxide biochemical changes in the liver had any physiological effect on the liver.

In order to test this, we shut off blood supply to the liver for one hour and then restored blood flow for 5 hours then measured the level of liver damage in the mouse. Remarkably, the liver was protected from injury from a disruption in blood supply. How could nitric oxide produced only in the heart protect the liver? Could nitric oxide be a hormone, similar to other hormones where they are produced in one specific organ but have systemic effects on all organs, tissues and cells?

At the time, nitric oxide was considered an autocrine or paracrine signaling molecule, meaning that it could only affect the cell in which it was produced (autocrine) or a neighboring (paracrine) cell, due primarily to its short half-life.

Through a series of additional experiments, we were able to demonstrate that the nitric oxide produced in the heart was oxidized to nitrite and nitrite itself, as we had previously published, protected all organs from injury. Furthermore, we were able to demonstrate that nitric oxide or some related metabolite would bind to glutathione, the master antioxidant in the body, and form S-nitrosoglutatione metabolite that would transfer and transport the biological activity of nitric oxide throughout the body.

This was the first demonstration that nitric oxide is a hormone. For me this was my "EUREKA" moment and the epiphany that changed everything. Although others in the field had contemplated that nitric oxide may be a hormone, our work was the first to actually demonstrate and reveal that **NITRIC OXIDE IS A HORMONE**. We published this study in the *Proceedings* of the National Academy of Science.

Based on our data and observations, this instructed me that all I had to do was produce nitric oxide gas in any biological compartment in the body and the human body would take care of the rest. As a biochemist, I knew how to make nitric oxide gas and I could do it in the mouth. All I had to do was invent and create an orally disintegrating lozenge that would produce a specified amount of nitric oxide gas over a specified period of time.

My first nitric oxide product technology was born. The year was 2007. Now with the understanding that nitric oxide is a hormone, we could replace the hormone nitric oxide similarly to replacing testosterone or estrogen. Testosterone and estrogen are produced in the gonads of men and women respectively. However, to replace testosterone and estrogen, we do not give pre-cursors or substrates and hope your body produces testosterone or estrogen. We give the actual molecule. Nitric oxide is no different.

In order to replace missing nitric oxide, we must give the actual molecule and the body will do the rest of the work. After all, we do not have to give testosterone shots in the testes where it is produced (thank God), we can give intramuscular injections or take oral troches or implant pellets that slowly release testosterone. We can do the same thing with nitric oxide. We just need to deliver bioactive NO gas in some compartment in the human body. The mouth is the most accessible, non-invasive compartment we could deliver NO.

The Secret of Nitric Oxide

Can Nitric Oxide Reduce Inflammation?

We all know inflammation drives chronic disease. The earliest stage of inflammation is when there is an increase in adhesion molecules inside the lining of the blood vessels and the blood vessels become like Velcro. Everything sticks including white blood cells, platelets become activated leading to blood clots and lots of bad things happen. It is also known that if we can prevent vascular inflammation, you can prevent vascular disease.

In collaboration with my friends and colleagues at LSU School of Medicine the Department of Molecular and Cellular Physiology, we designed an experiment where we could induce vascular inflammation and then treat with nitrite to see if nitrite could inhibit or reverse the vascular inflammation.

Again, we fed our rats an inflammatory diet that caused massive vascular inflammation. We could visualize this in real time by videoing the white blood cells rolling and sticking to the inside of blood vessels.

When we gave therapeutic amounts of nitrite in their drinking water at the same time they were eating an inflammatory diet, there was no inflammation and blood vessel function was restored. You can see the side-by-side comparison below where on the left there are a number of cells stuck to the lining of the blood vessel. The picture on the right shows the blood vessel more dilated with very few cells stuck.

We also tested the function of the endothelial cells in these blood vessels and found that when stimulated with acetylcholine, they would respond with an increase in nitric oxide production.

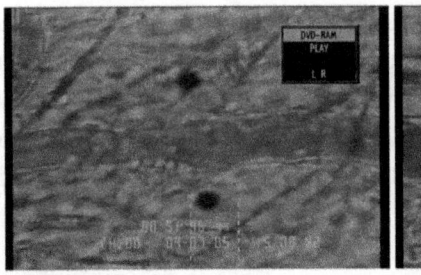 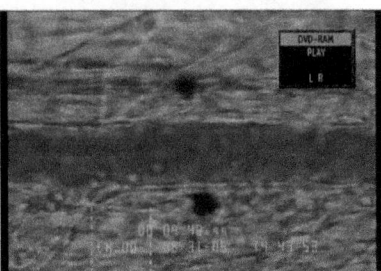

Vascular inflammation.   Treated with nitric oxide.

We had demonstrated that the nitrite in the drinking water could also improve the function of the NOS enzyme. Now we had evidence that nitrite, when used as a pro-drug could protect organs from injury, protect the blood vessels from inflammation and restore the structure and function of blood vessels. This seemed to be the "Holy Grail" in cardiovascular medicine. We published our results in 2009 in the *American Journal of Physiology*.

Can nitric oxide help in diabetes?
We also started to explore the role of nitric oxide in diabetes and insulin resistance. There is a growing epidemic of diabetes around the world. The number of people with diabetes has risen from 108 million in 1980 to more than 550 million in 2021 and expected to affect more than 643 million people by 2030. Insulin resistance and diabetes causes a number of systemic problems. These patients have elevated blood glucose, they produce too much insulin. High glucose and high insulin cause inflammation which leads to systemic issues in every major organ system. Glucose acts like a glue. Sugar is very sticky and when it sticks to proteins and enzymes it restricts their ability to move and change conformation.

Enzymes and proteins must be agile and able to move to do their job. When sugar sticks to proteins because there is too much sugar in circulation, this leads to dysfunction.

We can measure the amount of sugar stuck to hemoglobin by measuring HbA1c, a routine lab used to determine long-term diabetes management. If sugar sticks and binds to hemoglobin, it will also stick and bind to other proteins and enzymes, even the NOS enzyme.

Diabetic patients have higher incidence of macular degeneration in the eye, higher incidence of heart attack, stroke, peripheral neuropathy, loss of limbs due to amputation from poor wound healing, erectile dysfunction, chronic fatigue and many other disorders. At the time, the scientific community had a clear understanding on the effects of diabetes on nitric oxide production but not a good understanding on the effects of nitric oxide on diabetes.

We knew that if you develop insulin resistance and diabetes that this caused a down-regulation of the enzyme nitric oxide synthase. The body produced less of this enzyme. Furthermore, what enzyme was present, was

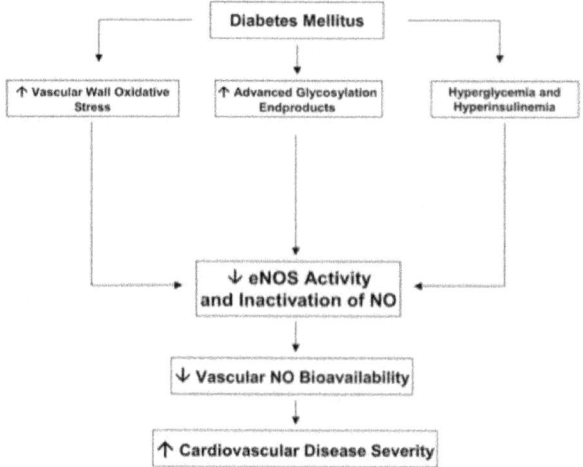

Endothelial Nitric Oxide Synthase (eNOS) and Diabetes.

not functional. This means that the enzyme that normally produces nitric oxide from L-arginine did not work. It made sense that if your body could not make nitric oxide, it would lead to all the symptoms and conditions mentioned above.

Another important observation came from looking at mice that were genetically engineered to lack the enzyme that makes nitric oxide. The mice that were born without the ability to produce nitric oxide actually developed insulin resistant type 2 diabetes early on in their life.

Their diabetes was not caused by their diet but simply by their inability to produce nitric oxide. It was not known at the time how nitric oxide was involved in insulin signaling and glucose uptake in cells. I felt this was a very important question to answer and if we could figure this out, then perhaps we could develop a safe and effective treatment for diabetes because obviously the current medications available are not working great with the ever-growing population of diabetics.

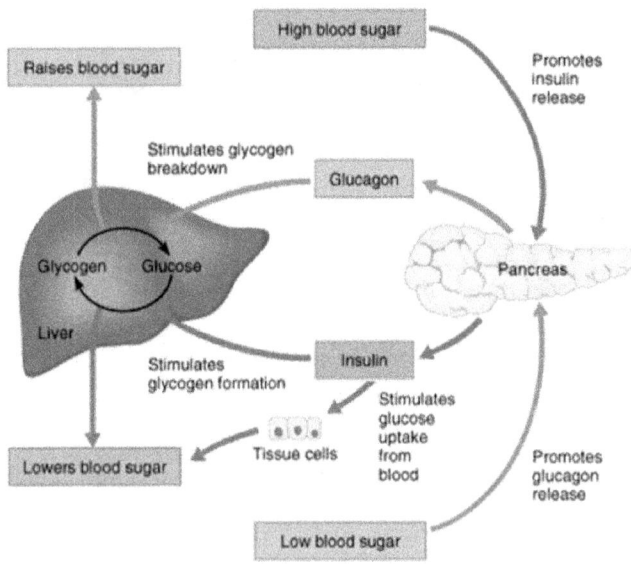

How the body regulates normal blood sugar.

In order to answer this question, we had to fully understand how insulin signaling works.

Let's briefly review. In normal health subjects, when we eat and our body senses an increase in blood sugar, it signals the pancreas to secrete insulin. Insulin is then the signal in the body that tells our fat cells, our liver and muscle cells to increase the uptake of glucose to clear it from the circulation. A simplified model is shown above.

We understood at that time that once insulin binds to the insulin receptor on certain cells, this initiates a number of intracellular signals that eventually tells a specific glucose transporter protein GLUT4, to move to the cell membrane and bring glucose into the cell and clear it from the circulation. In conditions of insulin resistance, apparently, the GLUT4 protein does not get the signal and therefore does not clear glucose from the circulation and bring it into the cell.

Our first question was, is nitric oxide involved in this signaling cascade? If it is, we know in diabetic patients, they cannot make nitric oxide and maybe this is the underlying problem.

The Secret of Nitric Oxide

Well, this is a simple enough experiment to design and test. Fortunately for us, there was a technology already available that tagged the GLUT4 protein with a green fluorescent protein that you could actually visualize within a cell. So, if the GLUT4 protein was getting the signal from insulin, we could see it moving in the cell under fluoroscopy. Pretty cool stuff.

We setup the experiment, we did not add anything to our control cells and we added nitrite and/or S-nitrosoglutatione (GSNO) a source of nitric oxide to the other cells. We found that the cells that had been given nitrite or GSNO, the GLUT4 protein was translocating to the membrane and there was an increase in glucose uptake, even without activation with insulin.

Did we just discover a new form of regulation of insulin signaling and glucose uptake? What happens in cell culture does not always translate to animal models of diabetes and animal models of disease rarely translate into humans and clinical medicine.

Next, we took diabetic mice and started treating them with sodium nitrite in their drinking water to see if our hypothesis and data from cell culture actually was in play in live diabetic mice.

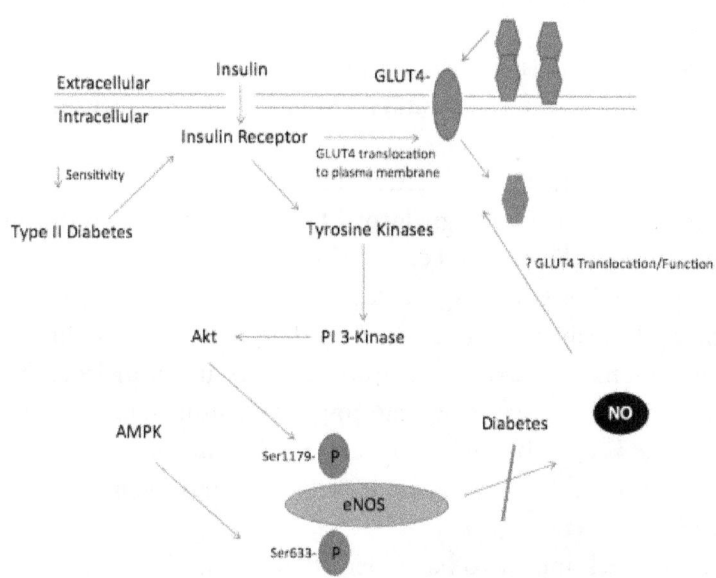

Insulin signaling inside a cell. The production of nitric oxide is required for glucose uptake by GLUT4. (Jiang *et al. Free Radic Biol Med.*, 2014 Feb:67:51-7.

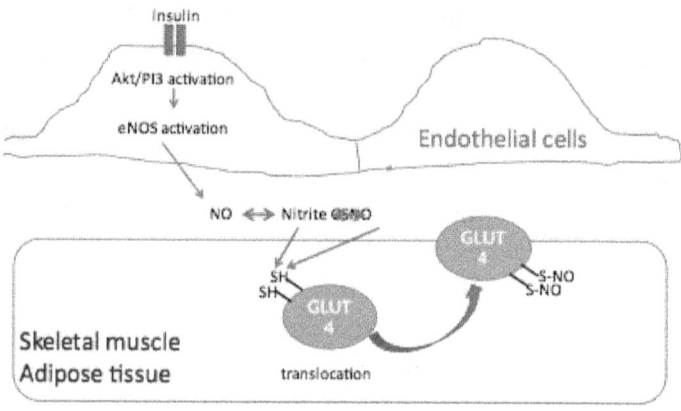

Jiang et al Free Radic Biol Med. 2014 Feb;67:51-7

Insulin signaling and glucose uptake are dependent upon nitric oxide Production.

We found remarkably that the mice receiving the nitrite in the drinking water had lower levels of insulin and lower fasting glucose levels. This completely made sense to me. As shown above, insulin stimulates a number of intracellular signals, primarily the AMP kinase (this is how metformin works by activating AMP kinase) and the PI3/Akt pathway. However, both of these proteins then stimulate and activate the enzyme that makes nitric oxide.

If the NOS enzyme is not functional and active, which is known to be the case in diabetes, then the signal stops, GLUT4 does not get the message and we develop insulin resistance.

This explained everything we know about diabetes, the systemic symptoms and the mechanism of the underlying disease. Incredible.

So, if we can fix the nitric oxide producing enzyme or provide the body with a source of nitric oxide, we can improve insulin signaling, improve glucose uptake and get better management of insulin and glucose levels in patients. This would be revolutionary in the management of insulin resistance and diabetes.

Our discoveries appear to have identified a new class of anti-diabetic medicines that involve nitric oxide drug technology. This indicates that if we can provide drug therapy to post-translationally modify the GLUT4 protein, then this is necessary and sufficient for improved glucose uptake and in the management of diabetes.

The GLUT4 protein is just one of many cellular targets of nitric oxide. If we provide nitric oxide, what other targets could we be hitting to further improve diabetes.

Well, we know that we can add NO to the hemoglobin of our red blood cells to improve oxygenation and improve blood flow. This is pretty important since diabetics typically have reduced blood flow and poor tissue oxygenation. From our previous studies and discoveries, we know that giving nitric oxide can reduce inflammation and oxidative stress. Diabetic patients are certainly inflamed and have a lot of oxidative stress. Now the pursuit was how do we best deliver a bioactive source of nitric oxide that is both safe in patients and effective to recapitulate all that nitric oxide does when it is produced endogenously.

CHAPTER 10
Traditional Medicines And Nitric Oxide
"The Chinese do not draw any distinction between food and medicine."
—Lin Yutang

About the same time, we were making some really important discoveries and publishing nearly a dozen papers a year, I was contacted by a Chinese physician who was working as an interventional cardiologist in Florida. He sent me an email and asked if Traditional Chinese Medicines that have been used for more than 1000 years very safely and effectively might provide a source of nitric oxide. I had no idea but indicated that we could easily test this theory.

Yaoping Tang, M.D. moved to Houston and he joined my lab shortly thereafter as a post-doctoral fellow. Complementary and alternative medicine (CAM) which includes traditional Chinese medicine (TCM) is the term for medical products and practices that are not part of the standard care in Western medicine. There is generally a lack of understanding of their mechanisms of action and/or the active compounds.

Rigorous, well-designed clinical trials for many CAM therapies are often lacking; therefore, the effectiveness of many of these types of therapies are uncertain and as a result are not recognized as mainstream therapy and certainly not approved by the FDA here in the U.S.

However, Traditional Chinese Medicine (TCM) is a form of CAM that remains the primary form of medicine throughout a large portion of Asia and Asian communities in the rest of world with a long history of safety and efficacy in a number of different diseases. In fact, one could argue that TCM is the earliest form of CAM. Defining CAM here in the U.S. is difficult because the field is very broad and constantly changing.

The National Institutes of Health now has a dedicated Center for Complementary and Alternative Medicine (NCCAM) due to the growing popularity of such approaches to ensure safety and promote rigorous clinical trials to demonstrate efficacy. NCCAM defines CAM as a group of diverse medical and health care systems, practices, and products that are not generally considered part of conventional medicine, as practiced by medical doctors and their allied health professionals. The boundaries between CAM and conventional medicine are not absolute, and specific CAM practices may, over time, become widely accepted.

Complementary medicine refers to use of alternative treatments together with conventional medicine, such as using acupuncture or herbal medicines in addition to usual care to help with disease management. Most use of CAM by Americans is complementary. Alternative medicine refers to use of CAM in place of conventional medicine. Integrative medicine combines treatments from conventional medicine and CAM for which there is some high-quality evidence of safety and effectiveness. It is also called integrative medicine.

Since many CAM based therapies are derived from TCM, we will provide a brief historical account behind the theory of TCM and how this has now been integrated into CAM approaches here in the U.S.

TCM has long been used as a major health care system in China and many other countries in Asia. TCM has its origin in ancient Taoist philosophy, which views a person as an energy system in which the body, mind, and spirit are unified into one when in harmony and are disrupted in disease.

TCM practice treats the patient as a whole, not as a part, and it emphasizes a holistic approach that attempts to bring the mind, body, and spirit into harmony. This is the complete antithesis of Western Medicine where there are specialists for each organ system that typically do not communicate with one another. TCM theory is extremely complex and originated thousands of years ago through meticulous observation of nature, the cosmos, and the human body.

In TCM theory, imbalance between yin and yang is a summation of all kinds of basic disease and disorders. There is a growing and sustained interest in TCM fueled by a combination of factors including recognition of the benefits, dissatisfaction with and ineffectiveness of traditional Western medicines, increasing commitment to holistic care, skepticism regarding adverse side effects, and increasing evidence for the personalized nature of various combinations of herbs for specific disorders.

The use of TCM is increasing in Western nations, mostly among people of Southeast Asian origin. Patients who use TCM in Western countries report that the main reason for using it is that TCM is a "more natural" and potentially safer alternative in the treatment of chronic illness than pharmaceutical drugs or surgery.

There is a growing population that prefer natural or holistic medicine than the standard prescription drugs. Of the approximately 500 herbs that are in use today, 50 or so are very commonly used alone or in combination. Rather than being prescribed individually, single herbs are combined into formulas that are designed to adapt to the specific needs of individual patients.

An herbal formula can contain from 3 to 25 herbs. Each herb has one or more of the four flavors/functions and one of five "temperatures" "氣" (pronounced "chi") (hot, warm, neutral, cool, cold). Herbal formulations work to balance the body from the inside out. Traditional herbal medicines include herbs, herbal materials, herbal preparations, and processed herbal products that contain parts of plants or other plant materials as active ingredients which assist with strengthening the vital energies (chi), blood, and fluids internally. They are typically administered as tablets, teas, pills, elixirs, soups, liquid extracts and broadly classified as dietary supplements here in the U.S.

When I first started learning about TCM and the concept of chi, I immediately thought that how they described chi sounded eerily similar to nitric oxide. Could chi actually be nitric oxide? We could find out. Recognizing and understanding NO activity of TCM may help explain centuries of treatment efficacy in a number of diseases and highlight new treatment options for conditions of NO insufficiency.

Unbeknownst to me, many Americans were already using some form of complimentary and alternative medicine in their daily lives. A 2002 survey of U.S. adults 18 years and older conducted by the National Center for Health Statistics (CDC) and the NCCAM indicated that 74.6% pf Americans had used some form of CAM, 62.1% had done so within the preceding 12 months, 54.9% used CAM in conjunction with conventional medicine and 14.8% sought care from a licensed or certified practitioner suggesting that most individuals who use CAM prefer to treat themselves.

The Secret of Nitric Oxide

The global CAM market was valued at $102 billion in 2021 and is projected to reach $437.9 billion by 2031. In 2004, a survey of nearly 1,400 U.S. hospitals found that more than one in four offered alternative and complementary therapies such as acupuncture, homeopathy, and massage therapy. Therefore, this industry and type of health care can no longer be ignored. Wouldn't it be cool if we could figure out how these medicines are actually working and advance this ancient science?

Identifying physiological systems or molecular targets that may be affected by TCM will help propel the field and industry forward and create a better safety and efficacy profile of certain CAMs. I felt confident with the tools and methods that we had in the lab we could answer these questions.

Once Yaoping was settled in, I sent him to a local acupuncture shop in the Texas Medical Center, close to our lab. I asked him to bring back any herb or combination of herbs that one would use to treat symptoms of nitric oxide deficiency such as high blood pressure, patients with previous heart attack, diabetes, etc. Yaoping brought back about a dozen different herbs in their unrefined natural form and other refined products offered commercially as a pill from pharmaceutical companies out of China. You can see the herbs in their raw form above along with their names and primary indication in the accompanying table.

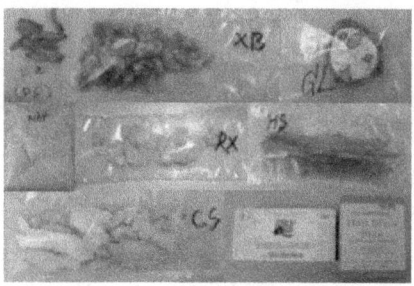

Once we received the herbs, we processed the herbs with a mortar and pestle to grind them up into powder form and then place them in alcohol or water to dissolve the powders. Once in solution we would inject them into our nitric oxide analyzer to see if we could detect any nitric oxide gas

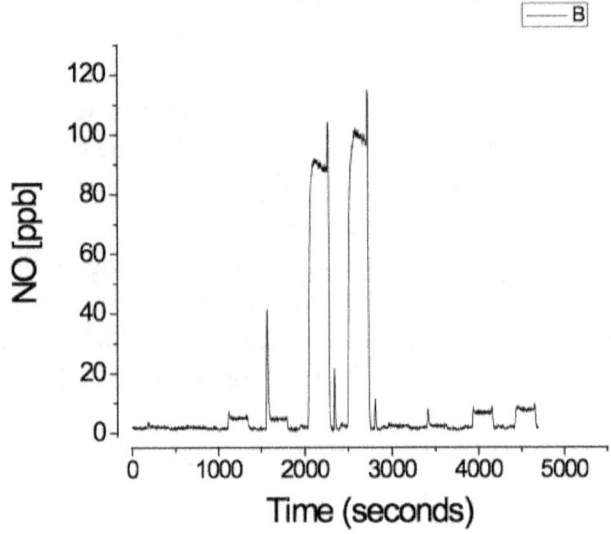

coming off the solutions of herbs. As you can see in the figure below, the first few samples, really did not produce any real nitric oxide signal.

We would let each sample run for 2-3 minutes then wash out the solution and then add a new one. You can see about the fourth sample at around 1000 seconds, we started to get a nitric oxide signal. As soon as we placed the herbal extract into the analyzer, it began generating nitric oxide gas that we could detect and quantify. It appeared as if it had a very good and predictable nitric oxide release profile. We washed that one herb out and injected a new one and we get a spike of NO that then comes down a bit but continuously produces nitric oxide gas.

I was starting to get excited at this point. To my knowledge, this had never been done or observed before. Since the two herbs that we had just tested had been used in combination for thousands of years because of their so-called synergistic effects, I asked Yaoping to add equal amounts of the two herbs into the reaction vessel at the same time. This started at about the 2000 second point in the graph. As you can see, the combination of the two herbs gave much higher levels of nitric oxide than the same amount of either of the herbs alone.

The Secret of Nitric Oxide

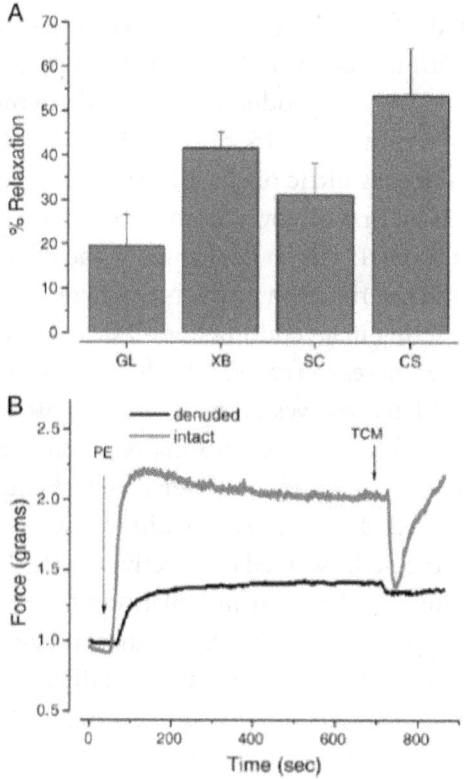

We could actually quantify the synergy that had been described for thousands of years based on patient observation and now by the ability of these herbs to amplify the nitric oxide output.

In somewhat disbelief, we washed out the solution and I asked Yaoping to repeat the exact solution again and we got the exact same result. We continued on with the rest of the herbs and some but not all produced nitric oxide under our experimental conditions. I realized we could deliver specific amounts of nitric oxide gas based on how we combined these different herbs. This is exactly what the ancient Chinese had been doing for thousands of years based on what they felt worked in their patients without any knowledge or objective ways to measure nitric oxide gas. This was fascinating and provided an explanation for how these herbs and medicine provided benefit to the patients.

Now that we were able to quantify nitric oxide activity coming from these herbal extracts, the next question was to determine if these herbs and tinctures could actually dilate isolated blood vessels as nitric oxide is known to do. So, we isolated a few strips of blood vessels from mice. We prepared them in an organ bath mounted on force transducers and then added the extracts that we demonstrated produced nitric oxide to the blood vessels.

As you can see above on page 115, the blood vessels relaxed and dilated in a very similar fashion as nitric oxide. Similar to the experiments of Dr. Bob Furchgott when he first discovered nitric oxide, we also intentionally rubbed off the endothelial cells to determine if the effects of these herbs were dependent upon the function of the NOS enzyme in the endothelial cells or if they were acting in an endothelium-independent mechanism.

As shown on the left here, you can see the degree of vasodilation by a few of the herbs. Some dilated the vessels by more than 50%. Below we show that the herbs dilated blood vessels no matter if they had a functional endothelium or not. Obviously, if a functional endothelium is in place, the herbs would lead to great degree of vasodilation but even in the absence of an endothelial layer, the herbs seemed to directly activate the smooth muscle leading to smooth muscle relaxation and dilation of the blood vessels. This indicated that even in people with endothelial dysfunction, these herbs were still providing a source of nitric oxide that could dilate blood vessels. This was adding the herbal extracts directly into an organ bath with isolated blood vessels. This is considered *ex vivo* or outside the body experiment.

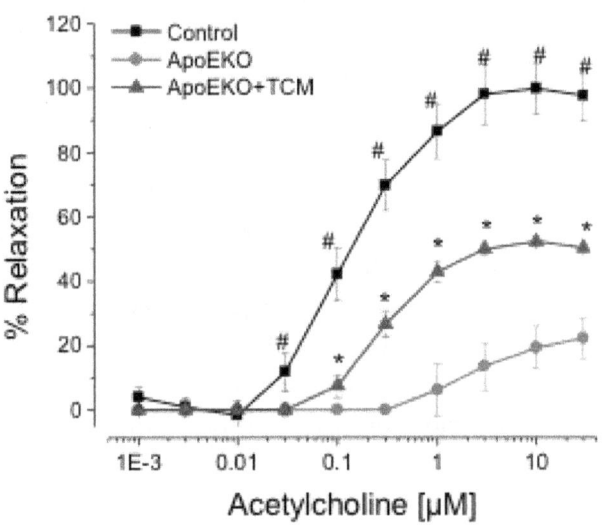

The next big question was, can these herbs work similarly when given orally to a live intact animal? We elected to use a specific strain of mice that are known to develop endothelial dysfunction and vascular disease due to a compromised ability to produce nitric oxide when activated or stimulated. Could these nitric oxide specific herbs overcome the inability to produce nitric oxide and correct endothelial dysfunction?

The beauty about scientific research is that you can ask any question you want and then design an experiment to give you answers. This is what is so fun. For this experiment, we took three different groups of mice. The first was our normal health mice that we use as our controls. The second group was the genetically modified animals that lack a specific ApoE protein.

These mice are known to develop atherosclerosis and have severe endothelial dysfunction. They were fed normal diet and not given anything other than water. The third group was the ApoE knockout mice but this group was given an oral dose of the TCM once daily for 30 days.

After 30 days, we sacrificed the mice, isolated their aorta, the large artery that leaves the left ventricle of the heart and delivers the blood to all parts of the lower body. Similar to the other organ bath experiments, we hung the blood vessels in our organ bath and mounted between force transducers to measure the degree of vasoconstriction or vasodilation. As shown in the figure above, when activated with acetylcholine, the blood vessels of the control mice, dilate very effectively since they can produce nitric oxide from the endothelium.

The NOS enzyme is functional. In the ApoE knockout, you can see they only have about 10% of the normal vascular function of the control mice. These mice have severe endothelial dysfunction and their ability to produce nitric oxide is severely compromised. However, when we fed these mice the TCMs orally for 30 days, we could recover about 50% of the endothelial function.

Now understand this is a genetic disorder in these mice. This is not caused by diet or any drug. But yet, the TCM herbs corrected by more than 50% their ability to produce nitric oxide in the lining of their blood vessels. This was remarkable.

There is no drug available or approved by the FDA that has been shown to do this. And these herbs are natural, not synthetic so they are certainly safe but even more efficacious than FDA approved drugs at correcting vascular dysfunction. This was really cool. We had demonstrated that certain herbs naturally produced nitric oxide. They were biologically active due to their ability to dilate blood vessels in isolation. They were orally viable and available given that the mice that were administered these herbs orally every day for 30 days showed significant improvements in their vascular health and their ability to produce nitric oxide. This told me that nature had a way to produce nitric oxide and if we could harness what nature has provided, then we could develop some really good nitric oxide product technology.

These were really cool observations and discoveries but does it make sense in what we know about the production and regulation of nitric oxide in the cardiovascular system and could this be a way to restore nitric oxide in patients that were compromised?

From our observations that the TCMs improve NO production in the endothelium, we could rationalize a mechanism to explain this. In healthy patients, NO is endogenously generated from the amino acid L-arginine and molecular oxygen in reactions catalyzed by a family of enzymes called NO synthases (NOS). There are three mammalian NOS isoforms: neuronal (nNOS), endothelial (eNOS), and inducible (iNOS).

Under physiological conditions, the dominant NOS isoform in the vasculature is eNOS. Endothelial dysfunction arises from down-regulation of eNOS expression and activity, and uncoupling of NOS generating free radicals.

In other words, when the NOS enzyme is uncoupled and not functional, it actually produces oxygen radicals and causes oxidative stress. We now recognize and appreciate the endothelial production of NO declines progressively with age and can be further reduce by poor diet and lifestyle. This becomes the basis for endothelial dysfunction and the etiology of a number of CVD related symptoms.

Restoring endogenous production of NO or providing an exogenous source of NO would be an attractive therapeutic option if this intervention could slow down the progression of endothelial dysfunction and reduce the risk of CVD. It appears that the TCM used in our experiment may be recoupling the NOS enzyme, perhaps by preventing the oxidation of important co-factors. They could also be upregulating their genetic expression. We did not probe deeper to answer this question but the fact that they could improve endothelial nitric oxide production was fascinating and important.

To explain the effects of vasodilation in the blood vessels that did not have a functional endothelium, we can explain by perhaps the actions of nitrite and nitrate that are found naturally in these extracts.

As described in previous chapters, an alternative pathway for NO generation was discovered about 30 years ago, wherein the inorganic anions nitrate and nitrite, most often considered inert end products from NO oxidation, can be reduced back to NO and other bioactive nitrogen oxide species. This nitrate-nitrite-nitric oxide pathway is regulated differently than the classic L-arginine-nitric oxide synthase pathway, and it is greatly enhanced during conditions that do not favor endothelial NO production such as low oxygen and low blood flow.

This makes sense since the human body is full of redundancy, meaning there is more than one pathway to produce such as essential molecule nitric oxide. During the course of my research and others, both nitrite and nitrate have become very attractive targets for therapies for nitric oxide. Nitrite and nitrate are now considered a major storage form of NO in both blood and tissues.

As we demonstrated several years earlier, administering both nitrite and nitrate protected tissues from injury and could restore NO homeostasis in mice that could not make nitric oxide. It appeared the TCMs did the same thing. We then began to measure the nitrite and nitrate in each of the herbal extracts from each herb. Some contained higher concentrations than others but appeared to contain enough that would be sufficient to generate nitric oxide. The nitrate-nitrite-nitric oxide pathway is boosted by an increase in the dietary intake of nitrate. Previous studies had already demonstrated that dietary nitrate supplementation, in the form of potassium nitrate or nitrate naturally found in beet root or other vegetables has been shown to reduce blood pressure, inhibit platelet aggregation and protect the heart from ischemia-reperfusion injury.

In order to metabolize any nitrate found in the herbal extract, the patient must first have the right oral nitrate-reducing bacteria. Bacteria are required to metabolize nitrate into nitrite since humans do not have this enzyme.

Once nitrite is produced, there are a number of endogenous systems in mammals capable of reducing nitrite to NO. We and others have published on this. For this system to proceed there must be enough substrate for reduction and the necessary bacteria and reductive machinery to reduce nitrate all the way down to NO. Dietary and enzymatic sources of nitrate are a potentially large source of nitrite and ultimately NO in the human body.

The nitrite in saliva is produced from nitrate by oral bacteria is converted to NO gas once swallowed after entering the acidic environment of the stomach, helping to reduce gastrointestinal tract infection, increase mucous barrier thickness, and increase blood flow to the stomach.

In addition to the simple acid chemistry of nitrite that happens in the stomach to produce nitric oxide, there are several enzymatic pathways for conversion of systemic nitrite to NO and other bioactive nitrogen species. Hemoglobin, myoglobin, neuroglobin, xanthine oxidoreductase, aldehyde oxidase, carbonic anhydrase and mitochondrial enzymes have all been identified with having a role in nitrite bioactivation. In most cases the enzyme systems only produce nitric oxide from nitrite in low oxygen environments. Therefore, for this system to generate enough bioactive NO, there must be sufficient nitrate and nitrite available for this inefficient reduction.

A consequence of endothelial dysfunction is reduced blood and tissue levels of nitrite available for reduction further comprising this alternative NO pathway. Since most of the TCMs are herbal extracts, we initially thought they may be good sources of nitrite and nitrate. Also, antioxidants and polyphenols have been shown to effectively reduce nitrite to NO. This combination of nitrite, nitrate and polyphenols could provide then a system for repleting NO homeostasis.

We did indeed confirm that all of the nitric oxide active herbal extracts contain high amounts of nitrate and also the capacity to reduce nitrite to NO. It appears that the TCM herbal extracts provide the entire system for producing nitric oxide, and we speculate this may be the reason for their therapeutic effects.

The described benefits of these ancient medications may be attributed to their inherent nitrate/nitrite content combined with their robust nitrate/nitrite reductase activity to generate NO independent of the L-arginine-NO pathway. Upon further research, it was revealed that potassium nitrate or saltpetre has been used for centuries. The first use of inorganic nitrate for treatment of patients with symptoms that appears to be angina was described in an 8th century Chinese manuscript uncovered at the Buddhist grotto of Dunhuang.

The patients were instructed to take Xiao Shi Xiong Huang San, hold it under the tongue for a time, and then swallow the saliva. Understand this was during a time when there were no antiseptic mouthwashes or fluoride being used to destroy the oral bacteria.

The significance of the instructions is that under the tongue, even in a healthy mouth, nitrate-reducing bacteria convert some of the nitrate into nitrite. Therefore, if the patient follows the physician's instructions fully, he or she will be taking nitrite, known to be effective in alleviating pain resulting from angina.

Chinese physicians in traditional medicine have more recently tested the therapeutic effects of Xiao Shi Xiong Huang San (the Nitrum and Realgar Powder), one of the Dunhuang prescriptions, on angina pectoris caused by coronary heart disease. Compared to nitroglycerin, Xiao Shi Xiong Huang San showed much higher efficacy and improvement in a clinical trial of 61 patients.

This means that these traditional medicines are more effective than the best medicines available here in the U.S. Mu-Fang-Ji-Tang (TJ-36), a traditional Chinese herbal medicine, is made from four natural traditional

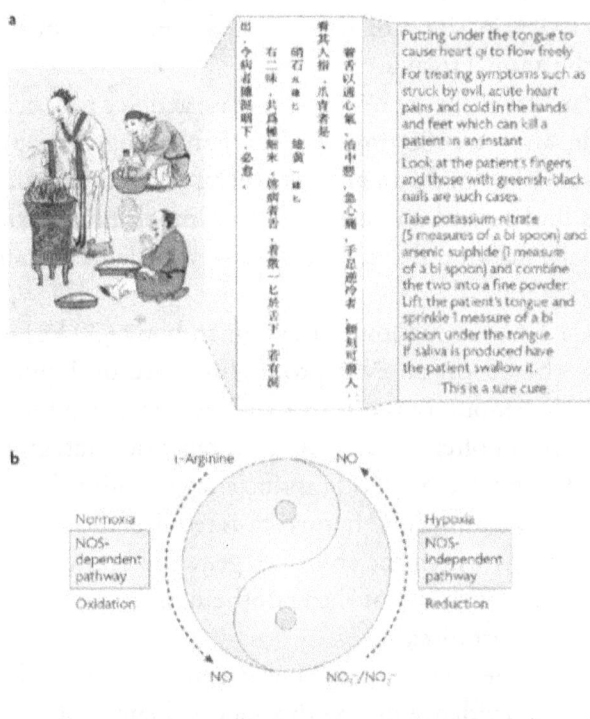

Nature Reviews | Drug Discovery

Chinese drugs: Panax ginseng radix, Cinnamomum cassia, Sinomenum acutum, and Cypsum fibrosum, which is said to have been used for more than 1800 years to treat heart failure in China.

Recent studies have shown that Mu-Fang-Ji-Tang (TJ-36) had protective effects against heart attack in a mouse model of congestive heart failure induced by viral myocarditis. Our studies have provided convincing evidence that many these TCM contain significant amounts of nitrate and nitrite and also active nitrite reductase activity in certain herbs known to have protective or therapeutic benefits to patients with CVD, such as the Danshen Root (radix salviae miltiorrhizae), Sanchi (radix notoginseng), and Hongshen (radix ginseng).

These herbs, with specific indications for cardiovascular disease can generate NO from nitrite, and relax blood vessels. The therapeutic benefits of these herbal medicines are providing an alternative source of NO to patients that may be unable to make NO from L-arginine owing to endothelial dysfunction.

There is an endogenous nitrite reductase activity in animal tissues, such as the liver and aorta, but this inherent biological capacity is low. The reductase activity in some of these herbal medicines may exceed that detected in the animal tissues.

It is estimated that the increased reductase activity may occur by orders of magnitude, almost 1000 times higher than endogenous production of NO. If we wanted to make an effective therapy for nitric oxide, we would first need to understand and calculate how much nitric oxide a healthy person normally makes and then figure out how to deliver this amount back to the patient.

The average NO production in the human body (70 kg) is 1.68 mmol NO per day (based on an NO production rate of 1 µmol/kg/h). By supplying the exogenous nitrate/nitrite and reductase activities, these herbal combinations could offer an alternative therapeutic strategy to combat or treat any condition related to NO insufficiency including heart disease and hypertension. Maintaining NO homeostasis requires the repletion of nitrite and nitrate through which the ability to generate NO can be restored to compensate for the inability of the endothelium to convert L-arginine to NO in coronary heart disease.

As we started reviewing the published literature, we actually found quite a bit of published evidence on the therapeutic benefit of certain Chinese medicines. Some studies have provided new evidence on Danshen, a commonly used herbal medicine for CVD in China, which may have a similar efficacy to the known NO donor nitroglycerin.

Danshen related Chinese herbal medicines have been widely used for treatment of coronary heart disease in the East, and clinical trials have been conducted in the United States. Danshen is a routine herbal medication for acute angina pectoris.

In addition, it may be effective for dyslipidemia, blood hyperviscosity syndrome, peripheral angiopathy (superficial thrombophlebitis, venous thrombosis, allergic arteriolitis), diabetes mellitus, and cirrhosis, and is also used for altitude sickness. Experimental studies have shown that Danshen dilates coronary arteries, increases coronary blood flow, and scavenges free radicals in ischemic diseases, reducing cellular damage from ischemia and improved heart functions, remarkably similar to known effects of NO and nitrite.

All of these observations had been published prior to our work but no one was able to provide an explanation on the mechanism of action of the observed therapeutic benefits. However, the nitrate/nitrite reductase activity in Danshen is relatively low.

Often, Danshen is mixed with other herbal products. One of which is an extract of cinnamon or borneol. Borneol is consumed excessively in China and Southeast Asian countries, particularly in a combined formula for preventing cardiovascular disease. Borneol exerts a concentration dependent inhibitory effect on venous thrombosis. The antithrombotic activity of borneol contributes to its action in combined formula for preventing cardiovascular diseases.

Our recent studies have shown that although the natural form of borneol itself contains very little nitrite and nitrate, when combined with the nitrate and nitrite rich DanShen, this creates an ideal synergistic system for producing nitric oxide. Another herbal medicine made from the root of Radix ginseng may also have synergistic effects with Danshen. Ginseng contains modest amounts of nitrate but has stronger reductase activity. Therefore, this may explain the mechanism behind the theory of synergy of specific combination of herbs.

We were also very interested in explaining the effects of the TCMS on promoting endothelial nitric oxide production. Some TCM may regulate NO production by exerting regulatory effects on the L-arginine/eNOS/NO signaling pathway. One of the compounds, Puerarin is a major active ingredient extracted from the traditional Chinese medicine Ge-gen (Radix Puerariae, RP).

It has long been used to treat cardiovascular diseases including coronary artery diseases (CAD), arrhythmia, and hypertension. We found reports that revealed that it increased serum nitrite concentration in rats with heart attack through an increased expression of the eNOS enzyme.

Tongxinluo (TXL), a mixture of traditional Chinese medicines, was shown to protect from injury after heart attack. TXL is composed of Radix ginseng, Buthus martensi, Hirudo, Eupolyphaga seu steleophage, Scolopendra subspinipes, Periostracum cicadae, Radix paeoniae rubra, Semen ziziphi spinosae, Lignum dalbergiae odoriferae, Lignum santali albi, and Borneolum syntheticum.

Owing to its efficacy and minimal adverse effects, TXL has been widely used in China to treat patients with acute coronary syndrome. The results show that TXL treatment can decrease creatine kinase elevation, improve coronary flow, and reduce infarct size. It appears that select TCM herbs alone and in combination can restore NO homeostasis both through an endothelium dependent manner by activating the L-arginine pathway and through an endothelium-independent manner through the nitrate-nitrite-NO pathway that may overcome endothelial dysfunction.

To further convince us the TCMs were indeed working through a nitric oxide pathway, we were interested to see if they could also reduce oxidative stress and inflammation that occurs when nitric oxide production is compromised. There is increasing evidence that in certain pathologic states the increased production and/or ineffective scavenging of reactive oxygen species (ROS) may play a critical role.

Medicinal plants are a source for a wide variety of natural antioxidants and may exhibit their effects via several proposed mechanisms, including inhibition of the activities of cyclooxygenase-2 (COX-2) working similar to aspirin or NSAIDS and nuclear factor-Kappa B (NF- kB), inhibition of angiogenesis, and activation of Nrf2-mediated antioxidant signaling all known to interface with the NO pathway.

Dang Gui has been shown to hold anti-inflammatory properties and antioxidant activities, especially when used concurrently with other herbs.

Drinking tea is a tradition that began in ancient China over 5000 years ago. Green tea from the leaves of Camellia sinensis is the second most consumed beverage in the world, after water. It is a well-studied herb for its effectiveness in chemoprevention, cancer therapy, and other benefits to overall health. The main components of green tea are polyphenols, known as catechins, which account for 30-42% of the solid weight in green tea leaves. The most abundant polyphenol in green tea is (-)-epigallocatechin-3-gallate (EGCG) which is also the most commonly studied green tea component. EGCG contributes to 10-50% of the total polyphenol contents in green tea and appears to possess the strongest antioxidant activity, about 25-100 fold more potent than vitamins C and E. Reducing oxidative stress and promoting endogenous antioxidant enzymatic defense systems very likely provides an additional benefit of traditional medicines. These antioxidants defenses will enhance endogenous NO production by keeping essential co-factors such as tetrahydrobiopterin (BH4) from becoming oxidized and also preserve and prolong NO activity once it is produced by preventing its scavenging by oxygen radicals.

This was a major discovery and very fun set of experiments. Once we published our results and the global scientific and medical community became aware of our findings, Yaoping and I became very famous and popular in China. (Tang, et al. Nitric Oxide Bioactivity of Traditional Chinese Medicines Used for Cardiovascular Indications. *Free Radic Biol Med* 2009 Sep 15;47(6):835-40.)

About a week after we published our data, I was invited to come to China and speak at many different medical and scientific conferences. Both Yaoping and I took off for China. I believe I gave seven speeches in 6 different cities all over China over a period of 8 days.

The Chinese community felt great appreciation that their centuries of science and medicine had finally been validated and verified with a mechanism of action. To summarize what we had discovered, some of the TCM and alternative medicines work by restoring nitric oxide signaling in the body. The NO donor-like herbs may serve as an alternative source of nitrate and nitrite or other NO-donors. They contain high activities of nitrite reductase that converts the inorganic anion into NO, which, in turn, relaxes blood vessels and prevents thrombosis.

There are also some TCM contain regulatory factors that influence the expression and activity of the nitric oxide synthase enzyme, and may interact with endogenous factors that modulate L-arginine/eNOS/NO signaling pathway. Our research is providing more evidence to understand specific activity of CAMs that will hopefully provide a mechanistic understanding of their clinical efficacy and allow for better combination of different herbs.

However, currently the use of CAM is influenced by legal restrictions, with shifts towards increasing regulation and formal recognition of CAM as means to treat or prevent disease. Our work reveals that traditional medicines have utilized nitric oxide for more than 4000 years.

However, it was never understood how these medicines worked based on a well described mechanism of action. Our research revealed that certain herbs and medicine have nitric oxide activity. Qi is the force that fuels life and in TCM is what controls energy and blood flow to all organs in the body.

We were the first to reveal that Qi is nitric oxide and can be restored by the rationale combination of certain herbs and medicine commonly used in China and other cultures that use herbal medicine. Yaoping spent about 4 years with me as a post-doctoral fellow and then was offered a position as Chair of Pharmacology at a major medical school in China. Yaoping invites me every several years to come to China to present and lecture to his physician and scientific colleagues. I am forever grateful for his time in my lab and the many contributions we made together.

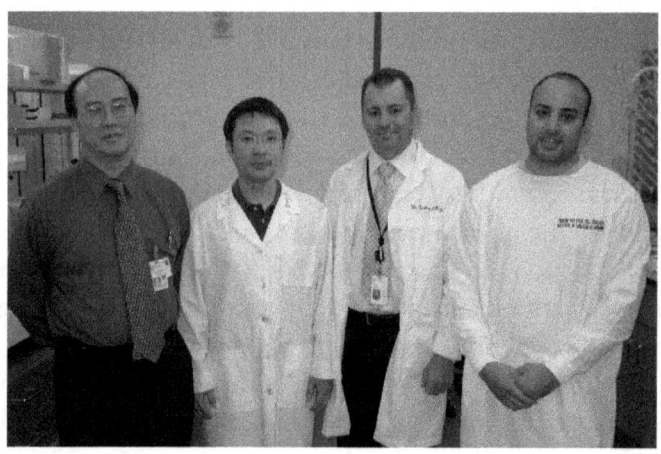

From the press release of the TCM study, left to right, Yong Jian Geng, M.D., Ph.D., Yaoping Tang, M.D., me, Harha Garg, M.D.

CHAPTER 11
Professional Challenges

"Trust is earned, respect is given and loyalty is demonstrated. Betrayal of any one of these is to lose all three."
—Unknown

I've learned over the course of my career that if you are doing things that really do not matter, people leave you alone. If you are doing really important work that has the potential to change the world, people develop an interest and, in some cases, will try to steal your ideas or try to stop you. In 2009, my research lab was very productive.

I had several post-doctoral fellows in my lab, several lab technicians and students working in the lab doing nitric oxide research. We were publishing 8-10 paper per year, gaining a really good understanding of nitric oxide production and mechanisms of action. I had recently been awarded an American Heart Association Grant. In collaboration with Baylor College of Medicine, we had been awarded a multi-million dollar grant for a rare urea cycle disorder in pediatric patients.

Earlier in 2007 I was awarded a Young Investigator Award at the University of Texas. I was working with the legends in Cardiology and Vascular biology including Denton Cooley, M.D., James T. Willerson, M.D. at Texas Heart Institute. I had submitted a number of invention disclosure to the Office of Technology Management and I felt very confident in my research program. I was working alongside a Nobel Prize winner as my department chair and had invitations to present our findings at major scientific meetings. Life was great and I was having fun doing research and making discoveries.

As we were working on the Traditional Chinese Medicine projects, Dr. Tang, was one of my post-docs in the lab who was leading the project. As

Denton Cooley, M.D. with me after my Young Investigator Award, 2007.

discussed in the previous chapter, we discovered that many of these herbs and medicine work through their ability to produce or stimulate nitric oxide production. This was very exciting.

We would present our data and findings at our departmental faculty meetings. In the Center for Cell Signaling with Dr. Murad as the Director and Chairman, we had lab meetings every Monday. Usually, we would rotate faculty members to present their findings and research to the group and we would discuss and give feedback, submit recommendations for new experiments and help drive the research for the center. When we first started evaluating the traditional Chinese medicines in lab meetings, there was a lot of interest. Many of the faculty members, post-docs, and lab techs were Chinese or of Asian descent.

I presented our findings showing that when you mixed certain herbal extracts in our nitric oxide analyzer, they produced nitric oxide gas. This was fascinating to me and to all others in the lab, including Dr. Murad. I was very open and honest about our findings and was looking for direction or indications if others had experienced similar results. I was not really offered much feedback from the group so we kept doing experiments using different extracts from different medicines and herbs. It was an exciting time and we had analytical equipment that many other labs did not have, including Dr. Murad's lab.

The Secret of Nitric Oxide

One weekend I was away on travel and I got a frantic phone call from Yaoping. He was working in the lab on a Saturday doing his experiments. Yaoping revealed that a post-doc, seasoned faculty member from Dr. Murad's lab had come into my lab while he was working and asked to use our analyzers to measure their samples. He also asked Yaoping to not inform me that he was using my instruments Of course, Yaoping did not agree to analyze the samples and indicated that he would have to speak with me and offer to formally collaborate. Afterwards, the post-doc, seasoned faculty member, threatened Yaoping that if he did not analyze their samples and help in their research, Dr. Murad would notify Yaoping's superiors back in China, have Yaoping deported and ruin his academic career.

Yaoping was obviously distraught and did not know what to do. I informed Yaoping that I would handle the situation once I returned to work on Monday. I was very upset and not exactly sure how I was going to handle the situation. I did not know how to interpret this. I'm always happy to collaborate with other labs and help in any experiments and data collection. Why were they not wanting to tell me?

I began to think about what was really going on in this situation and how was I going to approach my boss on this issue. I decided I needed some sort of evidence. After all, if there was something going on, who would the leadership at University of Texas believe, a post-doc, seasoned faculty member or a very young faculty member? The answer was obvious to me. In other words, I was dispensable and the post-doc, seasoned faculty member was not.

I decided to get a recorder and just record my conversation with the post-doc, seasoned faculty member about the incident. That way I had proof and it was not just his word against mine. This was a time before recorders on cell phones so I had to actually go purchase a pocket recorder from Radio Shack. On the way to work Monday morning, I stopped and bought a pocket size tape recorder and placed in my shirt pocket. It was small enough to be hidden and discreet. I tested it to make sure conversation could be heard and recorded. I then proceeded to the post-doc, seasoned faculty member's office and knocked on the door. He answered and asked me to come in. I informed him of the incident with Yaoping on Saturday in the lab and asked if he had any knowledge of what was going on. What proceeded from that point on was shocking. He asked that I close the door and take a seat. For the next hour, he informed me that he was involved in research in China at the Murad Research Institute in Shanghai where they were developing drugs and therapies around traditional Chinese medicine with nitric oxide activity.

In fact, many of the scientists and students in his lab at UT were from the Shanghai institute. He was concerned that my findings were in competition with his program in China. He advised me to stop all research on TCM and that Yaoping should not participate in any research using traditional Chinese medicine or he would have him deported. The postdoc, seasoned faculty member revealed many troubling situations during his hour-long monologue and was very deliberate in attempting to stop our research program. Fortunately, we had already conducted enough research to publish our results. We had a manuscript already in preparation.

I contacted one of the Editors at a scientific journal and indicated that I would need expedited review of our manuscript given the situation. I thought this was important to get our paper published and our invention disclosures submitted to the University since it appeared that some of our intellectual property was compromised and may have been sent to China.

Once we finished the meeting, I immediately took the recording to the Office of Technology Management where I was informed that I must report this incidence to the President of the University. I handed over the recording where the University transcribed the entire conversation. Afterwards, I went to my office and completed the manuscript on the nitric oxide activity of traditional Chinese medicine and submitted to a scientific journal for publication. Fortunately, the journal accepted our paper for publication in a very short time period. We went about our research in our lab but did not report any other findings in our departmental lab meetings.

The day after our paper was accepted for publication and it was available online, I received a letter. I could not believe it. I was just starting in my independent research career and I was being accused of scientific misconduct, breach of confidentiality and threats of being dismissed from my faculty position. My professional life was over, I thought. How could I recover from these accusations when I knew I did not do anything wrong? My only option was to stand strong with posture and confidence and stand my ground. I responded to the Director of the Institute of Molecular Medicine, Tom Caskey, M.D. with my own letter.

This started an inquiry into the accusation of scientific misconduct by the Executive Vice President of Research and my future in academia was at stake. The investigation by the University took weeks to complete and my future and career was in the hands of University officials who I trusted would be objective and not biased. I was very pleased to receive the letter from the EVP of research a few weeks later completely exonerating me of the very serious accusations.

One of the unintended consequences of this inquiry and accusations was a separate investigation into financial and research conflicts of interest with the University of Texas and the Shanghai Research Institute.

After the investigation into my scientific misconduct was completed and I was exonerated, I was asked by Dr. Caskey to take a week off so they could take care of some internal business that resulted from their own investigations I am not aware of any details from the investigation other than when I returned to work, the post-doc, seasoned faculty member was no longer employed by the University of Texas and his office was completely cleaned out several days later. In fact, the entire Center for Cell Signaling was dissolved.

I was still employed by the Institute of Molecular Medicine but I did not have a home within the Institute. I was offered a position to join the Texas Therapeutics Institute within the Institute of Molecular Medicine which was a perfect home for me. The TTI was created to commercialize discoveries into clinical therapeutics. That was exactly where my entire research program was focused. I spent the next 5 years at the Texas Therapeutics Institute within the Institute of Molecular Medicine with great leadership and focused direction on drug discovery. It appeared I had survived a very serious attack on my professional career from some very powerful forces. Little did I know this was just the first of many more to come.

The letter I received from Dr. Davies completely exonerating me of the accusations of the awful misconduct by the post-doc, seasoned faculty member was a huge relief for me. However, I still did not completely understand why all this happened or what I could have done differently to prevent this big misunderstanding. I was honest and transparent about the work we were doing and openly communicated our findings to the lab and Dr. Murad's research group. I also kept asking myself, why would someone take such a hardcore and risky stance and make such serious accusations about me and my work? Obviously, this indicated that the work we were doing trying to understand the mechanism of nitric oxide production by traditional medicine or botanicals was very important and we had made discoveries that others were after.

If it wasn't, then it would certainly not have caused such a response. Today, looking back I can understand why this was such a big deal. I had figured out how to make nitric oxide gas from natural products and this allowed me to dial in any level of nitric oxide I wanted based on how I combined certain components. This was the basis for everything I was going to do commercially to develop a safe and effective nitric oxide product. I felt as if I had achieved what everyone was working for in research and that is "to see what everyone else has seen, but to think what no one else had thought"—my favorite quote by Albert Szent-Györgyi, 1937 Nobel Prize winner in Physiology or Medicine. This has been my guiding light and principle throughout my entire research career. I am most proud that I have indeed seen what others have seen but thought what others have not thought.

CHAPTER 12
An Explanation on the Benefits of Certain Diets
"Let food be thy medicine, thy medicine shall be thy food."
—Hippocrates

Also, during our time investigating the Chinese medicines, we started working on quantifying the nitrate and nitrite content of certain foods commercially available here in the U.S. Foods like vegetables and cured meats.

Could it be that the Standard American Diet (SAD) diet did not provide sufficient nitrate and nitrite to provide any real source of nitric oxide production? Could certain dietary patterns such as the Mediterranean diet, Japanese diet and other dietary patterns known to prevent cardiovascular disease and cancer provide sufficient nitrate and nitrite to overcome nitric oxide insufficiency in patients? Well again, a very important question and one that we could test to get an answer.

Foundationally, there is clear evidence that diet can prevent, treat, cure and even reverse chronic disease. For years, scientists argued that certain diets were protective because of the antioxidants of certain foods and dietary patterns. However, use of antioxidants in clinical trials has failed to recapitulate the effects of a certain diets.

I was invited to give a lecture at Michigan State University in February of 2007 in the Department of Food Science. It was bitter cold those few days I was in East Lansing. I had a chance to visit with several of the Professor in the department both before and after my lecture.

One that stood out was Dr. Norm Hord. Norm was a registered dietician and had a Ph.D. in food science. After my lecture, he politely told me I was full of shit and that nitrite and nitrate are toxins found in cured meats that have been implicated in certain cancers.

I had received this type of feedback before at many of the meetings where I had lectured. Norm and I had a great conversation and we agreed we would work together to help provide some clarity. For the next few months, Norm and I would speak on the phone, we would agree on certain foods to measure to quantify the nitrate and nitrite content. We measured raw foods, we measured some food supplements, baby formulas, milk products and several other things. We found a very wide range of nitrate and nitrite content in different foods, supplements and baby formulas. We found that the food that historically had been proven to be healthy and have protection

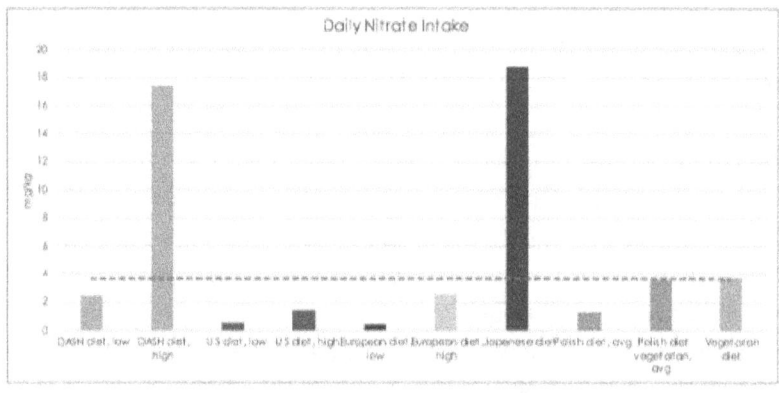

Comparison of Daily Nitrate Intake Values.

The data presented above was collected from published literature as follows: DASH, US, and European diets as cited in Hord *et al*, 2009; Japanese diet as presented, Sabka *et al*, 2010; Polish diets as presented and cited Miteket *et al*, 2013; and Vegetarian diet as cited in Lidder and Webb, 2012.

against high blood pressure and cardiovascular disease were the ones with the highest nitrate content.

We also took foods recommended by the Dietary Approaches to Stop Hypertension (DASH) diet. In our paper we published, we suggested that the cardioprotective benefits of certain diets such as the DASH Diet,

Mediterranean diet and others were due in part to the nitrate and/or nitrite content.

We revealed that the benefits of a Mediterranean diet, Japanese diet and Dietary Approaches to Stop Hypertension (DASH) diet all work through a common mechanism of action. These diets contain high amounts of inorganic nitrate and antioxidants that allow for the metabolism of nitrate into nitrite and nitric oxide. Other dietary patterns such as the Western diet are depleted of such nutrients and therefore do not provide any real health benefits.

Our next thought revolved around the idea that we could perhaps recommend specific servings of certain food based on their own nitrate and nitrite content. For example, since we knew green leafy vegetables such as spinach or celery contained a certain amount of nitrate, then we could calculate how much of that particular vegetable you would need to eat to get sufficient nitric oxide in the body once consumed.

In order to answer this very important question, we went to five different cities around the U.S. We went to New York, Raleigh, Dallas, Chicago and Los Angeles. We bought the same vegetables from the same retail grocer at each city and then brough it back to my lab for analysis. We also compared

Table 2. Mean nitrate (NO_3^-) concentrations[a] (ppm)[b] of raw vegetables classified as conventional from each city

Product category	Chicago	Dallas	Los Angeles	New York	Raleigh
Broccoli	271 ± 89 (61-822)	357 ± 50 (165-664)	512 ± 85 (164-1140)	279 ± 80 (29-1009)	553 ± 28 (374-680)
Cabbage	475 ± 46 (256-670)	256 ± 33 (63-434)	800 ± 142 (275-1831)	193 ± 28 (37-283)	364 ± 79 (72-882)
Celery	230 ± 19 (147-359)	2052 ± 156 (918-2973)	2651 ± 339 (608-4269)	88 ± 17 (20-157)	2201 ± 112 (1397-2727)
Lettuce	207 ± 32 (79-425)	1370 ± 93 (870-1909)	1051 ± 122 (422-1495)	568 ± 93 (321-970)	986 ± 185 (450-2171)
Spinach	647 ± 69 (162-875)	4923 ± 327 (2377-6473)	4138 ± 451 (2141-8000)	564 ± 174 (65-1545)	3155 ± 145 (2478-4168)

[a]Mean value with standard error; minimum and maximum nitrate values in parentheses.
[b]mg/kg of fresh weight.

Regional and Category Differences In
Conventional Vegetable Nitrate Values.

Table 3. Mean nitrate (NO₃⁻) concentrations[a] (ppm)[b] of raw vegetables classified as organic from each city

Product category	Chicago	Dallas	Los Angeles	New York	Raleigh
Broccoli	212 ± 35 (84-417)	430 ± 40 (225-683)	196 ± 47 (44-501)	167 ± 53 (11-502)	8 ± 2 (3-22)
Cabbage	53 ± 12 (2-107)	989 ± 166 (71-1472)	612 ± 85 (335-1365)	898 ± 191 (3-2114)	167 ± 18 (94-271)
Celery	310 ± 58 (26-597)	390 ± 139 (0.7-1453)	2022 ± 208 (1196-3589)	807 ± 208 (11-2053)	1023 ± 69 (598-1461)
Lettuce	100 ± 8 (58-159)	1367 ± 99 (989-2013)	1277 ± 73 (1029-1702)	780 ± 111 (347-1595)	692 ± 28 (567-869)
Spinach	459 ± 48 (238-744)	1610 ± 209 (488-2941)	2199 ± 237 (1075-3820)	1566 ± 384 (16-4089)	755 ± 101 (399-1362)

[a] Mean value with standard error; minimum and maximum nitrate values in parentheses.
[b] mg/kg of fresh weight.

Regional and Category Differences In Organic Vegetable Nitrate Values.

conventionally grown vegetables to those that were labeled organic. This was quite the effort but what we learned was so valuable.

We expected there to be some variability in the amount of nitrite and nitrate in the different vegetables but we did not appreciate the wide variation of nitrate in the same vegetable only grown in a different part of the U.S. We published our results in 2015 and the data from the tables are above.

What we learned is that if you live in Dallas or Los Angeles, you could eat 4-6 stalks of celery and get enough nitrate to normalize your blood pressure and produce nitric oxide. If you ate celery in New York or Chicago, you would have to eat 20-40 times more celery. There is no way we could ever make recommendations of how many servings of certain foods or vegetables because it depends on where you live and where the vegetables are grown.

When we compared conventionally grown vegetables to those grown organically, we also were very much surprised. As shown in the other table (below), organically grown vegetables appeared to have much lower nitrate than the same vegetables grown conventionally.

When we tried to understand and rationalize this, we had to investigate what is required for an organic label. In the U.S., organic means that the

The Secret of Nitric Oxide

Summary of changes in the Mineral Content of 27 Vegetables between 1940 and 1991

Year of Analysis	Mineral	Brassicas	'Bulb' Veg	'Fruit' Veg	'Leaf'	'Pods'	'Shoot' Veg	'Root' Veg	1940 Total	1991 Total	Change over 51 yrs
1940	Sodium	67.8	29.6	18.5	205.1	7	144.3	287.7	760		
1991	(Na)	21	16	14	191	1	61	83		387	Less 49%
1940	Potassium	922	641	976	1967	618	460	2098	7682		
1991	(K)	1030	570	730	940	550	460	2180		6490	Less 16%
1940	Phosphorous	194.4	81.1	76.9	240.7	130	52.6	239.5	1015.2		
1991	(P)	240	91	108	137	164	48	314		1102	Plus 9%
1940	Magnesium	55.8	31	37.8	113.2	53.2	22.2	105.1	418.3		
1991	(Mg)	54	18	36	67	53	11	81		320	Less 24%
1940	Calcium	349.3	226.7	85.5	908.8	48.1	70.6	299.4	1988.4		
1991	(Ca)	204	84	64	393	54	62	220		1081	Less 46%
1940	Iron	4.53	3.54	1.51	10.89	2.68	1.3	5.18	29.63		
1991	(Fe)	4	2.9	1.5	5.5	4	0.8	3		21.7	Less 27%
1940	Copper	0.41	0.3	0.35	0.67	0.32	0.25	0.72	3.02		
1991	(Cu)	0.11	0.13	0.05	0.09	0.07	0.06	0.21		0.72	Less 76%

Each analysis figure represents a cummulative figure obtained from individual tables - see Appendix 1

Ratio Changes:
- Ca:P 1:2 → 1:1
- Na:K 1:10 → 1:17
- Mg:Ca 1:4.8 → 1:3.4
- Cu:Fe 1:10 → 1:30

These statistics have been calculated by comparing and contrasting data first published in 1940 by McCance and Widdowson - 'Chemical Composition of Food', which was commissioned by the Medical Research Council - with that data published by the same authors in 1991 - The Composition of Food, which was commissioned by the Royal Society of Chemistry and the Ministry of Agriculture Fisheries and Food.

© Copyright D.E. Thomas 1/2000

Mineral Depletion of Foods Between 1940-1991.

food is grown without any added herbicides or pesticides and it does not permit nitrogen based fertilizers to be added to the soil. Farmers can use compost or manure, but not actual standardized nitrogen fertilizer. This started to make sense.

Without added nitrogen to the soil, there would be less nitrate in the soil and less nitrate assimilated in the vegetables grown in that soil. Now this created an interesting conundrum. Do we eat organic or not?

If you eat organic, you will not get enough nitrate in the vegetables to restore nitric oxide production. If you eat conventional, you may be exposed to herbicides or pesticides. I think the answer is to consume vegetables grown conventionally with added fertilizer but without the use of herbicides or pesticides.

I encourage people to shop local and support your local farmers and ask the right questions. Another issue is that most food requires nitrogen in order to assimilate other nutrients into the plant. There are data also showing that the foods grown in America have gradually declined in nutrient density since 1941. See the chart.

So, whereas we were only interested in a single nutrient, nitrate, it appears that most all minerals and nutrients are deficient in foods grown in America.

It was Linus Pauling who famously said, that "Most chronic diseases are caused by nutrient deficiencies." I think his hypothesis makes a lot of sense now.

Norm Hord and I continue to collaborate and have become really good friends. This is how science is supposed to be. Science must always be continuously questioned and challenged. This does not mean that the two scientists with two different views have to become enemies. After all, we are all after the truth.

Let's collaborate, design meaningful experiments to get meaningful answers and solve the controversy. That is how advancements and innovations are made. Ask relevant questions and then design the proper experiments to provide the answers. We cannot let ego or pride get in the way of science. Some of my most meaningful discoveries in science have been when I got the answers that I didn"t expect. That is what makes science so much fun.

CHAPTER 13
The Role of Bacteria and Stomach Acid in Nitric Oxide Production

"We mostly do not get sick. Most often, bacteria are keeping us well."
—Bonnie Bassler

The bacteria that live in and on our body outnumber our own human cells ten to one. The bacteria in our body are there to do things that human cells cannot do. These important metabolic processes contribute to human health.

Since we knew that the activation of dietary nitrate required certain and specific oral bacteria, we began investigations into the role of oral bacteria and their ability to produce nitric oxide in the mouth. This was an emerging field with others investigators showing nitrate-reducing bacteria in the mouth could produce nitrite and then once swallowed would generate nitric oxide in the stomach.

This is important because nitrate from vegetables must be metabolized by bacteria in order for it to become biologically active. Otherwise, nitrate is inert in humans and would just be excreted in feces, urine and sweat. The bacteria are responsible for converting inorganic nitrate into bioactive nitrite and nitric oxide. This process explains the cardioprotective benefits of certain diets.

We published in the *American Journal of Clinical Nutrition* in 2009 that the Dietary Approaches to Stop Hypertension (DASH) diet lowered blood pressure due to the nitrate content of those food choices and the ability of oral bacteria to reduce nitrate to nitrite and nitric oxide.

This also could explain the work of Drs. Dean Ornish and Caldwell Esselstyn who have used plant-based diets for decades to reverse heart disease and lower blood pressure. However, in speaking with Dr. Esselstyn he revealed that not everyone got the same benefits of a plant-based diet.

Some patients got better and some did not. How could this be? The answer came in understanding nitrate metabolism.

Nitrate is a naturally occurring molecule that is part of our atmospheric nitrogen cycle that plants then assimilate for growth and energy. The air we breathe is 78% nitrogen and through lightning storms and nitrogen fixing bacteria in the soil, this nitrogen is converted into nitrate.

Nitrate is responsible for the growth of plants and assimilation of other nutrients. This is the basis of nitrogen-based fertilizers to optimize plant growth. Without nitrate, plants do not grow and do not assimilate other important nutrients.

We now understand from our study on the difference between organic and conventional vegetables why organic is typically lower in nitrate. It is

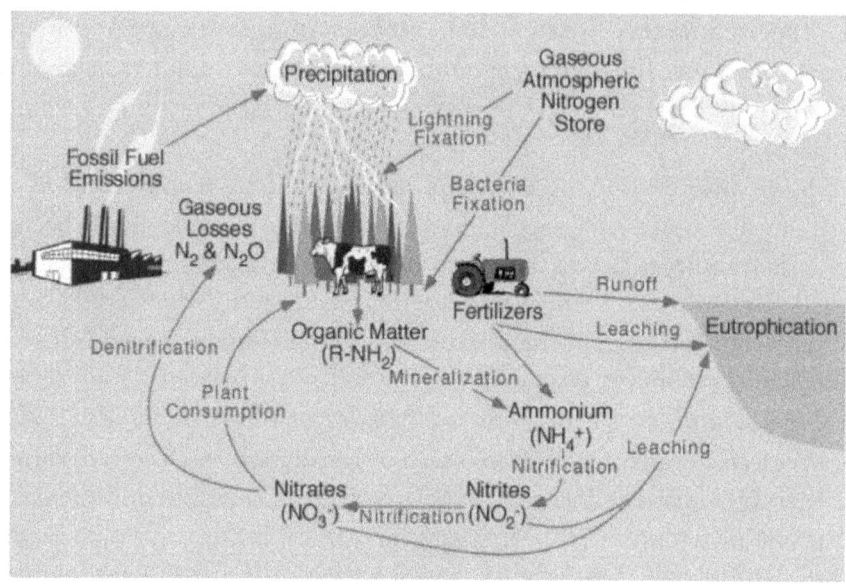

Atmospheric Nitrogen Cycle.
The story of nitrogen found in the atmosphere, where it exists as a gas (mainly N2), plays an important role for life. Most plants can only take up nitrogen in two solid forms: ammonium ion (NH4+) and the nitrate ion (NO3-). Most plants obtain the nitrogen they need as nitrate from the soil.
When released, most of the ammonium is often chemically altered by a specific type of bacteria (genus *Nitrosomonas*) into nitrite (NO2-). Further modification by another type of bacteria (genus *Nitrobacter*) converts the nitrite to nitrate. All nitrogen obtained by animals can be traced back to the eating of plants at some stage of the food chain.

The Secret of Nitric Oxide

because of the lack of nitrogen in the soil in organically grown vegetables. Nitrate is present in all vegetables but found in highest amounts in green leafy vegetables and root vegetables such as kale, spinach, arugula and beets.

Throughout decades of epidemiological research, it is obvious and apparent that a plant-based diet or by eating sufficient vegetables, there is less incidence of heart disease, cancer and basically all chronic disease. For years, scientists argued it was the antioxidant content of vegetables that was responsible for the beneficial effects but clinical trials using antioxidants have failed to reproduce the benefits of eating vegetables.

Most recently, nitrate has been proposed to be the component responsible for the health benefits of vegetables, but it is only active in the human body if it is first metabolized by oral bacteria. If you do not have the right oral bacteria, you get no nitric oxide benefit of eating vegetables.

Think about that for a second. Now dozens of clinical trials have proven nitrate can reproduce every single benefit of vegetables including reducing high blood pressure, improving exercise performance and endurance, preventing vascular inflammation, improving diabetes, obesity, Alzheimer's, kidney function, etc. Moreover, studies have shown that the Japanese diet has one of the highest amounts of nitrate, and Japan is one of the healthiest nations on earth and has more people that live over the age of 100 than any other nation. The Dietary Approaches to Stop Hypertension (DASH) diet works because of the nitrate content. Nitrate also explains the health benefits of a Mediterranean diet.

Furthermore, there is clear evidence on the mechanism of action of nitrate. It is metabolized into nitrite and nitric oxide and nitric oxide is what causes all of the health benefits above. If the science is so clear and undisputed, then why is cardiovascular disease still the number one killer of all men and women worldwide?

We now appreciate and understand that the lack of nitric oxide production and signaling in the human body is what is responsible for the onset and progression of cardiovascular disease and many other age-related diseases. In order to understand what may be going on with people that are nitric oxide deficient, we must first understand the process for producing nitric oxide from inorganic nitrate in the diet.

As mentioned in the previous chapters, there are two ways the body produces nitric oxide. The first to be discovered was through the utilization of L-arginine to make nitric oxide by the enzyme in the lining of our blood vessels. The other involves nitrate from the diet. How do we optimize nitric oxide production?

There are three steps and considerations to ensure you are getting sufficient nitrate that can then be metabolized into nitrite and bioactive nitric oxide.

THREE STEPS FOR NITRATE METABOLISM INTO NITRIC OXIDE

1. You must consume at least 300 mg of nitrate in a single meal in order to get the health benefits. Anything less, as shown in clinical trials, will not lower blood pressure or improve performance of any kind. So how many vegetables do you need to eat in order to get 300 mg of nitrate? This is impossible to predict based on our study several years ago showing there is much as a 50-fold difference in nitrate content of the same vegetable depending on where and how it is grown. Organically grown vegetables have on average about 5-10 times less nitrate than conventionally grown vegetables. It is estimated that Americans only consume roughly 150 mg of nitrate per day based on the Standard American diet. It is clear we are nitrate deficient as well as many Americans are deficient in magnesium, selenium, chromium, iodine and many other nutrients.

2. There are certain and specific nitrate-reducing bacteria that live in our mouth that are responsible for converting nitrate into nitrite and nitric oxide. These bacteria have been identified and studies also reveal that people who lack these bacteria cannot utilize nitrate from their diet to make nitric oxide and therefore do not get the benefits of a plant based or high vegetable diet. Lack of these bacteria are also associated with higher blood pressure and higher risk of many diseases. Why? As many as 200 million Americans use antiseptic mouthwash every day. Mouthwash has been shown to kill these good bacteria and prevent nitrate from being converted into nitrite and nitric oxide. This is roughly 2/3 of American population. Is it surprising now that 2 out of 3 Americans suffer from high blood pressure? I think not. We have an explanation for that. Furthermore, many Americans suffer from gingivitis, periodontal disease and oral infections that disrupt the good nitric oxide generating bacterial communities.

3. We need stomach acid to make nitric oxide from nitrate and nitrite. Nitrate is converted into nitrite by the oral bacteria. As a result, our saliva

The Secret of Nitric Oxide

becomes enriched and concentrated with nitrite. When we swallow our own saliva, the nitrite in the saliva is converted into nitric oxide when it reaches the acid environment of the stomach. However, if there is no stomach acid being produced, there is no nitric oxide generated and this leads to a condition of nitric oxide insufficiency. There are over 200 million Americans who are prescribed antacids every year. This does not even include the ones that can be bought over the counter.

Now taking each of these steps, and we can unequivocally explain why so many people are nitric oxide deficient. As demonstrated above, the standard American diet (SAD) does not contain sufficient nitrate in the foods we eat. Problem number 1.

Secondly, it has been clearly shown that the use of mouthwash eradicates the good bacteria in the mouth that is responsible for the metabolism of an inert molecule, nitrate into bioactive nitrite and nitric oxide. Data reveal that more than 200 million Americans use mouthwash on a daily basis, destroying the oral microbiome and shutting down nitric oxide production.

There are now multiple studies showing that the use of mouthwash causes an increase in blood pressure. We know that two out of three Americans have an unsafe elevation in blood pressure. This is the same number as those that use mouthwash daily. Use of mouthwash has been shown to inhibit the cardioprotective benefits of exercise.

We exercise to stimulate nitric oxide production but if we are using mouthwash, we lose the nitric oxide benefits of exercise. High blood pressure is the number one risk factor for the development of cardiovascular disease—the number one killer worldwide. Mouthwash use clearly causes an increase in blood pressure and increases risk of developing cardiovascular disease.

Now the third and final process in this step to produce nitric oxide is dependent upon stomach acid production. We need stomach acid to break down proteins into amino acids and to absorb trace minerals and nutrients. We also need stomach acid in order for the nitrite in our saliva to become nitric oxide gas when we swallow our own saliva.

If the lumen of the stomach is not acidic, then we do not get any nitric oxide produced from eating the proper diet or from exercise. Turns out shutting down stomach acid production is a really bad idea. Now that antacid drugs have been on the market for several decades, we are starting to get a clear understanding of their long-term effects and risks.

First of all, let's not forget that antacid drugs, proton pump inhibitors were only approved by the FDA for acute use for gastro-esophageal reflux disease. There were never approved to be used chronically. Yet, today, you can buy these drugs over the counter even without a prescription. Some people have been taking these drugs for years and never get off of them.

We've known for years now that people taking antacids have a higher incidence of osteoporosis. We understand this is because without stomach acid, the body cannot absorb basic vitamins and minerals such as boron or calcium.

A study published in 2015 revealed that people who have been taking antacids for 3-5 years had about a 40% higher incidence of heart attack and stroke. New data from 2023, reveal that people who have been taking antacids for 4-5 years had a 35% higher incidence of developing dementia.

Let's put this in perspective. One of the most common and popular over the counter drugs is causing osteoporosis, heart attack and stroke and even increasing dementia. What other data do we need to finally realize these drugs are not safe?

Mechanistically we know they shut down nitric oxide production explaining all of the side effects and risks of these drugs. Proton pump inhibitors such as Prilosec, Prevacid, Nexium, omeprazole, pantoprazole, etc. are dangerous, increase risks of heart attack, stroke and Alzheimer's. In order words, these drugs are deadly and should be taken off the market.

I also realize how difficult it is to live with acid reflux but the use of these drugs is actually killing the people who use them chronically. We must work to get people off of antacids. Unfortunately, you cannot just stop this class of drugs cold turkey. You must slowly wean off of them.

If you stop taking these drugs cold turkey you will get a rebound effect where the stomach produces too much acid at one time and it will cause more discomfort. Paradoxically, acid reflux disease is caused by the stomach's inability to produce stomach acid. It's never made sense to me why you would want to further inhibit stomach acid production.

Our entire digestive, endocrine and cardiovascular system depends on our ability to produce stomach acid. There are very important functions of stomach acid production that have nothing to do with nitric oxide. When we eat protein, either plant or animal protein, it has to be broken down into its constituent amino acids. Our body does not assimilate foreign proteins into our body. Instead, it takes the amino acids from plant or animal proteins and then uses those amino acids to make human proteins.

The breakdown of protein into amino acids is 100% dependent upon stomach acid production. Without stomach acid, the enzyme that breaks down the amino bonds in proteins, trypsin, is not active and therefore cannot digest proteins. When your body recognizes a foreign protein, it tries to get rid of it. If the foreign protein remains in the stomach or upper gut, then the body will try to expel it or expectorate. This is reflux. It is the body telling itself, it has a foreign invader and it needs to get out. If we have sufficient stomach acid, then the proteins are broken down into amino acids and there are no problems.

If we have undigested protein fragments emptied from the stomach into the intestines, the immune cells in our intestines recognize these protein fragments as foreign and tries to destroy them. We make antibodies against them and activate an immune response in the gut. The gut becomes leaky, the peptide fragments are absorbed across the gut and we develop auto-immune disease and food borne allergies.

It is my belief that most auto-immune diseases and food allergies can be traced back to insufficient stomach acid production due to the use of antacids especially early in life when prescribed to infants.

The second major problem related to insufficient stomach acid production is the loss of regulation of our body pH, making us more acidic and prone to certain cancers. As mentioned before, the stomach is designed to be a very acidic environment. When the contents of the stomach are emptied into the duodenum, the most proximal part of the intestines, the duodenum senses the very strong acid coming from the stomach.

This acid load then tells the pancreas to secrete sodium bicarbonate to buffer the strong acid coming from the stomach. It is the secretion of bicarbonate from the pancreas that then controls our body's ability to maintain cellular voltage and the proper buffering capacity.

In some cases of chronic use of antacids, the pancreas will become inflamed and not function properly which causes an issue with acid base imbalance and affect pancreatic function and lead to pancreatitis.

And finally, stomach acid is necessary for proper nitric oxide production. A specific type of antacid called proton pump inhibitors (PPIs) are really the worst of these medications. Drugs like omeprazole and pantoprazole are the most common. Not only do they shut down nitric oxide production from nitrate and nitrite but these drugs cause an increase in a molecule called asymmetric dimethyl L-arginine (ADMA).

ADMA acts as an inhibitor of the nitric oxide synthase enzyme in the lining of our blood vessels. There are only two ways the body produces nitric oxide, and PPIs inhibit both of those pathways.

Hopefully you are getting a sense of just how dangerous these drugs can be and should never be used long term. By now, you certainly appreciate the importance of nitric oxide and without it, we put our body at risk for a number of different chronic diseases. The evidence is already reported on increased risk of heart attack, stroke, bone fracture and dementia in patients that use PPIs. All of this can be explained by the loss of nitric oxide production.

So, what is the solution for those taking PPIs and other antacids? You must stop taking them by slowly weaning off of them. If you are currently taking PPIs follow this simple plan:

> 1. You must take an active nitric oxide product that generates nitric oxide for you. Your body has lost the ability to convert nitrate and nitrite into nitric oxide and your body has lost the ability to convert L-arginine into nitric oxide. Your only source of nitric oxide will be from a product that generates it on its own. That is what my products do.

> 2. Start cutting your dose of the antacid in half. Take half a dose for 10 days. After 10 days, take half a dose every other day. After that, you can stop taking them all together.

> 3. As you wean off over the next 2-3 weeks, take a tablespoon of apple cider vinegar before each meal. Vinegar is acetic acid and will help acidify the stomach so you can break down proteins into amino acids and actually absorb nutrients from the food you eat. Nutrients like B vitamins, iron, selenium, copper, zinc, iodine and others.

> 4 Since your body is depleted of many of the nutrients needed to actually produce stomach acid, you have to

The Secret of Nitric Oxide

supplement with the missing nutrients. Our parietal cells in our stomach need certain things to produce stomach acid. They need iodine, zinc, Vitamin B1, and sodium bicarbonate. I recommend any product that contains iodine (12.5mg), zinc (15mg) along with betaine hydrochloride and a few other good nutrients. This will ensure that your body has what it needs to regulate its own stomach acid production to properly break down proteins, absorb nutrients and produce nitric oxide.

I have used this approach for more than 15 years in people to get them off antacids and allow their body to heal.

Based on these three simple facts and observations, it is no surprise why Americans are the sickest people on the planet. Everything we do seems to disrupt nitric oxide production. It was also very clear to me that nitrate is not the answer as a means to restore and recapitulate nitric oxide production since one could not predict whether it would have any effect based on the presence or absence of certain oral bacteria. Now that we know how to generate nitric oxide using natural product chemistry that has been around for thousands of years, I now have enough information to develop a really innovative nitric oxide delivery system.

SECTION IV
BRINGING DISCOVERIES TO MARKET

CHAPTER 14
If it's to be, it's up to me
"The best way to predict the future is to create it."
—Peter Drucker

I had so much fun doing research, training post-docs and students and I felt like I was making an important contribution to science. However, the objective of all basic scientists is to be able to translate your findings into clinical medicine to treat, cure, prevent or diagnose human disease. Historically, it takes about 17 years for new discoveries to make it into clinical medicine.

However, most basic science discoveries never make it to market and are never introduced into clinical care. After about 5 years on faculty at the Institute of Molecular Medicine at UT Houston, I had submitted dozens of invention disclosures, the university had filed several patents based on my discoveries and then I felt we were in a holding pattern. I had figured out how to make nitric oxide. I had discovered that nitric oxide is a hormone. I have revealed that nitric oxide is foundational for many important biological functions.

The information from all the experiments and studies my lab had performed created a system for generating nitric oxide gas using natural products. I was trained in drug discovery and that was the mission of the Institute of Molecular Medicine, to develop safe and effective drugs. I also became aware that drugs typically take 10 years and on average about $800 million to get a drug approved and on the market.

Since my concept did not involve any synthetic molecule but rather natural products found in nature, I knew we could bring this product to market as a dietary supplement. After all, there were already dozens, if not hundreds of so-called nitric oxide dietary supplements on the market.

Even as far back as 2003, I had tried to work with existing dietary supplement companies to develop novel nitric oxide-based products. Once I filed my first patents at University of Texas, I was excited for the University to license my patents and technology to a company that would bring the technology to market.

Back in 2006 -2007 there were no drug companies really interested in nitric oxide or at least my concepts and technology around nitric oxide. Typically, universities license technology rights and patents to existing companies. At the time, there were no takers.

After about a year of frustrations, my neighbor at the time, Larry Covert, encouraged me to start my own company and he could help me raise money to fund the company. I did not have a background in business or any formal business degree or training. However, I believed and knew in my heart that the nitric oxide technology I had discovered would change the world.

I knew if it was going to happen, I was going to be the one to make it happen. Although the concept of starting my own company sounded simple enough, doing it was very difficult, especially since I had a full-time job at the University. Larry and I started a company, and we called it NitroSolvex. I earned a very modest salary as an assistant professor of molecule medicine and did not have much disposal income to fund much of anything. However, I knew I had to go and present at investor meetings all over. Larry introduced me to many groups including private equity groups, high net-worth families and a few asset management firms that had funded similar deals.

I met with existing companies that I had relationships with to introduce my product concepts to them to commercialize and bring to market. It would be much easier to find an existing company that has experience in product development and commercialization than for me to do it myself.

Although I had a lot of interest from several companies, no one was buying what I was trying to sell them. To reveal how naïve I was, I was trying to raise money for my patents and technology that the University actually owned. As an employee of the University, part of my employment agreement was the obligation to assign all patents and technology rights to the University. In other words, any discoveries that I made as an employee of the University belonged to the University.

After several meetings, Larry and I met with a high net worth individual out of Austin whom we met at the Doubletree Hotel in downtown

Houston. I presented our business plan and described to him the effects of nitric oxide and how our technology would change the world. He was immediately interested and indicated he wanted to invest $5,000,000. I was super excited.

I finally had the money to start a company and move forward with commercializing the technology and creating a product. The next day I went to the Office of Technology Management at UT Health Science Center and exuberantly revealed I had an investor, and we were ready to roll. The University quickly reminded me that I did not have any assets, nor did I have any rights to my patents or technology. My excitement quickly turned to disappointment and now what?

I was told that I had to have a license agreement from the University for my patents and technology to raise money and create any product for commercial purposes. Larry then introduced me to a wealth management firm, RAM Financial and the principals, Mark Reinking and Jason McGinty. Mark and Jason were wonderful people who immediately showed interest in our company. They agreed to come on board and help us raise money to fund the project. We created a company called NitroRam specifically to secure the license to my technology rights from the University. In February 2009, NitroRam executed a license agreement with UT for my patents and technology rights. Now we were in business and everyone was excited.

NitroRam was based out of Austin and I was still in Houston. I would drive back and forth to give my investment and business presentation to a room full of potential investors. It seemed that everyone to whom I presented was interested, excited about what I was doing.

However, after about 6 months, nothing happened. Based on the terms of the license deal with the University, there were milestones that NitroRam had to achieve to keep the license. I was growing frustrated and was running out of money traveling around trying to find manufacturing partners and trying to find additional investors. I was tired, burned out, broke and had lost hope that we would ever bring my nitric oxide technology to market. At one of my last investor meetings, I once again gave my "dog and pony" show to a room full of investors. It was one of my least enthusiastic talks. I quickly packed up my car and headed back to Houston. I was out of gas, out of money and barely had enough money to get me back home to Houston.

On the drive back home from Austin, I received a call from Mark Reinking indicating that there was interest from one of the people in the room that night. They were interested in investing but also in bringing in a team of people to run the company. However, they wanted to start a new company on our own and obtain the license agreement from UT.

NitroRam had the license to my patents from UT at the time. Furthermore, NitroRam owed the University of Texas milestone payments. This was a big deal for me since, as the inventor, I was entitled to 50% of any money paid to the University from my patent license. Any payment would surely help me at the time since I was dead broke.

NitroRam agreed to relinquish the license if the University would forgive the payments owed to the University. Now this really put me in a very awkward situation. I was really looking forward to receiving half of the payments owed and I needed it to survive. However, if NitroRam relinquished the license, then we could start a new company, secure the license from UT and then move forward with product development and commercialization.

After several meetings with UT, NitroRam agreed to give up the license and was forgiven the milestone payments owed to UT. This also meant that I would also be giving up half that was owed to me. It turned out to be a great decision since that company we started in 2009—and secured the license from UT in 2010—turned out to be one of the most successful and fastest growing companies in the U.S over the past 14 years.

CHAPTER 15
Putting the Pieces Together

"Your time is limited, so don't waste it living someone else's life. Don't be trapped by dogma – which is living with the results of other people's thinking. Don't let the noise of other's opinions drown out your own inner voice. And most important, have the courage to follow your heart and intuition. They somehow already know what you truly want to become. Everything else is secondary."
—Steve Jobs

Once NitroRam had relinquished the license from UT, I started a new company with my new partners. This new structure gave me more equity than I had in NitroRam and the four of us became equal partners. NitroRam maintained a small equity portion in the new company. The new partners invested around $350,000 and my uncle Randy Bryan put in around $200,000. We secured the license from the University of Texas Health Science Center at Houston and were officially in business.

Based on all of my research and observation at this point, I felt confident that I knew how to make nitric oxide and create products that could actually generate nitric oxide when consumed. If this were true, then I absolutely knew that I had the potential to change the world.

Drs. Murad, Furchgott and Ignarro had discovered the role of nitric oxide in the cardiovascular system but no one had discovered how to create nitric oxide gas in humans to overcome lack of endogenous production. Thinking back to our 2007 study where we showed that nitric oxide was a hormone and all we had to do was generate nitric oxide gas in a single biological compartment and then the signaling and hormone effects of nitric oxide would take care of everything else. What if I could produce nitric oxide at a certain dose over a specific period of time in the mouth? Could that be the way for us to deliver NO gas safely to humans and could it have systemic effects?

I knew how to recouple the NOS enzyme and restore endothelial nitric oxide production. I knew that I could pre-convert the nitrate to nitrite so it is not dependent upon the individual's microbiome to do it and I knew we could produce nitric oxide gas. Was it possible that we could correct nitric oxide production from both production pathways?

Collectively, the evidence suggests that the US diet is deficient in nitrate. Furthermore, common drug therapy and lifestyle decisions disrupt metabolism of nitrate into nitrite and nitric oxide. So how does one overcome inadequate nitrate consumption from our diet, variability between individual microbiome, mouthwash use, PPI use or achlorhydria (lack of stomach acid production)?

My idea was to use nitrite instead of nitrate along with the natural product chemistry I had discovered years earlier. I considered nitrate as a "pre-prodrug," nitrite as a "prodrug" and nitric oxide as the actual "active drug." Nitrite is the two-electron reduction product of nitrate that can be utilized and metabolized directly into nitric oxide by mammalian enzymes and is not dependent upon oral bacteria. In other words, it is directly bioavailable and bioactive when taken by humans.

Just like nitric oxide, nitrite is naturally produced in the body. It is produced directly from the metabolism of dietary nitrate by oral bacteria but also from the oxidation of endogenously produced nitric oxide by the enzyme nitric oxide synthase. Nitrite is found naturally in colostrum and breast milk, small amounts found naturally in green leafy vegetables and small amounts added to cured meats.

We estimated that nitrite intake from food varies from 0 to 20 mg/day. I was trying to develop a new concept in drug development called "restorative physiology," rather than pharmacology that was the typical approach. In order to do this, we had to understand how much nitric oxide a healthy person produces in any given day. We needed to know how much nitrate and/or nitrite was consumed through the diet in any given day based on normal consumption patterns.

Once we understood the absolute amount, I could then design products that could make up for the missing part and restore normal physiology. Years earlier it was reported that nitric oxide production rate measured with stable isotopes reveal that daily NO production varies between 0.15 and 2.2

µmol/kg/hour in healthy subjects. Knowing the chemical fate of nitric oxide being quickly oxidized to nitrite and nitrate through the reaction with oxygen and oxyhemoglobin respectively, we could now calculate the amount of nitrite and nitrate produced in any given day from NO production, and we could calculate how much was ingested from normal dietary patterns.

For a 70-80 kg person (154-176 lbs) this would equate to approximately 20-200 mg nitrite and nitrate daily. Due to approximately 5% reduction of nitrate (average of 150 mg per day in US diet plus 200 mg from oxidation of NO), this would equate to 17.5 mg endogenous nitrite production. Therefore, total daily nitrite exposure in a normal healthy individual on a Western diet is roughly 20-40 mg.

The same healthy individual consuming more of a vegetarian diet or DASH diet that included 400-1200 mg nitrate per day, endogenous nitrite production could exceed 70 mg per day. These nitrite levels are dramatically reduced in people with endothelial dysfunction, insufficient vegetable consumption or consuming vegetables without sufficient nitrate along with use of antibiotics/antiseptic mouthwash and/or PPIs. These data beg the question that if most people are nitrite deficient, can we safely and adequately supplement back what is missing? This approach is no different than Vitamin D for example. If labs demonstrate we are low in Vitamin D, then you supplement what is missing in order to normalize your levels. This has been our approach with nitrite and nitrate.

In order to get a sense of what had been tested in humans, I conducted a literature review of what was published in human clinical trials. There were a number of published studies in humans showing safety and efficacy of nitrite within a large range of doses.

There are only two concerns with toxicity by nitric oxide and sodium nitrite. It is hypotension, or an unsafe drop in blood pressure and a condition called methemoglobinemia. Methemoglobinemia is when the iron in hemoglobin in our red blood cells becomes oxidized to methemoglobin and it can no longer carry oxygen.

Patients become cyanotic or blue around the lips and they become hypoxic or deprived of oxygen. This is a deadly condition and very serious. There were studies using really high doses of sodium nitrite to test at what doses would nitrite become unsafe and intolerable. Sodium nitrite capsules at doses of 160 mg and 320 mg were used to determine toxicity and pharmacokinetics.

Nitrite even at a dose of 320 mg did not show any clinically toxic levels of methemoglobinemia (<15%). However, some subjects reported mild headache and nausea that resolved after a half-hour. This study also revealed that nitrite is 98% orally available.

In another study using sodium nitrite capsule in diabetics demonstrated that a single administration of 80 mg sodium nitrite was well tolerated with no significant changes in methemoglobin, sulfhemoglobin, pulse rate, laboratory tests, or other safety parameters with the possible exception of headache and a hot flush feeling in two of the 12 subjects (17%). The 80 mg nitrite dose led to a significant drop in systolic blood pressure with no effect on diastolic pressures. Plasma nitrite levels increased to 3-4μM or approximately 10 times higher than normal steady state. More chronic studies using 80-160 mg nitrite capsules for ten weeks in a randomized, placebo control, double blind study increased plasma nitrite acutely and chronically and was well tolerated without symptomatic hypotension or clinically relevant levels of methemoglobin. Endothelial function, measured by brachial artery flow-mediated dilation, was significantly improved without changes in body mass or blood lipids. Carotid artery elasticity (as measured by ultrasound and applanation tonometry) improved. These functional changes were related to 11 plasma metabolites identified by untargeted analysis with glycerophospholipids and fatty acyls, predicting these vascular changes with nitrite.

This was remarkable to me that just using nitrite at some pretty high doses could see such impressive changes in human physiology. Similarly, in another study using 80 and 160 mg nitrite capsules for 10 weeks showed improvement in performance on measures of motor and cognitive outcomes in healthy middle aged and older adults (62 ± 7 years). This meant that in older subjects, both their motor skills and ability to think and recall memory could be improved by nitrite.

These studies provide evidence that sodium nitrite supplementation is well tolerated, increases plasma nitrite concentrations, improves endothelial function, lessens carotid artery stiffening and improves motor and cognitive function in middle-aged and older adults, perhaps by altering multiple metabolic pathways.

Other studies have investigated sodium nitrite directly infused in critically ill patients with subarachnoid hemorrhage. Infusion of sodium nitrite over 14 days at a maximum dose of 64 nmol/kg/min (622 mg of nitrite per day for 14 days) showed no toxicity or systemic hypotension, and blood methemoglobin levels remained at 3.3% or less in all patients.

The authors state that the results of their study suggest that safe and potentially therapeutic levels of nitrite can be achieved and sustained in critically ill patients after a ruptured cerebral aneurysm. The effects of nitrite are not dependent upon oral nitrate-reducing bacteria and appear to be safe even as doses that far exceed daily human production. In order for me to develop a dietary supplement, I had to dial in a dose that one could ordinarily consume through normal dietary patterns.

The Food and Drug Administration (FDA) has oversight of dietary supplements in ensuring that they are safe and provide nutrients that are naturally found in our food supply and are part of our normal dietary patterns. As long as the products are safe, the FDA has no concerns.

The other regulatory consideration for dietary supplements comes from the Federal Trade Commission (FTC). Dietary supplements cannot be marketed or advertised to prevent, cure, treat, reverse or diagnose any disease. If companies are making unsubstantiated claims on their dietary supplement or making drug claims, the FTC has the authority to close down that business. Therefore, we had to play by the rules and make sure we were compliant with the regulatory rules.

The doses of nitrite used in all the published studies were typically more than one would normally consume in an ordinary diet. The doses used in those published studies would not fall under what would be considered a dietary supplement. The reason those studies used high doses of nitrite is in part due to the fact that nitrite is inefficiently reduced to NO along the physiological oxygen gradient and therefore more is needed to get any appreciable amount of NO produced, especially in people that are NO deficient.

I had published a study back in 2008 showing that oxygen inhibited nitrite reduction to nitric oxide. Therefore, under normal physiological conditions where there was sufficient oxygen, nitric oxide production from nitrite was very inefficient. As a result, one would have to dose higher doses of nitrite to get any nitric oxide production. Through the discovery of natural product chemistry of all the ingredients I had been testing in my lab, I identified an oxygen independent nitrite reductase which would now allow us to use much lower concentrations of nitrite to more effectively reduce nitrite to NO and therefore provide an exogenous source of NO in the oral cavity.

My company secured the license to my patents and intellectual property from the University of Texas on March 25, 2010. Upon execution of the license agreement, we entered into a sponsored research agreement with the University of Texas Health Sciences Center. This sponsored research agreement actually allowed me to use part of my time as a full-time Assistant Professor of Molecular Medicine to work on company related projects.

The sponsored research agreement clearly outlined that any inventions or discoveries made by me in my lab at the University of Texas belonged to the University. It was the work I had done years before and during this course of the sponsored research, that I identified specific ingredients that were necessary and sufficient for the generation of nitric oxide gas.

In other words, the University owned all the intellectual property and the rights to the technology. This turned out to be a very important issue that will come out years later. As we developed different prototypes of the nitric oxide lozenge, I would test it in my lab at the Institute of Molecular Medicine. The company did not have an official office and certainly did not have a lab or any other scientist working on product development. All of the work was performed by me as full-time faculty at the Institute of Molecular Medicine.

In fact, I was the science behind the company and my science was being conducted at the University of Texas Health Sciences Center at Houston. Under the sponsored research agreement, it was my job to figure this out using the analytical equipment in my lab at the Institute of Molecular Medicine. I knew from my trips to China that it was difficult to procure consistent finished products from China and many Americans did not trust ingredients or products out of China. So, I set out to find similar natural products here in the U.S. that may have similar nitric oxide activity as some of the Traditional Chinese Medicine.

The manufacturer that we had sought out began to send me ingredients from his trusted suppliers and I started testing these ingredients and their ability to produce nitric oxide under very specific conditions. I identified a specific ingredients and products that could donate electrons and lead to a more efficient production of nitric oxide. I spent the next year from January 2010 until almost August testing different ingredients and testing different prototypes of an orally disintegrating lozenge.

Since this work was performed under a sponsored research agreement with the University of Texas Health Sciences Center that very clearly stated that all work performed under this agreement belonged to the University and any discoveries or inventions made under this sponsored research agreement belonged to the University. It was clear to me that I and the University owned these discoveries and the rights to them.

When we first started the company, we rented a small one-bedroom apartment in Austin as our office. When we started it was primarily me and only one of the other partners doing most of the work. Now all we needed was a manufacturer that could take my product concepts and make it a reality.

I reached out to my friend Brazos Minshew who had been in product development and knew several manufacturers who could help us. Brazos introduced me to a manufacturing company who had developed an easy melt technology for dietary supplements. I flew out and spent several days with the manufacturer and explained my concept of creating a solid dose form of nitric oxide gas.

He felt confident he could make it. What we were trying to do had never been done before. My idea was to create a lozenge that when it was placed in the mouth and activated by saliva, it would start to release nitric oxide gas over a very specific period of time. Based on the work we had performed over the previous five years, I knew that it would provide enough nitric oxide through the lozenge—it would have systemic hormone effects. However, we had to generate enough nitric oxide to see an effect but not too much that might lead to an unsafe drop in blood pressure.

We worked together and after several months, we had prototypes developed that I tested in my lab at UT and it worked. The lozenge had a beautiful nitric oxide release profile. This was another amazing EUREKA moment. I had succeeded in making the first solid dose form of a bioactive nitric oxide gas. I had seen what everyone else had seen and thought what no one else had thought and succeeded at doing what people told me could not be done.

We launched the first nitric oxide product in August of 2010 and today have many products on the market that produce nitric oxide gas. If your body cannot make nitric oxide, my products make it for you. I had developed a hormone replacement technology for nitric oxide gas.

Now that the company had a product that could produce nitric oxide, we needed sales people to go out and sell the product. We brought in our first sales force in Susan Shaffer and Kristin Holt, former Dell employees who had experience in sales and marketing.

They would organize meetings at local pharmacy groups and a group of practitioners where I would come and educate them on nitric oxide. One of our first meetings I was scheduled to speak and educate was at People's Pharmacy. We had advertised and promoted and we were hoping several hundred people would show up. It was time to start the lecture and I walked out and there were two people in the audience. Despite the disappointment, I gave my lecture to these two wonderful and attentive people.

People's Pharmacy in Austin brought our product into their stores and it was our first major wholesale customer. Susan and Kristin would go around to local doctors' offices and convince them to use our nitric oxide product in their patient care.

We quickly realized we had a solution to a problem people did not know existed. In other words, we had a great product but consumers did not know why they would need nitric oxide for general health. There was very little awareness around nitric oxide in the general consumer market.

We needed a test to show that people needed nitric oxide. I developed a nitric oxide salivary test strip that would show most people were low in nitric oxide, and we could demonstrate that the lozenge could improve their levels. This was revolutionary.

I would periodically update the University of Texas on our product development. My superiors at the Institute of Molecular Medicine, including Dr. Tom Caskey, the Director of the Institute was not originally enthusiastic about our intention to bring to market a "dietary supplement."

After all, the University's mission is to develop drugs or medical devices. Dr. Caskey's concerns were noted. In order to appease him and the University that what we were doing was legitimate, we put our product through randomized, placebo controlled clinical trials, the same metric and rigor as drug products. Very few supplement companies put their products through randomized controlled clinical trials since they are very expensive and most dietary supplements do not provide much benefit nor have an effect on meaningful clinical endpoints such as blood pressure or modifying cardiovascular risk factors.

The Secret of Nitric Oxide

Now that I understood how the human body makes nitric oxide, I recognized what went wrong in people that could not produce it. The ultimate question was, can the technology I developed overcome the body's inability to produce it?

The premise of this technology is that if your body can't make NO due to endothelial dysfunction, oral dysbiosis, antiseptic mouthwash or PPI use, then this will provide an exogenous source of NO.

My first patented nitric oxide lozenge was designed to include ingredients and nutrients that could be achieved through normal dietary patterns. I rationalized that this amount would "supplement" what may be missing in the western diet but also provide a more efficient way to generate nitric oxide from nitrite than relying on the body to do it by itself.

Our first clinical trial found that it could modify cardiovascular risk factors in patients over the age of 40, significantly reduce triglycerides, and reduce blood pressure. Single administration of this lozenge leads to peak plasma levels of nitrite around $1.5\mu M$, similar to levels achieved just by exercising.

We had a patient population at Texas Children's Hospital with a condition called argininosuccinic aciduria (ASA), which is a very rare genetic disorder. These patients have a number of clinical problems including resistant hypertension, kidney disease, liver disease, blood clotting disorders and neurological problems. We tested a version of the nitric oxide lozenge in one of these 15 year-old patients. The nitrite lozenge led to a significant reduction in blood pressure when prescription medications were ineffective, improved renal function, cognition and reversed his heart disease within 5 months. The patient's kidney disease resolved in 5 days after he started taking the lozenge.

Another randomized controlled study using the nitrite lozenge reveals that a single lozenge can significantly reduce blood pressure, dilate blood vessels, improve endothelial function and arterial compliance in hypertensive patients. Furthermore, in a study of pre-hypertensive patients (BP >120/80 < 139/89), administration of one lozenge twice daily leads to a significant reduction in blood pressure (12 mmHg systolic and 6 mmHg diastolic) after 30 days along with improvements in functional capacity as measured by a 6-minute walk test.

In an exercise study, the nitrite lozenge significantly improved exercise performance by improving the time it takes a well-trained cyclist to ride a specific distance. Most recently, in subjects with stable carotid plaque, the NO lozenge led to a 11% reduction in carotid plaque after 6 months.

To put this in perspective, meta-analysis of trials using treatment with statins, cholesterol lowering medications (mean treatment duration of 25.6 months) reveal that a total of 7 trials showed regression and 4 trials showed slowing of progression of CIMT of approximately 2.7% after over 2 years.

In 2009, I had the great honor of presenting at the Karolinska Institute in the Nobel Forum where each year the Nobel Prize is announced.

Using the nitric oxide lozenge, the data show an average of 10.9% plaque regression after 6 months with no side effects. It seemed that every clinical trial we put this lozenge through it moved the needle providing unbelievable benefits. Similarly, this same patented technology in the form of our concentrated beet powder attenuates peripheral chemoreflex sensitivity without concomitant change in spontaneous cardiovagal baroreflex sensitivity while also reducing systemic blood pressure and mean arterial blood pressure in older adults.

These studies clearly demonstrate the safety and efficacy of low supplemental doses of nitrite in humans that can correct for any insufficiencies from dietary exposure, pharmacological inhibition by antiseptics or PPIs. I was presenting these findings at 20-30 medical and scientific meetings every year. People could hardly believe that a dietary supplement would have such profound effects on clinical medicine and able to correct many issues that were poorly managed by conventional medicine. This is the power of nitric oxide.

After about a year on the market, the company was starting to have success. I was speaking at large medical conferences in front of thousands of doctors educating them on nitric oxide. The company would have a booth in the exhibit hall where masses of doctors would come after my lecture with interest in selling our nitric oxide lozenges in their practices.

We continued to conduct more clinical trials on our product and every time we put it to the test, the product performed and people got better. We demonstrated that the lozenge would lower blood pressure when prescription medications were ineffective. We demonstrated it would improve performance and allow patients to walk further in a six-minute walk test. Their quality of life improved and people just felt better when taking it compared to placebo.

After about a year, we moved out of the apartment and leased an actual office space in a commercial office building. The company started hiring additional talent in marketing and we had a real company. I was continuing to do research on our technology in my lab at the University of Texas Institute of Molecular Medicine.

The University was becoming more accepting of my technology because they were receiving hundreds of thousands of dollars in royalty payments based on the sales of our product technology. In order to grow the company, we realized we had to have more than one product.

Around 2012, beet root juice was gaining traction in the sports and performance arena. In the 2012 Olympic games in London, many athletes were drinking beet root juice since there was published data showing it would increase nitric oxide production and improve their performance.

I quickly realized we could ride the beet wave with our nitric oxide product. After all, I knew this pathway better than anyone. I also realized that most beet root products did not have what it takes to produce nitric oxide I utilized my technology rights and know-how to make a fermented beet product that we positioned as a natural energy product to improve circulation and energy production.

I began to test all the beet root products on the market and quickly realized, most products did not produce any nitric oxide at all. These products were "dead beat" products. We could do better.

I flew to Florida and met with one of the largest beet suppliers in the U.S. I spent a week in their labs working with their scientists to develop a very powerful and potent beet product. We optimized their fermentation process so we could concentrate nitric oxide activity and pre-convert the inert metabolites in beets to a biologically active ingredient. We also had to make the product taste decent.

I hated the taste of beets and through research I realized beets are the third least liked vegetable on the planet. Products have to taste good in order for consumers to buy and continue to take. I worked with a number of flavor houses to make our beet powder taste decent. We successfully created a palatable, very effective nitric oxide generating beet product.

After about 5 years on the market, royalties to the University of Texas had reached millions of dollars. My technology was becoming one of the most successful technologies in the history of the University of Texas Health Science Center at Houston based on ongoing royalty payments. The payments I was receiving from the University were beginning to surpass my salary. I was making more money that I ever had before, the company was successful and life was grand.

CHAPTER 16
Nitric Oxide Diagnostics

"Diagnosis is not the end, but the beginning of practice."
—Martin H. Fischer

One of the first questions we encountered when we first started to market our nitric oxide lozenge was "how do I know if I need nitric oxide? Are there labs or tests that can determine my nitric oxide levels?" Another key finding from our focus groups and market research was most people had never heard of nitric oxide and did not understand why they would need to purchase a nitric oxide product.

Now we had to convince people that they needed nitric oxide or at least demonstrate in some way that they may be low. At that time there was no real test or lab to determine nitric oxide status in patients. It was not like cholesterol or Vitamin D where you could draw blood and test and then give the patient a number. In order to have success, I knew I had to develop a test to measure nitric oxide.

Based on my work from the previous 10 years, I knew I could develop a salivary test strip. Understanding that the use of salivary nitrite as a marker of endogenous NO generation, both from oxidation of NO and from dietary sources, is totally dependent upon the uptake and excretion of nitrate by the salivary glands and subsequent reduction of nitrate to nitrite by lingual bacteria, there are steps in the pathway that can become disrupted and lead to changes in salivary nitrite.

For the next few weeks, I developed the chemistry and created a semi-quantitative colorimetric test for testing nitric oxide activity in saliva. The chemistry has been known for decades and is called the Griess reaction. I needed to find a manufacturer to produce the test strip.

I found a manufacturer of urinary test strips that are diagnostic for urinary tract infections. Interestingly those tests use the exact same chemistry as I was using. For urinary tract infections, the presence of nitrite in the urine is indicative of bacteria in the urine. Nitrate is partially re-absorbed in the kidneys but the majority is excreted in the urine. Remember that nitrate is inert in humans and can only be metabolized by bacteria. If there are bacteria present in the urinary tract, those bacteria can reduce nitrate to nitrite. Therefore, the presence of nitrite in the urine indicates the presence of bacteria in the urine.

Well, this is the exact concept I was proposing. All we had to do was titrate the right concentration or dose that was relevant and significant for salivary conversation of nitrate to nitrite. I flew to New Jersey and met with the manufacture and its owner and I created the first and only non-invasive point of care diagnostic for nitric oxide. Now we had a way to demonstrate to people that they were deficient in nitric oxide and when taking our lozenge, we could restore and replete their nitric oxide.

I filed patents for this new discovery as a new point of care diagnostic for nitric oxide bioavailability. We were in business and ready to rule the world. Although the test strips have been quite useful there are a few caveats that we must understand so we can make the proper interpretation.

Let's review the chemistry and science behind the test strips.

Since nitric oxide is a gas that is produced and then gone is less than one second, it is very difficult to actually measure nitric oxide release in patients. However, I know how nitric oxide is metabolized once produced and which metabolites of nitric oxide production are most relevant to measure and detect. The major pathway for NO metabolism is the stepwise oxidation to nitrite and nitrate. For years, both nitrite (NO_2^-) and nitrate (NO_3^-)

Nitric Oxide Scale

Depleted   Low   Threshold   Target   High

(collectively, NOx) have been used as surrogate markers of NO production in biological tissues. In fact, NO status is not part of the standard blood chemistry routinely used for diagnostic purposes. This is simply unacceptable given the critical nature of NO in many disease processes.

The only true measure of endothelial NO production (endothelial function) is through flow mediated dilatation (FMD). FMD is a non-invasive ultrasound-based method where arterial diameter is measured in response to an increase in shear stress, which causes release of NO from the endothelium and consequent endothelium dependent dilatation. FMD has been shown to correlate with invasive measures of endothelial function, as well as with the presence and severity of the major traditional vascular risk factors.

Nitrite and nitrate have recently been shown to be biomarkers for cardiovascular and other diseases from both diagnostic and therapeutic aspects. However, it is not known if levels of nitrite and nitrate correlate with FMD. Several reports have demonstrated that plasma nitrite levels in humans progressively decrease with increasing cardiovascular risk load. Risk factors considered included age, hypertension, smoking, and hypercholesterolemia. All of these conditions are known to reduce the bioavailability of NO. Although a correlation exists in plasma, it is not known whether the situation is mirrored in the heart or other tissue of interest in specific disease.

The test strips are measuring salivary nitrite which can be used as a surrogate for nitric oxide availability in humans. Although this can be helpful in establishing a baseline for nitric oxide production and availability, there are certain limitations to the test strip. What we are measuring is salivary nitrite which reflects the presence of oral bacteria that metabolize nitrate to nitrite. Nitrate is found in green leafy vegetables but is inert, meaning it has no biological activity in humans.

However, there are oral nitrate-reducing bacteria that can metabolize nitrate in our saliva into nitrite, which is what the test strips are detecting. Nitrate can also be derived from the oxidation of endogenously produced nitric oxide that is then concentrated in our salivary glands. The nitrate in our salivary glands reflects how much nitrate is consumed in our diet and how much nitric oxide is produced in the lining of our blood vessels.

Through early cancer research, it was known that up to 25% of circulating nitrate is actively taken up by the salivary glands and concentrated 10- to

20-fold in saliva. In 1994, two independent groups demonstrated that nitric oxide gas can be produced in the stomach from swallowing our own saliva. NO gas was generated in the human stomach at high concentrations, and this production was dependent on gastric acidity that originated from salivary-derived nitrite.

Furthermore, NO generation was greatly enhanced after consumption of nitrate, which is found in some green leafy vegetables. We now understand how this works: Nitrate from our diet is absorbed in the gastrointestinal tract. Circulating nitrate that comes from nitric oxide production is actively taken up and secreted in saliva, and oral commensal bacteria reduce nitrate to nitrite. Salivary nitrite can now be assessed as a measure of total nitric oxide production capacity in humans.

I think it is worth reviewing how this works so people can begin to understand how the test strips work and how one can interpret the results. After ingestion of nitrate and effective absorption in the upper gastrointestinal tract, blood and salivary concentrations of nitrate become very high. However, nitrate is inert and will not produce any nitric oxide effects.

In the mouth there are certain bacteria, located in the deep crypts of the posterior part of the tongue, that can reduce or metabolize nitrate to nitrite by action of nitrate reductase enzymes. When we swallow nitrite rich saliva and it enters the acid environment of the stomach, nitric oxide gas is produced. This reaction is enhanced by low pH (more acid) and by reducing compounds, such as ascorbic acid and polyphenols.

Concentrations of NO gas in the stomach can be substantial and represent a bio-active source of NO distributed throughout the body. The nitric oxide produced in the stomach can be absorbed directly across the lining of the stomach but mostly it binds to glutathione, a major antioxidant in the body and transported as a more stable metabolite called S-nitrosoglutathione (GSNO). Part of the nitric oxide is also metabolized into nitrite and enters the systemic circulation. This is important because nitrite in our saliva has been shown to increase gastric mucosal blood flow and mucus thickness.

Salivary nitrite has antimicrobial effects to kill certain common food-borne pathogens such as E. coli, Salmonella, C. dificil and even H. pylori, the ulcer causing bacteria and other bad pathogenic bacteria. Nitrate reduction to nitrite is dependent on the oral bacteria because our own human cells do not convert nitrate to nitrite. We and others have identified these essential bacteria and now there is evidence that these bacteria are responsible for helping maintain normal blood pressure.

Nitrite and nitric oxide being produced by oral bacteria and in the lumen of the stomach have been shown to be involved in many important biologic processes, including regulation of blood flow, cell signaling, and energy production in the mitochondria, as well as tissue, responses to hypoxia or low oxygen. Furthermore, disruption of this nitrate-nitrite-NO pathway through the use of oral antiseptic mouthwash or overuse of antibiotics has been shown to cause an increase in systemic blood pressure due to disruption in nitric oxide production.

The fact that this pathway can be fueled by exogenous nitrate and nitrite leads to interesting therapeutic and nutritional implications but also for diagnostics. Our diet is a main provider of exogenous nitrate, and vegetables are especially rich in this anion. This has prompted us and several other research groups to investigate the possibility that nitrate may be involved in the well-established beneficial effects of a diet rich in vegetables on cardiovascular disease.

Understanding that the use of salivary nitrite as a marker of endogenous NO generation, both from oxidation of NO and from dietary sources, is totally dependent upon the uptake and excretion of nitrate by the salivary glands and subsequent reduction of nitrate to nitrite by lingual bacteria, there are steps in the pathway that can be disrupted and lead to changes in salivary nitrite. Each step is described below:

1. Sufficient nitrate ingestion in our diet. The standard American diet only provides about 150mg of nitrate per day. Clinical studies reveal that we need at least 300-400 mg of nitrate per day.

2. Nitrate uptake in the salivary glands: This initial step represents the key process in nitrate clearance from the circulation. It was recently reported that the sialic acid co-transporter is involved in nitrate uptake into salivary glands. Functional defects in the protein such as during Salla disease and infantile sialic acid storage disorder (ISSD) will certainly have an impact on salivary nitrite concentrations. Whether these patients become NO deficient is still not known.

3. Nitrate secretion by salivary glands: The volumes of saliva produced vary depending on the type and intensity of stimulation, the largest volumes occurring with cholinergic stimulation. Loss of salivary gland secretory activity because of radiation treatment for head and neck cancers or surgical removal of salivary glands (parotidectomy) and autoimmune disease (e.g., Sjogren's syndrome) or xerostomia can have consequences on salivary nitrite concentrations.

4. Oral bacterial nitrate reduction: Humans lack a functional nitrate reductase so salivary nitrate reduction is dependent upon oral commensal nitrate-reducing bacteria. We and others have identified several bacteria that are necessary and sufficient for nitrate reduction. Several bacteria have been identified for oral nitrate reduction: *Veillonella, Actinomyces, Rothia, Staphylococcus,* and *Propionibacterium*. Our most recent metagenomic analysis reveals 14 distinct bacteria that statistically differentiate optimal nitrate reduction from humans from those with no nitrate reduction. These include *Granulicatella adiacens, Haemophilus parainfluenzae, Actinomyces odontolyticus, Actinomyces viscosus, Actinomyces oris, Neisseria flavescens, Neisseria mucosa, Neisseria sicca, Neisseria subflava, Prevotella melaninogenica, Prevotella salivae, Veillonella dispar, Veillonella parvula,* and *Veillonella atypica*. The optimal community would reduce the maximum amount of nitrate, while also allowing nitrite accumulation to maximize the amount of bioactive nitrite available in the saliva of the host. Use of antiseptic mouthwash treatment to disrupt the oral microbiota reduces both oral and plasma nitrite levels in healthy human volunteers and is associated with a sustained increase in both systolic and diastolic blood pressure. Use of fluoride in toothpaste kills good bacteria and causes a disruption in salivary nitrite production.

5. Oral pH: Healthy oral pH is between 6.5 and 7.5. The pKa of nitrite is 3.4 so any condition that lowers the pH in the oral cavity may destabilize nitrite and affect the use of

salivary nitrite as a measure of NO activity. People with acidic saliva will show low nitrite on the test strip.

All the above conditions must be met in order for nitrite to accumulate in the saliva and made available for sampling and quantification. It is likely that any disruption of any of these steps will lead to a state of NO insufficiency. Although there are no false negatives on the saliva test strips, there are false positives that we must account for.

Patients with an active oral infection, symptomatic or asymptomatic, will show an increase in salivary nitrite and turn the test strip dark pink. This is due to a local immune response in the mouth, and this is not reflective of total body systemic nitric oxide production. This is the primary reason I do not use the test strips anymore.

Several years ago, I abandoned the patents on the test strips and today there are several companies that continue to sell the technology I developed. The test strips can be misleading. Therefore, we rely on symptoms of nitric oxide deficiency.

If a person has high blood pressure, erectile dysfunction, diabetes, dementia (loss of memory), exercise intolerance, autoimmune disease, or any systemic inflammation, these patients are deficient in nitric oxide, regardless of what their test strips may show. The test strips I developed in 2010 became the first point of care diagnostic for nitric oxide status in humans. Now we have a way to test nitric oxide status in people and if low, we could show a need for nitric oxide products. However, the test strips are best positioned to determine the presence or absence of nitrate-reducing bacteria.

CHAPTER 17
Is This What Nature Intended?
"Look deep into nature, and then you will understand everything better."
—Albert Einstein

As you may imagine I was starting to be ridiculed and attacked by some of my academic colleagues. Other competitive companies were taking issue with me and my science. The German philosopher Arthur Schopenhauer once said that all truth passes through three stages. First, it is ridiculed. Second, it is violently opposed. Third, it is accepted as being self-evident.

I quickly realized I was in the second stage of this process. I had already been ridiculed by some of my colleagues and now my product and my science are being violently opposed. I knew if I could stay the course and

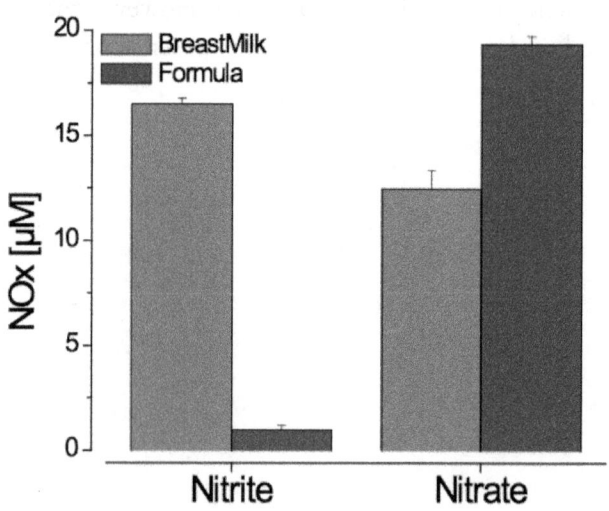

continue to advance science and provide indisputable evidence to back what I was doing, that eventually it would be self-evident. If supplementing deficient nitrite and nitrate in populations is a viable strategy for combatting cardiovascular disease or any condition associated with insufficient nitric oxide availability, are there examples in epidemiology or in specific populations that can provide justification for such? The answer may come in the form of Nature's most perfect food, breast milk.

Back in 2008 when my son Lincoln was born, my wife and I were having a discussion as we were leaving the hospital about the difference between breast milk and the formula milk the hospital sent us home with. We obviously were committed to breast feeding all our kids since we knew the health disparities between breast fed and formula fed babies.

When we left the hospital, I collected a few drops of colostrum from my wife's breast. We were 2 days post-partum, so it was still the almost clear colostrum. I took it to the lab, and I analyzed it using my high-performance liquid chromatography (HPLC) instrument and also compared it to the formula that was sent home with us from the hospital.

As shown on page 174, the nitrite concentration in the colostrum was orders of magnitude higher than what was in the formula. Based on this observation in one person, I then proceeded to get an institutional review board (IRB) approval to test the breast milk in many other new mothers. I secured the IRB from the University of Texas Health Science Center and

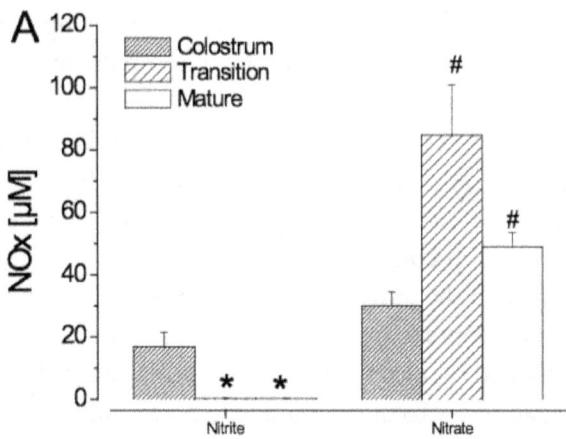

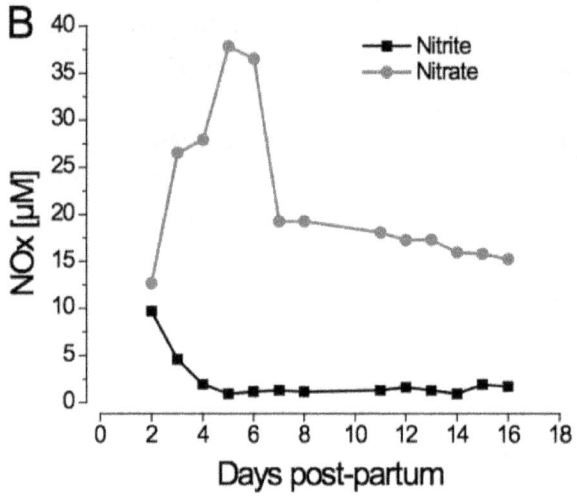

Memorial Hermann hospital. I collaborated with a very pleasant OB/GYN Pamela Berens, M.D. who delivered babies at Memorial Hermann hospital.

She helped me enroll and consent new mothers to participate in the study and helped me collect samples while they were still in the hospital.

We were hoping to get different stages of milk. Normally, days 1-3 days post-partum, the milk is considered colostrum. After day 4 until around day 14, it is called transition milk and from day 14 on it is considered mature milk. The consistency and biological/nutrient make-up of the milk changes over the course of time. Over the next few months, I would be notified by Dr. Berens that we had a patient who consented to giving us some breast milk. I would send my students or go myself and pick up the sample and then bring it back to the lab for analysis.

At the end we had collected over 50 samples and tracked 2 nursing mothers that gave us breast milk samples every day for 16 days. This gave us a more consistent time course from single donors. The data seemed to hold true that the colostrum contained the highest amount of nitrite, and it seemed to disappear in the transition milk and almost gone in mature milk. However, the nitrate content appeared to increase over time from colostrum to transition milk and then come back down in mature milk.

When we began to try to understand why breast milk would change in composition of nitrite and nitrate, we began to appreciate just how smart the human body is. Remember, babies are born mostly sterile. They get inoculated with bacteria during birth through the birth canal and vagina and when we touch or kiss the babies, we inoculate them with good bacteria. It typically takes about 5-7 days for the gut microbiome to get established in the infants. During the time the infants do not have the proper microbiome and bacteria to metabolize nitrate to nitrite, the breast milk has already converted nitrate to nitrite and provides the baby directly with nitrite that is biologically active. Once the microbiome is established after several days, breast milk provides nitrate and allows the baby's own microbiome to metabolize nitrate to nitrite and nitric oxide. This was brilliant.

The composition of human breast milk is adapted to fit the nutritional needs of the infant and provide immunologic protection during maturation of the immune system. The quality and characteristics of breast milk change over time. This change in composition is thought to be due partly to the changing gut microflora in the baby and the changing metabolic demands as the baby grows.

Colostrum, the early milk made by the mother's breasts, is usually present after the fifth or sixth month of pregnancy. Once the baby is born, it is present in small amounts for the first three days to match the small size of the baby's stomach. This precious colostrum should be given to the newborn as soon as possible after giving birth. It is this precious colostrum that contains the highest amount of nitrite of any of the milk products tested. Colostrum is designed to meet a newborn's special needs. Breast milk will change and increase in quantity about 48 to 72 hours after giving birth. Our data suggests that the ratio of nitrite and nitrate also changes in order to meet the changing metabolic demands on the infant.

Indeed, the pattern of nitrate and nitrite composition of human milk suggests that nitrate and nitrite also serve immunomodulatory and gastroprotective roles. Therefore, it is reasonable to surmise that nitrite must be supplied through human milk to the newborn to derive the resulting vascular, immunologic and gastroprotective benefits. The beneficial effects of NO in adult stomachs on gastric mucosal integrity and blood flow from the reduction of nitrate to nitrite to NO are known.

At birth, the gastrointestinal tract of the infant is sterile, and it is then rapidly colonized by bacteria originating from the mother and the environment. The first colonizing bacteria are aerobic bacteria, such as staphylococci, enterococci, and enterobacteria. Then, anaerobic bacteria, such as Bacteroides, Bifidobacterium, and Clostridium species, gradually colonize the gastrointestinal tract. The infant microbiota is also established from bacteria such as Bifidobacterium and Lactobacillus found in human milk. The high concentration of galacto-oligosaccharides in human milk provides optimal growth conditions for Bifidobacteria species which are a prevalent microbe in the infant's intestinal microbiome.

We now appreciate that reduction of nitrate to nitrite requires the commensal bacteria that normally reside in our body. However, in newborn infants this pathway has not developed. After the establishment of the infant's oral microbiome on the lingual surface as well as intestinal colonization by bacteria, the infant, like the adult, supplies the gastrointestinal tract with a constant source of nitrite by entero-salivary circulation of nitrate. Therefore, breast milk high in nitrite relative to nitrate overcomes the natural deficiency early in life. At later stages of development nitrate becomes the predominant anion when a symbiosis exists with the colonized bacteria. There appears to be a complimentary system whereby the nitrite in breast milk can be reduced to NO even before the colonization of bacteria in the infant.

This is extremely important to understand. Studies have demonstrated many important health benefits to breastfeeding as opposed to formula feeding. It provides many health advantages beginning at birth and continuing throughout a child's life. Many of the health problems today's children face might be decreased, or even prevented, by breastfeeding the infant exclusively for at least the first six months of life. The longer the mother breastfeeds, the more likely the child will get the health benefits of breastfeeding.

Many studies show that breastfeeding strengthens the immune system. Infants who are breastfed exclusively for six months have a more developed immune system than those who are not exclusively breastfed. Breastfeeding has also been shown to reduce the risks of infants developing asthma and allergies as well as childhood leukemia. Cardiovascular disease risk is also reduced through the reduction of obesity, blood pressure and cholesterol in babies that are breast fed. Breast feeding as an infant also provides benefit later in life.

Breast-fed children are less likely to contract many diseases later in life, including juvenile diabetes, multiple sclerosis, heart disease, and cancer before the age of 15. In fact, breast fed babies have been shown to have a small reduction in blood pressure later in life. Breastfeeding during infancy is also associated with a reduction in the risk of ischemic cardiovascular disease later in life. All these benefits sound as though they could be due to nitric oxide in some form or fashion.

We decided to take on a full study to measure the nitrite and nitrate content of breast milk and compare it to several different infant formulas. We also reported that putting nitrite in formula milk could actually improve necrotizing enterocolitis.

To calculate an absolute amount or dose of nitrite that breast milk was providing to the newborn baby, we first had to determine how much breast milk a newborn baby consumes. Normal daily infant breastmilk intake is 2-3 ounces per pound per day or 200 ml/kg. That translates into 14-21 ounces or 400-630 ml of milk for a typical 7-pound (3 kg) infant. Taking an average of 50 µmoles/liter concentration of nitrite or 2300 µg/liter, total daily nitrite exposure to nursing infants is roughly 1.2 mg/kg or about 4 mg nitrite for a 7–10-pound baby. For an 80-90 kg (176 - 198 lbs.) adult that would equate to 96-108 mg nitrite dosing. What we were using was much less but still had amazing therapeutic benefits.

Interestingly, commercial infant formulas lack any nitrite and have very little nitrate. The health disparities between breast fed and formula fed babies are well known. We and others showed that supplementing nitrite that is missing in formulas can protect from necrotizing enterocolitis. These data clearly demonstrate that nitrite missing in formulas is present in breast milk, and when supplemented back into formula affords protection.

Perhaps it is the missing nitrite in formula that accounts for some of the differences from that in breast milk. Breast or formula milk serve as primary sources of calories and nutrients in infants and children and may take several forms.

Human breast milk is recommended to serve as the exclusive food for the first six months of life and continue, along with safe, nutritious complementary foods, for up to two years. Breast milk is nature's most perfect food. In fact, the U.S. Centers for Disease Control and Prevention in 2010 acknowledged "Breast milk is widely acknowledged as the most complete form of nutrition for infants, with a range of benefits for infants' health, growth, immunity and development."

Breast milk is a unique nutritional source for infants that cannot adequately be replaced by any other food, including infant formula. It remains superior to infant formula from the perspective of the overall health of both mother and child. The reduction in adult-onset diseases may be due to the early influence of the nitrite/nitrate composition of breast milk. These data provide exactly the information that I was hoping to find. It appeared that what I was doing with nitrite and the natural product chemistry in our lozenge was exactly what nature was doing and what was intended.

Another important observation we had published in 2007 provided additional support that our approach was indeed physiological and recapitulated what nature does naturally. People that live in Tibet at an altitude of 12,000 feet above sea level have found a way to adapt to living at low oxygen.

The low atmospheric pressure at high altitude causes lower arterial oxygen content in most humans. However, Tibetan highlanders maintain normal

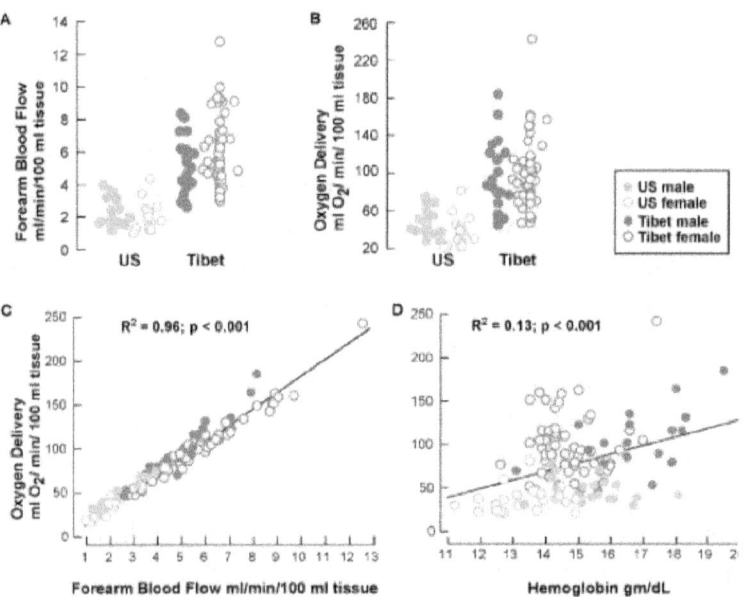

Hemodynamics and oxygen delivery among Tibetan and sea level populations, (A and B). Tibetan forearm blood flow (A) and oxygen delivery (B) were greater than sea level controls, (C).
The greater forearm blood flow of Tibetans compared with the sea level population accounts for the greater oxygen delivery, (D).
Higher hemoglobin concentrations of Tibetans as compared with sea level population contributes modestly to greater oxygen.

The Secret of Nitric Oxide

levels of oxygen use as indicated by basal and maximal oxygen consumption levels that are consistent with what one would experience at sea level. Hypothetically, the unavoidably low supply of oxygen in the air and the blood could be offset by increasing blood flow to improve oxygen delivery.

Could the adaptation to low oxygen due to high altitude be from an increase in nitric oxide production to not only improve red blood cell oxygenation but also improve blood flow and circulation?

Blood-flow is determined by numbers, length, and diameter of blood vessels that in turn are largely determined directly or indirectly by levels of nitric oxide. In our 2007 study, we published that Tibetans have a much higher production of NO. This increased NO production caused an increase in oxygen delivery even though they were breathing in less oxygen with each

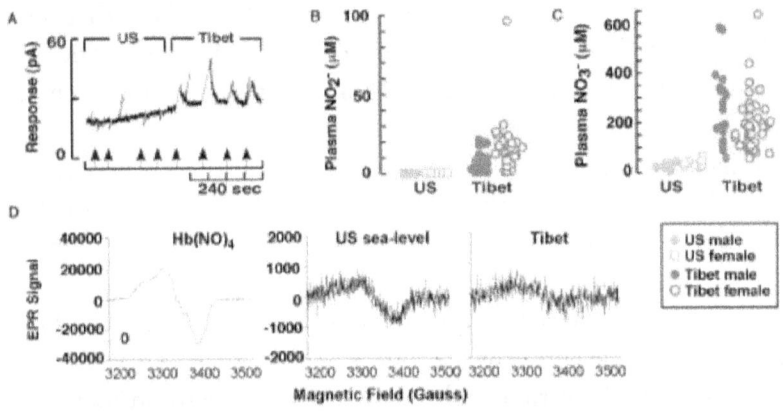

NO production in the circulation of Tibetan and sea level populations. (A) Amperometric detection (pA) of plasma NO release from nitrite. Arrows identify sample injections. (B and C) Tibetan nitrite (B) and nitrate (C) levels in plasma samples were higher than sea level controls (D) EPR determination of HbFeIINO in red blood cell samples. EPR spectra of teh tetranitrosyl HbFeIINO standard is shown in Left. EPR spectra of blood obtained from a Tibetan particpant (Right) revealed lower levels of HbFeIINO complex than blood obtained from a sea level volunteer (Center). Data shown are representative of the mean values of the population samples.

breath. This suggests that Tibetan highlanders offset hypoxia with higher systemic blood flow and higher levels of circulating, biologically active metabolites of NO. After synthesis by the endothelium, NO rapidly undergoes reaction in the blood to form products that have circulatory and metabolic effects, including nitrite, nitrosothiols and NO bound to hemoglobin.

From our studies we found that Tibetans living at 12,000 feet above sea level had forearm blood flow more than double that of people living at sea level. We also reported that their circulating concentrations of nitrite and nitrate were 10-50 times higher than those living at sea level. These data highlight blood flow and its regulation as central components of Tibetans' adaptation to high-altitude hypoxia. They do this through increasing nitric oxide production and increasing their circulating levels of nitrite and nitrate. What an amazing response by the human body to adapt to low oxygen by increasing nitric oxide production.

Could this be why athletes train at high altitude to improve their nitric oxide production to enhance their performance? Data show that when healthy individuals first go to altitude, there circulating levels of nitric oxide metabolites decrease within the first 24-48 hours and some even stay decreased for several days or weeks.

In healthy people, circulating nitric oxide metabolites increased back to baseline and even increased after 48 hours. Those that developed high altitude sickness and even high-altitude pulmonary edema stayed low for the entire duration of the altitude exposure. Could this also explain why some people get altitude sickness and others do not? Could it be due to their ability to produce nitric oxide?

If people go to high altitude and their body is unable to produce nitric oxide because of endothelial dysfunction or because they are using mouthwash or antacids or not eating the right diet to provide the body with nitrite or nitrate, then they are unable to adapt to the low oxygen environment and they get sick and some even develop high altitude pulmonary edema, a deadly condition.

Could we provide nitric oxide and adapt to high altitude for them? This was the whole basis for my discoveries and product development. If your body cannot make nitric oxide, then our product technology does it for you.

Years ago, I developed a product called Altitude Adapt that we sold at many different ski resorts in Colorado to help people with mountain sickness. One Christmas, my family and I went snow skiing in Aspen Colorado. We were on the gondola going up to the top of the mountain and

The Secret of Nitric Oxide

a lady sharing a ride with us pulled out her lozenges and commented how life changing this product had been for her and her family.

She mentioned that typically when they come for vacation, they must spend the first 2 days adapting to the altitude before they can actually enjoy their ski vacation. Now with this product, they take it immediately when they land, and they can begin skiing the very next day and feel great with no effects of the altitude.

What are the chances that a random stranger in Aspen Colorado was taking my product and could not say enough good things about it as I was riding along just listening? I just smiled and never revealed that I was the guy who invented that lozenge.

I had a similar experience in flying to Denver a couple of years later. The guy next to me took my lozenges out of his backpack and took one. I asked him what that was and he said it was the best nitric oxide product on the market. He took it every day but especially when flying and when going to high altitude. He said he never travels without it. I knew what I was doing was having an impact on people's lives.

Shortly after we launched the product, I was attending a Miami Heat basketball game in Miami and was the guest of Pat and Chris Riley. Pat was no longer coaching but was an executive with the Heat team. This was a time when the Heat were dominating the game with LeBron James, Chris Bosh and Dwayne Wade. Pat mentioned during the game that his players have a difficult time playing in Denver due to the altitude.

These guys are in great shape and certainly produce nitric oxide, but they fly in only one day before their game and this does not allow sufficient time for their body to adapt to the altitude. During halftime we went to the executive suite, and I mentioned to Pat that I had a product that would provide nitric oxide and allow the players to adapt to the high altitude almost immediately. They were playing Denver the next week. We provided the team with products that they took with them to Denver and took before the game.

The entire team had an incredible response to the lozenge, and no one had trouble adapting to the altitude and they dominated the Nuggets that game. It did not take long for words to spread around the NBA. It turns out every team struggles in Denver.

Nitric oxide product technology is now used by more than 100 NCAA and professional teams including NFL, MLB, NBA, NHL and even the

U.S. Olympic teams. This concept of providing nitric oxide through product technology was slowing changing the game in athletics, human performance and medicine.

Again, this provided us with the exact evidence I needed to be able to demonstrate that what I was doing with my product technology was exactly what nature had intended and we could mimic physiology by providing a source of nitric oxide. Providing nitrite and nitric oxide directly to people from a lozenge was very similar to what happens to newborn babies when they breast feed and to adult humans when they ascend to altitude.

The products I had developed increased circulating levels of nitrite and nitric oxide metabolites as what happens in healthy people when they train at altitude. Acclimatization to living at high altitude and reduced oxygen is through increased nitric oxide production with 20-50 times higher circulating nitrite and nitrate than those that live at sea level.

It is our normal physiological response for people who live at or near sea level, increasing their NO production and plasma levels of nitrite and nitrate as they ascend to altitude. Increasing nitrite and nitrate availability is a physiological response to low oxygen and the adaptive response to allow us to acclimate to different environments.

In other words, increasing steady state concentrations of nitrite and nitrate appears to be a natural physiological response that allows the body to adapt to changing oxygen environments, whether environmental or physiological. If people were unable to produce nitric oxide to acclimate to high altitude, then my products would do it for them.

CHAPTER 18

From Academia to Entrepreneurship

"Courage is resistance to fear, mastery of fear—not absence of fear."
—Mark Twain

I've learned that life has a way of body checking you. Just when things seem to be going well, life throws you a curve ball. One of my biggest challenges at the time was balancing my full-time academic job with helping support the company and its commercial success. As part of my employment agreement at UT, I was required to provide 100% of my salary and research budget from outside grants. I had been fully funded for the first 6-7 years of my academic appointment from my American Heart Association grant, partial funding from my collaborations at Baylor College of Medicine and from my start-up funds from the University.

The time I was spending at the company was interfering with my ability to write and submit grant applications for funding. I was quickly running out of funding for my research program. The fact that my grant applications were reviewed by a committee of my peers created another hurdle. Most of my peers in academia and at the National Institutes of Health, where the majority of research funding comes, were aware of my commercial success with my companies.

I cannot say without a doubt but I do believe my commercial success inhibited my ability to secure NIH grants and research funding for my academic program. Academia is very competitive with many investigators competing for the same grant money. If funds are awarded to your competitor, then there are less funds available for similar projects.

The other problem I encountered was my conflict-of-interest management plan. All Universities encourage their faculty to invent, innovate and create technology that will advance patient care and improve healthcare. However, if you do that, then the university appoints a team of your peers to help you manage the conflict of interest. The conflict arises when the research you are doing as an employee of the University has the potential to enrich you personally through financial gain. By rules, you cannot use government resources or employment for personal financial gain.

Conflicts of interest are allowable, but they must be managed by the University and must be fully disclosed on any publications, grant applications or any public disclosure. I was assigned a management team of my peers appointed by the Vice-President of Research. They would advise me on what I could and could not do with regards to my research program. Some of the members advised that I discontinue doing nitric oxide research altogether. Was I supposed to start an entire new line of research when all I had done for the previous 15 years was nitric oxide?

As you may imagine, I had a major problem with people telling me what I can and cannot do. I actually met with the President of the University on multiple occasions and informed him of the restrictions the University was placing on my research program. I had a little bit of confidence and posture since my royalties were now exceeding what the University was paying me in salary. I was able to walk away if I had to. I did not need the academic position anymore, at least not financially.

I met with my management committee once or twice a year. Each time, they put additional restrictions on my research program. I became curious how members of my committee had managed their own conflicts since they oversaw managing mine. At one of the meetings, I asked the Chair of my conflict-of-interest management committee how he managed his conflicts while being employed at UT. To my utmost surprise, the guy who was managing my conflicts of interest plan never had a conflict of interest. What? How could someone with no personal experience in managing conflicts of interest instruct me on how to manage mine? This had to be some kind of joke. This infuriated me. I kindly went around the table and asked the same questions to all the other members of my committee.

Not a single person on my committee had ever had a conflict of interest during their time at UT. I grabbed my things and walked out of the room, and as I was leaving, I instructed the committee that when they assembled a committee of people experienced in managing a conflict of interest, I would listen. Until then, I am out. Shortly thereafter, I received a letter from the Vice President of Research informing me that I had been assigned a new committee. I met with the new committee only once or twice before I had had enough of others "managing" my research program.

In 2014, with the impending loss of funding for my research program, along with the frustrations of restrictions on my research, I resigned from the Institute of Molecular Medicine. It was a happy but sad day. I was happy to not have to deal with the constant conflicts and having to write grant applications, but I was sad to leave academic research. It was time to move on to the next phase of my career and personal development.

To maintain some level of involvement, I took an honorary adjunct Assistant Professor position at Baylor College of Medicine in the Department of Molecular and Human Genetics. I kept that position for about 5 years. Looking back, leaving Academia was tough. I did not realize it at the time, but it takes enormous courage to leave behind a 15-year career for the unknown. Many people spend their entire lifetime in Academia. It is a wonderful profession with decent pay, complete intellectual freedom, awards and recognitions for the most productive professors, ability to teach, train and inspire future physicians, scientists and health care practitioners, peer esteem and in some cases fame and recognition. You have the ability to promote within the ranks and become part of the leadership of the Institutions. It is a great career. I only know a select few of my colleagues who have had the courage to leave academia to pursue industry and to chase the dream of commercializing their own discoveries. Most people are fearful of leaving that safe place of tenure, job security and comfort. I have found that no reward comes without risks. I was willing to take that risk. It was a very calculated risk but there was still some fear. Looking back, it was one of the best decisions I could have made.

My position at Baylor College of Medicine allowed me to continue to do research but with no responsibilities to the College. This allowed me to spend more time at the company, helping the company grow and providing more time for lecturing and education. At the same time, my appointment allowed me to continue to do research in the nitric oxide field.

The company now had dozens of employees and was growing very rapidly. I quickly learned of the different personalities at the company when I started spending more time there. I was the face of the company, the inventor of the technology upon which the company was founded and featured on nationwide radio and television commercials and advertising, and I was making more than half a million dollars a year on royalties.

In 2017, the company decided to no longer attend or support medical trade shows where I was speaking. I realized that my position and participation in any of the company activities was over. I was neither an employee of the company nor was I ever an employee of the company. I was not a consultant for the company and the company was not paying me anything. My next thought was what am I going to do to keep active in the nitric oxide field when I felt as if I was basically being pushed out of my own company. I was beginning to understand how Steve Jobs felt when he was once alienated from the company he started. I started looking for new opportunities while maintaining my research at Baylor College of Medicine.

In early 2017, the President of our company requested a meeting with me. He informed me that the company was raising money to fund the growth of the company. There was a private equity company interested in investing but one of their requirements was that I become a consultant to the company and that I sign a non-compete. I respectfully declined the offer. I did not want to re-engage in any way with the company. He indicated that the company could not continue without outside funding from this investment group. If the company's future success was based on this outside funding, then I felt I had to do it. All of us shareholders were able to sell a portion of our shares to the private equity group and then they invested the necessary growth capital into the company. It seemed everyone was happy.

After the first few months, I realized they were not interested at all in my consulting services or having any involvement at all in the company. It was during this time that the company began developing other products that were not based on my patents or technology rights and going in a different direction. I felt that I could no longer contribute to the science of any products that did not involve nitric oxide.

My concern was for my own academic reputation and peer esteem in the nitric oxide field. I had spent nearly two decades building a reputation as a credible and reputable scientist who made products that produce nitric oxide that anyone could detect, quantify and verify. I had become the face of our company's nitric oxide products. I felt I could not afford to have my science and credibility compromised by products that did not provide

The Secret of Nitric Oxide

consistent nitric oxide activity compared to how we had formulated our original nitric oxide products.

This was supposed to be the best time of my life. The company was growing exponentially, I was making millions of dollars in royalties, and I had complete time freedom to do what I wanted to do. I had purchased an 800-acre ranch and built a new home on it and had several hundred heads of cattle. I had a wife and 3 healthy boys at home. My only complaint in life was the lack of any real involvement in the company I started in 2009. I felt uncomfortable that I was unable to continue my passion for innovation and development of nitric oxide product technology, and I was absolutely isolated from the company that I had formed. I was still involved in some academic research at Baylor College of Medicine in Houston.

Early in the morning of December 16, 2018, I received the worst news any parent could receive. Our oldest son, Grant who was 20 years old at the time was killed in an automobile accident the previous night. I was at the airport in Las Vegas returning home from speaking at an Anti-Aging Medicine conference. My wife called me at 5 am Vegas time while I was about to board the plane and informed me. She had been trying to text Grant all night to make sure he was home in time for Church. As she was getting dressed in our bathroom, she noticed two Texas Department of Public Safety (DPS) cars pulling into our driveway. She immediately knew what had happened. Her gut told her Grant had died. She met the officers outside and they did indeed confirm our worst fears.

Grant went out with his high school buddies that night. He was home for the Christmas break from college where he was playing basketball at Schreiner University in Kerrville, Texas. It was around midnight and Grant was asleep as a passenger in a truck with his best friend driving. Around 3:30 am they headed home and the driver was intoxicated, going very fast and missed a turn and ran head on into a tree. Grant was killed instantly. It appears he was asleep and did not know what happened. We were told he felt no pain, felt no fear due to being asleep and died instantly upon impact.

This changed our lives forever. No human being is prepared to get this type of news. Our two younger boys, Lincoln 10 at the time and Conley who was 8 were both devastated. Their older brother and their hero, was gone. Now it seemed that everything I was worried about with the company did not matter. Nothing else mattered. Life has a way of putting things in perspective. How was our family to heal from this devastating tragedy? I had to be the strong foundation for Kristen and the boys. However, I was an absolute mess mentally. I've always been pretty good at appearing strong and in control, but this was the most tragic and devastating event in my entire life and I was weak. I felt like I had no control of any aspect of my life. For the next few days, we were planning the funeral and trying to cope with a completely new life without Grant.

It was also during this time that I was trying to negotiate an amendment to my consulting agreement to allow me to do things in the nitric oxide field that were outside the scope of work of the company.

I took a chance and called the principal from the private equity firm and had a conversation with him. Prior to Grant's death, I had arranged a call with the private equity partner to discuss my desire to amend my consulting agreement. The call which I scheduled weeks before, was scheduled while we were picking out caskets for Grant at the funeral home. Not an ideal time for a business call but the call had been scheduled for several weeks.

At first, he seemed resistant to any of my requests and was taking a hard nose approach. After a few minutes, I informed him that we were at the funeral home planning to bury our son. His demeanor immediately changed and was receptive to my requests. He was very accommodating and was willing to have my agreement amended, especially after hearing the news of our son's death. With his support, I met with the company's lawyer and got a new amended agreement executed that allowed me to develop my topical nitric oxide technology for skin care and beauty. This seemed like a good negotiation. I would not compete with the company in selling nutritional products or dietary supplements, and I could continue to innovate and create nitric oxide products that would change people's lives. Once the private equity group had agreed to have my consulting agreement amended, I had to meet with the company's lawyer in order to draft up an agreement that was agreed upon. Everyone agreed and we moved on. Looking back, I was not in a proper mental state to sign any contract.

I later found out that private investigators from what may have been a competing group had been following me for the past several months. I felt so violated and betrayed. I had kind of always thought someone was watching me just because of several strange things that happened over the previous few months. Now I was on alert. Over the next few months, I caught a private investigator following me on the interstate in Florida around midnight.

I was driving back from the American Academy of Anti-Aging Medicine meeting in Orlando Florida and had been driving for about 5 hours. I was feeling tired and sleepy and was going to pull over and book a hotel along interstate 10 outside of Tallahassee Florida. As I was exiting the interstate, I quickly recognized I was being followed. I always keep a licensed gun in my car in between my legs. I felt threatened and that my life was in danger. I took a few turns into a neighborhood around midnight, and he followed. I quickly dashed through the neighborhood, pulled into a driveway, turned off my lights and when he passed, I got in behind him and begun to follow the car that had been following me.

I called the police and notified them of the situation. The truck quickly sped off at more than 100 miles per hour going down interstate 10. I was in hot pursuit. I got pictures of the license plate, ran the plates and turned out to be a private investigator out of Jacksonville Florida. How many private investigators get caught?

I knew then that this had escalated into a very dangerous situation and I feared for my safety. Several months later when returning from a trip to California, I caught another private investigator pulling into the driveway of my ranch as I was pulling in behind him. Once he realized it was me, he quickly put his truck in reverse, almost ran me over and then sped off. Just like before, I took off after him.

We were doing 120 mph down a farm to market road. There was no way his Ford F-150 was going to outrun my sports car. We reached the end of the road at a stop sign and I bailed out of my car to approach the truck. He was obviously nervous and asked I leave him alone. He showed me his badge and admitted that he had been sent to follow me.

I have people following me in Florida. I have people following me and trespassing on my ranch. I later realized that there were plans to cause me to have a fatal car accident in Florida during one event. I now knew that nothing would ever be the same. I notified my family and kids and alerted them to always be on the lookout. Again, I felt completely violated that I wasn't even safe at my own home. For the next few months, my kids were not comfortable even riding around our 800-acre ranch in fear that someone was after us and spying on us. This was unimaginable.

I contacted the local Sherrif's office and had 24-hour surveillance of my home for a period of several weeks. I had guys that worked for me on the ranch come around on weekends when I was away to make sure my family was safe.

CHAPTER 19

Diversification and Risk Management

"He who is not courageous enough to take risks will accomplish nothing in life."
—Muhammad Ali

Now that I had an agreement to go out and develop other nitric oxide technologies that did not compete with the products at my first company, I was excited to continue the innovation and product development. Earlier around 2015, I aspired to develop nitric oxide drugs. However, the capital requirements and diligence for drug development are much different than dietary supplements. To continue my quest for bringing safe and effective product technology in every major market segment around the globe, I realized I had to manage my risks and separate different products in different segments into different companies.

There is a wide range of risks and opportunities between drugs, cosmetics, skin care products and dietary supplements. The regulatory affairs are worlds apart and the capital required to launch is much higher for drugs than supplements and cosmetics. In 2018, I started a drug company, Nitric Oxide Innovations. My intent was to pursue my original objective and goal of getting a nitric oxide drug approved and on the market. Knowing that drugs take ten years and around $800 million to get to market, I knew it was a long road ahead. But a journey of a thousand miles begins with a single step.

My company from 2009 had the license for my patents and technology rights to be used in nutrition and dietary supplements. I was pursuing the same patents and technology rights for drug development. Although I had the structure of a drug company, I was not actively pursuing drug development at that time. I had also learned from my efforts from years earlier that I had to first secure the license for my patents from UT. I knew the drug development would take many years and more money than I had at the time. I felt I had other priorities that I could focus and continue to innovate. While I contemplated how I was going to move forward with the drug company, I started a new project developing a topical nitric oxide serum.

The idea of developing a topical nitric oxide serum originated back in 2009 when I submitted an invention disclosure to the University of Texas on developing a topical nitric oxide for erectile dysfunction. I thought if I could deliver nitric oxide to the sex organs, perhaps we could enhance blood flow and improve erectile function.

On a more personal note, back in 2014, my dad had developed a very serious hemorrhoid problem. My dad is paraplegic from his car accident back in 1984. We took him in for hemorrhoid surgery and afterwards his surgeon advised him to take a hot sitz bath or to sit on a heating pad for half an hour several times a day. Dad borrowed a heating pad from a neighbor and started to sit on it for half an hour to an hour to help with his post-surgical recovery.

Turns out that having a diabetic, paraplegic use a heating pad causes a third-degree burn on his backside. Dad did not even know he was burnt. After about 24 hours, dad developed a fever with cold chills. He went to take a bath to warm up and realized that he had skin and flesh coming off his backside.

He called the ambulance, and they immediately came to pick and up and quickly recognized the severity of his situation. I was in Scottsdale Arizona speaking at a medical event when I received a call from dad's phone, and it was the paramedic transporting him to Brook Army Medical Center (BAMC) in San Antonio. BAMC is one of the world's premier wound care and burn centers in the U.S. I got a call from one of the surgeons assigned to dad's case and he notified me that my dad might not survive this injury due to high risk of infection in that area and because he was nearly 65 years old, paraplegic, diabetic with many other co-morbidities.

God has a cool way of intervening at just the right time. At the event where I was lecturing with Jerry Tennant, M.D., I had just heard a lecture from Mark Starr, M.D. who presented a case of a third degree burn that completely healed with no scarring using a device that Dr. Tennant had invented called a biomodulator along with humic and fulvic acid on the wound. Now this was in a very healthy younger person. Could my dad achieve the same results being older, diabetic and paraplegic? I quickly

The Secret of Nitric Oxide

notified Dr. Tennant and his staff of what had just happened to my dad.

Barbara Evans, one of the organizers and team members of Dr. Tennant's team, sent me home with a device, and I was going to follow the protocol that Dr. Starr had used on the wound case he had just presented. I immediately flew home, got in my car and drove to San Antonio to visit dad. They had just finished the skin graft and had performed a colostomy on dad to divert his fecal waste away from the wound to prevent infection. Dad was in his room on intravenous antibiotics and not doing well at all.

At night, once all the nurses and doctors had left the room, I started treating dad's wound with a gauze soaked in humic and fulvic acid, and then I used the Tennant biomodulator on the wound. After about a half hour treatment I would cover the wound with a nitric oxide generating gauze with hopes of getting blood flow and circulation to the newly grafted skin over the burn. The doctors informed us that the wound would take at least 6-9 months to heal if it healed at all. Chances were still high that dad may not even survive the injury due to infection and sepsis.

The next morning the nurses and doctors came into his room to clean and dress the wound and it was remarkable how much the wound had healed just overnight using the humic/fulvic along with biomodulator and nitric oxide gauze.

The wound was a nice pink color indicating there was sufficient blood supply and circulation. I did not reveal anything that I was doing in fear the doctors would instruct me not to mess with their patient. I continued this protocol every day for a week or two.

Within 3 months the wound had completely healed, the skin graft was successful, and dad was discharged and sent home with a completely healed third degree burn. His doctors and surgeons could not believe how his burn had healed and healed so quickly. It was unlike anything they had ever seen. This was again confirmation that what we were doing with nitric oxide would change the world and how we treated some complex patients and cases that otherwise would have poor prognosis and outcome. As we were leaving and taking dad home, I revealed to the hospital staff and doctors that I had been using nitric oxide on the wound to help with the healing. Of course, they knew what nitric oxide was, but they did not have the ability to provide nitric oxide in their hospital to burn victims or for the treatment of other wounds. Although they were impressed with the results of the healing, they really showed no interest in trying to find a way to introduce it into BAMC so other patients may benefit.

I realized there would be some resistance to what we were trying to do introducing nitric oxide-based therapies into hospital systems and making this part of the standard of care. We were all so thankful that dad was home and recovering from what could have been a deadly burn. Being paraplegic for several decades, I had always dealt with decubitus and pressure ulcers on dad's feet and backside and we would continuously monitor his skin for breakdown.

About 6 months after he was released from BAMC with the burn, dad developed a bad ulcer on his right butt cheek just over his ischium (tail bone). The skin began to break down and once it revealed itself, it was a stage 4 bed sore. It quickly got infected, and he was again hospitalized. He was given intravenous antibiotics to kill the infection and was given a wound vac to help heal the wound.

The wound care center and doctors told us that this wound would likely not heal and that he may eventually succumb to the infection and not survive. Well, we had certainly heard this story before, and we overcame all those odds. After 10 days in the hospital, dad was released and sent home with instructions to change out wound vac every 48 hours and to keep an eye on the wound for infections. I took control of dad's wound care.

I would change out the wound vac and dress every 48 hours. Every other day, when I changed out the wound vac dressing, I would clean the wound bed with saline. I used an infrared light on it for 20 minutes. I used the humic and fulvic acid along with the Tennant biomodulator and then put wound vac back on and I would repeat this protocol every 48 hours. With no other choice, I begin creating a nitric oxide releasing wound dressing. I would create a 4x4 gauze that I implanted with nitric oxide generating components and then I would stick the gauze into the wound and cover it up. The idea was that when the gauze became moist inside the wound, it would begin generating nitric oxide gas within the wound.

I took dad to the best wound care doctors in the area and all of them told us that the wound would not heal due to his age, his paraplegia and all his co-morbidities. Within a matter of days of starting the nitric oxide generating dressing, we noticed the wound looked much better with a bright pink color indicating more blood flow. The infection appeared to be resolving, and we could see tissue growth and the wound started to fill in. This was incredible.

There was evidence in the literature that nitric oxide could kill certain bacteria, but I had never really explored it. Nitric oxide appeared to be the perfect medicine for wound care. It would kill the infection present in most wounds, and it would increase blood flow to allow for tissue granulation and wound healing. The wound was beginning to show some progress.

As I was traveling quite a bit, we hired a nurse to come and change out wound dressing when I was away. One evening I came home after 5-6 days of travel. As I was walking into dad's house, I smelled an awful odor. It smelled like death. I walked into dad's bedroom where he was asleep and shaking with a fever. I woke him up and looked at his wound. It was severely infected. When I started cleaning the wound, I found a gauze pad that had not been removed by the nurse since I was gone, and it was nasty and necrotic.

Fearing that dad might become septic, I had an ozone generator that I had recently bought. I used the ozone gas to insufflate the wound bed and gave dad intravenous ozone gas to help kill the infection. I also treated the wound with the topical nitric oxide. I deliberately made a very high dose of nitric oxide within the gauze to help kill the infection. Once I finished the wound dressing, dad got out of bed and in his wheelchair. As he was wheeling from the bedroom and into the kitchen, he yelled at me that he could not see and felt faint.

I quickly ran to him, and he was ghost white. I felt his pulse and I could barely palpate his very weak pulse. I took his blood pressure, and his blood pressure would not even register on the blood pressure monitor. I knew that I had overdosed him on the nitric oxide that I had put in his wound. The overproduction of nitric oxide from the wound dressing had dropped his blood pressure to very dangerous levels. I quickly picked dad out of his wheelchair and carried him to his bed. He was going in and out of consciousness. I elevated his feet, instructed my wife to go get dad a soda or some caffeinated beverage. I immediately began to pump his legs, lowered his head to try to maintain enough blood pressure to keep him awake and alive.

We pumped him full of fluids and after about 20 minutes, his blood pressure started coming back. Within a few hours he had returned to normal blood pressure. This made me realize that we had to be very careful with nitric oxide product technology. Too little nitric oxide was bad and now I have had personal experience that too much NO was also very bad. I had nearly killed my dad by administering too much nitric oxide to his wound bed. Within a few days, he immediately got better. We continued this protocol for several weeks but obviously using much lower concentrations of nitric oxide in the wound.

The wound was making some progress, but it was slow. It was at this time that I was learning from attending a few dental events that people with root canals or with metal fillings or metal teeth had a hard time healing. Dad had a silver tooth right in front due to his bull riding days where he got hooked in the mouth and knocked out his tooth and he had several root canals and several teeth with mercury amalgam fillings.

I took dad to Marble Falls Texas to Dr. Stuart Nunnally, one of the leading biological dentists that I had met several months earlier. Dr. Nunnally cleaned up the infected root canaled teeth, replaced the silver tooth with a bio-compatible implant and removed all the mercury amalgam fillings and replaced with a safe composite filling. Dr. Nunnally and his staff also gave dad IV ozone and treated his wound with ozone as well.

After his dental visit, Dad made a remarkable recovery. He felt better and his wound seemed to get better. Over the next few months, the wound continued to get better. We could see tissue growth and the nurse was measuring the internal dimensions of the wound, and it was getting smaller and smaller. The wound care doctors could not believe the wound was healing.

Once we got the wound 80% healed, I took my dad to my good friend, James Davis, M.D., a pain management physician whom I had met at a stem cell event a few years earlier. Dr. Davis performed liposuction on dad and spun down the fat tissues to isolate his own stem cells. Once the stem cells were isolated, Dr. Davis then injected the fat derived stem cells into the wound and then delivered several million stem cells intravenously.

This is called stromal vascular fraction or SVF, a technique developed and optimized by the Cell Surgical Network. Within 10 days, the wound was 90% healed. There was enormous tissue growth from the stem cell treatment. Once we got enough tissue growth to almost heal the wound, I took dad to a plastic surgeon who performed a surgical flap where he moved muscle and tissue to completely close the wound. The wound that all doctors told us would not heal, was completely healed.

All his wound care doctors were amazed and could not believe that we had healed this non-healing wound. This was a great victory for me and for my dad personally but also made me realize how important nitric oxide could be for skin applications.

Recognizing that tens of thousands of people die each year due to non-healing infected wounds, I felt an obligation and a responsibility to develop this product and bring it to the market. It was too important not to pursue. It was not nitric oxide alone that healed this wound. It was the application of ozone insufflation, red light therapy, protocols for stem cell deployment by the Cell Surgical Network and most importantly the faith and hope of a father and his son and by the Grace and Mercy of our Lord Jesus Christ, the ultimate healer.

Once I knew how to make a shelf stable product that delivered nitric oxide gas, I quickly adapted this to skin care and cosmetics. I knew that developing the topical drug would take many years and tens of millions of dollars to go through the FDA clinical trials. However, the barrier to entry into the skin care/beauty market was much lower and a billion-dollar market. I spoke at the International Cell Surgical Conference for several years and met many wonderful physicians and scientists in the regenerative medicine practice. I met many plastic surgeons, dermatologists and other medical specialists that quickly recognized how important nitric oxide would be if applied topically. This was the same group that helped my dad and did the stem cell procedure for my dad's wound.

One such physician was Greg Chernoff, M.D. Greg is a triple board-certified plastic, facial and reconstructive surgeon. Greg and I, along with Susan Shaffer, who had recently departed from our previous company met and discussed a new business involving nitric oxide and cosmetics and skin care. The three of us met and developed a go-to market strategy. Within a couple of months, we had our prototypes of our dual chamber nitric oxide releasing serum. We put the product to the test. It released nitric oxide that we could detect with a gas phase nitric oxide analyzer. It was amazing.

Once applied to the skin you could see the nitric oxide working by turning the skin a light pink color by increasing blood flow and circulation to wherever the serum was applied. The commercial product was working exactly like the makeshift product I had made for my dad's wound. Dr.

Chernoff conducted a few clinical trials using the serum and the results were transformative. In his more than 30 years in aesthetics and plastic surgery, he had never seen a product do what our nitric oxide product technology was doing. Dr. Chernoff went on to publish 5 clinical trials showing the remarkable effects of our nitric oxide serum.

We called the company Pneuma Nitric Oxide. *Pneuma* is the Greek word for "breath of life" and *pneuma* was the word used by the Roman physicians, Galen around 100 AD to describe the "energy that animated the human." That is exactly what nitric oxide was. It is the breath of life, and it is what is required for life.

We launched a dual chamber nitric oxide activating skin serum in May of 2019. The skin care and beauty industry had never seen anything like this. Most skin care products hide or mask blemishes on the skin. Our serum was the first skin care/beauty product that gets to the root of the problem, which is insufficient blood flow. The skin is an organ just like any other organ. Without sufficient blood supply, the organ fails. When the skin fails, you lose the barrier function, you lose hydration, you become susceptible to infections and acne and your skin begins to sag, fine lines and wrinkles appear, and you look old. Nitric oxide can fix all those problems. Our serum delivered on that promise.

In March of 2020, COVID-19 became the worldwide headlines. Up until this point, I had not done much with my drug company. In April of 2020, I realized that the people that were getting sick and dying of COVID were those patients that were deficient in nitric oxide. Those were the elderly with underlying conditions such as high blood pressure, diabetes, previous heart attack, kidney disease, smokers and especially African Americans.

All these symptoms were symptoms of nitric oxide insufficiency. Studies were published in 2005 that demonstrated that nitric oxide could inhibit the corona virus from replicating. I immediately began to mobilize resources to get our nitric oxide drug program up and running so we could help with the COVID crisis.

I was introduced to Bob Arnot, M.D. who was recently appointed as part of the coronavirus task force at the White House. Dr. Arnot introduced me to John Somberg, M.D., who had experience conducting clinical trials for the Food and Drug Administration (FDA). I contacted Patheon ThermoFisher, one of the world's largest drug manufacturers. Within 3 weeks, we had a clear plan to get a nitric oxide COVID drug developed and into FDA clinical trials.

With the help of Dr. Somberg, we submitted our investigative new drug (IND) application to the FDA in June 2020. In 30 days, we had approval to move forward with the study. We submitted our institutional review board (IRB) in August of 2020 and had our IRB approved in October 2020.

Patheon had our clinical trial material manufactured and tested for stability by November 2020 and at the beginning of December 2020, we had our FDA clinical trial underway, and patients enrolled. What typically takes at least 24 months for drug development and clinical trial design and approval, we did in less than 6 months.

The FDA required us to monitor the first 100 patients for one hour after we dosed our nitric oxide drug to ensure there was no unsafe drop in blood pressure or any adverse events. Not surprising to me, there was no unsafe drop in blood pressure and no safety signal whatsoever. Enrollment in our drug study was very slow because there was a lot of fear around COVID. Our drug study required 840 patients, half on placebo and half getting the active drug. We designed our study and powered our study to decreased hospitalization and death by 20%.

However, as we all know, COVID disease changed dramatically over the course of 2020-2022. It became a less virulent infection with much milder symptoms than the original COVID virus. As a result, people who were infected were no longer going to the hospital and death rates were dropping. Furthermore, there was not a lot of focus on early-stage therapeutics by the FDA or the administration in 2021-2022. All efforts and focus were on vaccines. We realized we were going up against some major players and a lot of resistance to our nitric oxide drug.

After all, if the FDA approved a safe and effective drug for COVID-19, all the emergency use authorization and vaccine mandates would go away. In early 2023, we elected to stop our drug study since COVID was no longer a real threat and it was clear we were not going to hit our endpoints for our clinical study. The good news is that we demonstrated our nitric oxide drug is completely safe, and it made COVID patients better. We will table our viral drug Noviricid until the next respiratory virus outbreak.

We treated over 500 sick, highly susceptible, high-risk patients on a number of prescription medications and our nitric oxide drug showed no signs of being unsafe. This was a great safety study for our nitric oxide drug.

Based on the safety of our oral nitric oxide drug, Bryan Therapeutics, Inc. is now developing drug studies for several conditions including ischemic heart disease, ischemic non-obstructive coronary artery disease, Alzheimer's Disease, heart failure and we are moving our topical nitric oxide technology into clinical trials for diabetic and non-healing ulcers.

The drug company secured a license from the University of Texas Health Sciences Center in Houston. The indications are endless for nitric oxide-based therapies.

SECTION V
THE FUTURE OF HEALTHCARE

CHAPTER 20
NITRICEUTICAL®

"Innovation distinguishes between a leader and a follower."
—Steve Jobs

Although nitric oxide is a growing market segment, there is still not much global awareness around nitric oxide. Several market reports have estimated the nitric oxide supplement industry to be in the tens of billions of dollars annually.

The problem with people that become nitric oxide deficient and may need nitric oxide products that work is that their body has lost the ability to convert nutrients into nitric oxide gas. These people are commonly not deficient in amino acids like L-arginine or L-citrulline; they have lost the ability to utilize those amino acids to produce nitric oxide. There are literally hundreds of nitric oxide products on the market. Most of these products date back to 1998 after the discovery of nitric oxide won the Nobel Prize in Medicine.

The effectiveness of beet-based products in supporting nitric oxide production can vary depending on factors such as nitrate content and formulation. Consumers should research and select products that align with their health goals. There are, however, a few beet root products that have known amounts of nitrate. There are also products that contain potassium nitrate in a capsule that are sold as a nitric oxide product. But if you are using mouthwash, antibiotics, antacids and have poor oral hygiene, these products may not work for you.

* * *

The nitric oxide supplement industry is diverse and product formulations vary. Reviewing the scientific literature can help consumers identify products that best meet their needs. Once I started learning what products were out there being marketed as nitric oxide products, I realized there are 3 main categories of these products:

1. Products that contain L-arginine and/or L-citrulline.
2. Beet root-based products.
3. Nitrate-based products.

One of my priorities has always been to find a way to differentiate my nitric oxide products based on the most recent science and research from all the other products. After focusing on nitric oxide research for many years, I developed my own product line to further explore innovative solutions in the field. I had to create a product category that would differentiate what I was doing with every other nitric oxide product on the market.

* * *

How could I create a differentiated product that was safe but also effective at producing nitric oxide? I had to create a new category of products. People are familiar with nutriceuticals, which are nutrients sold as dietary supplements that provide health benefits. The word nutraceutical has been used for decades to represent nutrients meant to replace or replete missing nutrients that may be missing for optimal health. This can be Vitamin C, Vitamin D, zinc, iodine, selenium, etc. These are all important nutrients that can be used to supplement one's diet to reach optimal levels.

The suffix "ceutical" means something of healing or therapy, so nutraceutical means nutrients meant to heal or provide therapy. Similarly, pharmaceuticals refer to drugs that are meant to heal or provide therapy. I have always been interested in nitric oxide-based therapeutics that can provide a source of nitric oxide to help restore our body's most important signaling molecule. Therefore, I coined and trademarked the term

The Secret of Nitric Oxide

"NITRICEUTICAL®" to refer to nitric oxide-based products that generate nitric oxide to provide healing or therapeutic benefit.

* * *

Nitriceuticals are products where the goal is to support nitric oxide production, leveraging research-driven approaches to enhance efficacy. This is a new product category based on my research and innovations over the past 20 years. Now that we understand that nitric oxide is a hormone, we can develop product technology that generates nitric oxide gas in the human body. We can do this in the form of a lozenge that releases nitric oxide gas as it is dissolving in the mouth that is completely independent and does not rely on the oral microbiome or stomach acid. We can do this through powder forms that when dissolved in water and taken as a shot generate nitric oxide gas. We can also do this topically as a novel skinceutical. There is no other way to deliver nitric oxide outside a clinical setting.

Nitric oxide is a gas. Nitric oxide is a signaling molecule and hormone that once produced initiates many important biological processes. All my products are NITRICEUTICALS® that actually produce nitric oxide gas when dispensed or taken that we can quantify and verify with a gas phase nitric oxide analyzer.

I've spent more than 25 years in nitric oxide research and discovery, published hundreds of peer reviewed papers, written several books and given more than 300 lectures around the world on nitric oxide. It is important for consumers to understand how nitric oxide supplements function and to make informed choices based on available scientific research.

Federal regulations based on the Dietary Supplements Health and Education Act of 1994 established rules and guidelines for marketing dietary supplements. All companies are allowed to make "structure/function" claims meaning these products can help support certain functions of the body. Therefore, all companies in the dietary supplement space can say the same thing.

Educating consumers on nitric oxide science is a key focus, ensuring that individuals can make well-informed decisions when selecting supplements.

Trust the science and the companies that conduct research and have experience and expertise in the nitric oxide field. Nothing is more important for your health than ensuring your body makes enough nitric oxide and to restore endogenous NO production.

We know how to make nitric oxide. More than 200,000 scientific publications reveal just how important this molecule is. Without it, you get sick. With it, you have good health, free of disease. It's that simple. Now you have no excuses. Look for "NITRICEUTICAL®" products that deliver on the brand promise of NO.

My line of products are from the n1o1 brand, NO2U brand and we are building out other brands for different demographics. Understanding the difference in product technology is important. I get emails from people telling me that nitric oxide did not work for them, and they failed to get a benefit from nitric oxide. This is a misinterpretation. Nitric oxide always works and provides benefit when delivered at the right dose.

The major problem with the health of most Americans is sugar. Sugar is a toxin. Sugar is a poison. Sugar is one of the most addictive substances on earth. Have you ever spilled a sugary beverage such as a soda or juice and then come back the next day and notice how sticky it is?

Sugar is sticky. Glucose in the body is glue. Notice, GLUcose and GLUe. Same root, same meaning. Sugar or glucose sticks to proteins, enzymes and all other molecules in the body. We know sugar sticks to hemoglobin, and we can measure this as an indication of long-term glucose control. We call this Hemoglobin A1c. This is not unique to hemoglobin.

Sugar sticks to the nitric oxide synthase enzyme and all other enzymes, protein and molecules. For proteins and enzymes in the body to do their job, they must be able to move freely and undergo conformational changes. When sugar is stuck to them, they are stuck and cannot move freely. Consequently, the enzymes, proteins and molecules become dysfunctional. This is part of the reason people with diabetes have so many systemic problems. None of their enzymes can work because they are glued together and stuck by the excess sugar.

Stimulator and activator molecules such as grape seed extract, resveratrol, polyphenols, insulin and other molecules do not and cannot have the same effects when administered to a diabetic with high sugar. We see the same thing when these molecules or ingredients are delivered in a hydrated sugar matrix that have become a fad delivery system for many vitamins and nutrients.

Understand what may be affecting product response or patient response to products or supplements based on how they are delivered and the person into whom they are delivered. My goal is to educate enough people to help quality products and companies thrive. Nitric oxide must be in a delivery form factor that produces nitric oxide gas. If your body cannot produce nitric oxide, then it must be provided for you. Once people start to understand the science of nitric oxide, they will quickly recognize products that work for them.

CHAPTER 21
The Future Of Healthcare

"The people who are crazy enough to think they can change the world are the ones who do."
—Steve Jobs

Today, we recognize that nitric oxide is one of the most important molecules produced in humans. The loss of nitric oxide is responsible for most, if not all, age-related diseases. In fact, the major diseases are poorly managed by conventional drug therapies. The science of chronic disease is very clear. There are 4 hallmarks of all chronic disease, and it doesn't matter if it is Alzheimer's Disease, cardiovascular disease, diabetes, neurological disease, kidney disease, liver disease, pulmonary disorders or any other clinical issue. Those 4 common problems are:

1. Decreased blood flow, hypoxia and/or ischemia
2. Inflammation
3. Oxidative stress
4. Immune dysfunction

You should now recognize from reading this book that nitric oxide corrects all four of these common hallmarks of all chronic disease. Therefore, nitric oxide-based therapies can completely and profoundly change the way we treat patients and manage chronic disease. Let's just review each of these to reveal how simply restoring nitric oxide can address each.

Decreased blood flow and oxygen delivery to organs, tissues and cells are the root cause of all diseases. Hypoxia refers to low oxygen delivery. You can have sufficient blood flow but without proper oxygen delivery, the cells cannot function.

Ischemia is when there is a disruption in circulation or blood flow. Ischemia occurs during a heart attack or an ischemic stroke when a blood clot blocks the blood vessels and anything downstream the clot will not get any blood supply. This leads to tissue death. Nitric oxide when produced causes blood vessels to relax and dilate which opens up the blood vessels so they can accommodate more blood and oxygen delivery. Nitric oxide is the main vasodilator produced in the body. Without sufficient nitric oxide production, the blood vessels do not dilate and over time they become chronically constricted which leads to high blood pressure or hypertension.

Hypertension is the number one risk factor for cardiovascular disease. The high pressure in the arteries causes them to harden (arteriosclerosis) and leads to further damage. The functional loss of nitric oxide production is called endothelial dysfunction. When you provide nitric oxide or restore the endogenous production of nitric oxide, the blood vessels dilate and lead to improved blood flow and oxygen delivery. This tells us that the body never stops responding to nitric oxide, it just loses its ability to produce it. You cannot overcome low blood flow without correcting nitric oxide production.

Inflammation is a word that most everyone has heard. Inflammation is the driver of disease, and most Americans are inflamed. Inflammation has been called the silent killer, especially as it related to cardiovascular disease. Most people do not feel vascular inflammation. It is the inflammation inside

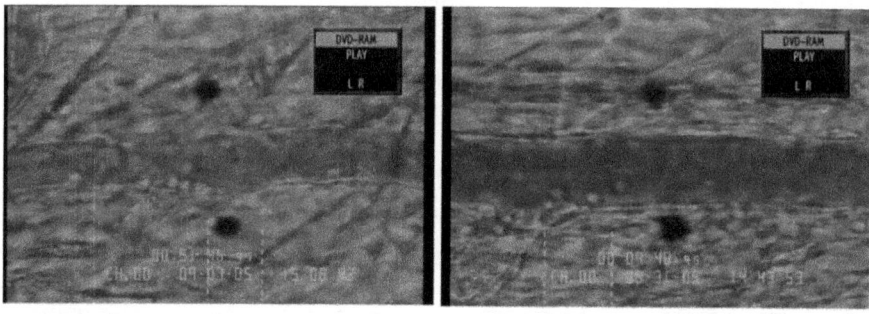

On the left is an artery without sufficient nitric oxide. You can see the blood vessel is constricted and there are several immune cells stuck to the blood vessel and some that have even migrated across the endothelium. The picture on the right is your blood vessel on nitric oxide. The blood vessel is more dilated and open. The immune cells do not stick to the inner lining of the blood vessel, and we get better blood flow with less inflammation.

The Secret of Nitric Oxide

the blood vessels that lead to plaque instability, plaque rupture leading to heart attack and stroke.

The first and earliest stages of chronic disease called microvascular inflammation are when our immune cells and platelets start to stick to the lining of the blood vessels. Nitric oxide produced by the lining of our blood vessels, the endothelium, is what keeps adhesion molecules from being expressed on the blood vessels. When we lose the ability to produce nitric oxide, there is an upregulation of adhesion molecules which attracts our immune cells to stick to the inside lining of our blood vessels, platelets become activated which causes the blood to clot and this leads to an eventual obstruction in the blood vessels and causes stenosis or an obstruction of the arteries.

As shown in the picture on page 212, we can look at blood vessels and see how inflamed they are. Using real time intravital microscopy, we can visualize and count how many immune cells are sticking to the blood vessels. The picture on the left is from a blood vessel that is extremely inflamed from an inflammatory diet. The picture on the right is the same blood vessel after eating an inflammatory diet but given nitric oxide and restored the production of nitric oxide in the lining of the blood vessel. This was a very important experiment because it revealed to us that even in severe

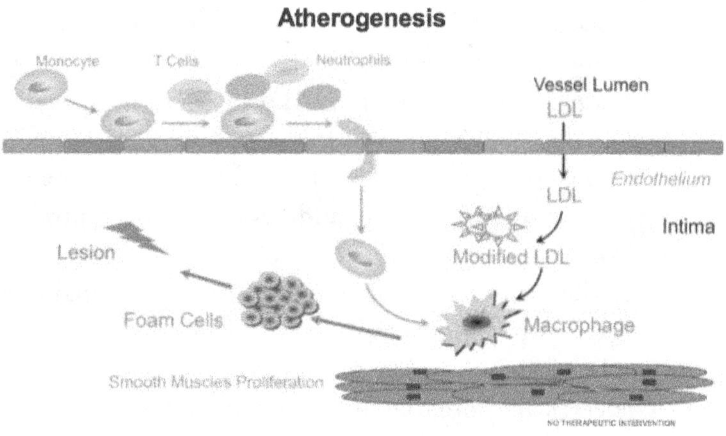

A cartoon representation of vascular inflammation. Immune cells stick to the lining of the blood vessels, then migrate through and then cause oxidative stress and immune dysfunction leading to cardiovascular disease.

inflammation, nitric oxide would completely suppress it, even with no change in the diet.

Science also reveals to us that if you can stop the monocytes and neutrophils from sticking to the lining of the blood vessels, you can completely prevent and treat cardiovascular disease. You cannot do this without restoring the production of nitric oxide. Fortunately for those reading this book, I know how to do that, and we have product technology that can do this for you. However, you can do this on your own.

You can change your diet and eat more foods that are high in antioxidants. You can eat more green leafy vegetables, provided you don't use mouthwash or antacids. You can start exercising more and collectively, this will improve your nitric oxide production.

The key to combatting cardiovascular disease, early death and becoming sick and disabled is to make sure you do not lose the ability to produce nitric oxide.

Oxidative stress is another major contributor to chronic disease and one of the four hallmarks. Oxidative stress refers to the production of oxygen radicals which steal electrons and cause oxidation. Think of this as rusting from the inside out. There are three main sources of oxidative stress in the human body:

> 1. NADPH oxidase (nicotinamide adenine dinucleotide phosphate oxidase) is an enzyme that is normally dormant and only becomes activated when during inflammation or infection. The activated NADPH oxidase generates superoxide which has roles in animal immune response to kill bacteria or other pathogens. The problem occurs when the enzyme remains active and continuously produces superoxide.
>
> 2. The mitochondrial electron transport chain can produce superoxide and oxygen radicals when the mitochondria are not functioning properly. There has to be an electrical potential maintained across the inter-mitochondrial membrane to allow for cellular energy production of ATP. When there is a leakage of electrons across the membrane, this leads to superoxide and oxygen radical production. Mitochondria are a major source of

oxidative stress if they are not working properly. Not only are the cells not getting efficient energy production, but the cells are damaged due to all the oxidative stress.

3. Nitric oxide synthase enzyme when uncoupled and dysfunctional produces superoxide instead of nitric oxide. This happens when you give a high dose L-arginine to an uncoupled enzyme. That is why taking L-arginine can be harmful in some patients.

You may ask how nitric oxide can correct the three main sources of oxidative stress. Well, science is very clear and there are a number of very important scientific studies that have been published clearly demonstrating how nitric oxide corrects all three. Firstly, if the cell can produce sufficient nitric oxide, the NO that is being produced modifies the NADPH oxidase enzyme and causes it to go from an active state back to a dormant state. When this happens the enzyme no longer produces superoxide, and the cell can recover from the oxidative stress. Without nitric oxide, the NADPH oxidase enzyme remains active and continuously causes oxidation and oxidative stress.

There is also sufficient scientific evidence that nitric oxide can help recouple the electron transport chain of the mitochondria and suppress superoxide production. Nitric oxide can modify certain complexes of the electron transport chain and prevent the leakage of electrons thereby maintaining the electrical potential of across the inner membrane. Nitric oxide also improves the efficiency of oxygen utilization for energy production. Without nitric oxide, mitochondria become dysfunctional and continuously produce superoxide causing more oxidative stress.

Paradoxically, the enzyme that normally produces nitric oxide, can produce superoxide when the NOS enzyme becomes uncoupled and dysfunctional. Too much oxidative stress causes oxidation of a very important molecule called tetrahydrobiopterin or BH4. When BH4 becomes oxidized, it causes the NOS enzyme to uncouple and can no longer produce nitric oxide. It then turns into a superoxide synthase. You can see how things quickly get out of control if our body has too much oxidative stress. Oxidative stress shuts down nitric oxide production and without nitric oxide, we have uncontrolled oxidative stress. We published a seminal paper back in 2009 showing how our nitric oxide technology can recouple the NOS enzyme by protecting BH4 from becoming oxidized. It appears to be self-fixing.

Immune dysfunction is a major problem in chronic diseases. Our immune system is designed to protect us from infection and to help with tissue repair. Immune dysfunction occurs when our immune system loses its ability to regulate itself or when it loses the ability to recognize foreign matter vs. human tissues. This is the basis for auto-immune disease when our own immune system starts attacking our own cells.

Auto-immune diseases such as Lupus, rheumatoid arthritis, Hashimoto's thyroiditis, psoriasis, Sjogren syndrome, Grave's disease, Celiac disease, multiple sclerosis, myasthenia gravis just to name a few are all caused by our immune system attacking our own body. Macrophages are a type of white blood cell that play an important role in the human immune system and carry out various functions including engulfing and digesting microorganisms; clearing out debris and dead cells; and stimulating other cells involved in immune function.

There are different types of macrophages called M1 and M2 macrophages. M1 macrophages inhibit cell proliferation and causes tissue damage while M2 macrophages promote cell proliferation and tissue repair. M2 are protective and M1 are damaging. M2 macrophages are anti-inflammatory, regulate tissue repair and regeneration, involved in angiogenesis or the formation of new blood vessels and are generally considered the good guys. M1 macrophages are pro-inflammatory, and when they lose their regulation contribute to chronic inflammation.

Part of the tissue repair and acute inflammatory response is the switching of M1 to M2 macrophages to turn off the inflammation and repair any cells and tissues that were affected by any infection or inflammatory response. It just so happens that nitric oxide is responsible for the conversion of M1 to M2. So, if your body has lost its ability to produce nitric oxide, the M1 macrophages never get the signal to convert to M2 and we are left with a chronic inflammatory condition with severe immune dysfunction. If we can restore the production of nitric oxide, evidence suggests that we can switch M1 to M2 and shut down the inflammatory response and turn off the immune dysfunction seen in all chronic diseases.

Now let's marvel at just how smart the human body is. If we can give the body nitric oxide or restore the body's ability to make nitric oxide, then we can increase blood flow, reduce inflammation, inhibit oxidative stress and shut down immune dysfunction. This basically gets to the root cause of all chronic diseases. This means that there is really no disease or drug indication where nitric oxide at the right dose would not provide therapeutic benefit.

This really gets me excited because there have been efforts over the past 30 years by companies to develop safe and effective nitric oxide drugs. To date, no company has been successful at bringing nitric oxide drugs to market. Where my technology and companies are today puts us light years ahead of any other company trying to develop nitric oxide drugs.

There have been several fortuitous events or real blessings that allowed us to get to where we are. In normal times, it takes on average 10 years and more than $800 million to get a drug through FDA clinical trials and on the market. This is why most early-stage biotech and drug companies fail. It is very difficult to raise hundreds of millions of dollars from investors when historically 95% of these companies never make it past phase 1 which is designed to demonstrate safety of the drug.

We all know COVID was a complete disruption to the world economy and our own lives. One of the blessings of COVID was that it forced the U.S. government and the FDA to fast-track drugs that could have an impact on COVID disease. In response to the novel COVID-19, the administration at the time instructed the FDA to quickly create in March 2020 the Coronavirus Treatment Acceleration Program (CTAP), which was designed to help facilitate the development of drugs and biologics (other than vaccines) for COVID-19 therapeutics. As previously described, we quickly filed an investigative new drug (IND) application for our nitric oxide drug. Our IND was approved in July 2020, and we began treating COVID patients in December 2020.

The first 100 patients were considered a phase 1 study. We had to monitor the patients for up to one hour after dosing them to ensure there wasn't an unsafe drop in blood pressure or any other side effects. We enrolled over 550 sick, highly susceptible patients, many on numerous different medications, and we did not have a single adverse event with our drug. There was no safety signal whatsoever.

All drugs have side effects but what we were doing was different. Our drug technology was not a synthetic compound that inhibited some biochemical reaction like most other drugs. We delivered a naturally produced molecule as doses that could mimic or recapitulate what the body would normally do. In this case, we did not expect, nor did we see any side effects. This is how drug discovery and drug design should work. Give the body what it needs, and the body heals itself.

It just happens that most people that are sick or susceptible to chronic illness cannot produce sufficient nitric oxide. So, we must give it to them directly through our drug and product technology. We continue to move our drugs forward and hopefully will soon have nitric oxide drugs approved and on the market.

Ischemic Heart Disease

Atherosclerotic heart disease (ASHD) affects 126 million individuals globally. In the U.S., the prevalence of ASHD is 1,584 per 100,000 or approximately 53 million individuals in the U.S. The CDC reports 696,962 deaths per year due to heart disease with the majority due to ASHD. In the U.S. there are 605,000 first time heart attacks and a total of 805,000 heart attacks or myocardial infarctions per year.

In 2021 there were approximately 9 million patients in the U.S. with anginal symptoms. Anginal therapy is important to relieve chest pain and increase the amount and duration of activities a patient can perform without chest pain or angina. It is believed that by reducing the frequency and duration of ischemia, the incidence of heart attacks can be reduced though this has not been proven for all angina treatments.

Beta blockers reduce mortality in patients with ischemic heart disease that have had a previous heart attack. While calcium channel blockers and organic nitrates have been shown to reduce angina, those therapies have not been shown to reduce heart attacks and prolong life. One major problem with organic nitrate therapies is the development of tolerance over time. In carefully controlled studies it is known that organic nitrates work for a few hours but there is no benefit after the 6-hour dose. This reveals that cornerstone therapy of chest pain (angina) is not effective long term.

Today interventional cardiology has taken on these patients. Patients with angina often undergo angioplasty and stenting. Those patients with angina often have repeat procedures or are referred for coronary artery bypass surgery (CABGS). Angina may persist after stenting or CABGS and patients are placed on nitrate, beta blocker and/or a calcium channel blocker therapy. Given the problem with nitrate tolerance, the utility of nitrate therapy is questionable. Our nitric oxide drug which does not develop tolerance will provide a new safe and effective therapy for ischemic heart disease.

Ischemic non-obstructive coronary artery disease (INOCA)

There is a growing number of patients with ischemic, non-obstructive coronary artery disease (INOCA) for which there is no effective treatment. These patients with signs of obstructive coronary artery disease including angina, and shortness of breath, upon angiogram reveal no major obstructions in the large coronary arteries.

It turns out that up to 70% of patients undergoing an invasive assessment of chest pain do not show obstructive coronary artery disease. INOCA patients present with chest pain and have an increased incidence of cardiovascular events, repeat hospitalizations, reduced quality of life and a higher mortality compared to patients without INOCA.

The etiology of INOCA has been found to involve coronary vasospasm and/or small vessel coronary occlusion disease. The arteries coming off the main arteries are not well dilated and thus the heart is not getting enough oxygen to supply the heart muscle. INOCA is more common in women than men.

The treatment of INOCA is most unsatisfactory. This was an obvious indication for our NO drug since we knew it could dilate small vessels. The pathophysiology involves inadequate endogenous nitric oxide production or release. Organic nitrate therapies are ineffective due to tolerance developing. Alternative anti-anginal therapies such as beta blockers and ivabradine are ineffective.

In fact, beta blockers may worsen INOCA since blocking beta mediated coronary dilatation can worsen angina and underlying ischemia. Calcium channel blockers may be beneficial, but do not completely alleviate symptoms or the underlying pathophysiology. Currently it is estimated that there are 3-4 million affected individuals with INOCA in the U.S. We feel confident that our orally disintegrating nitric oxide lozenge will provide substantial improvement in symptoms, providing an anti-anginal indication for this population.

The development of anti-anginal drugs is well understood with considerable precedents set at FDA. We currently have clinical trials designed to investigate our nitric oxide drug for INOCA.

Alzheimer's Drug Program

Alzheimer's disease is the most common form of dementia, a progressive neurologic disease that slowly destroys memory and thinking skills and eventually the ability to carry out activity of daily living. Currently there is no therapy that has been satisfactorily shown to slow or stop the progression of Alzheimer's disease.

Recently a research team led by Feixiong Cheng Ph.D. from the Cleveland Clinic Genomic Medical Institute using computational methodology reported that in a review of a large database (7 million patients) that patients taking Viagra (sildenafil) had a 69% reduction in the incidence of Alzheimer's disease. This is very interesting and exciting since drugs like Viagra work through an increase in blood flow.

Sildenafil is an inhibitor of phosphodiesterase 5 (PDE5) an enzyme that prevents the breakdown of cGMP. When nitric oxide is produced in the body, it leads to an increase in cGMP. By increasing cGMP due to NO production, sildenafil can improve blood flow through vasodilation.

Our thoughts are that if you do not have sufficient blood flow to the brain, you can't get the good stuff, oxygen and nutrients, to the cells of the brain and there is a build-up of metabolic waste. These are the amyloid plaques and tau protein tangles that are present in Alzheimer's patients. Therefore, the amyloid plaque that develops in Alzheimer's patients is a consequence of their disease and not necessarily a cause of disease. That is the primary reason that all drugs targeting the amyloid plaques, and the misfolded proteins have failed in clinical trials.

It is the wrong target to get to the root cause of Alzheimer's Disease. Nitric oxide signals through the increase in production of cGMP resulting in smooth muscle relaxation and vasodilation. The increase in brain blood flow provides the elimination of protein degradation products. Vascular abnormalities often precede Alzheimer's dementia. Imaging through MRI and SPECT scans often reveal hypoperfusion or reduced blood flow in patients with dementia and Alzheimer's.

Alzheimer's has also been referred to as Diabetes Type 3 where there is insulin resistance and impaired glucose uptake in the brain. Just so happens nitric oxide increases cGMP production, cytochrome P450 activity and heat shock protein 70. Heat shock protein may play a protective role in Alzheimer's. Additionally, heat shock protein 70 plays a crucial role in preventing protein misfolding and in inhibiting protein aggregation involving a class of proteins potentially involved in Alzheimer's disease pathogenesis.

Another potential mechanism for NO being beneficial in Alzheimer's is the improvement in neuron excitability by improving the function of voltage-gated potassium channel activity. Science reveals that our nitric oxide drug therapy will decrease the beta amyloid through the increase in activity of genes involved in antioxidant defense, detoxification, autophagy and cytoprotection.

In April of 2023, I gave a lecture at the Personalized Lifestyle Medical Institute at the invitation of Dr. Jeff Bland. I presented our work on nitric oxide. Afterwards, David Perlmutter, M.D., approached me and was excited about the potential of nitric oxide to combat Alzheimer's and other neurological disorders. Dr. Perlmutter and I had several discussions regarding the science of NO and how it may correct all aspects of Alzheimer's disease. Dr. Perlmutter agreed to come on board our drug company, Bryan Therapeutics, Inc, to lead our drug trials on Alzheimer's.

I have been a huge fan of Dr. Perlmutter for many years. I first met him in 2011 at the Integrative Health Symposium in New York and we had developed a friendship since then. Now we have one of the world's top neurologists and Alzheimer's experts on board, leading our efforts to cure one of the world's most feared diseases. We feel confident our nitric oxide release drug will be beneficial in Alzheimer's patients based on known mechanisms of nitric oxide below:

1. Increase in cGMP and improvement in cerebral blood flow.
2. Decreased inflammation, oxidative stress, and immune dysfunction.
3. Improvement in insulin sensitivity and energy metabolism.
4. Activate neuroprotective signaling and prevent misfolding of proteins.

Wound care and Diabetic Ulcers

My experience with treating my dad's wounds and pressure ulcers successfully with nitric oxide inspired me to bring a topical nitric oxide drug to market. The field of wound care has seen little advance in many years. We still treat wounds today the same way we did more than 50 years ago.

In total, chronic wounds (e.g., pressure injury, vascular ulcers, and diabetic ulcers) affect between 2.4 and 4.5 million people in the United States, causing a significant humanistic and financial burden. The extended healing time utilizing currently available treatments, topicals and bandages, leaves the patient at a much greater risk of developing a potentially devastating infection. This can lead to hospitalization or death, and a higher cost of treatment. Furthermore, limited wound care resources are overburdened, and institutions face greater liability.

ETIOLOGY OF CHRONIC WOUNDS
- Hallmark of any pressure injury or diabetic wound is ischemia/insufficient blood flow.
- Hallmark of many chronic or potentially fatal wounds is presence of infection.
- Lack of blood flow to the wound bed preventing immune response and proper healing.
- Patients with co-morbidities associated with poor circulation are at greatest risk of slow healing and chronic wounds.

Topical nitric oxide products produce nitric oxide gas. Nitric Oxide is a fast-acting molecule that is generated when the contents of both chambers are mixed. The images below and top of the next page illustrate how blood flow improves at the site of application within seconds.

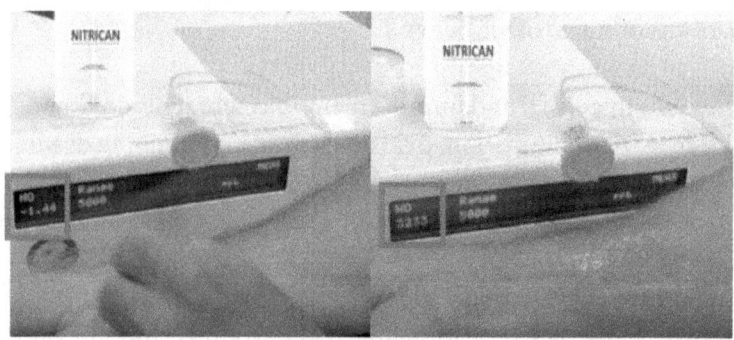

Utilizing a Nitric Oxide detector to verify the production of NO. Note the NO generation resulting in an increase of blood flow at the site of application turning the skin pink within seconds.

The Secret of Nitric Oxide

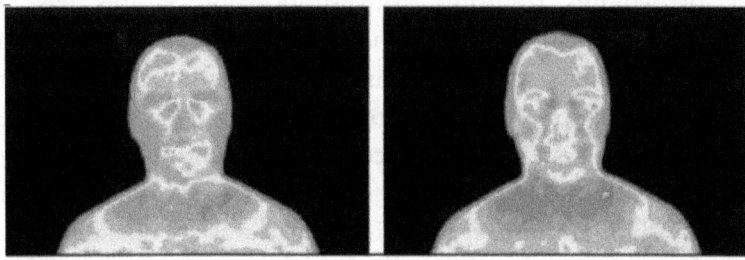

Utilizing infrared photography to illustrate the increase of blood flow before and 30 seconds after application of the topical nitric oxide on the face, neck and chest.

Nitric Oxide generation is the result of a patent pending process and the combination of very specific ingredients. The dual chamber pump bottle conveniently dispenses the serum and the most active form of Nitric Oxide. We can verify nitric oxide release by using a gas phase nitric oxide analyzer to detect the production of NO. Note the NO generation resulting in an increase of blood flow at the site of application, turning the skin pink within seconds. Also using infrared photography (thermography) to illustrate the increase of blood flow before and 30 seconds after application of our topical nitric oxide on the face and neck and chest.

The main stay of wound care therapy is negative pressure using a wound vac combined with topical and oral antibiotics to kill any infections. Wounds due to pressure injury, vascular ulcer, diabetes ulcers, trauma or secondary to surgical procedures affect between 3 to 6 million people in the U.S. Wounds can cause significant disability, pain and be a nidus for infection.

The longer the healing process, the greater the likelihood of infection and the greater the patient burden, the greater risk of developing deadly sepsis from the wound. Chronic diabetes and/or ischemic ulcers are a very considerable source of disability as well as a source of infection, often leading to hospitalization and at times death. There is indeed a high societal cost of these conditions. Improvement in wound healing would decrease the societal cost, patient suffering and potential for infection.

One may ask why wounds are so difficult to heal and a festering source for infection. Wounds most often occur in areas with insufficient blood supply. Blood supply resulting in adequate oxygenation is critical for effective and rapid wound healing. But patients with diabetes, ischemic ulcers, trauma, or wounds resulting from surgical procedures have poor vascularization of the surrounding areas decreasing the likelihood of healing.

The wound is often open permitting bacterial colonization. The bacterial presence along with poor blood supply, compromises the effectiveness of the body's immune system to gain access to the wound. These problems all combined to make wound healing difficult and thus favor the development of progressively more serious infections. Without adequate circulation, covering the wound may facilitate the development of anerobic infections and thus potential sepsis. Just keeping the wound clean and awaiting the body's natural healing capacity for healing often proves inadequate for complete wound healing, especially with infected wounds.

We believe that improving the vascularization of the wound while killing any resident infection in the wound will increase the rate of healing, as well as the completeness of the healing process. It just happens that nitric oxide does both of these. Due to the success of our topical serum in cosmetics and skin care, we had several physicians begin to use the serum on wounds, surgical site infections and non-healing ulcers.

The results were unlike anything seen in wound care in decades. I feel confident that our topical nitric oxide drugs will revolutionize wound care and save the lives of millions of people. Nitric oxide-based drugs and therapeutics are certainly the future of medicine. Nitric oxide is required for stem cell mobilization and differentiation so even the future of regenerative medicine and the use of stem cells is dependent upon nitric oxide.

I hope that with our model of drug discovery and drug development utilizing the concept of restorative physiology rather than pharmacology, we can begin to develop drugs that are safe without side effects and address the root cause of human disease. If you give the body what it needs, it will heal itself.

Our strategy is to give the body nitric oxide so that it can deliver oxygen and nutrients to every cell in the body and allow the body to do what it is designed to do. In this case, there will be no side effects. This is the future of drug development and treatment of every major human disease known.

CHAPTER 22
Learnings From Failure, Challengess And Persistence
"Success consists of going from failure to failure without loss of enthusiasm."
—Winston Churchill

The longer I live the more I realize how my life has been directed by God. I could never have imagined that everything and every situation I have endured throughout my life was preparing me for the next phase. I live with no regrets. Every action, decision and person with whom I have interacted has served a purpose in my life's journey.

Obviously, there are some people that have had a severe negative impact on my life and on my life's work. There are others that I could not have survived without. My divorce, although traumatic and heart breaking at the time, ended up being a blessing.

My first marriage introduced me to the Catholic faith and I became Catholic. I loved the structure, discipline and personal relationship with God. I also learned about courage. We both knew we were unhappy, but we had the courage to pull the trigger and initiate the divorce. For that I am thankful. You learn who your real friends are in the worst of times but also in the best of times.

People whom I thought were my friends and partners completely betrayed me. Those are the toughest lessons. Nothing is more difficult than having someone you trust and respect lie to you, betray you and then try to destroy you and your life's work. However, every success story shares this similar experience. In a world of good vs. evil, I have certainly witnessed the evil of people and their ill intent. My faith in God, trust in doing what is right to serve others has always seen me through the toughest and darkest of times. My driving forces are fear of disappointment and fear of hurting other people's feelings. I recognize this about myself and fortunately or unfortunately it drives my decisions.

Each of us is driven by different motivations. Fear is the most motivating factor on earth, but fear does not have to be a bad thing as long as it does not debilitate you—if it is what motivates you. We are reminded in Isaiah, "So do not fear, for I am with you; do not be dismayed, for I am your God, I will strengthen you and help you; I will uphold you with my righteous right hand."

The move from full-time academia to full-time entrepreneur was a difficult transition. It was a situation of do or die. I felt comfortable that I could survive on the income from my patent royalties, but I had no real job or income. I had to make our companies successful. The scary part was I knew that companies with great products and great technology many times failed. I also realized that many companies with inferior products succeeded. I knew I had the best products on the planet that would change people's lives. All I had to do was assemble the right team and right people to get our message out there and educate the market. Even though I had many lawsuits against me for speaking the truth, I became a trusted voice in the nitric oxide field. I had my business partner since 2010, Susan Shaffer leading and running the companies. I was attracting top talent in medicine and science to lead our drug discovery program. I had one of the most qualified and experienced cardiologists running our clinical trials, John Somberg, M.D.

Dr. Somberg has conducted dozens of FDA clinical trials and has received FDA approval on dozens of new drugs. Through Dr. Somberg, we developed a great relationship with the FDA and have received great guidance on our drug studies and on the design of our clinical trials. Now, through our meetings with the FDA, we know exactly what we need to do for our drug programs: I just had to go raise the money to get it done and let the drugs perform as I know they will.

The most difficult part of all of this, for me, was understanding those who had tried to impede our progress. I just keep my head down and try not to be distracted or lose focus on what I am trying to do. I know and I've always known that nitric oxide-based therapies and product technology had the potential to change the world and make people better.

There are very few career options and jobs that give people the opportunity to change people's lives for the better daily. Over the course of the 15 years that I have been involved in entrepreneurship and commercializing my discoveries, I have received hundreds and probably thousands of emails, phone calls and text from people who claim I have saved their lives or have made some profound impact on their lives or someone they love. That is the power of nitric oxide and that is the power of the nitric oxide technology that I have been privileged to bring to the market. There is an old saying that if you change one person's life, you have changed the world. That one person's world has certainly changed. I'm most proud and grateful for the many lives we have changed.

The good news is that we are just getting started. The field of nitric oxide is still in its infancy. Although there are now over 200,000 published scientific papers on nitric oxide, its application and utility in medicine and everyday life have not yet materialized. Science is clear. There is really no disease where nitric oxide at the right dose at the right time in the right patient would not be beneficial. The only remaining piece is to educate and inform the masses, both consumers and health care practitioners, on the importance of nitric oxide. That is the primary objective of this book.

It is my hope that from reading this book, you leave with an appreciation of the power of nitric oxide but also a clear understanding of how nitric oxide is produced in the human body so all of you can make informed and educated decisions on how to personally improve and restore your nitric oxide.

I've been very fortunate and blessed to be the first and only person to develop a solid dose form of bioactive nitric oxide gas. I've had many mentors and colleagues over the years that I have learned from. As Isaac Newton famously said in 1675, "If I have seen further, it is by standing on the shoulders of giants."

There have been many giants in the field of nitric oxide that made many seminal discoveries. I've been privileged to learn from them, to train under them and to collaborate with them. I have seen what others have seen and I have thought what others have not thought and I have done what many said was impossible. I believe that has been the key to my success to date is that I have thought differently. I have survived the ridicule, the violent opposition and strong forces against me, and most importantly I have stuck to science and revealed its fundamental truth in human physiology. The future of medicine is dependent upon nitric oxide. We must maintain and defend the integrity of the science of nitric oxide and hold those companies accountable that continue to exploit the field by providing products that do not have any nitric oxide activity nor provide any nitric oxide benefit to the consumers.

The two most important dates in one's life are the day you are born and the day you realize WHY you were born. Although it took me a while to figure out my path in life and my WHY in life, I feel as if I am on the right path. We have accomplished a lot over the past few decades, but we have so much more work to do.

I hope this book inspires and motivates everyone who reads it but more importantly I hope the information shared in this book opens your eyes to the importance of nitric oxide. Knowledge is power only if it is acted on. So, every day I wake up to a new day full of optimism. Every day for me starts with prayer and gratitude. As I sit in my infrared sauna, I open my hallow app, listen to the scripture and focus on how I can be better than I was yesterday. Every day I want to be a better person than I was the day before. Success is a journey, not a destination.

I always reflect on the day before, prepare a mental game plan for the day ahead and how I am going to execute my plan. No matter how bad life gets, I recognize that it can always be worse. No matter how good life gets, I recognize it will not always continue and there will certainly be some not so good times in the future. I have been blessed beyond what I probably deserve and for that I am extremely grateful. Today I live with a servant's heart and do my best to serve others. My hope is to leave a legacy from the brief time I have on this earth and more importantly to have life everlasting.

CHAPTER 23
What's Next?

"First they ignore you, then they laugh at you, then they fight you, then you win."

—Muhatma Gandhi

As I finished the final draft of this book for publication, a more than 3-year lawsuit is over. Both parties agreed to settle just prior to our trial date. I am proud that I stood firmly and fought vigilantly. It is not easy to stand on principle, especially when it costs millions of dollars in legal fees. What is important for me is that people now know that I will always fight for what is right.

I will defend my science and reveal the truth. I will not compromise my principles and beliefs even though it may be very expensive to defend. I wanted to set a precedent for me and my companies.

There is nothing that will or can stop me from making sure my nitric oxide products are accessible to every person around the globe. This includes drug therapy, dietary supplements, skin care and beauty products, oral care including toothpastes and mouth rinses, medical devices and diagnostics in every product category around the world.

We have been very successful at bringing nitric oxide supplements and skin care products to market. In fact, my products are the most successful products on the market. However, still too few people are looking for nitric oxide-based supplements. I've spent many years speaking on the importance of the oral microbiome and nitric oxide production.

I have finally cracked the code on developing a nitric oxide friendly toothpaste and mouth rinse that will help eradicate the pathogenic oral bacteria while supporting and maintaining a healthy and diverse microbiome. Everyone brushes their teeth (at least I hope) and two out of three Americans use mouthrinse. I truly believe our oral care line of products will have a major impact on global health. It is clear that fluoride-based toothpaste and antiseptic mouthwashes are completely destroying the oral microbiome, leading to a loss of nitric oxide and causing rapid acceleration of disease.

A simple switch to our nitric oxide friendly oral care products will end this practice. We and others have shown that using mouthwash destroys the microbiome, leading to loss of nitric oxide production and increase in blood pressure. Now we have an oral solution that can support and improve the oral microbiome, enhance nitric oxide production and perhaps (I'm betting yes) that we can help improve and support healthy blood pressures. Think about that. Simply by changing your toothpaste and using our biome friendly mouth rinse, we can get an improvement in blood pressure. With high blood pressure being the number 1 risk factor for the number 1 killer of men and women worldwide, this simple solution will transform public health and perhaps finally lead to a reduction in cardiovascular disease.

Pets are a part of many people's lives. We are in the process of developing a line of nitric oxide pet products for our furry pet friends. As an owner of thoroughbred race horses, we are developing a line of products to enhance performance in all mammals. We have even seen instances of a reduction in pulmonary bleeds in race horses. If we can get horses performing better without bleeding and eliminate the need for diuretics, like Lasix during races, the sport and the horses will be much better for it.

Nitric oxide will not fix, solve or cure every major illness or all suffering around the world, but what it will do is give the body an opportunity to heal and respond better to all other treatment modalities. I wake up each day with excitement for what we are doing for public health.

The U.S. election of 2024 reveals that most Americans want a change and want to make America healthy again. We are moving our drugs through the FDA and hopefully within a short few years, we will have safe and effective nitric oxide drugs approved and on the market for physicians to give to their patients. In the meantime, I will continue to educate, inform and reveal the real science of nitric oxide so consumers can make informed decisions and choose products that actually work.

The health of Americans and the future of medicine will be fundamentally improved by taking steps to restore nitric oxide production and by integrating nitric oxide-based product technology into your daily regimen. My goal is to build a global nitric oxide centric company that offers safe and efficacious products in every major product category around the world. My companies are not for sale. I am not building a global company for some larger pharmaceutical company to buy us up and then shelve the technology.

Nitric oxide is a disruptive technology. When people can address the root cause of their illness, condition or disease through our approach of restorative physiology, patients can begin to wean off of prescription drugs. This has never occurred before in the history of Western medicine. The approach of big pharma is to get every person on as many medications as possible.

Remember, medicine is a business. In fact, one of the largest global markets. The goal of any business is to acquire as many customers as possible and keep those customers as long as possible. Today, our medical system is designed to do just that. When we begin to wean patients off of drugs, then this begins to disrupt the market share of many pharmaceutical companies. Nitric oxide product technology can and will do just that. My goal is to make sure people all over the world have the most up-to-date scientific and medical information so they can become empowered to take control of their own health and hopefully avoid the need for medication. Don't get me wrong, there will always be a need for certain medications for a short period of time. However, the human body is not designed to be subjected to a synthetic compound for the duration of a lifetime. The scientific and medical community can do better and we will do better.

The truth is that the secret to your best health is already inside you. It is nitric oxide and this single molecule can transform how you heal, how you age and how you perform. This is not just about science in a lab. The science is proven, clinically translated and has already changed the lives of millions of people. Imagine a world where optimized nitric oxide becomes as common as taking a daily vitamin—a world where we are not just extending lifespan but improving health span, the years we live free from disease and full of vitality. The science is here. The tools are here. The future of wellness is brighter than ever and it starts at the cellular level and the molecular level with nitric oxide.

People always ask me what is next for me and what keeps me going. Although I have lived a very full life, full of many victories but far more defeats and failures than victories and successes, I feel my life is just beginning. I have survived the absolute worst events that any human can ever encounter. Yet here I am today not only surviving but thriving and I feel as empowered as I have ever been. The old saying that what doesn't kill you makes you stronger is valid. I have struggled from time to time but none of those events killed me. They made me question my actions and what I could have done to make things different. We cannot change past decisions or what resulted from those decisions. All we can do is learn from our past experiences and integrate those learnings going forward. Today, I feel as if there is nothing I cannot accomplish and there is nothing that can or will get in my way. I have weathered the storm. With the Grace and Mercy of God, I have survived, but more importantly I have thrived and will continue to thrive.

If you found this book valuable, please share this book with a friend or family member. Keep up with the latest scientific breakthroughs by following my YouTube channel at drnathansbryanNitricOxide.

Thank you for taking time to read and learn about nitric oxide. Our most valuable asset is our time and health. I appreciate you sharing your time with me and hopefully I've provided valuable information to improve your health.

CASE REPORTS OF LIFE CHANGING EFFECTS OF NITRIC OXIDE

1. Nitric oxide lozenge brings back elderly woman in coma.

Case Study: When we first launched our nitric oxide lozenge, I often donated products to a few of my physician friends. One was a physician in my hometown of Caldwell Texas. His 99-year-old grandmother was found unresponsive and unconscious in her home. She was brought to the emergency room in an ambulance. She had Do Not Resuscitate (DNR) orders, so they admitted her and gave her supportive care with supplemental oxygen. She was found to have heart arrhythmia, low blood pressure and low respiration rate. She remained unconscious. She was only a few weeks away from her 100th birthday. Her grandson and her physician decided to give her the nitric oxide lozenge since there was really nothing else, they could do. He crushed it up and placed it in her mouth and then squirted a little bit of water in her mouth to help dissolve the powder. He then left and went to nurses' station. About 20 minutes later, the nurse came running to let him know that grandma had woken up and was alert. He went back into the room, she was alert, her heart was in normal sinus rhythm, her blood pressure was normal, and her respiration was normal. The nitric oxide appeared to restore blood flow to her heart to restore electrical conductance. After hearing this, I was confident we had a product that would change the world.

2. Nitric oxide lozenge saves the life of a 15-year-old patient with resistant hypertension, kidney disease, heart disease and liver disease.

Case Study: *In February of 2010, a 15-year-old pediatric patient presented at Texas Childrens Hospital with blood pressure of 210/115 mmHg. He was admitted into the pediatric intensive care unit. The patient had a history of argininosuccinic aciduria, an inborn error in metabolism that caused a urea cycle disorder and elevated ammonia.*

He was on several different anti-hypertensive prescription medications that were not managing his blood pressure. In collaboration with Baylor College of Medicine, we have been researching this condition for several years. We discovered that these patients were deficient in nitric oxide due to their lack of an enzyme that is necessary to regulate NO production. Based on our research, his physician started giving him isosorbide dinitrate, a drug that is metabolized into nitric oxide.

After 4 days on this drug, his blood pressure came down and he was sent home. He did well for several months and then developed tolerance to the isosorbide, meaning that he no longer responded to this type of medication. In February 2011, the patient came back to Texas Childrens Hospital taking isosorbide (20 mg) 4 times a day and his blood pressure was still 185/110 mmHg. We made the patient a nitric oxide generating lozenge and started him on the lozenge. Within 4 hours, his blood pressure had normalized to 135/85 mmHg. This was remarkable since no other medication would work on this patient.

This was a case where the nitric oxide lozenge saved this kid's life since it was the only thing that would normalize his blood pressure. Furthermore, his kidney disease resolved in 3 weeks and his heart disease reversed after 5 months. This was another revelation on the life-saving effects of nitric oxide on complex medical situations.

This revealed to us that even in the case of a genetic disorder, nitric oxide still had a remarkable effect. The body never loses its ability to respond to nitric oxide, it simply loses its ability to produce it. We published this study in the *American Journal of Human Genetics* in 2011. It made headline news and led to a small documentary on this case.

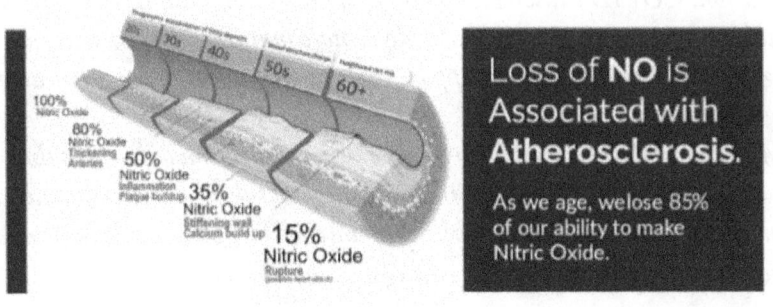

3. The body cannot deliver oxygen without nitric oxide, even when supplemental oxygen is administered. A problem in COVID patients is not oxygen availability, it is oxygen delivery.

Case Study: *In 2020, my drug company, Nitric Oxide Innovations got an investigational new drug (IND) application approved by the U.S. FDA to make a nitric oxide lozenge into a drug for the treatment of COVID-19. In October 2020, we had our investigational review board (IRB) approved and our drug manufactured.*

We started enrolling patients in our drug study in Nov 2020. We would give the patients a pulse oximeter so they could measure their blood oxygen saturation. COVID causes a loss of oxygen saturation, and it is important to be able to monitor it. We could also do remote monitoring of their blood oxygen saturation through an app on their phone linked to our telehealth program.

We would have patients with blood oxygen saturation of low 80s that would increase to high 90s within 10 minutes of taking our nitric oxide drug. Even though this was a double blinded placebo-controlled study, we could tell which patients were on the active drug and which were on the placebo.

The Secret of Nitric Oxide

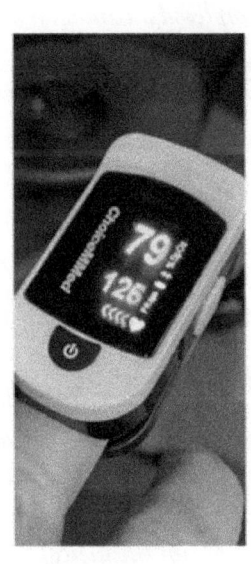

Baseline COVID patient.

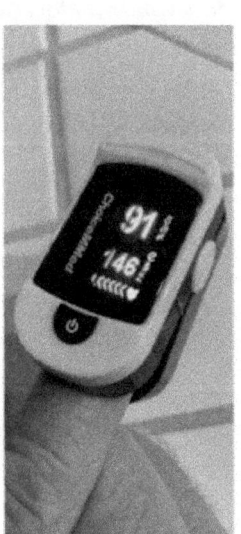

8 minutes past NO treatment.

4. Nitric oxide lozenge reverses vascular disease.

Case Study: *We had a patient report back to us that based on an ultrasound, he had nearly 80% occlusion of his carotid arteries, the arteries that go up the next and feed the brain. He started taking the nitric oxide and 6 months later he had 15% occlusion changing nothing else but just taking the lozenge.*

Based on this observation, we completed a clinical trial in 11 patients and found that in 6 months there was an average of 11% plaque regression using nitric oxide. This has never been observed before even using prescription medication.

5. Nitric oxide helps Navy Seal team adapt to high altitude and be combat ready in Afghanistan.

Case Study: *Our former Texas Governor Rick Perry invited me to the Governor's mansion one morning for coffee and to meet with a group of active Navy Seals. They informed me their base camp was about 3000 feet in the mountains of Afghanistan. Their helicopter would take them on missions into the mountains and they would rappel from the helicopter in the cover of the night. Many times, there were elevations of 10-12,000 feet above sea level where the oxygen concentration is much less. They would have to be combat ready as soon as they landed into enemy territory, but many times they would suffer from acute mountain sickness since they had not had time to acclimate.*

We sent the nitric oxide lozenges with them to use on these high-altitude missions. They would take the lozenge on the ride up and then by the time they repelled, the nitric oxide had allowed their bodies to acclimate, and they were immediately combat ready. For me, protecting and supporting our armed forces is one of the most important things we do.

6. The nitric oxide lozenge helps elderly patients with history of transient ischemic attacks and strokes.

Case Study: *One of our prominent physicians and endocrinologist, Dr Joseph Prendergast, was using the nitric oxide lozenge in his clinical practice. He had an elderly lady come into his office with angina, brain fog, and lightheaded with chronic headaches.*

Her medical history revealed she had coronary artery disease, history of transient ischemic attacks (TIAs) and chronic migraines. He informed her of the nitric oxide and gave her one to take while she was in the exam room with him. Within seconds of putting the lozenge in her mouth, she asked, "What is this you just gave me? I feel better than I have in years."

Even he was shocked that the lozenge would work so quickly and relieve her ischemic heart pain of angina. Her brain fog and light headedness went away. He explained to her that the lozenge generated nitric oxide gas which then opened the blood vessels and allowed for better delivery. Both he and she became big fans that day.

7. Topical Nitric oxide heals non-healing wounds and facilitates healing like never seen before.

Case Study: Nitric Oxide is a potent anti-microbial effectively killing most bacteria commonly found in an infected wound. (P. Aeruginosa, MRSA, etc).

CLINICAL STUDY DATA
Excerpts from published clinical studies.

The Utilization of a Nitric Oxide Generating Serum for Improving Vascularity in Wound Healing

SURGICAL CASE REPORTS | ISSN 2613-5965, Surgical Case Reports doi: 10.31487/j.SCR.2020.09.04. Volume 3(9): 2-4.

Objective: Poor vascularity in injured or operated tissue predisposes the patient to poor healing. Many disease states such as diabetes mellitus, atherosclerosis, and Raynaud's Disease exhibit delayed or compromised healing. Post-radiated tissue is another example of poor healing potential. Any surgical wound, local, regional, or free flap reconstruction, can see delayed healing or lack of healing with poor blood supply. We used our topical nitric oxide several different wounds to determine its healing effects.

Results: Without exception, the study population showed a more rapid and improved quality of healing in the wounds that were treated with Nitric oxide generating serum as compared to control sites.

The Secret of Nitric Oxide

Rapid re-epithelialization, wound contraction, less bruising and edema were commonly seen. Neo-vascularization was more rapid in surgical flap cases. Burn wounds healed dramatically.

In a diabetic foot ulcer that was not healing for the previous one year, the topical nitric oxide heals in 30 days.

A young girl who was bitten in the mouth by her dog, after surgery, the physician applied the topical nitric oxide twice daily for 30 days—complete healing and very good scar remediation by using the serum.

A 56-year-old male after surgical excision of a basal cell carcinoma where the NO serum led to complete recovery 7 days applying twice daily.

A 52-year-old female who suffered a 2nd-degree burn that was non-healing for 2 months. She started applying the topical nitric oxide and within 7 days remarkable healing and within 21 days the wound was completely healed with very little scarring.

The topical nitric oxide generating serum is currently used by plastic and reconstructive surgeons in the US, Canada, Europe, and Australia for diabetic, pressure injury, post-surgical healing, burns, skin grafts and a wide variety of skin conditions.

NON-HEALING SACRAL WOUND

A 64 year-old wheelchair bound male Paraplegic. Non-healing wound treated by two wound care specialists referred from Yale Health, New Haven, Ct. One and a half years of no progress with multiple debridement sessions and use of santyl ointment and bandages.

Patient discontinued care of wound specialists and applied topical nitric oxide 3x daily. No skin sloughing or debridement was required. Wound completely healed in 6.5 months using the nitric oxide topical serum.

ATV ACCIDENT AND DEGLOVING OF RIGHT FOOT

In June of 2018, my 8-year-old son Conley was a passenger in our Polaris Ranger side-by-side. My other son, Lincoln, was driving too fast and took a turn and turned the Ranger over. Both boys were ejected from the Ranger but unfortunately the Ranger landed on top of Conley's foot. He was trapped.

Lincoln had to run about a mile through the pasture to come get me. When I found Conley, I was thankful he was alive. We lifted the Ranger off his foot and witnessed the destruction to his foot. I had to apply a tourniquet with my belt to stop the bleeding and then I rushed him to the local rural emergency department.

After irrigating and cleaning wound in Emergency room, and after some pain medication, we took a 90-minute ambulance ride to Texas Childrens Hospital. My son had surgery about 14 hours after the accident to close the wound. The surgeons were concerned that he may require multiple surgeries including plastic surgery to completely close the wound. They were also concerned about permanent damage and partial loss of function.

We spent 4 nights in Texas Childrens hospital. I used my nitric oxide releasing bandages on the wound as soon as he came back to his room from surgery. The next day, the wound looked remarkable, and the surgeons were amazed at how well the wound was healing.

They agreed they would watch the wound and if it continued to heal, then perhaps there was no need for additional surgery. We continued to use the serum daily on the surgical site and the wound completely healed with no loss of function and very little scar formation.

The effects of our topical nitric oxide on a number of different wounds including trauma convinced me this would change the wound care industry forever. The effects of nitric oxide led to faster healing time, higher quality healing with fewer infections with great scar remediation, improved survival rates, lower costs of treatment and reduced liability to wound care center, nursing homes and insurance companies.

HOME ON THE RANCH

January 2023

GLOSSARY OF TERMS ON NITRIC OXIDE

CAD	coronary artery disease
CVD	cardiovascular disease
DASH	Dietary Approaches to Stop Hypertension
DNR	Do Not Resuscitate
ED	erectile dysfunction
EDRF	endothelium derived relaxing factor
FDA	Food and Drug administration
GTP	guanosine triphosphate
IND	Investigational New Drug
INOCA	ischemic, non-obstructive coronary artery disease
IRB	Institutional Review Board
NO	nitric oxide
NANC	non-cholinergic, non-adrenergic
OTC	over the counter
PDE	phosphodiesterase
Ph.D.	Doctor of Philosophy
PVN	periventricular nucleus
SNO	nitric oxide synthase
TCM	Traditional Chinese Medicine
TIA	transient ischemic attack

SCIENTIFIC PUBLICATIONS
ORIGINAL RESEARCH ARTICLES

[1] Joshi MS, Ferguson TB, Han TH, Hyduke DR, Liao JC, Rassaf T, Bryan N, Feelisch M, Lancaster JR Jr.
Nitric oxide is consumed, rather than conserved, by reaction with oxyhemoglobin under physiological conditions.
Proc Natl Acad Sci USA. 2002 Aug 6;99(16):10341-6

[2] Feelisch M, Rassaf T, Mnaimneh S, Singh N, Bryan, NS, JourdHeuil D, Kelm M.

Concomitant S-,N-, and heme nitros(yl)ation in biological tissues and fluids: implications for the fate of NO in vivo.
FASEB J. 2002 Nov;16(13):1775-85.

[3] Rassaf T, Bryan NS, Kelm M, Feelisch M.

Concomitant presence of N-nitroso and S-nitroso proteins in human plasma.
Free Radic Biol Med. 2002 Dec 1;33(11):1590-6.

[4] Rodriguez J, Maloney RE, Rassaf T, Bryan NS, Feelisch M.

Chemical nature of nitric oxide storage forms in rat vascular tissue.
Proc Natl Acad Sci USA. 2003 Jan 7;100(1):336-41.

[5] Rassaf T, Bryan NS, Maloney RE, Specian V, Kelm M, Kalyananraman B, Rodriguez J, Feelisch M.

NO adducts in mammalian red blood cells: too much or too little?
Nat Med. 2003 May;9(5):481-3.

[6] Kleinbongard P, Dejam A, Lauer T, Rassaf T, Schindler A, Picker O, Scheeren T, Godecke A, Schrader J, Schulz R, Heusch G, Schaub GA, Bryan NS, Feelisch M, Kelm M.

Plasma nitrite reflects constitutive nitric oxide synthase activity in mammals
Free Radic Biol Med. 2003 Oct 1;35(7):790-6.

[7] Bryan NS, Rassaf T, Rodriguez C, Maloney R, Saijo F, Rodriguez J, Feelisch M.

Cellular targets and mechanisms of nitros(yl)ation: A first insight into their nature and kinetics in vivo
Proc Natl Acad Sci USA 2004 March 23;(101);4308-4313.

[8] Bryan NS, Rassaf T, Rodriguez J, Feelisch M.

Bound NO in human red blood cells: fact or artifact?
Nitric Oxide. 2004 Jun:10(4):221-8.

[9] Tao L, Gao E, Bryan NS, Ou Y, Liu HR, Hu A, Christopher TA, Lopez BL, Yodio J, Koch WJ, Feelisch M, Ma XL.

Cardioprotective effects of thioredoxin in Myocardial ischemia and reperfusion: the role of S-nitrosation.
Proc Natl Acad Sci USA 2004 Aug 3:101(31):11471-6.

[10] Janero DR, Bryan NS, Saijo F, Dhawan V, Schwalb, DJ, Warren MC, Feelisch M.

Differential nitros(yl)ation of blood and tissue constituents during glyceryl trinitrate biotransformation in vivo.
Proc Natl Acad Sci USA 2004 Nov 30:101(48):16958-63

[11] Zamora R, Bryan NS, Boyle P, Wong C, Milsom AB, Jaffe R, Feelisch M, Ford HR.

Nitrosative stress in an Animal Model of Necrotizing Enterocolitis
Free Radic Biol Med. 2005 Dec 1:39(11):1428-1437.

[12] Bryan NS, Fernandez BO, Garcia-Saura MF, Bauer SM, Milsom AB, Rassaf T, Maloney R, Bharti A, Rodriguez J, Feelisch M.

Nitrite is a signaling molecule and regulator of gene expression in mammalian tissues
Nature Chemical Biology, 2005 Oct (1); 290-297.

[13] Peyrot F, Fernandez BO, Bryan NS, Feelisch M, Ducrocq C.

N-Nitroso Products from the Reaction of Indoles with Angeli's Salt
Chem Res Toxicol. 2006 Jan;19(1):58-67.

[14] Elrod JW, Greer JJ, Bryan NS, Langston W, Szot JF, Gebregzlabher H, Janssens S, Feelisch M, Lefer, DJ.

Cardiomyocyte-Specific Overexpression of NO Synthase-3 Protects Against Myocardial Ischemia-Reperfusion Injury
Arterioscler Thromb Vasc Biol. 2006 July;26(7):1517-23.

[15] Wang X, Bryan NS, MacArthur PH, Rodriguez J, Gladwin MT, Feelisch M.

Measurement of nitric oxide levels in the red cell: Validation of triiodide based chemiluminsence with acid-sulfanilamide pretreatment
J Biol Chem. 2006 Sept 15;281(37):26994-7002.

[16] Duranski MR, Elrod JW, Calvert JW, Bryan NS, Feelisch M, Lefer DJ.

Genetic Overexpression of eNOS Attenuates Hepatic Ischemia-Reperfusion Injury Am J Physiol Heart Circ Physiol 2006 Dec;291(6):H2980-6.

[17] Bryan NS

Nitrite in NO Biology: Cause or Consequence? A Systems-Based Review
Free Radic Biol Med 2006 Sept;41(5):691-701.

[18] Bryan NS, Grisham MB

Methods to Detect Nitric Oxide and its Metabolites in Biological Samples
Free Radic Biol Med 2007 Sep 1;43(5):645-57.

[19] Erzurum SC, Ghosh S, Janocha A, Xu W, Bauer S, Bryan NS, Tejero JB, Hemann C, Hille R, Stuehr D, Feelisch M, Beall C.:

Higher blood flow and circulating NO products offset high-altitude hypoxia among Tibetans
Proc Natl Acad Sci USA 2007 Nov 6;104(45):17593-8

[20] Bryan NS, Calvert, JW, Elrod JW, Duranski MR, Gundewar S, Ji SY, Lefer DJ

Dietary Nitrite Supplementation Protects Against Myocardial Ischemia-Reperfusion Injury

Proc Natl Acad Sci USA 2007 Nov 27;104(48):19144-9

[21] Elrod JW, Calvert JW, Gundewar S, Bryan NS, Lefer DJ

Nitric Oxide Promotes Distant Organ Protection: Evidence for an Endocrine Role of Nitric Oxide
Proc Natl Acad Sci USA 2008 Aug 12;105(32): 11430-35

[22] Bryan NS, Calvert JW, Gundewar S, Lefer DJ

Dietary Nitrite Restores NO Homeostasis and is Cardioprotective in eNOS Deficient Mice
Free Radic Biol Med. 2008 Aug 15;45(4):468-74

[23] Feelisch M, Fernandez BO, Bryan NS, Garcia-Saura MF, Bauer S, Whitlock DR, Ford PC, Janero DR, Rodriguez J, Ashrafian H

Tissue processing of nitrite in hypoxia: an intricate interplay of nitric oxide-generating and -scavenging systems.
J Biol Chem. 2008 Dec 5;283(49):33927-34.

[24] Mujoo K, Sharin VG, Bryan NS, Krumenacker JS, Sloan C, Parveen S, Nikonoff LE, Kots AY, Murad F

Role of nitric oxide signaling components in Differentiation of embryonic stem cells into myocardial cells.
Proc Natl Acad Sci U S A. 2008 Dec 2;105(48):18924-9.

[25] Harg H, Bryan NS

Dietary Sources of Nitrite as a Modulator of Ischemia-Reperfusion Injury
Kidney Int. 2009 Jun;75(11):1140-4

[26] Perlman DH, Bauer SM, Ashrafian H, Bryan NS, Garcia-Saura MF, Lim CC, Fernandez BO, Infusini G, McComb ME, Costello CE, Feelisch M

Mechanistic Insights Into Nitrite-Induced Cardioprotection Using an Integrated Metabonomic/Proteomic Approach.
Circ Res. 2009 Mar 27;104(6):796-804

[27] Stokes KY, Dugas TR, Tang Y, Garg H, Guidry E, Bryan NS

Dietary Nitrite Prevents Hypercholesterolemic Microvascular Inflammation And Reverses Endothelial Dysfunction
Am J Physiol Heart Circ Physiol. 2009 May;296(5):H1281-8.

[28] Bryan NS, Bian K, Murad F

Discovery of the nitric oxide signaling pathway and targets for drug development
Front Biosci. 2009 Jan 1;14:1-18.

[29] Bryan NS

Cardioprotective Actions of Nitrite Therapy and Dietary Considerations
Front Biosci. 2009 Jan 1;14:4793-808

[30] Hord NG, Tang Y, Bryan NS

Food Sources of Nitrates and Nitrites: The Physiological Context for Potential Health Benefits
Am J Clin Nutr. 2009 Jul;90(1):1-10

[31] Tang Y, Garg H, Geng YJ, Bryan NS

Nitric oxide bioactivity of traditional Chinese medicines used for cardiovascular indications
Free Radic Biol Med. 2009 Sep 15;47(6):835-40.

[32] Sanghani PC, Davis WI, Fears SL, Green SL, Zhai L, Tang Y, Martin E, Bryan NS, Sanghani SP

Kinetic and cellular characterization of novel inhibitors of S-nitrosoglutathione reductase
J Biol Chem. 2009 Sep 4;284(36):24354-62.

[33] Milkowski A, Garg HK, Coughlin JR, Bryan NS:

Nutritional Epidemiology in the Context of Nitric Oxide Biology: A Risk-Benefit Evaluation for Dietary Nitrite and Nitrate
Nitric Oxide. 2010 Feb 15;22(2):110-9.

[34] Lim CC, Bryan NS, Jain M, Garcia-Saura MF, Fernandez BO, Sawyer DB, andy DE, Loscalzo J, Feelisch M, Liao R:

Glutathione Peroxidase Deficiency Exacerbates Ischemia-Reperfusion Injury in Male but not Female Myocardium: Insights into Antioxidant Compensatory Mechanisms.
Am J Physiol Heart Circ Physiol. 2009 Dec;297(6):H2144-53.

[35] Lundberg JO, Gladwin MT, Ahluwalia A, Benjamin N, Bryan NS, Butler A, Cabrales P, Fago A, Feelisch M, Ford PC, Freeman BA, Frenneaux M, Friedman J, Kelm M, Kevil CG, Kim-Shapiro DB, Kozlov AV, Lancaster JR Jr, Lefer DJ, McColl K, McCurry K, Patel RP, Petersson J, Rassaf T, Reutov VP, Richter-Addo GB, Schechter A, Shiva S, Tsuchiya K, van Faassen EE, Webb AJ, Zuckerbraun BS, Zweier JL, Weitzberg E:

Nitrate and nitrite in biology, nutrition and therapeutics
Nat Chem Biol. 2009 Dec;5(12):865-9.

[36] Saijo F, Milsom AB, Bryan NS, Bauer SM, Vowinkel T, Ivanovic M, Andry C, Granger DN, Rodriguez J, Feelisch M:

On the dynamics of nitrite, nitrate and other biomarkers of nitric oxide production in inflammatory bowel disease
Nitric Oxide. 2010 Feb 15;22(2):155-67.

[37] Hord NG, Ghannam J, Garg HK, Berens PD, Bryan NS:

Nitrate and nitrite content of human, formula, bovine and soy milks: implications for dietary nitrite and nitrate recommendations Breastfeeding Medicine 2010 Oct 19.

[38] Tang Y, Jiang H. Bryan NS

Nitrite and Nitrate: Cardiovascular risk-benefit and metabolic effects Curr Opin Lipidol. 2011 Feb;22(1):11-5.

[39] Jourd'heuil FL, Lowery AM, Melton EM, Mnaimneh S, Bryan NS, Fernandez BO, Park JH, Ha CE, Bhagavan NV, Feelisch M, Jourd'heuil D:

Redox-sensitivity and site-specificity of S- and N- denitrosation in proteins. PLoS One. 2010 Dec 21;5(12):e14400.

[40] Bryan NS: Processed Meats and Coronary Heart Disease:

Perspective and Context. Circulation. 2011 Jan 25;123(3):e16; author reply e17.

[41] Zand J, Lanza F, Garg HK, Bryan NS.

All-natural nitrite and nitrate containing dietary supplement promotes nitric oxide production and reduces triglycerides in humans. Nutr Res. 2011 Apr;31(4):262-9.

[42] Mian AI, Du Y, Garg HK, Caviness AC, Goldstein SL, Bryan NS.

Urinary nitrate might be an early biomarker for pediatric acute kidney injury in the emergency department. Pediatr Res. 2011 Aug;70(2):203-7.

[43] Dyson A, Bryan NS, Fernandez BO, Garcia-Saura MF, Saijo F, Mongardon N, Rodriguez J, Singer M, Feelisch M.

An integrated approach to assessing nitroso- redox balance in systemic inflammation. Free Radic Biol Med 2011 Jun 14

[44] Aranke M, Bryan NS, Mian AI.

Towards nitric oxide based diagnostics: call to action. Trends Mol Med. 2011 Nov;17(11):614-6.

[45] Erez A, Nagamani SC, Shchelochkov OA, Premkumar MH, Campeau PM, Chen Y, Garg HK, Li L, Mian A, Bertin TK, Black JO, Zeng H, Tang Y, Reddy AK, Summar M, O'Brien WE, Harrison DG, Mitch WE, Marini JC, Aschner JL, Bryan NS, Lee B.

Requirement of argininosuccinate lyase for systemic nitric oxide production. Nat Med. 2011 Nov 13;17(12):1619-26

[46] Garcia-Saura MF, Saijo F, Bryan NS, Bauer S, Rodriguez J, Feelisch M.

Nitroso-Redox Status and Vascular Function in Marginal and Severe Ascorbate Deficiency. Antioxid Redox Signal. 2012 Feb 5

[47] Mian AI, Bryan NS, Zaidi AK.

Translational Research in the developing world: molecular medicine goes global. Trends Mol Med. 2012 Mar;18(3):135-7.

[48] Nuñez De González MT, Osburn WN, Hardin MD, Longnecker M, Garg HK, Bryan NS, Keeton JT.

Survey of residual nitrite and nitrate in conventional and organic/natural/uncured/indirectly cured meats available at retail in the United States. J Agric Food Chem. 2012 Apr 18;60(15):3981-90.

[49] Parthasarathy DK, Bryan NS.

Sodium nitrite: The "cure" for nitric oxide insufficiency. Meat Sci. 2012 Mar 10.

[50] Jiang H, Tang Y, Garg HK, Parthasarathy DK, Torregrossa AC, Hord NG, Bryan NS.

Concentration- and stage-specific effects of nitrite on colon cancer cell lines. Nitric Oxide. 2012 Apr 5.

[51] Nagamani SC, Campeau PM, Shchelochkov OA, Premkumar MH, Guse K, Brunetti-Pierri N, Chen Y, Sun Q, Tang Y, Palmer D, Reddy AK, Li L, Slesnick TC, Feig DI, Caudle S, Harrison D, Salviati L, Marini JC, Bryan NS, Erez A, Lee B.

Nitric-oxide supplementation for treatment of long-term complications in argininosuccinic aciduria. Am J Hum Genet. 2012 May 4;90(5):836-46.

[52] Jiang H, Torregrossa AC, Parthasarathy DK, Bryan NS.

Natural product nitric oxide chemistry: new activity of old medicines. Evid Based Complement Alternat Med. 2012;2012:873210.

[53] Bryan NS.

Application of nitric oxide in drug discovery and development. Expert Opin Drug Discov. 2011 Nov;6(11):1139-54. [46]

[54] Jiang H, Parthasarathy D, Torregrossa AC, Mian A, Bryan NS.

Analytical Techniques for Assaying Nitric Oxide Bioactivity J Vis Exp. 2012 Jun 18;(64):e3722

[55] Mujoo K, Nikonoff LE, Sharin VG, Bryan NS, Kots AY, Murad F.

Curcumin induces differentiation of embryonic stem cells through possible modulation of nitric oxide-cyclic GMP pathway. Protein Cell. 2012 Jul;3(7):535-44.

[56] Torregrossa AC, Aranke M, Bryan NS. Nitric oxide and geriatrics:

Implications in diagnostics and treatment of the elderly. J Geriatr Cardiol. 2011 Dec;8(4):230-42.

[57] Bryan NS, Alexander DD, Coughlin JR, Milkowski AL, Boffetta P.

Ingested nitrate and nitrite and stomach cancer risk: An updated review. Food Chem Toxicol. 2012 Aug 4;50(10):3646-3665.

[58] Bryan NS.

Pharmacological therapies, lifestyle choices and nitric oxide deficiency: A perfect storm. Pharmacol Res. 2012 Dec;66(6):448-56.

[59] Bryan NS, Torregrossa AC, Mian AI, Lindsey Berkson D, Westby CM, Moncrief JW.

Acute effects of hemodialysis on nitrite and nitrate: potential cardiovascular implications in dialysis patients. Free Radic Biol Med. 2013 Jan 29;58C:46-51.

[60] Mian AI, Aranke M, Bryan NS.

Nitric oxide and its metabolites in the critical phase of illness: rapid biomarkers in the making. Open Biochem J. 2013;7:24-32.

[61]Chintalgattu V, Rees ML, Culver JC, Goel A, Jiffar T, Zhang J, Dunner K Jr, Pati S, Bankson JA, Pasqualini R, Arap W, Bryan NS, Taegtmeyer H, Langley RR, Yao H, Kupferman ME, Entman ML, Dickinson ME, Khakoo AY.

Coronary microvascular pericytes are the cellular target of sunitinib malate-induced cardiotoxicity. Sci Transl Med. 2013 May 29;5(187):187ra69

[62] Jiang H, Torregrossa AC, Potts A, Pierini D, Aranke M, Garg HK, Bryan NS.

Dietary Nitrite Improves Insulin Signaling Through GLUT4 Translocation. Free
Radic Biol Med. 2013 Oct 21;67C:51-57.

[63]Hyde ER, Andrade F, Vaksman Z, Parthasarathy K, Jiang H, Parthasarathy DK, Torregrossa AC, Tribble G, Kaplan HB, Petrosino JF, Bryan NS.

Metagenomic analysis of nitrate-reducing bacteria in the oral cavity: implications for nitric oxide homeostasis. PLoS One. 2014 Mar 26;9(3):e88645.

[64]Oostindjer M, Alexander J, Amdam GV, Andersen G, Bryan NS, Chen D, Corpet DE, De Smet S, Dragsted LO, Haug A, Karlsson AH, Kleter G, de Kok TM, Kulseng B, Milkowski AL, Martin RJ, Pajari AM, Paulsen JE, Pickova J, Rudi K, Sødring M, Weed DL,

Egelandsdal B. The role of red and processed meat in colorectal cancer development: a perspective. Meat Sci. 2014 Aug;97(4):583-96.

[65] Premkumar MH, Sule G, Nagamani SC, Chakkalakal S, Nordin A, Jain M, Ruan MZ, Bertin T, Dawson BC, Zhang J, Schady D, Bryan NS, Campeau PM, Erez A, Lee B.

Argininosuccinate lyase in enterocytes protects from development of necrotizing enterocolitis. Am J Physiol Gastrointest Liver Physiol. 2014 Jun 5.

[66] Hyde ER, Luk B, Cron S, Kusic L, McCue T, Bauch T, Kaplan H, Tribble G, Petrosino JF, Bryan NS.

Characterization of the rat oral microbiome and the effects of dietary nitrate. Free Rad Biol Med 2014 Dec;77:249-57

[67] Pierini D, Bryan NS.

Nitric oxide availability as a marker of oxidative stress. Methods Mol Biol. 2015; 1208:63-71.

[68] Justice JN, Gioscia-Ryan RA, Johnson LC, Battson ML, de Picciotto NE, Beck HJ, Jiang H, Sindler AL, Bryan NS, Enoka, RM, Seals DR.

Sodium nitrite supplementation improves motor function and skeletal muscle inflammatory profile in old male mice. J Appl Physiol (1985). 2015 Jan 15;118(2):163-9.

[69] Bryan NS.

The potential use of salivary nitrite as a marker of NO status in humans. Nitric oxide 2015 Feb 15;45:4-6

[70] Sindler AL, Cox-York K, Reese L, Bryan NS, Seals, DR, Gentile CL.

Oral nitrite therapy improves vascular function in diabetic mice. Diab Vasc Dis Res. 2015 Feb 12.

[71] Nuñez de González MT, Osburn WN, Hardin MD, Longnecker M, Garg HK, Bryan NS, Keeton JT.

A survey of nitrate and nitrite concentrations in conventional and organic-labeled raw vegetables at retail. J Food Sci. 2015 May;80(5):C942-9.

[72] Bryan NS.

Nitric Oxide Enhancement Strategies. Future Sci OA. 2015 Aug 1;1(1):FSO48

[73] Bryan NS, Ivy JL.

Inorganic nitrite and nitrate: evidence to support consideration as dietary nutrients. Nutr Res. 2015 Aug;35(8):643-54

[74] DeVan AE, Johnson LC, Brooks FA, Evans TD, Justice JN, Cruickshank-Quinn C, Reisdorph N, Bryan NS, McQueen MB, Santos-Parker JR, Chonchol MB, Bassett CJ, Sindler AL, Giordano T, Seals DR.

Effects of sodium nitrite supplementation on vascular function and related small metabolite signatures in middle-aged and older adults. J Appl Physiol (1985). 2015 Nov 25.

[75] Justice JN, Johnson LC, DeVan AE, Cruickshank-Quinn C, Reisdorph N, Bassett CJ, Evans TD, Brooks FA, Bryan NS, Chonchol MB, Giordano T, McQueen MB, Seals DR.

Improved motor and cognitive performance with sodium nitrite supplementation is related to small metabolite signatures: a pilot trial in middle-aged and older adults. Aging (Albany NY). 2015 Nov;7(11):1004-21.

[76] Jiang H, Polhemus DJ, Islam KN, Torregrossa AC, Li Z, Potts A, Lefer DJ, Bryan NS.

Nebivolol Acts as a S-Nitrosoglutathione Reductase Inhibitor: A New Mechanism of Action. J Cardiovasc Pharmacol Ther. 2016 Jan 8

[77] Bryan NS, Tribble G, Angelov N.

Oral Microbiome and Nitric Oxide: the Missing Link in the Management of Blood Pressure. Curr Hypertens Rep. 2017 Apr;19(4):33

[78] Raizada MK, Joe B, Bryan NS, Chang EB, Dewhirst FE, Borisy GG, Galis ZS, Henderson W, Jose PA, Ketchum CJ, Lampe JW, Pepine CJ, Pluznick JL, Raj D, Seals DR, Gioscia-Ryan RA, Tang WHW, Oh YS.

Report of the National Heart, Lung, and Blood Institute Working Group on the Role of Microbiota in Blood Pressure Regulation: Current Status and Future Directions. Hypertension. 2017 Jul 31. pii: HYPERTENSIONAHA.117.09699

[79] Bock JM, Ueda K, Schneider AC 4th, Hughes WE, Limberg JK, Bryan NS, Casey DP.

Inorganic nitrate supplementation attenuates peripheral chemoreflex sensitivity but does not improve cardiovagal baroreflex sensitivity in older adults. Am J Physiol Heart Circ Physiol. 2017 Sep 29:ajpheart.00389.2017

[80] McMahon TJ, Bryan NS.

Biomarkers in Pulmonary Vascular Disease: Gauging Response to Therapy. Am J Cardiol. 2017 Oct 15;120(8S):S89-S95

[81] Bryan NS.

Functional Nitric Oxide Nutrition of Combat Cardiovascular Disease. Curr Atheroscler Rep. 2018 Mar 17;20(5):21

[82] Kho J, Tian X, Wong WT, Bertin T, Jiang MM, Chen S, Jin Z, Shchelochkov OA, Burrage LC, Reddy AK, Jiang H, Abo-Zahrah R, Ma S, Zhang P, Bissig KD, Kim JJ, Devaraj S, Rodney GG, Erez A, Bryan NS, Nagamani SCS, Lee BH.

Argininosuccinate Lyase Deficiency Causes an Endothelial-Dependent Form of Hypertension. Am J Hum Genet. 2018 Aug 2;103(2):276-287

[83] Araujo-Gutierrez R, Van Eps JL, Kirui D, Bryan NS, Kang Y, Fleming JB, Fernandez-Moure JS.

Enhancement of gemcitabine cytotoxicity in pancreatic adenocarcinoma through controlled release of nitric oxide. Biomed Microdevices. 2019 Feb 21;21(1):23

[84] Tribble GD, Angelov N, Weltman R, Wang BY, Eswaran SV, Gay IC, Parthasarathy K, Dao DV, Richardson KN, Ismail NM, Sharina IG, Hyde ER, Ajami NJ, Petrosino JF, Bryan NS.

Frequency of Tongue Cleaning Impacts the Human Tongue Microbiome Composition and Enterosalivary Circulation of Nitrate. Front Cell Infect Microbiol. 2019 Mar 1;9:39

[85] Bryan NS, Lefer DJ.

Update on Gaseous Signaling Molecules Nitric Oxide and Hydrogen Sulfide: Strategies to Capture their Functional Activity for Human Therapeutics. Mol Pharmacol. 2019 Jul;96(1):109-114

[86] Waheed S, Kalsekar AG, Kamal AK, Bryan NS, Mian AI.

Association of Plasma Levels of Nitric Oxide Oxidative Metabolites with Acute Stroke in Patients Presenting to the Emergency Department of a Low-Middle Income Country. Emerg Med Int. 2019 Jun 2;2019:9206948.

[87] Banez MJ, Geluz MI, Chandra A, Hamdan T, Biswas OS, Bryan NS, Von Schwarz ER

A systemic review on the antioxidant and anti-inflammatory effects of resveratrol, curcumin, and dietary nitric oxide supplementation on human cardiovascular health. Nutr Res. 2020 Jun;78:11-26.

[88] Rossman MJ, Gioscia-Ryan RA, Santos-Parker JR, Ziemba BP, Lubieniecki KL, Johnson LC, Poliektov NE, Bispham NZ, Woodward KA, Nagy EE, Bryan NS, Reisz JA, D'Alessandro A, Chonchol M, Sindler AL, Seals DR.

Inorganic Nitrite Supplementation Improves Endothelial Function With Aging: Translational Evidence for Suppression of Mitochondria-Derived Oxidative Stress. Hypertension 2021 Apr;77(4):1212-1222.

[89] Fernandez-Moure JS, Van Eps JL, Scherba JC, Haddix S, Livingston M, Bryan NS, Cantu C, Valson C, Taraballi F, Kaplan LJ, Olsen R, Tasciotti E.

Polyester Mesh Functionalization with Nitric Oxide-Releasing Silica Nanoparticles Reduces Early Methicillin-Resistant Staphylococcus aureus Contamination. Surg Infect (Larchmt) 2021 Apr 30.

[90] Lion RP, Vega MR, Smith EO, Devaraj S, Braun MC, Bryan NS, Desai MS, Coss-Bu JA, Ikizler TA, Akcan Arikan A.

The effect of continuous venovenous hemodiafiltration on amino acid delivery, clearance, and removal in children. Pediatr Nephrol. 2022 Feb;37(2):433-441.

[91] Bryan NS, Burleigh MC, Easton C.

The oral microbiome, nitric oxide and exercise performance. Nitric Oxide. 2022 Aug 1;125-126:23-30

[92] Bryan NS.

Nitric oxide deficiency is a primary driver of hypertension. Biochem Pharmacol. 2022 Dec;206:115325.

[93] Bryan NS, Ahmed S, Lefer DJ, Hord N, von Schwarz ER.

Dietary nitrate biochemistry and physiology. An update on clinical benefits and mechanisms of action. Nitric Oxide. 2023 Mar 1;132:1-7.

[94] Bryan NS, Molnar J, Somberg J.

The Efficacy of Nitric Oxide-Generating Lozenges on Outcome in Newly Diagnosed COVID-19 Patients of African American and Hispanic Origin. Am J Med. 2023 Oct;136(10):1035-1040.e11.

BOOKS

[1] Bryan NS (Editor):

Food, Nutrition and the Nitric Oxide Pathway. DesTech Publishing – Pennsylvania ISBN: 978-1-932078-84-8, September 2009

[2] Bryan NS and Loscalzo J (Editors)

Nitrite and Nitrate in Human Health and Disease – Springer Humana Press New York ISBN: 978-1-60761-615-3, May 2011

[3] Bryan NS and Loscalzo J (Editors)

Nitrite and Nitrate in Human Health and Disease Second Edition– Springer Humana Press New York ISBN: 978-3-319-46189-2, Jan 2017

BOOK CHAPTER CONTRIBUTIONS

[1] Bryan NS, Murad F

What is Nitric Oxide? In Food, Nutrition and the Nitric Oxide Pathway (Ed) Bryan NS DesTech Publishing – Pennsylvania ISBN: 978-1-932078-84-8, September 2009

[2] Grisham MB, Bryan NS

Dysregulated NO and Disease In In Food, Nutrition and the Nitric Oxide Pathway (Ed) Bryan NS DesTech Publishing – Pennsylvania ISBN: 978-1- 932078-84-8, September 2009

[3] Bryan NS, Hord NG

Food Sources of nitrite and nitrate: The Physiological Context for Potential Health Benefits In Food, Nutrition and the Nitric Oxide Pathway (Ed) Bryan NS DesTech Publishing – Pennsylvania ISBN: 978-1-932078-84-8, September 2009

[4] Huffman R, Bryan NS

Nitrite and Nitrate in the Meat and Food Industry In Food, Nutrition and the Nitric Oxide Pathway (Ed) Bryan NS DesTech Publishing – Pennsylvania ISBN: 978-1-932078-84-8, September 2009

[5] Bryan NS, Hord NG

Regulations gone awry: Addressing public concerns In Food, Nutrition and the Nitric Oxide Pathway (Ed) Bryan NS DesTech Publishing – Pennsylvania ISBN: 978-1-932078-84-8, September 2009

[6] Bryan NS, Hord NG

Diet and Endothelium – A Concert in NO Homeostasis In Food, Nutrition and the Nitric Oxide Pathway (Ed) Bryan NS DesTech Publishing – Pennsylvania ISBN: 978-1-932078-84-8, September 2009

[7] Bryan NS

Paradigm Shift: From Toxic Food Additive to Indispensible Nutrient In Food, Nutrition and the Nitric Oxide Pathway (Ed) Bryan NS DesTech Publishing – Pennsylvania ISBN: 978-1-932078-84-8, September 2009

[8] Bryan NS and Van Grinsven H

The Role of Nitrate in Human Health, in: Donald, S.(Ed.), Advances in Agronomy, Academic Press, 153–182. 2013 ISBN: 9780124072473

[9] Harsha K. Garg and Bryan NS

Inorganic Nitrite and Nitrate are Bioactive Food Components Conferring Nitric Oxide Activity in vivo In Functional Foods for Chronic Diseases Volume 5 Diabetes and Related Diseases (Ed) N. Abate & D.K. Martirosyan Food Science Publisher – ISBN-10: 0976753561, July 2010

[10] Bryan NS and Loscalzo J

Introduction In Nitrite and Nitrate in Human Health and Disease (Ed) Bryan NS and Loscalzo J. Springer-Humana Press ISBN 978-1-60761-615-3 May 2011.

[11] Berens P and Bryan NS

Nitrite and Nitrate in Human Breast Milk: Implications for Development In Nitrate and Nitrite in Human Health and Disease (Ed) Bryan NS and Loscalzo J. Springer-Humana Press ISBN 978-1-60761-615-3 May 2011.

[12] Bryan NS and Lancaster JL

Nitric Oxide Signaling in Health and Disease In Nitrite and Nitrate in Human Health and Disease (Eds) Bryan NS and Loscalzo J. Springer-Humana Press ISBN 978-1-60761-615-3 May 2011.

[13] Bryan NS and Loscalzo J

Looking Forward In Nitrite and Nitrate in Human Health and Disease (Eds) Bryan NS and Loscalzo J. Springer-Humana Press. ISBN 978-1-60761-615-3 May 2011.

[14] Bryan, N.S., van Grinsven.H.

The Role of Nitrate in Human Health, in: Donald, S.(Ed.), Advances in Agronomy, Academic Press, 153–182.
ISBN: 9780124072473; 2013

[15] Parthasarathy, D and Bryan, N.S.

Curing: Physiology of Nitric Oxide, in: Dikeman, M (Ed.) Encyclopedia of Meat Sciences 2nd Edition, Elsevier Publishing; 2012

[16] Pierini, D and Bryan, N.S.

Nitric Oxide Availability as a Marker of Oxidative Stress in: Armstrong, D. (Ed.), Advanced Protocols in Oxidative Stress III, Humana Press, 2014

[17] Bryan, N.S.

Nitric Oxide Enhancement Strategies, in: Friedman, A and Friedman J. (Eds), Development and therapeutic applications of nitric oxide releasing materials Future Science Ltd 2014

[18] Bryan, N.S.

An Overview of Nitrite and Nitrate: New Paradigm of Nitric Oxide. Debasis Bagchi (Ed), Sustained Energy for Enhanced Human Functions and Physical Activity

[19] Bryan, N.S., Schwarz, E.

Vascular Biology and Vascular Aging for the Clinician in Cardiovascular Medicine Textbook: An Integrative, Metabolic and Functional Medicine Approach. Mark Houston, M.D. (Ed) Wolters Kluwer Health, Inc.

[20] Chernoff, G., Bryan, N.S.

Mesothelial Stem Cells and Stromal Vascular Fraction: Use in Functional Disorders, Wound Healing, Fat Transfer and Other Conditions in Facial Plastic Surgery Clinics in North America. New Trends and Technologies in Facial Plastic Surgery. J Reagan Thomas, M.D. (Ed). Elsevier ISSN: 1064-7406

[21] Bryan, N.S.

Safe and Effective Use of Nitric Oxide Based Supplements and Nutrition for Sports Performance in Nutrition and Enhanced Sports Performance: Muscle Building, Endurance and Strength, 2nd Edition. Debasis Bagchi (Ed). Elsevier

[22] Bryan NS.

Inorganic Nitrite and Nitrate: Dietary Nutrients or Poisons in Nitrate Handbook Environmental, Agricultural, and Health Effects Edited by Christos Tsadilas, First Edition, 2022 Boca Raton, Fl CRC Press.

[23]Bryan NS.

Ernst Von Schwarz, Vascular Biology and Vascular Aging for the Clinician in Personalized and Precision Integrative Cardiovascular Medicine by Mark Houston, LWW 2019

[24]Bryan NS., Ernst Von Schwarz

The Role of Nitric oxide Supplements and Foods in Cardiovascular Disease in Nutrition and Integrative Strategies in Cardiovascular Medicine. Houston and Sinatra, Editors. CRC Press 2021

AUTHORED BOOKS

[1] Nathan S. Bryan:

Blood and Tissue Nitric Oxide Products: Formation and Physiological Significance – ISBN: 3639178092; Aug 2009

[2] Nathan S. Bryan & Janet Zand with Bill Gottlieb

The Nitric Oxide (NO) Solution Good for you Books Publishing – ISBN: 978-0-615-41713-4; November 2010

[3] Nathan S. Bryan & Caroline Pierini:

Beet the Odds – ISBN: 978-1-9888135-0-2; 2013

[4] Nathan S. Bryan:

Functional Nitric Oxide Nutrition: Dietary Strategies to Prevent and Treat Chronic Disease – ISBN: ISBN: 978-1-948719-00-1 (p) ISBN: 978-1-948719-01-8 (e) 2018

[5] Nathan S. Bryan

The Secret of Nitric Oxide: Bringing Nitric Oxide to Life –Brick Tower Press; Feb 2025

INVITED LECTURES

INTERNATIONAL
[1] Physiological Basal Nitrosation Levels: The Art of the Method (Invited Lecture) Heinrich-Heine University Division of Cardiology, Pulmonary Diseases and Angiology; Dusseldorf Germany June 2002

[2] Nitrite-Mediated Blood and Tissue Nitros(yl)ation – Society for Free Radical Biology and Medicine Meeting – St Thomas Virgin Islands Nov 2004

[3] Nitric Oxide Enhancement Restores Endothelial Function and Combats Adverse Effects Of Homocysteine – Trivita Medical Advisory Board Meeting – Invited speaker, Vancouver BC August 2007

[4] Dietary Nitrite and Nitrate Contribute to Cardiovascular Health and Disease –– Invited Plenary Speaker Lisbon Portugal - Feb 20-24, 2008

[5] Dietary Nitrite and Nitrate as Indispensable Nutrients International Meeting on the Role of Nitrite Physiology, Pathophysiology and Therapeutics – Invited speaker, June 18-19, 2009, Nobel Forum, Stockholm Sweden

[6] Inorganic Nitrite and Nitrate as Novel Therapeutic Agents to Restore NO Homeostasis
The Ninth Conference of Chinese Integrated Medicine on Cardiovascular Diseases in China – Invited speaker, September 5, 2009; Tianjin, China.

[7] Inorganic Nitrite and Nitrate as Novel Therapeutic Agents to Restore NO Homeostasis – Invited speaker, Guangxi Traditional Chinese Medical University – Ruikang Hospital September 7, 2009; Nanning, China

[8] The Nitrate-Nitrite-Nitric Oxide pathway – Invited Speaker Nitrate-Nitrite-Nitric Oxide: New Perspective for Health before World Health Organization and France National Academy of Medicine, Thursday, March 31st, 2011, Hôpital Pitié-Salpêtrière, Paris FRANCE

[9] Nitric Oxide index of Foods: defining the context for health benefits of dietary nitrite and nitrate while mitigating risk – Invited Speaker Nitrate-Nitrite-Nitric Oxide: New Perspective for Health before World Health Organization and France National Academy of Medicine, Thursday, March 31st, 2011, Hôpital Pitié-Salpêtrière, Paris FRANCE

[10] Emerging Health Benefits of Nitrite and Nitrate: A Change in Paradigm – Keynote Speaker International Congress of Meat Science and Technology – Montreal Canada Aug 12-17, 2012

[11] Emerging Health Benefits of Nitrite and Nitrate: A Change in Paradigm – Mapleleaf Foods, Toronto, Canada Sept 24, 2012

[12] Nitric Oxide Deficiency and Restoration: New Discoveries in Cardiovascular and Sexual Health – Orthomolecular Medicine Conference, Sao Paulo Brazil May 9-11, 2013

[13] Dietary Nitrite and Nitrate: From Menace to Marvel – Canadian Nutrition Society Annual Meeting, Quebec City May 30-June 2, 2013

[14] An Update on Nitric Oxide Research: New Innovations and Product Solutions – Canadian Health Food Association Sept 4, 2013

[15] Why Dietary Nitrite and Nitrate May Be Good for You - Centre for Advanced Studies at The Norwegian Academy of Science and Letters, Oslo Norway Nov 6-7, 2013

[16] New Paradigm for Regulation of Endogenous Nitric Oxide Production in Humans: The Oral Systemic Link – Karolinska Institute, Stockholm Sweden Nov 8, 2013

[17] What is Nitric Oxide and Why Should You Care? - Canadian Health Food Association; Toronto ON, Sept 12, 2014

[18] Nitric Oxide Deficiency & Restoration; New Discoveries in Cardiovascular & Sexual Health – Canadian Health Food Association; Vancouver BC, April 10, 2015

[19] GSNO Reductase as a Therapeutic Target – International Nitric Oxide Conference, Sendai Japan, May 20-22, 2016

[20] The Role of Nitric Oxide in the Management Of Hypertension, Inflammation and
Cardiovascular Disease – Functional and Regenerative Medicine Auckland, NZ June 7, 2017

[21] The Role of Nitric Oxide in Primary Care - General Practice Conference and Medical Education, Rotorua, NZ, June 8-11, 2017

[22] Erectile Dysfunction is Endothelial Dysfunction: Understanding the Symptoms that Lead to Heart Disease- General Practice Conference and Medical Education, Rotorua, NZ, June 8-11, 2017

[23] Nitric Oxide, So What? - General Practice Conference and Medical Education, Rotorua, NZ, June 8-11, 2017

[24] Nitric Oxide in Heart Disease - General Practice Conference and Medical Education, Rotorua, NZ, June 8-11, 2017

[25] What is NO and Why Should you Care? - General Practice Conference and Medical Education, Rotorua, NZ, June 8-11, 2017

[26] Evidenced Based Therapeutic Strategies for Anti-Aging Medicine – A4M Dubai, January 19-21, 2018

[27] Oral Microbiome, Nitric Oxide and Systemic Health – World Dental Forum – Dubai, April 2-4, 2018

[28] The Physiological and Therapeutic Role of Nitric Oxide - Dubai External Counterpulsation Symposium and Workshop, Dubai, UAE, Sept 8-9, 2018

[29] The Effect of Light Therapy on Nitric Oxide – Global Wellness Summit – Cessena Italy, Oct 6-8, 2018

[30] Nitric Oxide in Acute Care - 21st National Health Sciences Research Symposium Emergency Care: Time & Life Matter – Aga Khan University, Karachi Pakistan, Nov 9-11, 2018

[31] The Role of Nitric Oxide in Anti-Aging and Regenerative Medicine – Anti-Aging Medicine Conference, Mexico City, Mexico Feb 15-17, 2019

[32] New Paradigm in the Regulation and Production of Nitric Oxide in Humans:
Translating Basic Science – Behai, China Aug 17, 2019

[33] New Paradigm in the Regulation and Production of Nitric Oxide in Humans:
Translating Basic Science – Guangxi University of Chinese Medicine, Nanning, China Aug 17, 2019

[34] Functional Nitric Oxide Nutrition to Restore Vascular Function: Optimization of Brain Perfusion and Detoxification – Third International Forum on Nutritional Medicine, Beijing China October 2019

[35] The Role of Nitric Oxide for Optimal Health – Regenerative Medicine Congress, Mexico City, Sept 13, 2020.

[36] The Use of Nitric Oxide Generating Lozenge to Prevent Rapid Progression of COVID-19 and Other Health Benefits – Kathmandu Nepal, Norvick International Hospital, Aug 2021.

[37] Importance of Nitric Oxide in Health, Hormones and Circulation – Arsinal, Andorra, Biohacking and Longevity Convention July 5-7, 2024

[38] The Role of Nitric Oxide in Regenerative Medicine - 10th International Congress on Longevity and Integrative Therapies, keynote lecture – Sao Paulo Brazil; Nov 16, 2024

[39] Are You Building Bridges or Walls to Traditional Medicine? – Dubai, UAE; Health 2.0; Dec 5, 2024

NATIONAL
[1] Formation and Physiological Significance of Blood and Tissue Nitrosation/Nitrosylation Products – Invited Seminar Speaker LSU Health Sciences Center June 2004

[2] Dietary Nitrite Contributes to Cardiovascular Health and Disease – Institute of Food Technologists – Invited Speaker Chicago IL July 2007

[3] Dietary Nitrite and Nitrate ContribSute to Cardiovascular Health and Disease – Worldwide Food Expo, Plenary speaker – Chicago, IL Oct 2007

[4] Dietary Nitrite and Nitrate Contribute to Cardiovascular Health and Disease – Invited Speaker LSU Health Science Center Dept of Molecular and Cellular Physiology – Jan 23, 2008

[5] Dietary Nitrite and Nitrate Contribute to Cardiovascular Health and Disease – invited Speaker Michigan State University Dept of Food Science and Human Nutrition – Feb 30, 2008

[6] Nitrites: Essential to Health? A New Story About an Old Antimicrobial. International Association for Food Protection Annual Conference – Invited speaker, Aug 6, 2008, Columbus Ohio.

[7] Dietary Nitrite and Nitrate as Indispensable Nutrients Kraft Meat Summit – Invited speaker, June 25, 2009 Madison Wisconsin

[8] Dietary Nitrite and Nitrate as Indispensable Nutrients University of Wisconsin Dept of Animal Science – Invited speaker, June 26, 2009 Madison Wisconsin

[9] Inorganic Nitrite and Nitrate are Bioactive Food Components Conferring Nitric Oxide Activity in vivo – Invited speaker, Functional Foods Conference Dec 4-5, 2009 Denton Texas

[10] Nature's NO: Novel Strategies to Restore Nitric Oxide Homeostasis – Invited Speaker, Wake Forest Nitrogen Oxide Meeting, Farmington, PA, May 28-30, 2010 – Nemacolin Resort

[11] Dietary Nitrite and Nitrate: From Menace to Marvel – Invited Speaker – Invited Speaker, Reciprocal Meat Conference, Lubbock Texas June 20-23, 2010

[12] Nitric Oxide in Health and Disease – Invited speaker, Austin Functional Medicine Group – Oct. 28, 2010 Austin, TX

[13] Nitric Oxide in Health and Disease – Invited Speaker, San Antonio Functional Medicine Group – Nov. 3, 2010, San Antonio Tx

[14] Approaches for Diagnosing and Restoring Nitric Oxide Production in Humans – Invited Speaker – Wake Forest University Translational Science Center – April 4, 2011, Winston-Salem NC.

[15] Nitric Oxide: The Overlooked Molecule in Patient Care – Invited Speaker – CME lecture – American Academy of Anti-Aging Medicine Conference – April 7, 2011 Orlando Fl

[16] Nature's NO: Harnessing the Therapeutic Potential of The Nitrate-Nitrite-Nitric Oxide Pathway from Natural Products – Invited Speaker – Approaching the Clinic: Nitrite and Nitrate Conference – May 11-13, 2011 Atlanta GA

[17] Nitric Oxide in Health and Disease – Invited speaker, Pastoral Medical Association – May 21, 2011 Austin, TX

[18] Nitric Oxide Diagnostics and Therapeutics – Invited Speaker – International Conference and Exhibition on Clinical Research: Dermatology, Opthalmology and Cardiology – San Francisco, CA July 5-6, 2011-07-25

[19] Nitrite and Nitrate in Health and Disease: A Paradigm Shift – Invited Speaker - Joint Annual Meeting: ADSA and ASAS 2011 July 12, 2011 New Orleans, LA

[20] Nitric Oxide: The Miracle Molecule – Invited Speaker – Synergy Medical Group July 22-23, 2011 Salt Lake City, Utah

[21] Nitric Oxide in Health and Disease: A New Paradigm for Healthy Living – Invited speaker – Exxon Annual Safety Meeting; Heart Health Aug. 8, 2011 Houston, TX

[22] Nitric Oxide in Health and Disease: An update on Current Research – Invited Speaker, Synergy Medical Group – Phoenix AZ Oct 28, 2011

[23] Nitric Oxide in Health and Disease: An Overview of Current Research – Invited Speaker - 14th International Congress of BioEnergetic Medicine, Nov 4, 2011 Orlando Fl.

[24] Nitric Oxide: The Overlooked Molecule in Patient Care – Keynote Lecture, CME - 19th Annual World Congress on Anti-Aging and Aesthetic Medicine Las Vegas, NV – December 8-10, 2011

[25] Nitric Oxide in Health and Disease: An Overview of Current Research – Invited speaker – Hawaii Spa Marketplace, Honolulu HI Jan 23, 2012

[26] A Novel Method for Nitric Oxide Production – Invited speaker – American Academy of Ozonotherapy, Dallas, TX Feb 17-18, 2012

[27] Nitric Oxide in Health and Disease: An Overview of Current Research – Invited speaker – Crossroads Apothecary, Columbia, MD March 16, 2012

[28] Novel Strategies to Diagnose and Restore Nitric Oxide Production in Humans – Invited Speaker – Hawaii Institute of Molecular Education, Las Vegas NV June 5-6, 2012

[29] Nitric Oxide Signaling: Its Physiological Importance to Nitrite, Nitrate and Nitrosation Reactions – Institute of Food Technologies, Las Vegas, NV June 28, 2012

[30] Nitric Oxide in Health and Disease: An Overview of Current Research – Empowered Doctors, Miami, FL Aug 8, 2012

[31] Nitric Oxide in Health and Disease: An Overview of Current Research – Leadership and Longevity Conference, Green Bay WI Oct 25-26, 2012

[32] Nitric Oxide in Health and Disease: An Overview of Current Research – Heart Institute of Southern California; Temecula, CA Jan 31, 2013

[33] Nitric Oxide in Health and Disease: An Overview of Current Research – Physician training, Newport Beach CA Feb 2, 2013

[34] Nitric Oxide in Health and Disease: An Overview of Current Research – Heart Attack and Stroke Prevention Alliance, Dallas TX Feb 16, 2013

[35] Nitrite and Nitrate in Health and Disease – Invited Lecture University of Colorado, Dept of Integrative Physiology, Boulder, CO Feb 25, 2013

[36] Nitric Oxide Generating Bacteria Affect Cardiovascular Health of Host: Linking Oral Health to Cardiovascular Disease – Holistic Dental Assn, Washington, DC April 19, 2013

[37] Nitric Oxide Deficiency & Restoration: New Discoveries in Cardiovascular & Sexual Health – Age Management Medicine Group, Hollywood FL, May 2, 2013

[38] An Update on Nitric Oxide Research – Baylor College of Medicine, Dept of Obstetrics and Gynecology Aug 19, 2013

[39] The Role of Nitric Oxide in Pain, Inflammation and Arthritis – Florida Chiropractors Assn, Orlando FL Aug 24, 2013

[40] Oral Microbial Nitric Oxide Production Linking Oral Health & Cardiovascular Disease – International Academy of Biological Dentistry and Medicine, Houston, TX, Oct 11-13, 2013

[41] New Paradigm on the Production and Regulation of Nitric Oxide: Advancements
in Diagnostics and Therapeutics – Invited Lecture Houston Methodist Research
Institute, Department of Cardiovascular Sciences, January 24, 2014

[42] Revolutionary Advancement in Nitric Oxide(NO): Renewal beyond L-Arginine. The Premise for Health, Cellular Anti-Aging, Prevention & Disease Management; American Academy of Ozonotherapy, Dallas TX March 26, 2014

[43] New Paradigm for Regulation of Endogenous Nitric Oxide in Humans: The Oral Systemic Link, Dallas TX April 12, 2014.

[44] Nitric Oxide, Menopause and Female Sexual Arousal Disorder – Invited Lecture – CME at the American Academy of Anti-aging Medicine; Orlando FL May 17, 2014.

[45] The Truth About Dietary Nitrates and Mechanisms for Nitric Oxide Production in Humans at the Collegiate and Professional Sports Dietician Association (CPSDA); Scottsdale AZ, May 20, 2014

[46] The Role of Nitric Oxide in Gastrointestinal Health and Chronic Disease - 12th Annual Restorative Medicine Conference Santa Fe, NM, Oct 8-12 2014

[47] The Truth About Dietary Nitrates and Mechanisms for Nitric Oxide Production in Humans – The Food and Nutrition Conference and Expo, Atlanta, GA Oct 20, 2014

[48] The Role of Nitric Oxide in Cellular Aging: Telomeres, Mitochondria and Stem Cells – Academy of Comprehensive Integrative Medicine Sante Fe, NM Oct 24, 2014

[49] Advancements in Nitric Oxide Diagnostics and Therapeutics: Combatting Sexual Dysfunction for Men and Women – Age Management Medicine Group, Las Vegas NV Nov 7, 2014

[50] The Role of Bacteria in Anti-Aging Medicine: Nitric Oxide and Beyond – American Academy of Anti-Aging Medicine, Las Vegas, NV Dec 12, 2014

[51] Clinical Use of Nitric Oxide Therapy – American Academy of Ozonotherapy, Dallas TX Feb 20, 2015

[52] Sodium Nitrite: The Cure for Cardiovascular Disease – Iowa State University, Department of Animal Science Seminar Series, Ames, IA March 27, 2015

[53] Nitric Oxide Supplementation: The Good, the Bad and The Ugly – Austin Functional Medicine, Austin, TX March 12, 2015

[54] Chiropractic Nitric Oxide Nutrition – Fetterman Chiropractic Organization, Milwaukee, WI, April 18, 2015

[55] Nitric oxide Supplementation: Biochemistry and Physiology – Weber Medical Symposium, Boca Raton, FL April 25, 2015

[56] Sodium Nitrite: The Cure for Cardiovascular Disease – Kemin, Des Moines, IA April 27, 2015

[57] Nitric Oxide and Stem Cell Therapy – American Academy of Anti-Aging Medicine, Hollywood FL May 8, 2015

[58] New Paradigm in the Regulation and Production of Nitric Oxide in Humans:
Translating Basic Science – LSU Health Science Center at New Orleans, New Orleans, LA May 11, 2015

[59] Improving Clinical Outcomes in Vascular Disease by Enhancing Nitric Oxide Production – Professional Compounding Centers of America, Houston, TX June 11, 2015

[60] Nitric Oxide in Regenerative Medicine – Cell Surgical Network, Beverly Hills, CA June 27, 2015

[61] Chiropractic Nitric Oxide Nutrition – Fetterman Chiropractic Organization, Toledo, WI, April 18, 2015

[62] Nitric Oxide and Sexual Function: New Discoveries And Innovations in Diagnostics and Therapeutics - American Naturopathic Medical Association, Las Vegas NV, August 29, 2015

[63] Chiropractic Nitric Oxide Nutrition – Fetterman Chiropractic Organization, Green Bay, WI, September 24, 2015
[64] Chiropractic Nitric Oxide Nutrition – Fetterman Chiropractic Organization, Stevens Point, WI, April 18, 2015

[65] Vascular Inflammation and Nitric Oxide: Bridging Diagnostics to Personalized Therapies – Cleveland Heart Lab Continuing Medical Education, August 8, 2015

[66] Erectile Dysfunction is Endothelial Dysfunction: Understanding the Symptoms that Lead to Heart Disease – Age Management Medicine Group, Las Vegas, NV November 6, 2015

[67] The Role of Nitric Oxide in Regenerative Medicine – Select Biosciences, San Diego, CA November 9, 2015

[68] The Role of Nitric Oxide in Health and Aging: From Telomeres to Sexual Function - American Functional Medicine Association Atlanta, GA, November 13, 2015

[69] Chiropractic Nitric Oxide Nutrition – Fetterman Chiropractic Organization, La Cross, WI, December 5, 2015

[70] Inflammation and Sexual Dysfunction: Nitric Oxide as the Common Denominator – American Academy of Anti-Aging Medicine, Las Vegas, NV December 12, 2015

[71] The Role of Nitric Oxide in Regenerative Medicine – Cell Surgical Network, Rancho Mirage, CA February 20, 2016

[72] Erectile Dysfunction is Endothelial Dysfunction: Understanding the Symptoms that Lead to Heart Disease – Tennessee Osteopathic Medical Association, Chattanooga, TN, April,28 - May 1, 2016

[73] The Role of Nitric Oxide in Regenerative Medicine – Cell Surgical Network, Beverly Hills, CA June 4, 2016

[74] Role of Nitrate-Reducing Oral Bacteria on Systemic Blood Pressure: Mechanisms of the Oral-Systemic Link – National Institutes of Health NHLBI Working Group, Bethesda MD June 10, 2016

[75] Nutritional Strategies for Restoration of Nitric Oxide in Humans – International and American Associations of Clinical Nutritionists, Jacksonville, Fl August 11-13, 2016

[76] The Role of Oral Bacteria in Systemic Nitric Oxide Production in Humans: The Mechanism Behind the Oral-Systemic Link – The International Academy of Oral Medicine and Toxicology, Reno, NV Sept 9-10, 2016

[77] Dietary Nitrite and Nitrate: From Menace to Marvel – Plenary Lecture, Functional Food Conference, Harvard Medical School, Boston MA Sept 22-23, 2016

[78] Erectile Dysfunction is Endothelial Dysfunction: Understanding the Symptoms that Lead to Heart Disease – American Functional Medicine Association, Atlanta, GA Nov 10-12, 2016

[79] The unknown nutrient: Discovery of the health benefits of dietary nitrate – International Conference on Food Chemistry and Technology, Las Vegas, NV, Nov 14-16, 2016

[80] The Role of Nitric Oxide in Regenerative Medicine – Cell Surgical Network, Jacksonville, Fl, Feb 2-4, 2017

[81] The Role of Nitric Oxide in Regenerative Medicine – Academy of Regenerative Practice, Ft. Lauderdale, Fl, Feb 24-26, 2017

[82] The Role of the Oral Microbiota in Hypertension – American Academy of Anti-Aging Medicine, Hollywood, Fl, April 7-8, 2017

[83] Dietary Nitrite and Nitrate: From Menace to Marvel – Grocers Manufacturers Association, Washington, DC, April 20, 2017

[84] Hypertension, Inflammation and Nitric Oxide – Age Management Medicine Group, Orlando, FL, April, 27-30, 2017

[85] Oral Microbiome and Nitric Oxide: Mechanisms into the Oral Systemic Link – Ground Rounds NOVA Southeastern University, Ft. Lauderdale, Fl, May 12, 2017

[86] Clinical Applications of Nitric Oxide – Regenerative Medicine Business Summit, St. Cloud, MN, May 19, 2017

[87] Dietary Nitrite and Nitrate: From Menace to Marvel – Keynote Lecture, International Conference on Food & Nutrition, Las Vegas, Nevada, USA May 22-24, 2017

[88] Nitric Oxide is Required for Stem Cell Mobilization and Differentiation – Cell Surgical Network, Beverly Hills, CA June 2-3, 2017

[89] The Role of Nitric Oxide in Oxidative Stress & Pain – Florida Academy of Pain Medicine, Orlando, Fl, June 16-18, 2017

[90] Dietary Nitrate and Nitrite: Risk Benefit Analysis for Human Health and Performance – International Society of Sports Nutrition, Phoenix, AZ July 22-24, 2017

[91] The Role of Nitric Oxide in Health and Disease; Keynote – Florida Food and Nutrition Symposium, Fort Lauderdale, FL. July 16, 2017

[92] Oral Microbiome and Nitric Oxide: The Missing Link in the Treatment of Hypertension – American Naturopathic Medical Association, Las Vegas, NV. August 25-27, 2017

[93] Vascular Inflammation: Cooling the Heat with Nitric Oxide – Innovision Media, Minneapolis, MN. Sept 22-23, 2017

[94]T he Clinical Use of Nitric Oxide in Dental Medicine – International Association of Biological Dentistry and Medicine, Houston, TX. October 19-21, 2017

[95] The Role of Nitric Oxide in Regenerative Medicine – MedRebels Cell Therapy Training, Austin, TX. Oct 26-28, 2017

[96] The Role of Nitric Oxide in Regenerative Medicine – Pacific Regenerative Medicine Conference, Honolulu, HI. Nov 6-7, 2017

[97] The Role of Oral Bacteria in Gut and Brain Health – Innovision Media, Clearwater, FL. Nov 10-11, 2017

[98] The Role of Nitric Oxide in Regenerative Medicine – Academy of Regenerative Practices, Weston, FL. March 2-3, 2018

[99] Functional Nitric Oxide Nutrition – Florida Academy of Nutrition and Dietetics – Keynote Lecture, Fort Lauderdale, FL. March 10, 2018

[100] Nitric Oxide Past, Present and Future: Cardiovascular Implications in Adaptation to Space Travel – Grand Rounds NASA. April 10, 2018

[101] The Effects of Nitric Oxide on Performance And Cardiovascular Health – Sports, Cardiovascular and Wellness Nutrition (SCAN) Conference, Keystone, CO. May 4, 2018

[102] Nitric Oxide Overview: History of Discovery And Fundamentals of Production - WholeHealth Integration Summit: Linking Mind-Body-Mouth-Airway-Sleep – Washington DC, May 18-19, 2018

[103] Nitric Oxide is the Requisite Signal For Stem Cell Function – Cell Surgical Network, Beverly Hills, CA, June 1-3, 2018

[104] The Role of Nitric Oxide in Bio-Energetic Medicine - Tennant Institute
Dallas, TX – Sept 13-15, 2018

[105] Chiropractic Nitric Oxide Nutrition – Fetterman Education, Wassua, WI, Sept 29, 2018

[106] The Role of Nitric Oxide in Vascular Function – Worldlink Medical Congress, Oct, 5-7, 2018

[107] Strategies to Optimize Regenerative Medicine Outcomes: the Role of Nitric Oxide - Med Rebels Regenerative Medicine Symposium, Austin, TX Oct 25-27, 2018

[108] The Role of Nitric Oxide in the Treatment and Prevention of Chronic Disease – Can Chronic Disease be Reversed Medical Conference, Orlando, FL, Feb 1-2, 2019

[109] Strategies to Optimize Regenerative Medicine Outcomes: the Role of Nitric Oxide – Academy of Regenerative Practices, Westin, FL. March 22-23, 2019

[110] How Not to Die From Cardiovascular Disease: My Story of Discoveries and Life Lessons Learned Along The Journey – Burleson County Chamber of Commerce Keynote Lecture, Caldwell, TX April 12, 2019

[111] How Not to Die From Cardiovascular Disease: My Story of Discoveries and Life Lessons Learned Along The Journey – Washington County Chamber of Commerce Keynote Lecture, Caldwell, TX June 5, 2019

[112] Strategies to Optimize Regenerative Medicine Outcomes: the Role of Nitric Oxide – Breakthrough Discoveries in Regenerative Medicine, Beverly Hills, Ca. June 22, 2019

[113] Strategies to Optimize Regenerative Medicine Outcomes: the Role of Nitric Oxide, Aesthetic Conference, Las Vegas Nv July 11-14, 2019

[114] Physiology and Supplementation of Nitric Oxide for the Treatment of Peripheral Neuropathy - The Association of Extremity Nerve Surgeons (AENS) 2019 Annual Symposium – Atlanta, GA Nov 8-10, 2019

[115] Nitric Oxide and Mental Health – Keynote Address, American Academy of Anti-Aging Medicine Annual Conference, Las Vegas, NV Dec 12-14 2020

[116] Nitric Oxide and Chronic Disease: You Can't Live Without It – Can Chronic Disease Be Reversed, 3rd annual Conference, Tampa Bay, Fl, Feb 13-15, 2020

[117] The Role of Nitric Oxide in Regenerative Medicine – International Cell Surgical Society, Las Vegas, NV, June 4-5, 2020

[118] The Role of Nitric Oxide in Optimal Health – Allen Family Drug, Dallas Tx, Aug 2020

[119] Functional Nitric Oxide Nutrition – Fetterman Chiropractic Organization, Milwaukee, Wi, October 17, 2020

[120] Translation of Nitric Oxide Based Therapies – U.S. Neuropathy Centers, Atlanta, Ga, Dec 2020

[121] The Role of Nitric Oxide in Optimal Health – International Cell Surgical Society, Las Vegas, NV, June 3-5, 2021

[122] The Role of Nitric Oxide in Regenerative Aesthetics – Aesthetics Show, Las Vegas, NV, July 7-11, 2021

[123] Nitric Oxide: A Natural Therapy for Chronic Disease – American Naturopathic Medical Association, Las Vegas, NV Aug 27-30, 2021

[124] Innovations in Nitric Oxide Based Therapies For Human Disease – International Academy of Oral Medicine and Toxicology, Bellevue, WA, Sept 23-26, 2021

[125] Functional Nitric Oxide Nutrition – Fetterman Chiropractic Education, Sept 25, 2021

[126] Physiology and Supplementation of Nitric Oxide for the Treatment of Peripheral Neuropathy – Association of Extremity Nerve Surgeons, Golden, CO Nov 5-7, 2021

[127] Light Therapy and Nitric Oxide: From Skin Health to Hypertension – AmSpa, Las Vegas, Jan 27-30, 2022

[128] Nitric oxide as the oral systemic link: From COVID-19 to heart attacks – International Academy of Oral Medicine and Toxicology, New Orleans, LA, March 3-6, 2022

[129] How to Optimize Nitric Oxide in the Human Body – Biohacking Congress, Las Vegas, NV March 19-20, 2022

[130] Nitric Oxide and Chronic Disease: You Cannot Live Without It – Senergy Medical, Dallas, Tx March 24, 2022

[131] Nitric Oxide as a Prevention and Treatment of Cardiovascular and COVID19 - American Osteopathic Society of Rheumatic Diseases, Las Vegas, NV March 25, 2022

[132] Functional Nitric Oxide Nutrition – Fetterman Chiropractic Education, Milwaukee, WI, April 1, 2022

[133] Nitric Oxide for the Prevention and Treatment of Cardiovascular Disease with a Splash of Covid 19 – Congress of Medical Excellence, Dallas, TX April 3, 2022

[134] How to Optimize Nitric Oxide in the Human Body, The Wellness Way, Orlando, Fl. April 9, 2022

[135] How to Optimize Nitric Oxide in the Human Body, How Do You Health, Austin, TX. April 22, 2022

[136] Menopause and Female Sexual Arousal Disorder – American Academy of Anti-Aging Medicine, Hollywood, Fl, April 28-30, 2022

[137] Nitrate for Athletic Performance: Understanding the How and Why – Academy of Nutrition and Dietetics, May 11, 2022

[138] Optimization of Ozone Therapy with Nitric Oxide – American Academy of Ozonotherapy, Denver, CO, June 2-3, 2022

[139] The Essential Requirement of Nitric Oxide in Regenerative Medicine – International Cell Surgical Society, June 9-11, 2022

[140] How to Optimize Nitric Oxide in the Human Body – Biohacking Congress, Boston, MA June 11-12, 2022

[141] Nitric Oxide and Chronic Disease: You Cannot Live Without It – Senergy Medical, Dallas, Tx June 23, 2022

[142] Nitric oxide as the oral systemic link: From COVID-19 to heart attacks -International Academy of Biological Dentistry and Medicine, July 9, 2022

[143] Nourishing the Skin Inside and Out with Nitric Oxide – Aesthetics Show, July 11, 2022

[144] Nitric Oxide Biochemistry and Translation to Clinical Medicine – Quicksilver Scientific, Denver, CO Aug 30, 2022

[145] How to Optimize Nitric Oxide in the Human Body – Biohacking Congress, Miami, Fl Oct 21, 2022

[146] Nitric Oxide is Required for Cellular Regeneration – American Academy of Anti-Aging Medicine, Las Vegas, NV, Dec 9, 2022

[147] Nitric Oxide and Performance – Mr. Olympia, Las Vegas, NV, Dec 16, 2022

[148] How to Optimize Nitric Oxide in the Human Body – Biohacking Congress, Austin, TX, Feb 4, 2023

[149] Cracking the Code of Clinical Translation of Nitric Oxide Science – Keynote Lecture, Gordon Research Seminar, Ventura, CA, Feb 11, 2023

[150] Cracking the Code of Clinical Translation of Nitric Oxide Science – Gordon Research Conference, Ventura, CA, Feb 13, 2023

[151] Role of the Oral Microbiome in Maintaining Systemic Blood Pressure – Holistic Dental Assn, Las Vegas, NV March 31,2023

[152] Nitric Oxide: Connecting Oral and Systemic Health – Integrative Dental Medicine Scholar Society, St. Petersburg, FL, April 20, 2023

[153] Nitric Oxide: Beyond Hypertension – Personalized Lifestyle Medicine Institute, Chicago, IL, April 22,2023

[154] Nitric Oxide: The Master Regulator of Acute and Chronic Inflammation – American Academy of Anti-Aging Medicine, Orlando, Fl, May 19, 2023

[155] Nitric Oxide in Regenerative Medicine – International Cell Surgical Society, Las Vegas, NV June 1-3, 2023

[156] Biohacking your Brain and Sex Organs with Nitric Oxide - Biohacking Conference, Orlando, Fl, June 22-24, 2024

[157] Nitric Oxide: Connecting Oral and Systemic Health – American Academy of Oral Systemic Health, Dallas, Tx Aug 24, 2023

[158] Importance of Nitric Oxide in Health and Disease – Raadfest, Anaheim, Ca, Sept 7-10, 2023

[159] Basic Understanding of Nitric Oxide in Humans – Fetterman Chiropractic, Milwaukee, Wi, Sept 22, 2023

[160] Nitric Oxide as a Hormone – American Academy of Anti-Aging Medicine Bio-Identical Hormone Replacement Symposium, Chicago, Il, Sept 30, 2023

[161] The Microbiome and Nitric Oxide: Connecting Oral and Systemic Health – Pioneering the Microbiome Symposium, Hollywood, Fl, Oct 21, 2023

[162] Nitric Oxide: How to Restore Endogenous Production – Health Freedom Symposium, Scottsdale, AZ Nov 5, 2023

[163] Better Circulation for Better Health and Safety – Truckers Health Network Symposium, Mesa, Az Nov 10, 2023

[164] The Synergy Between Telomerase and Nitric Oxide – American Academy of Anti-Aging Medicine, Preconference workshop, Las Vegas, Nv, Dec 13, 2023

[165] The Key to Longevity: Regulating Telomeres, Stem Cells and Mitochondria, Las Vegas, Nv, Dec 14, 2023

[166] Basic Understanding of Nitric Oxide in Humans – Fordham Page Nutrition Study Club, Washington DC March 1, 2024

[167] Basic Understanding of Nitric Oxide in Humans – Fetterman Chiropractic, Wasau, Wi March 2, 2043

[168] The Role of the Oral Microbiome in Regulating Systemic Blood Pressure – Holistic Dental Assn, Herndon, Va April 12, 2024

[169] Improvements in Sexual Performance and Cognition with Nitric Oxide – Changing Life and Destiny Annual Congress, Plano, TX April 12-14, 2024

[170] The Race for Longevity Begins with the Search for Nitric Oxide – Changing Life and Destiny Annual Congress, Plano, TX April 13, 2024

[171] Nitric Oxide Signaling to Overcome Metabolic Disease – American Academy of Anti-Aging Medicine, West Palm Beach, Fl, May 5, 2024

[172] Nitric Oxide, Blood Pressure and Totality of Care – Integrative Dental Medicine Scholar Society, Knoxville, TN, May 18, 2024

[173] Biohacking your Brain and Sex Organs with Nitric Oxide – Biohacking Conference, Dallas, TX May 30, 2024

[174] Nitric Oxide in Regenerative Medicine – International Cell Surgical Society Conference, Las Vegas, NV, June 8, 2024

[175] Dentistry's Role in Regulating Nitric Oxide and Blood Pressure – American Dental Association, Chicago, Il, June 21, 2024

[176] Nitric Oxide: The Foundation for Longevity and Optimal Health – RaadFest, Anaheim, Ca. Sept 6, 2024.

[177] Nitric Oxide As A Hormone: Understand How to Replace a Missing Gas – American Academy of Anti-Aging Medicine; Los Angeles, CA Sept 20, 2024

[178] Enhance IV Therapy and Cellular Uptake with Nitric Oxide – American Academy of Anti-Aging Medicine, Boston, MA. Oct 24, 2024

[179] Basic Mechanisms of Nitric Oxide Production and Signaling – American Academy of Anti-Aging Medicine Preconference Workshop, Las Vegas, NV Dec 12, 2024

[180] Strategies to Restore Nitric Oxide Production - American Academy of Anti-Aging Medicine Preconference Workshop, Las Vegas, NV Dec 12, 2024

[181] Longevity and Health Span Begins in the Mouth - American Academy of Anti-Aging Medicine, Las Vegas, NV Dec 13, 2024

MEETING PRESENTATIONS

INTERNATIONAL
[1] Detection of Basal Levels of N-Nitrosamines and S-Nitrosothiols Throughout the Organ System – International Conference on Nitric Oxide Prague, Czech Republic June 2002

[2] Arginosuccinate Lysate is An Essential Regulation of Nitric Oxide Production
Nitric Oxide Gordon Conference – March 1-6, 2009 Barga, Italy

[3] Metagenomic Analysis of Bacteria from Human Tongue Scrapings Reveals Novel Bacterial Communities that Contribute Nitrite and Nitric Oxide to the Host – International Nitric Oxide Conference, Edinburgh, Scotland July 22-26, 2012

[4] Emerging Health Benefits of Nitrite and Nitrate: A Change In Paradigm – International Congress on Meat Science and Technology, Montreal, Canada, August 12-17, 2012

NATIONAL
[1] On the Occurrence of Endogenous Nitros(yl)ation Products in Blood and Tissue – Experimental Biology Conference, San Diego CA, April 2003.

[2] Vitamin C Deficiency Evokes Redox Signaling via Nitrite – Society for Free Radical Biology and Medicine Meeting – Austin TX Nov 2005

[3] A NObonomic Approach to Unraveling Complex Nitric Oxide Biology – Department of Integrative Biology and Pharmacology, The University of Texas Houston Medical School – Department Seminar Series, Nov 2006

[4] Alterations in Dietary Nitrite Modulate the Severity of Ischemia-Reperfusion Injury – Society for Free Radical Biology and Medicine Meeting – Denver CO Nov 2006

[5] Dietary Nitrite Supplementation Restores NO/nitroso Homeostasis in Endothelial Dysfunction and Atherosclerosis – Second International Meeting on the Role of Nitrite in Physiology, Pathophysiology and Therapeutics – Bethesda MD Sept 2007

[6] Dietary Nitrite and Nitrate Contribute to Cardiovascular Health and Disease – UT Houston Institute of Molecular Medicine Seminar Series – Oct 2007

[7] Novel Strategies to Replete NO Homeostasis: Emerging New Paradigms – UT Health Science Center Institute of Molecular Medicine Oct 9, 2009

[8] Concentration and Stage Specific Effects of Nitrite on Colon Cancer – American Institute for Cancer Research – Oct 2010 Washington DC

[9] Concentration and Stage Specific Effects of Nitrite on Colon Cancer – Society for Free Radical Biology and Medicine Conference – Nov 17-21, 2010; Orlando Fl

[10] Novel Combination of Beet Root and Hawthorn Promotes Nitric Oxide Production and Lowers Triglycerides in Humans – Seventh International Conference on Functional Foods for Chronic Disease – Dec 3-4, 2010, Dallas Tx.

[11] Unique Combination of Beet Root and Hawthorn Berry Promotes Nitric Oxide Production and Lowers Triglycerides in Humans – Experimental Biology Meeting – April 10, 2011 Washington DC

[12] Nitric Oxide and Diabetes: Cause and Effect – American Academy of Anti-Aging Medicine – Continuing Medical Education, Orlando FL, May 18-19, 2012.

[13] The Implications of Nitric Oxide Production and its Relation to Cardiovascular Heath – International Academy of Oral Medicine and Toxicology, Minneapolis, MN Sept 21-22, 2012

[14] ATP Energy Production is Linked to Nitric Oxide - The Importance for Sexual and Exercise Performance - 20th Annual World Congress on Anti-Aging and Aesthetic Medicine Orlando FL – April 11-13, 2013

[15] Nitrite and Insulin Signaling – Fifth International Nitrite and Nitrate Meeting – Pittsburgh, PA May 4-6, 2013.

[16] The Role of Nitric Oxide in Cellular Aging: Telomeres, Mitochondria & Stem Cells
– American Academy of Anti-Aging Medicine, Las Vegas NV Dec 13-15, 2013

[17] The Role of Nitric Oxide in Inflammation, Arthritis & Pain Mediation – Florida
Chiropractic Association, Destin, FL Feb 7-8, 2014

[18] Revolutionary Advancements in Nitric Oxide – Integrative Healthcare Symposium – New York New York Feb 20-22, 2014

[19] The Therapeutic Effects of a Nitric Oxide Generating Lozenge that Utilizes Natural Product Chemistry – International Nitric Oxide Conference, Cleveland OH, June 19, 2014

[20] Therapeutic Effects of a Nitric Oxide-Generating Lozenge that Utilizes Natural Product Chemistry - Controversies and Advances in the Treatment of Cardiovascular Disease The Fourteenth in the Series, Beverly Hills CA Nov 20, 2014

[21] Therapeutic Effects of a Nitric Oxide-Generating Lozenge that Utilizes Natural Product Chemistry - 30th Annual "Interventional Cardiology" symposium, Snowmass, CO March 5, 2015

[22] Nitric Oxide Restoration: How to Find a Product that Works – Scripps Natural Supplement Conference, San Diego, CA January 27, 2016

[23] Nitrite, the Microbiome and Blood Pressure – Nitric Oxide Gordon Conference, Ventura, CA Feb 19-24, 2017

[24] The Oral Microbiome and Hypertension – Experimental Biology, APS, San Diego CA, April 22, 2018

[25] Natural Product Chemistry and Nitric Oxide Production: New Strategies for NO Based Therapeutics – Experimental Biology, ASPET, San Diego CA, April 22, 2018

[26] Evidence for Consideration of Dietary Guidelines for Nitrite and Nitrate – Functional Food Conference, Session Chair, San Diego CA, April 24, 2018

[27] The Contribution of Oral Anaerobes to Hypertension: Is There NO Link? - The 14th Biennial Congress of the Anaerobe Society of the Americas, Las Vegas, NV July 9-12, 2018

[28] Dietary Nitrite and Nitrate: From Menace to Marvel - Symposium: Is It Time to Change the Paradigm for Food Toxicology? Nitrate as a Case Study, Institute of Food Technology Annual Meeting, Chicago, July 17, 2018

[29] Nitric Oxide and Heart Disease: New discoveries and innovations in diagnostics and therapeutics - Annual Biotechnology Congress, Vancouver, BC – July 23, 2018

[30] Nitric Oxide is the Requisite Signal For Stem Cell Function - American Association of Stem Cell Physicians, Miami, FL August 10-12, 2018

[31] Inherent Inefficiencies of Nitrate And Nitrite Reduction to NO Limit Their Therapeutic Utility – Nitric Oxide Gordon Conference, Ventura, CA Feb 3-8, 2019

[32] Strategies to Optimize Regenerative Medicine Outcomes: the Role of Nitric Oxide – American Association of Ozonotherapy, Denver, CO, May 2-4, 2019

[33] Evidence for Use of Functional Nitric Oxide Nutrition in Primary Care – Functional Food Center Conference, San Diego, CA. May 9-10, 2019

[34] Strategies to Optimize Regenerative Medicine Outcomes: the Role of Nitric Oxide – American Academy of Anti-Aging Medicine, Orlando, Fl. May 16-19, 2019

[35] Nitric Oxide Functionality in Cellular Regeneration – International Cell Surgical Society Annual Meeting, Beverly Hills, Ca May 31 - June 2, 2019

[36] Nitric Oxide Functionality in Cellular Regeneration – The Aesthetics Show, Las Vegas, NV. July 11-14, 2019

MEETING ORGANIZER

Third International Meeting on the Role of Nitrite Physiology, Pathophysiology and Therapeutics, June 2009, Stockholm Sweden

Fourth International Meeting on the Role of Nitrite Physiology, Pathophysiology and Therapeutics, May 2011, Atlanta GA

10th International Conference on the Biology, Chemistry and Therapeutic Applications of Nitric Oxide – Sept 16-20, 2018, Oxford UK

14th International Conference of the Biology, Chemistry and Therapeutic Applications of Nitric Oxide – April 22,27, 2026; Austin, TX

MEDIA EVENTS

Television
KTRK ABC Houston – TV interview with Health Correspondent Christi Myers – November 2007
CNN – Telephone interview with Health Correspondent Elizabeth Cohen – December 2007
Feedstuff – TV interview with Trent Loos – April 2008
KTRK ABC Houston – TV interview with Health Correspondent Christi Myers – October 2010
Feedstuffs – TV interview with Sarah Muirhead – December 2010
KTBC FOX Austin – TV interview – April 2011
KENZ ABC San Antonio – TV interview with Wendy Rigby – May 2011
Media Training – 2012
PBS – Healing Quest TV series – August 2013
iHealthtube – December 2014
Immortality Now – May 2015
Top 100 Magazine – Cover story
Inspire Magazine
Fortune Magazine Article

INTELLECTUAL PROPERTY
Dozens of issued US Patents
Canada Issued patent
New Zealand issued patent
Mexico issued patent
Korea issued patent
6 patents pending worldwide
Stock owner and Advisor – SAJE Pharma
Founder, CEO – Pneuma Nitric Oxide, LLC, Austin, TX
Founder, CEO – Nitric Oxide Innovations, LLC, Austin, TX
Founder, CEO – Bryan Nitriceuticals, LLC, Austin, TX
Founder, CEO – Nitric Oxide Research Institute, LLC, Austin, TX
Founder, Chairman and CEO – Bryan Therapeutics, Inc, Austin, TX

Acknowledgments

There have been so many people that have helped me through life and to get to a stage where I am able to write a book about my personal life and my professional journey through science and discovery. My wife, Kristen, has been patient and supportive and has stood firm through all the good times and bad. She has raised our boys in my many absences as they have grown into wonderful, respectful young men. My business partner Susan Shaffer has led our companies from my big ideas into successful and realizable products that are changing lives every day.

I have many mentors that have guided me and taught me along my journey. Martin Feelisch is responsible for my training and education on nitric oxide. Martin taught me how to be a good scientist and to follow my curiosity and not always conform to the scientific method. Tienush Rassaf, M.D., Ph.D., who worked alongside me for the first years of my training was an incredible friend and mentor. The late Drs. James T. Willerson and C. Thomas Caskey, both whom encouraged me early on to follow my science and supported taking my academic research into drug and product technology. Drs. Bruce Butler and Christine Flynn Weaver at the Office of Technology Management at the UT Health at Houston who helped me early on with my discoveries and invention disclosures and all aspects of commercialization of discoveries.

I'm extremely thankful for the early pioneers in the nitric oxide field to whom I look up. Their work created the field and provided the framework for my line of research. These include Lou Ignarro, Jonathan Stamler, Jack Lancaster, David Lefer, Salvador Moncada, Ferid Murad, Jon Lundberg, Eddie Weitzberg, Nigel Benjamin, Amrita Ahluwalia, Dennis Stuehr and Mark Gladwin.

My mom and dad have been incredible sources of support and inspiration along with my brothers, Marty and Justin. Thanks to all my friends and family that lent me money to survive the lean times when it appeared I would not survive. Bill Huff has been a great friend who has supported my commercial efforts and made many wonderful introductions. I am forever thankful to my trusted agent and friend Alan Morell and Creative Management Partners who have represented me and my companies over the past 5 years. Most of all, I must thank God for the many blessings, the continuous guidance, wisdom, strength and courage.

In Memoriam
Grant W. Peimann
April 14, 1998 – December 16, 2018

About the Author
Nathan S. Bryan, Ph.D.

Dr. Bryan earned his undergraduate Bachelor of Science degree in Biochemistry from the University of Texas at Austin and his doctoral degree from Louisiana State University School of Medicine in Shreveport where he was the recipient of the Dean's Award for Excellence in Research. He pursued his post-doctoral training as a Kirschstein Fellow at Boston University School of Medicine in the Whitaker Cardiovascular Institute. After a two-year post-doctoral fellowship, in 2006 Dr. Bryan was recruited to join faculty at the University of Texas Health Science Center at Houston by Ferid Murad, M.D., Ph.D., 1998 Nobel Laureate in Medicine or Physiology. During his tenure as faculty and independent investigator at UT, his research focused on drug discovery through screening natural product libraries for active compounds. His nine years at UT led to several discoveries which have resulted in over a dozen issued US and international patents and many more pending worldwide.

Specifically, Dr. Bryan was the first to describe nitrite and nitrate as indispensable nutrients required for optimal cardiovascular health. He was the first to demonstrate and discover an endocrine function of nitric oxide via the formation of S-nitrosoglutathione and inorganic nitrite. Through the drug discovery program in natural product chemistry, Dr. Bryan discovered unique compositions of matter than can be used to safely and effectively generate and restore nitric oxide in humans. This technology is now validated in several published clinical trials. These discoveries and findings have transformed the development of safe and effective functional bioactive natural products in the treatment and prevention of human disease and may provide the basis for new preventive or therapeutic strategies in many chronic diseases.

Dr. Bryan has been involved in nitric oxide research for the past 25 years and has made many seminal discoveries in the field. Dr. Bryan is a successful entrepreneur and founder, chairman and CEO of Bryan Therapeutics, Inc., a privately-held, clinical-stage biotechnology company that is actively engaged in the discovery and development of nitric oxide-based therapies. BTI has active drug development programs in heart disease, Alzheimer's Disease and topical drugs for diabetic ulcer and non-healing wounds. Dr. Bryan's consumer line of products are some of the most successful nitric oxide products on the market. Dr. Bryan is an international leader in molecular medicine and nitric oxide biochemistry.

www.N1o1.com
www.drnathansbryan.com
www.bryantherapeutics.com
Instagram: @drnathansbryan
Twitter: @drnitric
LinkedIn: drnathansbryan

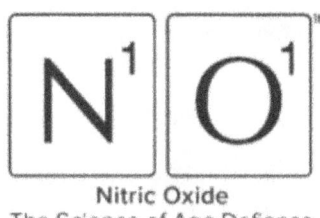

For more information about nitric oxide products, please follow the link through the QR code below.

For sales, editorial information, subsidiary rights information
or a catalog, please write or phone or e-mail
Brick Tower Press
Manhanset House
Shelter Island Hts., New York 11965, U.S.
Tel: 212-427-7139
www.ibooksinc.com
bricktower@aol.com
www.IngramContent.com

www.ingramcontent.com/pod-product-compliance
Lightning Source LLC
Chambersburg PA
CBHW070830240925
32979CB00018B/1117